# VEN

"Peopled with intriguing characters, the world of *Vengeance Born* is unique and filled with compelling mystery. I'm looking forward to seeing where Kylie Griffin takes that world next."

—Nalini Singh, *New York Times* bestselling author

"A great debut novel; Kylie Griffin has me hooked. This story grabbed my attention and raced down several dangerous, intense, enthralling paths, making it very hard to put down. The tale of Annika and Kalan is set in a well-thought-out, fascinating world filled with danger, intrigue, betrayal, passion, revulsion, tenderness—Griffin has given her readers a whole gamut of emotions to feel and leaves her readers with the hope for more stories set in this compelling universe. It's not only good on the first read, it's still good on the second; this is definitely one for my keeper shelves."

—Jean Johnson, national bestselling author of
*Finding Destiny*

"Kylie Griffin builds a compelling and fascinating world that pulled me right in!"
—Joss Ware

"In *Vengeance Born*, Kylie Griffin spins an intriguing story of two races who are mortal enemies, and the half-breeds that are despised by both, who must transform their cultures. The book has solid world building, sympathetic characters, and a twisty story line. I'm looking forward to the next in the Light Blade series."

—Robin D. Owens, national bestselling author of
*Hearts and Swords*

*Berkley Sensation titles by Kylie Griffin*

**VENGEANCE BORN**
**ALLIANCE FORGED**

# ALLIANCE FORGED

## KYLIE GRIFFIN

BERKLEY SENSATION, NEW YORK

THE BERKLEY PUBLISHING GROUP
Published by the Penguin Group
Penguin Group (USA) Inc.
375 Hudson Street, New York, New York 10014, USA
Penguin Group (Canada), 90 Eglinton Avenue East, Suite 700, Toronto, Ontario M4P 2Y3, Canada
(a division of Pearson Penguin Canada Inc.) • Penguin Books Ltd., 80 Strand, London WC2R 0RL,
England • Penguin Group Ireland, 25 St. Stephen's Green, Dublin 2, Ireland (a division of Penguin
Books Ltd.) • Penguin Group (Australia), 250 Camberwell Road, Camberwell, Victoria 3124, Australia
(a division of Pearson Australia Group Pty. Ltd.) • Penguin Books India Pvt. Ltd., 11 Community
Centre, Panchsheel Park, New Delhi—110 017, India • Penguin Group (NZ), 67 Apollo Drive,
Rosedale, Auckland 0632, New Zealand (a division of Pearson New Zealand Ltd.) • Penguin Books
(South Africa) (Pty.) Ltd., 24 Sturdee Avenue, Rosebank, Johannesburg 2196, South Africa

Penguin Books Ltd., Registered Offices: 80 Strand, London WC2R 0RL, England

This book is an original publication of The Berkley Publishing Group.

This is a work of fiction. Names, characters, places, and incidents either are the product of the author's
imagination or are used fictitiously, and any resemblance to actual persons, living or dead, business
establishments, events, or locales is entirely coincidental. The publisher does not have any control over
and does not assume any responsibility for author or third-party websites or their content.

PUBLISHING HISTORY
Berkley Sensation trade paperback edition / July 2012

Library of Congress Cataloging-in-Publication Data

Griffin, Kylie.
Alliance forged / Kylie Griffin.—Berkley sensation trade paperback ed.
p. cm.
ISBN 978-0-425-25601-5
I. Title.
PS3607.R54836A45 2012
813'.6—dc23
2012012364

PRINTED IN THE UNITED STATES OF AMERICA

10  9  8  7  6  5  4  3  2  1

*To Kendra and Michelle:*
*How could I have done this without*
*your wonderful emails and special brand of pestering?*
*You do realize payback's a bitch?*

# ACKNOWLEDGMENTS

Ask any author starting out on their publishing journey and I bet most will say that their second book was the hardest to write. This one certainly was for me. To the little voice in my head throwing in comments—see, I did it. Again. Don't doubt; just write!

Again, to my comrades-in-arms—my editor and agent—Leis and Elaine, thank you for helping make this book the best it can be and for your unwavering support. I've learned so much from both of you!

To the kids in my class (past and present), and some of you know who you are—you provided the inspiration for Tovie, Rissa, and the other young characters. So, yes, there are some of you in my books. Also to the parents and staff of MPS who've encouraged and supported me over the years—many, many, many hugs! Special thanks to Dee—you're a fantastic beta reader.

And to those who are reading this series—a huge thank you for buying these books. I hope that the characters and their stories have entertained you—if they have, then it's mission accomplished, my job is done . . . until the next book!

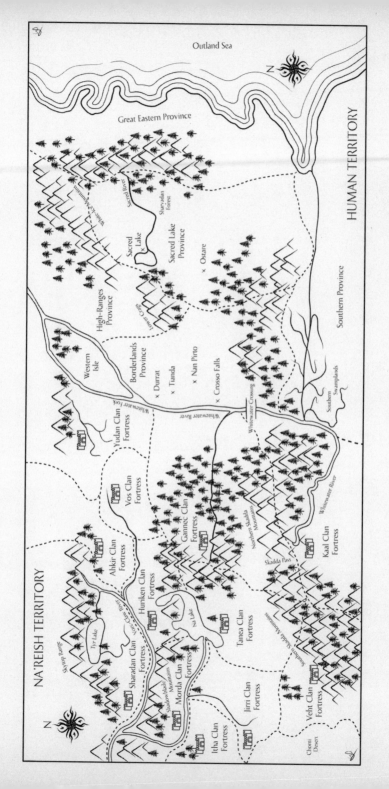

# Chapter 1

"HELP!"

The note of panic in the child's high-pitched cry had Kymora scrambling to her feet, the half-mended shirt falling from her hands to the ground. Her fingertips brushed over the coarse-textured wattle and daub wall of the croft until she found her staff. Sweeping the staff in front of her, she stepped out from the shade into the biting warmth of the afternoon sun.

"Evie, over here!" she called, recognizing the voice. Three strides and the hard sound under the heel of her boot told her she stood in the middle of the pathway among the row of huts lining either side of it.

At the edge of her mind, the young shepherdess's aura flared, brushed hers, but she was too far away for Kymora to read it accurately. The rapid thump of boots on hard-packed ground grew louder as they came in her direction.

A hollow wooden scraping came from her left, the door to the house being pushed open. An earthy, wild, wind-swept scent wafted through the air. The odor varied *Na'Chi* to *Na'Chi* but the rich base note of the half-human, half-demon race was always the same.

"Kymora, what's wrong?"

She shook her head. "I don't know, Lisella."

The door creaked and a hand touched her elbow. The half-blood woman's gesture let her know she was there beside her, a courtesy all the *Na'Chi* had learned in the weeks she'd been living with them.

"*Temple Elect!* They're killing the flock!"

The child's aura was a seething mass of darkness edged with the roughness of barely contained terror. Had she been able to see, Kymora had little doubt Evie's face would have borne a wide-eyed, fearful expression. The ability to read auras compensated for the absence of that sense.

She stretched out her hand to the child, tempted to hurry to the girl but the ground was too uneven. Each row of huts had been built half a dozen steps apart, leaving a corridor for foot traffic, but with young children using the pathways as play areas, even the smallest hole or hollow dug by little hands made traversing the thoroughfares hazardous.

Such a small thing challenged her independence and left her feeling vulnerable, a sensation she disliked. A lot. There were times, like this, when her blindness left her feeling like she was a child again, learning to cope with her disability when she'd first lost her sight. For now, it stopped her from rushing to comfort the child.

She grunted as the ten-year-old barreled into her. Small arms reached around her waist and squeezed tightly. She smoothed a hand over the girl's trembling body; the harsh sound of her gasping only reinforced the terror she could feel beneath her hands.

"Shh, you're safe," she crooned. "Tell me what you saw."

"Rahni and I were watching the fl-flock from the rocks when we s-s-saw men coming over the hill." The girl shuddered. Her aura pulsed so viciously Kymora fought not to wince. "They were so qu-quick . . . we couldn't stop 'em. They started k-killing the bleaters. . . ."

Lisella moved closer. "Geanna and Eyan were the watchers today," she murmured. "Why didn't they spot them first?"

A cold knot of unease curled in Kymora's stomach. *Na'Chi* senses were three times as acute as humans'. Disregarding that, the scouts were highly skilled warriors and never derelict in their responsibilities. What had happened to them? "How many were there, Evie?"

"I'm not sure, maybe ten. They're c-coming this way!"

Kymora's stomach clenched. With the appearance of the *Na'Chi* in human territory, the myth associated with their rumored existence had been dispelled, shocking many. After five hundred years of war with the *Na'Reish*, many had assumed they were just like the power-hungry demons, especially when it became known that they possessed traits similar to their *Na'Reish* heritage—particularly the need to consume blood.

Some hostility was to be expected, but a physical attack on the *Na'Chi*? Surely these renegades had read the missives sent out by the Blade Council explaining that the *Na'Chi* had received the blessings of the *Lady*, their deity?

Why would anyone risk censure for breaking the laws of sanctuary by attacking the *Na'Chi*?

"And Rahni, where's he?" Lisella's soft voice came from down low, as if the *Na'Chi* woman had crouched to be on eye level with the child, and drew Kymora's attention back to the present.

"He's gone to warn those gathering berries."

Relief surged through Kymora with that news. The young *Na'Chi* teenager tended to act first and think later. For him to err on the side of caution meant a large number of men were making their way toward the village. She inhaled a steadying breath, frowned, and then drew in a deeper one. A faint acrid odor stung her nostrils.

"Lisella, do you smell smoke?" she asked. Lisella's boots scuffed the ground as she moved farther away from the side of the house.

"*Mother of Mercy*, I can see it!" A tremor of anger threaded her voice. "They're burning the crops! Evie, find Giron. He's working in the crafters' hut. Tell him to find Varian. He's in the Sharvadan Forest training with the Light Blades."

"Yes, Lisella."

Kymora released the girl and listened to her run off into the village. A hot breeze caressed her face. The odor of smoke grew stronger.

"Lisella, the children." Goose bumps lifted along her arms. Today there were more of them than adults in the village. Would there be enough time for them all to escape? "They're going to take longer to get up the mountain path and to the caverns."

Months of work were being destroyed by the flames, and not just with the crops. She'd been working for weeks to convince the more reluctant members of the *Na'Chi* that integration into human society would help each race accept one another. To establish that bond, she'd convinced crafters and Light Blade warriors to live with them and share their skills with one another.

With the ranks of Light Blade warriors at an all-time low, and the *Na'Reish* border raids for blood-slaves increasing, the *Na'Chi's* expertise was needed. With their own limited numbers, they'd spent the last twenty years learning to hide and ambush the *Na'Reish*—techniques the Light Blades needed now. She knew her brother, Kalan, hoped that by having them learn these specialized skills, it'd prove an advantage in any future confrontation with the *Na'Reish*.

She grimaced. This attack would only reinforce the *Na'Chi's* fears and misgivings now. The *Na'Reish* demons outnumbered them all two to one. Humans and *Na'Chi* needed each another if they were going to survive any conflict with them.

The breeze picked up strength. The scent of smoke saturated the air. It took very little to imagine the flames engulfing the houses.

Kymora tightened her grip on her staff. "We need to split up and warn everyone."

"Kymora, your brother wouldn't like you left unguarded."

"The children should be seen to first."

"As leader of the Temple, you can't risk your safety." A twinge of guilt raced through Kymora at Lisella's gentle censure. The *Na'Chi's* hand patted her shoulder. "Let's warn people together. We need to move fast and you'll do that better with someone beside you."

Kymora gritted her teeth. She might be blind, and it would hamper the speed of her escape, but it didn't mean she was helpless. Why was Lisella ignoring the fact that she could defend herself and had done so since her early teens? While she was a good friend, there were times Lisella was as overprotective as some of the other *Na'Chi* were disdainful of her disability. A trait inherited from their *Na'Reish* heritage.

"We don't have time to argue. Nor will I need your help." Kymora thumped the butt of her staff on the ground. "You know this isn't just for decoration. Get everyone to the safety of the caverns. I'll check the houses around here and follow with whomever I find."

"You're as stubborn as Varian." While the woman grumbled, she could hear a tolerant smile in Lisella's voice. "Be careful. You know what he'll do if you come to harm."

Duty and honor formed the backbone of the *Na'Chi* warrior-leader, something she'd realized from almost the first time they'd met in the *Lady's* Temple and Varian had claimed sanctuary for his people from her. When it came to protecting those under his care, he was ruthless, and in the last few months, he'd informed her in no uncertain terms that she fell within those boundaries living with them in the rugged foothills overlooking Sacred Lake. She inhaled a steadying breath.

"I can take care of myself." She made a shooing motion. "Go warn the others. I'll start here. Go!"

Gathering her skirt in one hand, Kymora moved as swiftly as she could, calling out as she reached each house, warning those within so they could begin their escape. The scuff of boots along the pathway and the occasional curt instruction assured her the exodus was progressing.

The *Na'Chi* had spent all their lives hiding from patrols in *Na'Reish* territory. Escaping detection was their specialty, and achieving it was done in silence. While they'd enjoyed much more freedom inside human territory, they'd limited their contact with humans and now were forced to fall back on ingrained survival habits. Something they shouldn't have to do. Her jaw tightened and her temper flared. It wasn't right.

A soft sob caught the edge of her hearing. Kymora turned and felt her way along the wall of one house. "Is someone there?"

"*Temple Elect!* Everyone's gone. . . ."

Kymora tried to place the very young voice. "Why didn't you go with them, Tovie?"

"I was on the necessary. . . ." The six-year-old *Na'Chi* boy hiccupped. "Henna didn't wait for me. . . ."

"Search the houses! Kill any *Na'Chi* you find!"

The nearby shout drew a whimper from the child, and a chill coursed through Kymora. Who were these attackers? She pulled Tovie closer, her arm tightening around his shoulders, the danger to his life stark and immediate. He had to flee. Now.

Strangers' voices, all men, called to one another. They hadn't wasted any time, covering the distance between the crops and the village in just a few minutes.

From the hails and chatter, the search seemed methodical, organized, rather than haphazard and random. Not something expected of farmers or townsfolk, more like disciplined warriors. Light Blades.

Renegades. Kymora's pulse leapt. Surely not. If they were Light Blade warriors, how could those sworn to serve the *Lady* do something like this? It went against the tenet of protecting the *Lady's* children, and *She'd* declared the *Na'Chi* as her children. Light Blades were supposed to stand against injustice not instigate it.

"The bad men will hurt me, won't they?" the boy asked, his solemn question too worldly wise for his age.

"I won't let them." Kymora ran a reassuring hand over the side of his face. The wetness of tears coated her fingers.

Precious seconds bled away as she tilted her head. The warmth of sunlight hit her right cheek. At this time of day, Tovie needed to go right to find the uphill mountain path that would lead him to the others. She prayed the *Na'Chi* and everyone else had made it to safety without being seen.

"Tovie, you need to get to the forest, then make your way to the caverns. Keep behind this row of houses and use all the boulders along the edge of the gully to stay out of sight."

"Like Rissa taught us in hidey-go-seek?"

*Lady* bless the healers' apprentice for teaching the *Na'Chi* children that game. Kymora smiled. "Yes, exactly like that. Ready?"

A small hand gripped hers. "But what about you?"

Her stomach knotted. As tempting as it was, she couldn't risk his life by expecting him to help her. There was no way she was going to be able to keep up with the boy, not without both of them being spotted and caught.

Pottery shattered nearby; the violent sound seemed too deliberate to have been an accident. Wood splintered, the noise just as startling and shocking. Under her hand, Tovie flinched. She hugged the boy tightly.

Were the intruders looting or destroying the *Na'Chi's* possessions? Belongings they'd made by hand with the crafters. Kymora regretted the loss. Hours of painstaking work destroyed in less than a heartbeat. Through the wattle and daub wall of the house next to them, someone uttered a curse.

"I'll be all right. When you see Lisella, tell her I stayed behind. Go on now," she whispered, mouth close to his ear. "Keep low and run!"

The child took off.

A small spurt of unease curled in her stomach at her decision to remain behind. Should she stay hidden or reveal herself? Surely the renegades would be less likely to harm a human than a *Na'Chi*? Regardless, Tovie needed time to make his escape.

Sweat prickled the sides of her face and under her arms as she fingered the amulet around her neck. The indented circle etched into the middle represented the sun and cycle of life, the wavy beams the symbols of strength, a gift of life the *Lady* bestowed upon them all.

"*Mother of Mercy*, help me stand against the ignorance of hatred," she murmured, and made her way back to the main pathway running through the village.

"Faral, have you found any sign of the demons?"

Kymora tightened her grip on her staff. The man was no more than a stone's throw away, the ripe odor of manure in the air indicating he was near the animal enclosure. The gravelly voice wasn't one she recognized, but then there were thousands of Light Blade warriors and she didn't know them all.

A muffled reply in the negative came from a distance. Taking a fortifying breath, she tapped her way from the cool shade of the house and used the heat and angle of the sun on her face to guide her down the pathway.

"The *Na'Chi* are all gone." She mustered all her confidence to keep her voice raised and strong. "These people have been given sanctuary within human territory. You're breaking the *Chosen's* covenant. Who are you?"

A door hit the wall of the house as if someone had flung it open, and hasty footsteps scuffed the ground. "Veren?" Another male voice, higher pitched. Even without sensing his wavering aura, the tremor in it betrayed the man's nervousness. "Is she one of them?"

"I'm Kymora, the *Temple Elect*." Kymora held her ground as run-ning footsteps converged from several directions. *Lady's Breath*, how many of them were there? Surely her title as leader of their religious order would protect her? She swallowed against a throat suddenly gone dry. "The destruction you've caused is intolerable."

"The *Lady's* Handmaiden?" The nervous man's sudden intake of breath came from her left. "Veren, we weren't told there'd be any humans here . . . especially not her!"

"Who told you that, countryman?" Kymora asked.

"Hold your tongue, Faral," snarled the gravelly voice. Stale sweat and the iron tang of blood wafted on the gentle breeze, becoming stronger with the nearing sound of footsteps. "I don't care if she's the *Temple Elect* or my mother. Anyone who supports those demons betrays us. . . ."

The darkness in his tone made her shiver. Kymora opened her mouth to rebuke him. Something struck her in the face, hard enough to buckle her knees and send her to the ground. She lost her grip on her staff, heard it land at her feet.

Stunned, she sprawled there. Tears burned in her eyes. Small pebbles and debris pricked through the material of her dress, but the sting of them poking into her was nothing compared to the pain throbbing in her cheek. It radiated into her jaw, paralyzing the side of her face.

"Veren, you can't do that! She's the *Lady's* Handmaiden!" Faral's pulsing aura reflected Kymora's shock. "What about the tenet of respect . . . ? She deserves better than this!"

His reference to the *Lady's* ideology consolidated her suspicion. There was a chance these were Light Blade warriors.

Fingers tangled in her hair and jerked her head upward. She cried out, one hand reaching up to relieve the pressure, the other clawing over hot dirt and rough-bladed grass, searching. She found the end of her staff, closed her fingers around it. With a cry, she swung hard.

It cracked against something soft and a howl of pain rent the air. She was released.

"*Lady of Light!*" Veren's hoarse curse shook with anger.

She scrambled away from him. Her boot caught on the hem of her dress, it tore, and she stumbled before righting herself.

"You dare attack a Handmaiden?" Adrenaline gave her strength even though she wasn't able to disguise the quaver in her voice. She lifted a shaking hand to her aching jaw. "You swore to serve the *Lady* by protecting the innocent and those in need, to respect those who served *Her* in *Her* Temple. Everything you've done here today is wrong!"

"The only thing wrong is allowing those half-bloods to live among us!" another voice retorted behind her. She swung around. "Councilor Davyn warned us . . ."

"Shut up, Bennic. . . ." Veren hissed.

So these men were supporters of Davyn? The ex-Councilor had manipulated others for years, driven insane by his need to avenge his daughter's death at the hands of the *Na'Reish*. What twisted, venomous lies had he told them? Her brother and the Blade Council needed to know about this.

"Faral, does your family know you're a part of this? Would they approve of you attacking defenseless children? Of killing those who've done you no harm?" she asked. Were they all fanatics or could she count on the support of some of them? "Are you willing to sacrifice your honor and bring shame to your family by defying the *Lady's* will? The *Chosen's* mandate? You'd risk having your rank revoked?"

"Where's the honor in a leader and priestess who ally themselves with a race who will use us as blood-slaves," the third man declared, his deep voice rich with righteous anger.

"The *Na'Chi* don't enslave humans."

Veren snorted. "So, that half-blood whore of Kalan's didn't drink his blood?"

Frustration burned through Kymora's veins at the accusation. Annika's feeding from Kalan had saved her life after being stabbed by Davyn, his plot to prove she was the animal he assumed her to be thwarted. Despite trying to keep that incident low-key, neither Kalan nor the Blade Council had been able to stop gossip. Bless the *Lady* only a select few knew how the *Na'Chi* suffered the blood-addiction rather than the usual enslavement of human to demon. She inhaled a calming breath.

"The messages you sent out to every town and village . . . Is it true all Light Blades have demon blood in them?" Faral's question held such confusion and uncertainty. His emotions were so tangible his aura throbbed.

"The history annals of *Chosen* Zataan revealed that truth. Copies were sent with the messages. Didn't you read them for yourself?"

"Lies! The messages held lies!" Scorn and derision laced Bennic's deep voice. "If Light Blades or those with Gifts are supposed to be of demon-get, then where are the body markings on our skin? Why don't we crave blood?"

Kymora shivered, the stark confirmation of their Light Blade identity established with his words. She turned toward him. "Master Healer Candra believes the traits have weakened over time, or that some never inherited them."

"Dominant traits and inherited features? Passed on through bloodlines? You make us sound like livestock," he hissed. "Our Gifts are *Lady*-given and have nothing to do with demon blood!"

"Then how do you account for Annika being able to heal and kill with a touch?" she argued. "Sensing human emotions, connecting with animals, manipulating energies . . . the *Na'Chi* all possess skills as varied and as similar to our own Gifted." Their auras swirled and contorted with dark tendrils of hostility and resistance. "How can you ignore the *Lady's* words? She's accepted them as *Her* children as much as you or I."

"Veren? You told us Kalan made up that lie, that the *Lady* would never utter such blasphemous words. You said Davyn declared the *Na'Chi* were as dangerous to us as the *Na'Reish* and had to be killed so our people would no longer be divided . . . so the Blade Council could focus on the *Na'Reish* threat across the border." Faral's bewilderment held a hint of anger. "What's the truth?"

Kymora's heart pounded on hearing the lies told to Faral. How many other Light Blades had been led astray by Davyn's deception?

"What does your heart tell you?" she countered. "Think of your families, your homes. The Council will place sanctions on anyone who supports you because of what's happened here today, but I can speak on your behalf if someone has misled you."

"Don't listen to her." Bennic's voice deepened further with his reprimand. "She's trying to divide us."

"The truth, Faral, is that the *Na'Chi* will turn on us. No alliance will hide their true nature. They're just like the *Na'Reish*," Veren stated. His rasping laughter sent a shiver along her back. "As for the Council placing sanctions on us, you need to bear witness, and that's not going to happen, priestess."

Despite the heat of the sun beating down on her, coldness spread throughout Kymora. Dear *Lady*, was he going to kill her? Would the others stand by and watch? Slowly she repositioned her feet to widen her stance and brought her staff across her body in a relaxed but ready position.

"Do you really think you can fight us off?" Ugly laughter mocked her again. "You're blind, *Temple Elect*."

Her heart hammered in her chest. Five was the best she'd ever managed to defend herself against, and then only for a short time. Her breathing quickened. Why hadn't she listened to Lisella and accepted her help?

She kept her voice firm and steady. "If you know I can fight, then you know it means I'm not helpless."

"It's nine against one. Even sighted you'd be hard-pressed to prevail against us."

Kymora swallowed hard and drew on every shred of strength she possessed, determined to face the impossible. *Lady* willing, she would survive. She had to. The Blade Council needed to know of the threat to the *Na'Chi*.

"Veren, no. . . ."

"If you can't stomach this, Faral, then leave." Her attacker stepped closer. She sensed others closing in on her. "Let those loyal to the cause deal with this."

Goose bumps prickled over Kymora. The cause? Davyn's cause? The ex-Councilor's influence was a greater threat than the Blade Council had anticipated. Veren's use of the term *cause* suggested more than the few gathered around her. How many others were there committed to seeing the *Na'Chi* dead and the alliance fail?

"*Lady* protect *Your* servant," she murmured.

If Veren believed her blindness made her an easy target, he'd soon discover just how thorough her training with the Temple guards had been, and how very wrong his assumption was.

They all would.

# Chapter 2

FEAR reeked of a pungent bitterness that lingered in the nostrils, but Varian wasn't able to detect even a whiff of it on the gentle breeze. He did, however, catch the sharp spicy scent of anticipation. His opponent lay somewhere ahead, concealed, waiting, hoping to ambush him. Well, he was one *Na'Chi* who wouldn't be walking into a trap.

"Where are you hiding?" he murmured.

With eyes narrowed, he scanned the sunlight-dappled clearing ahead. A large fallen tree lay partway across it, years of rot and weathering scarring its gnarled length. An animal trail paralleled the downed tree but the debris along its path was undisturbed, the moss coating its bark intact. He hadn't expected to see any telltale marks or tracks; the warrior was cunning and unpredictable, more so with the pressure of being hunted by half a dozen *Na'Chi.*

"You're here somewhere." In the thicker forest to Varian's left, a patch of darkness flickered. Adrenaline rushed through his veins.

There, in the deeper shadows, he could make out the semiprone form of a body. He bared his teeth in a savage grin. "Found you."

Remaining crouched behind the rocky outcrop, Varian glanced to his right. Pressed up against the side of another tree, a young scout with dark hair twisted into multiple braids and dressed in brown was barely visible. Violet eyes, very much like his, locked on him. Varian pointed in the direction of the hidden intruder, then swirled one finger in the air.

The scout nodded sharply, slid to the ground, and crawled away using the dense brush to his advantage. Zaune would circle around the clearing and either force their opponent into moving from his position or flush him out into the clearing.

Capturing the human was preferable, but Varian doubted this one would go down without a fight. With three other warriors already tracked and taken, he was the last one to be run to ground.

It wasn't often he met someone with a skill similar to his scouts, but this one had learned fast and led them on a merry chase all over the mountainside all afternoon. His grin widened in grudging respect for the warrior's abilities.

A trilling war cry broke the quiet of the forest. Varian heard a muffled curse, then the impact of a body hitting another. From the shadowed thicket to his left, two tangled forms rolled into the clearing, each grappling with the other, trying to get the upper hand. Fists struck flesh in dull thuds, in rapid succession, accompanied by painful grunts.

Chunks of dirt flew from beneath their flailing limbs as the two scuffled for position. The dark blond warrior ended up on top, pinning the leaner Zaune to the forest floor with his greater weight.

Varian sensed the rapid buildup of energy within the human warrior, the familiar hum of it grazing his senses. The Light Blade possessed the kinetic power to kill through any weapon or even the touch

of a bare hand, the skill a Gift from the *Lady* and a counterbalance
to the *Na'Reish's* immense physical strength.

Moving swiftly, Varian stepped out from behind the rocky outcrop and came up behind the pair. The older man blocked and
deflected Zaune's desperate strike and placed a hand on his chest.
Triumph flashed across his face.

"You're dead!" he hissed, then the warrior flung himself to one
side, almost as if he sensed Varian's presence, and rolled to his feet
in a defensive half crouch. "I knew there had to be more than one of
you," he panted, chest heaving, his deep blue-eyed gaze never leaving
him as Varian circled left around the clearing.

Sweat shone on the warrior's begrimed face and soaked his torn
shirt, and some of his long blond hair had pulled free of the tie at his
neck during the scuffling.

"That's four of your scouts I've bested today, *Na'Chi*," he taunted.
The precise way he mirrored Varian's every step contradicted his dishev-
eled appearance of exhaustion. There was plenty of fight left in him yet.

"And you think to add me to that tally?" Varian asked. The warrior wasn't armed, but even without a blade, he could kill with his
Gift. "You can try."

Varian leapt and caught the man around the knees and took him
to the ground again. A well-placed elbow impacted his ribcage, startled a grunt out of him, and loosened his hold enough for his opponent to twist. Varian blocked a blow meant for his head. Half a
heartbeat later two more scouts joined the fray.

"Contain him, don't kill him!" he ordered.

A curse ripped from the human. He fought hard, twisting and
bucking. It took all three of them to flip him onto his stomach and
pin him to the ground.

"Concede?" Varian gripped the warrior's wrists against the small
of his back, straddling his full weight across the man's legs to stop
him kicking.

Another heated expletive singed the air. "*Lady's Breath*, I should've known you'd have more than one partner hidden around the clearing." Beneath them, the warrior finally stilled. "A mistake I won't make again. I concede, this time." Self-disgust laced his tone.

Varian met his scouts' gazes and gave a nod. "Don't be so hard on yourself, Arek." They released the man and moved back from him. "Your skills have improved in the few months you've been training with us."

The Light Blade warrior rolled onto his back, his lips curving in a twisted half smile. "A compliment? From you?"

"He's been known to give them." Zaune scrambled to his feet, no longer "dead," and dusted off his breeches. "He's a hard taskmaster but fair. So consider yourself one of the privileged few."

Varian shot Zaune a dry look as he held out his hand to Arek. The man took it, accepting his help to rise. "So, how many others wait out there, eh?"

Varian whistled. The remaining scouts revealed themselves.

"Two more? You had ten scouts searching for me? Just like a full *Na'Reish* patrol?"

"You were ready for this test." Varian clapped him on the shoulder. "But we're going to have to work on you concealing your scent. The *Na'Reish* will detect it as easily as we did."

"*Mother of Mercy*, you *Na'Chi* and your enhanced senses." Arek shook his head. "They give you the advantage."

"And your Gift of using energy to kill with a touch? I think that balances the odds, Light Blade."

"So, will you teach me how to mask my scent now?"

"Not today. We've trained hard, and knowing Lisella, she'll have organized a farewell meal for those returning to Sacred Lake tomorrow—"

"*Lady* help us if we're late for that," Zaune commented, his eyes sparkling despite his somber tone.

Arek snorted. "Indeed. I don't know whose tongue is sharper when displeased, hers or Kymora's."

An unbidden smile curved the corners of Varian's mouth at Arek's description of the two women. Growing up together, many of the scouts around him had been on the wrong side of Lisella countless times, and the human priestess might be blind, but she rarely missed a thing, her hearing as keen as a *Na'Chi's*. Both possessed warm hearts, but when their tempers sparked they were a sight to see.

"Varian!"

The distressed cry had him pivoting on his boot heel. Pounding footsteps running through the forest grew closer. A young *Na'Chi* boy, his cheeks ruddy with exertion, burst into the clearing. Varian caught him as he stumbled to a halt.

"Giron, what's wrong?"

The boy's wide-eyed gaze met his, their violet color flecked with bright yellow. "The village—" he gasped, his fingers biting into Varian's forearms. "Intruders . . . fire!"

"An assault?" Uneasiness skittered along the length of his back.

"Evie said someone killed the bleaters . . . and there's smoke. . . ."

Fury, colder than a knife blade, ripped through Varian at the thought of his people under attack. The imprisonment of Councilor Davyn, Corvas, and Yance after their betrayal of the High Council had sparked as much unrest as the *Na'Chi's* appearance in human territory. Despite the new Blade Council's support, he'd wondered how long it'd take the dissenters to gather the courage to go from verbal protests to attacking them.

Varian gently pushed the boy toward the scout. "Zaune, stay with Giron until he recovers, then head for the caverns. The others will seek shelter there."

The *Na'Chi* had the skills to evade detection, but the humans living with them weren't as savvy. Lisella would organize and guide them there, but the children and Kymora would slow them down. His skin prickled at the thought. Whether they escaped detection depended on how much of a head start they received.

As much as he respected and admired Kymora's self-taught independence, her disability would impede her. Fleeing into the foothills, while attempting to elude pursuers, would be next to impossible. She'd never make it to the safety of the caverns.

A hard knot formed in his stomach. No amount of confidence in her skills could unravel it. He met Arek's gaze, and the furious concern swirling within their blue depths told him the Light Blade was thinking the same thoughts. Varian blew out a sharp breath.

"We'll head downhill, straight through Greyshard Pass," he said. "It's the quickest route."

"And the most dangerous," Arek countered. "We risk turning our ankles or worse on the rocky scree."

"We'll just have to be careful."

"I knew the humans would attack us!" hissed one of the other scouts, his expression darkening. "I warned you they would. I've been saying it ever since that Blade Council meeting when they turned against us. We can't trust them, Varian!"

"Trust who, *Na'Chi*?" Arek growled. The spicy scent of his anger saturated the air. "My warriors and I? The crafters and townspeople who've come to live with you? Do you now distrust us?"

"You humans have never been comfortable living with us!" Rystin declared, his jaw set. "Are you going to deny that?"

"Of course not." Arek's mouth flattened into a thin line. "But we all knew there would be problems during the transition."

Varian's respect for the Light Blade grew. A couple of months ago, when the Light Blades had first come to live with them, Arek's temper would've bested him and he'd have had to intervene in a fight to stop the argument.

"Putting aside preconceptions learned over a lifetime doesn't happen overnight." Arek's gloved hands flexed. "Everyone who came to your village did so with an open mind. Surely you can acknowledge the progress that's been made. . . ."

"Enough!" Varian sliced the air with a hand. "Arguing is wasting our time."

"We need to defend ourselves." Rystin's low-voiced statement drew support from several of the *Na'Chi*.

Varian ground his teeth together. The attack was already fueling the fears and dissatisfaction of those *Na'Chi* resistant to living with the humans. It would provide Rystin with a valid excuse to demand they seek a more isolated location to live. Or even worse, a return to *Na'Reish* territory and a life of hiding from the demons and human-slaves who despised them for their mixed heritage. Everything inside him rebelled at that thought. Being hunted down and killed was not the future he'd envisaged for his people.

"Rystin, rest easy." He kept his voice soft, calm. "Kalan declared any supporter of the disgraced Councilors as rebels."

"And he will deal with them, I assure you," Arek vowed. "The *Lady's Chosen* granted you the right to defend yourselves against anyone who threatened you." A promise made in front of the Blade Council when Kalan had agreed to their petition of sanctuary. Arek's reminder eased some of the tension. "Although, I pray to the *Lady* it doesn't come to that." Though his face was harsh, the Light Blade warrior's blue eyes reflected equal amounts of warning and regret. "Killing the rebels will only do more harm than good. Keep that in mind, Varian."

Varian's gut churned. With the *Na'Reish* demons invading more frequently across the border for blood-slaves, fighting among themselves was a huge risk. Kalan, the *Lady's Chosen*, would end up battling a war on two fronts. A war neither of them could afford if they wanted to survive. Varian inclined his head, acknowledging the human's warning.

"Time's wasting." He glanced at his scouts. "Let's move!"

"VEREN, she's the *Temple Elect!*" Faral's voice came closer to Kymora. "If we harm her, we ignore and dishonor our vows to the *Lady!*"

Kymora shuddered at the thought of so many warriors abandoning their faith to believe the lies of a madman. She was relieved Faral sounded as appalled as she felt. In nearly a thousand years, only two other warriors had been stripped of their responsibilities, such was the honor of being chosen to join the ranks of Light Blade warriors. Perhaps there was hope yet that some of the rebels would realize the truth.

Veren's snort was loud. "We've broken no vows. The *Lady's* words are clear. 'Corruption is insidious and cunning. It creeps and works its way into the souls of the lax and complacent. Those who embrace it shall suffer the consequences of their actions. Watch carefully, act swiftly before its shadow consumes you all.'" His voice rang with fervent belief. "Corruption began the moment an alliance with those demons was suggested. We're acting before it consumes everything we abide for."

"I don't agree with the Council's decision to harbor the demons, but what you're doing is wrong!" Faral's tone firmed. "I won't let you do this."

Veren made a dismissive sound. "Where are the *Na'Chi, Temple Elect?*"

"What makes you think I'd tell you? You've already admitted to wanting to kill them," she countered, and took a small step backward, closer to Faral. Thank the *Lady* at least one of them had a conscience.

Veren growled the same instant an undulating *Na'Chi* war cry rent the air. Another and another followed, each coming from a different direction as if they were scattered around the village.

Bless the *Lady*, Giron had found the scouts. She gasped, relief swamping her.

"Pair up!" Veren ordered. "Search the perimeter. Don't hesitate to kill them."

The metallic hiss of blades being drawn from sheaths sent a chill coursing through Kymora. When a hand grasped her arm, she instinctively twisted.

"Handmaiden, it's Faral. Let me guide you away from here," he pleaded. "While the others are distracted."

Her scalp crawled at the thought of trusting a man who'd been prepared to kill her less than an hour ago, but what other choice did she have? She gave a curt nod, gambling his intentions were sincere. If he wasn't, then the odds of gaining her freedom were certainly better fighting him rather than all the rebels.

He whirled her around and she began to run, hoping, praying their path was clear and smooth.

"Faral!" Veren's shout raked across every nerve, and her muscles surged to life, lent her speed. Despite the adrenaline rush, her breath hitched short and sharp, and she stumbled numerous times over unfamiliar ground.

"Turn left. . . ." Faral kept his instructions short. "We'll head west, through the houses."

She tried to remember the path they'd already taken to figure out where she was, but he'd rushed her through too many twists and turns. She bit her lip to stop a sob. *Lady's Breath*, where was she?

Kymora tried to focus her thoughts, quell her rising panic. "Where's Veren?"

"He follows with another."

Fear raked cold fingers the length of Kymora's spine. If the renegades caught them, they were both dead. The ground beneath her boot dipped suddenly. She stumbled, crying out as her arm and shoulder yanked painfully in its socket.

Faral kept her on her feet and moving, but then he jerked to a halt, and she found herself pushed behind him. Her pulse pounded in her throat as she gasped in a breath, afraid that Veren had found them.

"Release the *Temple Elect* and I'll let you live!"

The deep, resonant voice, although rough and harsh, was so familiar and such a blessing to hear. "Varian! He saved my life." She clutched a fistful of Faral's shirt in her hand. "Faral, the *Na'Chi* is my friend."

A roar of anger came from behind them. "Betrayer!"

Veren's rage reached out to her, thrumming and vibrating like a living thing. The sensation lifted the hairs on the back of her neck. Faral moved beneath her hand, turning to face the new threat.

"Run, Handmaiden, run!" he urged and pushed her away from him.

Kymora swept her staff out in front of her, trying to gain an impression of the ground as she heard him draw his blade.

"To me, Kymora!" Varian's order gave her a direction. "Hurry!"

She ran as men's curses filled the air. A sob bubbled in her throat as she collided with a hard body. Her legs lost their strength and threatened to buckle. Large hands gripped her shoulders. A clean, earthy scent combined with the tang of sweat filled her nostrils. "Varian, thank the *Lady*."

"Drop your staff."

She did and found herself swept up into his arms and cradled against a warm, broad chest. His shirt was damp in places, and when she wrapped her arms around his neck, the bare skin of his neck was hot with exertion. She didn't care. The sensation of feeling safe was immediate.

"Hold on," he ordered, and then, with the sounds of weapons clashing behind them, he started to run.

# Chapter 3

SOME of the tension consuming Varian eased as Kymora's arms tightened around his neck, the softness of her curves pressing against him. He inhaled her sweet, sunshine and flowers scent and let it wash through him, allowing it to calm his anger and settle the killer inside him.

His demon half had come too close to breaking free on seeing her surrounded by so many enemies as he'd descended on the village from the pass. Equal amounts of fury and fear had consumed him as he'd issued orders for them to split up and capture as many rebels as possible.

No stranger to either emotion, he often used both to his advantage in a confrontation, but this time the rage and fear seething inside him ran so deep it'd disturbed him on a level he'd only ever felt for those in his *Na'Chi* family.

He didn't usually trust others so swiftly. Had their friendship progressed so quickly that he viewed her like family? Perhaps it was his promise to Kalan, her brother, to protect her while she lived among the *Na'Chi*. Kymora's safety would ensure that the alliance between humans and the *Na'Chi* continued smoothly. This would certainly justify his protective feelings for her and was the only explanation that made sense.

"Varian, we're going downhill. Lisella and the others went uphill to get to the caverns." Kymora's warm breath brushed past his ear. "Where are we headed?"

"The river." He heard her breath catch. As light as she was in his arms, he knew they had only so much time before the renegades caught up with them. "I won't risk taking you back through the village until the rebels are dealt with. We'll backtrack and join the others once we've lost our pursuers."

"Faral?"

Varian spared a glance over his shoulder, jaw tightening as he saw the man go down, impaled by two blades. "He's only bought us a few minutes' reprieve."

He scanned the stark landscape ahead. The narrow escarpment was little more than a rocky terrain, too open, too exposed, with few bushes to hide from view behind, but a lone group of boulders ahead offered possible cover.

Dodging behind the rocky outcrop, he heard Kymora whisper a prayer for the downed warrior, and marveled at her generous soul. The moment the village had been attacked, the human had forfeited his forgiveness and compassion.

If he wasn't so set on finding a safe home for his people, the attackers never would have lived to see another sunrise. Eliminating those who threatened them was as ingrained a practice as keeping silent in enemy territory. It had been the only option living under the noses of the *Na'Reish*. But an alliance required compromise, as Arek had quite rightly reminded him. So, as much as it grated, he'd given the order to capture and contain the rebels. Kalan and the Blade Council could deal with them.

Underfoot the ground grew rockier, the barren patch of dirt replaced by loose scree of gravel and debris, unstable enough to turn an ankle. Varian blinked sweat from his eyes and slowed. The undulating terrain would soon end in a narrow shelf of rock that ran parallel to the river.

"They're coming." Kymora's quiet warning held a thread of fear. "Veren knows we're trying to get to the river."

Her hearing was as keen as his. A discovery he'd made the first time they'd met, when he'd approached her in the *Lady's* Temple to ask for sanctuary for the *Na'Chi*. Her blindness had surprised him but he'd quickly discovered Kymora had learned to adapt and fine-tune her other senses. The strength of one balancing the deficiency of another, a fascinating dichotomy that drew him to her.

Focusing, he could hear the renegade leader issue an order for the other man to head them off, herd them away from the escarpment. These humans knew the countryside as well as he did if they knew where to cut off their escape, a disturbing revelation.

Ignoring the burn of fatigue in his thigh muscles, Varian increased his pace, the need to get to the escarpment first outweighing the risk of turning an ankle. The sharp crack of a rock smashing into another, as if someone had slipped on the uneven pathway, brought a round of curses from one of the two men chasing them.

His breath rasped in and out of his lungs by the time he reached the shrub-lined lip, but it wasn't so loud he couldn't hear the dull rush of water below them. Its fresh scent filled his nostrils. This close, the breeze provided cool relief against his sweaty face.

Easing Kymora's feet to the ground, he kept himself between her and the edge. "Two steps behind me is a sheer drop-off to the river below."

Barely a stone's throw wide, the expanse would be easy to traverse if they had a raft or boat, but its speed and depth made it impossible to cross on foot. Squinting against the reflected glare of sunshine off the surface of the water, he peered over to estimate the drop.

"We're going to have to jump." Even though Kymora's expression remained neutral, her nails dug into his skin. "It's no higher than your brother's dwelling balcony to the water below."

A shout echoed off the boulders around them. Another swift glance showed Veren and the other renegade closing on them, barely three dozen paces away, both with daggers drawn.

"Ready?" he asked.

White lines of tension bracketed Kymora's mouth as she turned her sightless emerald gaze in his direction. "Varian, I can't."

Her soft voice trembled and the sharp scent of fear emanated from her even though she struggled to contain it. It tugged at something deep inside him. Taking the rebels on wasn't an issue, but he wasn't willing to risk Kymora's life if one of them slipped past him.

Varian laced his fingers among hers. "I won't let go of you."

Her tongue wet her bottom lip and she took a breath to protest. They didn't have time to argue. He snatched her from her feet and leapt over the edge.

Kymora's scream caught in her throat as Varian threw them both from the escarpment. Her stomach dropped sharply as they both fell, the wind rushing past her face as noisy as the water tumbling over the riverbed below. The sensation of falling was terrifying, but worse was the utter helplessness of not being able to control what was happening. Losing her independence occurred frequently in her nightmares, but she did everything to ensure it never happened in real life.

Sound exploded in a blast of air bubbles and cold water, a shock after standing in the sun's warmth. As the liquid closed in around her, Kymora resisted the urge to fight free of Varian's grip. The current immediately grabbed them, so strong it tore a boot from her foot. With a quick push, she toed off the other, then kicked hard for the surface, her progress helped as Varian tugged on her arm.

Surfacing, she gasped for air and shook her hair from her face. The undercurrent tugged hard at her dress, and she tightened her hold on his hand. She could swim but rarely chose to. The water was one environment she had no control over.

"I've got you." Varian's arm wrapped around hers from behind, supporting her. "Lay back, let the current float us downstream."

Muscles so tight and every instinct protesting relinquishing control to him, it took conscious effort to lean back and release his arm. She dug her fingers into the one wrapped around her waist.

The thought of not being able to touch the riverbed with her feet made her teeth chatter. She couldn't feel the rocks or anticipate where obstacles might lay. She bit her lip hard. Drawing in a slow breath, she tried to focus on the warmth and strength of Varian's body cradling hers, and not on the submerged perils ahead of them.

"Doesn't look like the renegades want to join us for a swim," he said, his voice raised loud enough for her to hear over the hiss of the water. "They're following us along the edge of the cliff."

"Do you think they'll keep up?" She forced the question past stiff lips and focused on his words.

"We're moving too fast downstream and there's a bend coming up. They'll lose sight of us shortly."

She released her breath. That would alleviate one threat, if only for a while. She doubted Veren would give up searching for them, but at least they'd have some distance and a river between them.

A strange, rushing sound caught her attention. She tensed. "Varian, what's up ahead?"

"A set of rapids near the bend. The water is smoother on the inside. I'll try and move us over there."

Knowing he needed to concentrate, she resisted the urge to ask him how rough they were. She wasn't sure she wanted to know any-way. It was a wonder Varian couldn't feel just how hard her heart was beating through their two layers of clothes.

A wave splashed over her chest and face. They submerged. Water filled her mouth and nose. She jackknifed and fought to sit up as Varian's legs gave a strong kick, then they broke through the surface. She gasped in a shocked breath.

"Easy, I've still got you." Varian's voice in her ear was laced with tension. "Relax."

Another drop, much deeper than the first, had her digging her fingernails into his forearm as they went under again, only this time they were flipped facedown, then buffeted around and around.

Under the surface, the tinny roar of water pounding against stone deafened her, added to her confusion. *Mother of Mercy*, which way was up? Varian's legs brushed hers as he gave a powerful kick. Thank the *Lady* for *Na'Chi* strength. They surged upward. Lungs burning, she flailed with one arm, hunting for the surface. They both emerged coughing and sucking in fresh air.

Her limbs began to shake. Being separated from Varian was all too easy to imagine. Logic told her he was doing everything he could to keep them safe. With every movement, she could feel his muscles flexing, contracting, guiding the direction they drifted, fighting the current to keep them afloat. But one hard jolt against a submerged rock, being sucked into a small whirlpool, or even tumbling over rapids could do it.

"Breathe deeply, Kymora. Slow your breathing."

"I can't." She shuddered. This was too much like her nightmares. In them her fear became a living entity, so thick it often smothered her like a blanket, or rising water. She always woke before it overcame her but not before she reached the brink of torment. Just like now. "Let me go."

She hardly recognized the thready, high-pitched voice as her own. Varian's arm tightened around her. She struggled harder, her breath coming in desperate gasps.

"Kymora, relax."

She elbowed him and he grunted. Her pulse thundered in her ears. She needed to get out of the water. *Now.*

"Tread water." Varian's sharp command and movement upright penetrated her panic. "Turn."

Somehow she managed to loop an arm around his neck and they ended up face-to-face. Hot tears prickled in her eyes. *Mother of Light,* what was she doing?

"I'm sorry. . . ." Her voice broke.

She could hear his rapid breathing above the sound of the rushing water. The power in his legs was the only thing keeping them above the surface. Hers were tangled in the folds of her dress, useless, a dead weight that threatened to drag them to the bottom.

"Use the fear to strengthen you. Don't let it win." The sense of urgency in his tone sharpened her focus. What could he see ahead that she couldn't? "Climb onto my back. Now!"

The thread of steel in his voice quelled her flare of panic and spurred her to try. Submerging again to duck under his arm was the worst, but she clung to his shirt and emerged to wrap her arms over his hard-muscled shoulders, plastering herself along the length of his back.

"Kick hard, Kymora." His muscles bunched, and with his arms free, she could feel them moving through the water a lot faster.

Kicking through material that wrapped around her legs was hard, but it was better than floating helplessly on her back. The sense of control helped ease the fear clawing her insides.

"Nearly there . . ." His breathless reassurance ended in a grunt. His body jerked as if he'd hit something. They stopped moving. Beneath her, his every muscle and limb felt like steel, rigid and hard as he held them steady against the current. "We've reached the bank. The boulder has a lip"—he gasped in a breath—"a hand span above the water level. It's flat on top. Reach up . . . feel for it."

Kymora slid a hand along his arm, over his fingers until she could feel the pitted surface of the rock. She found a crack and wedged her fingertips in it, hoping her trembling muscles wouldn't jeopardize her hold.

"You get out first."

"Are you sure?"

"Yes." Her teeth wouldn't stop chattering. Transferring her weight to the hand gripping the boulder she forced herself to let Varian go. Her stomach dropped like a stone to the bottom of the river with the loss of contact. The absence of his body heat made the water swirling around her seem much colder.

Biting her lip to stop herself from crying out, she found a second handhold, then scrambled with her legs to find purchase on the submerged rock wall. Panting hard, she pressed her cheek against wet rock. She was on her own, her nightmares resurrected. Far too real.

"Please hurry." Whether he heard her or not above the sound of rushing water, she had no idea.

Gritting his teeth, Varian flung his arm over the edge and hauled himself out of the water. His body shook with the effort, but the terror etched on Kymora's face gave him the strength he needed to pull himself the rest of the way. Water streamed off him as he scrambled to his knees on top of the water-worn boulder. He leaned over the edge and grasped her wrists.

"I've got you!" Kymora stared up at him, her sightless gaze wide, and her cheeks pinched and pale. The sharp, bitter scent of her fear coated his nostrils. It was much, much stronger now.

Not that he blamed her. The journey down the river had taken an enormous amount of nerve to make. Relying on him to help her swim downstream took a level of trust he'd never have given another. The respect he felt for her rose another notch.

"You can let go now, Kymora. I've got you."

Bracing himself, he hauled her clear of the water and onto the rock in one swift movement. The momentum took them backward and he went with it, curling his arms around her to cushion her fall. He ended up flat on his back with her cradled on top of him.

Varian laid his head back on the rock and closed his eyes, content to feel the warmth of the sun on his face as he sucked in huge breaths, one after the other. Every muscle felt overheated and rubbery. His limbs were as heavy as some of the boulders lining the riverbank.

For the moment, he didn't care. They'd outdistanced the rebels. They were safe. Kymora was safe. That was all that mattered. Until he realized how badly she shook. Her shoulders twitched, and where she lay against him, he could feel her hiccupping, as if she were crying. Not a sound came from her though.

The sharp stab in the center of his chest, like someone had pricked his heart with a knife blade, caught him off guard. "Kymora?" Her tears twisted his insides tighter than the braids at his temples.

*Comfort her.*

He hesitated. He wanted to but didn't know how. He hadn't had a lot of practice being with others or easing their fears. You had to be around them and spend time with them to do something like that. But as Kymora continued to tremble, his conscience demanded he do something.

Gingerly, he tightened his arms around her. He shifted so they were seated on the boulder with her cradled between his spread legs, and placed a hand on her back to rub it. The gesture felt awkward and uncomfortable, but it was something he'd seen Lisella do with younger children. He just hoped it would work with Kymora because he didn't know what else to do.

She tucked her head beneath his chin and pressed her cold cheek against his chest. Her spasmodic breaths were warm against his wet skin. She tucked her hands between their bodies, then wrapped her arms around his waist, squeezing him as if she were afraid he'd let her go.

Water dripped from his hair into his eyes but he ignored it. "Shh, I'm here."

Being needed as a scout or warrior was an entirely different feeling from providing someone with a source of emotional comfort. As strange as it felt, a part of him liked it.

Peering across the white-tipped waves rushing downstream, he wished he knew what to say to make her feel better. Talking about her fear would probably embarrass her. If the situation were reversed, he knew he'd hate the thought of anyone seeing him so vulnerable.

"Kymora, you're safe." He kept his voice quiet, calm. "We both are."

He frowned. Had she heard him? Her fingers gripped handfuls of his sodden shirt. He could feel her nails digging into his back. Smoothing wet strands of her black hair from her face, he saw that she'd bitten her lip so hard she'd drawn blood. He grazed the back of his finger over her cheek, his stomach clenching at the bruise beginning to darken her flesh.

She'd been struck. He almost demanded she tell him which rebel had hit her, but he contained the urge, fighting to control his renewed fury at the thought of her in danger. Had he been sure of where the others were, and more certain of Kymora's safety, he'd have rescinded his capture-and-contain order concerning the rebels. They deserved death for threatening the lives of his people and the humans.

Had his scouts and the Light Blades been successful against the rebels? Were Lisella and the others safe? He had to get back to the village, but Kymora was still trembling and shivering in his arms.

Unsure of what to do, Varian just held her and ran his hand along her hair. Even wet the strands were soft as they brushed against his skin. It felt good just touching her, something he'd wanted to do since their momentous meeting in the *Lady's* Temple.

His stroking slowed as he recalled Lisella pressing a gentle kiss to the crown of a child's head. Did he dare? Would Kymora accept such a gesture from him? More importantly, was it appropriate? Varian swallowed hard and wondered if she could hear how hard his heart was beating.

Hunting, tracking, fighting, training, disciplining, killing; those were all areas he excelled in. Situations like this were way out of his experience. Comfort and care belonged to people like Lisella. Kymora needed someone like her, not him. He ground his teeth together. What was he supposed to do?

"We need to find shelter, a place to hide." Action. Now that was something he could deal with. He kept his voice low, gentle. "We never made it around the bend in the river and we're too exposed to stay here on the riverbank."

Peering around the rocky scree, the low angle of the sun and the lengthening shadows told him they had barely an hour of daylight remaining. As much as he wanted to get back to the village, Kymora wasn't ready to face a long, arduous trek, especially one that contained another river crossing. Not yet.

While he didn't know this section of the foothills well, the jagged ridge that ran parallel to the riverbank was the same one that ran behind the village. The caverns there had provided them with temporary accommodations while the village was being built. Varian gathered Kymora into his arms again.

"We'll find a cave to shelter in for the night. If we're lucky, it'll be deep enough for us to build a fire and shield the light." His thigh muscles ached in protest as he pushed to his feet, but he ignored the pain. "There's plenty of wood to scavenge in the forest. . . ."

They were going to need that fire come nightfall. While the day had been hot, the lateness of the season meant the evenings cooled off. Spending a night in wet clothes wasn't ideal.

With her in his arms, he headed for a sandy egress and made his way up the riverbank. As he reached the fringe of the forest, he continued listing all the things he could think of that would make their overnight stay more comfortable. Collecting dry leaves for a bed, setting a snare in the hope of catching dinner; he even mentioned how he hated walking in soggy boots.

Anything to keep Kymora's attention focused outward. And if he were honest, it kept his mind off inappropriate thoughts such as how much he was beginning to like having her soft, warm body in his arms.

# Chapter 4

THE line of captured renegades bore a range of facial expressions, some downright hostile as they glared at their *Na'Chi* guards, another couple seemed afraid, while one or two had the presence of mind to look ashamed.

Arek fisted his gloved hands as he watched his Light Blade warriors binding the rebels' hands and feet. Because they'd gone in unarmed against them, two of his warriors had suffered defensive wounds, one rebel lay dead after refusing to surrender, and another had been found stabbed outside the village.

None of the renegades deserved to wear the *Lady's* sun amulet around their necks. Every single one of them had resisted. Very little sympathy for any blood or bruises adorning them mixed with the white-hot anger seething inside him.

Using a begrimed sleeve, he wiped sweat from his brow. "Are they all accounted for?"

Glancing away from where the rebels sat lined up against one of the village houses, his gaze connected with several *Na'Chi*, then settled on Zaune's. The young scout had joined them toward the end of the battle with worrying news from Lisella. Kymora had not made it to the shelter of the caves, and their search of the village for her had proved futile.

Kalan and Kymora were closer than any brother and sister he knew, so delivering such news to his friend wasn't something he looked forward to doing. The man had enough to worry about with the increasing frequency of attacks by the *Na'Reish* on the border, not to mention brewing unrest within human territory that could easily explode into civil war. Arek sighed softly. This incident certainly wasn't going to help that situation anytime soon.

"We're not sure if they're all here," Rystin replied. The dark-haired scout's violet eyes were flecked with black. His scowl matched Arek's mood. "Varian's also disappeared."

"Second . . ."

The weak, hoarse call came from the injured man found at the edge of the village. His face seemed familiar but Arek couldn't place him. The warrior obviously recognized him, as he'd called him by his title. Slumped against the wall of a house, the man tried to straighten but hadn't the strength. Each breath he took gurgled in his chest and was painful to listen to.

Arek covered the distance between them and crouched beside him. The thick metallic tang of blood mingled with sweat and the foul stench of human waste. The wound low on his abdomen seeped a dark red, almost black liquid.

Arek grimaced. A bowel wound. That accounted for the putrid odor. The other was higher up in his ribs. Both were mortal.

"Second, there are two more. . . ." Pain contorted his weathered features as he stretched out a bloody hand to grip his arm. "They tried to kill the *Temple Elect*."

"There were twelve of you?" He squeezed the man's hand as his eyes fluttered closed. "Stay with me, warrior."

"Twelve . . . yes." His head dipped, then lifted. His blood-flecked lips twisted in a grimace. "Veren and Torant . . . I tried to stop them. . . ."

The wounds were from his friends, not from the recent battle? Arek frowned. "Did you see what happened to the *Temple Elect*?"

"One of *them* took her. . . ." He inclined his head toward the scouts. "She claimed he was her friend."

Arek sucked in a short breath. "A *Na'Chi* about my height, black hair, with temple braids?"

"Yes." A racking cough stained his mouth with bright, frothy blood. The man wiped it from his lips with the back of his hand. Dark brown eyes met his, a glassy sheen to them but sharp enough to reflect the knowledge that he knew he had little time left in this world. "Veren and Torant gave chase. . . . The *Na'Chi* and *Temple Elect* leapt off the cliff . . . to escape them. . . ."

"Varian and Kymora jumped from the escarpment?" Zaune's tone reflected his surprise. "Can Kymora swim?"

"Yes, but she hates the water." Arek frowned. Kymora only ever swam close to the shoreline and never in anything higher than waist deep. "Take five men, a mix of your scouts and mine. Find their tracks—"

"You're giving us orders?" Rystin stiffened where he stood. "Who put you in charge, human?"

Arek ground his teeth hard. "If the *Na'Chi* don't want to help, that's fine. I'll send my warriors out alone, but with you, Varian and Kymora will be found a lot quicker."

"Rystin, it doesn't matter who gives the orders; they'd be the same if they came from you or me, wouldn't they?" Zaune cocked one dark eyebrow. "Varian and Kymora's safety comes first, eh?"

Rystin stared at Arek for several long heartbeats, his gaze hard, intense, then he turned on his heel and walked away.

Zaune shook his head and glanced at Arek. "He's still not sure about the alliance. . . ."

"He's not the only one," Arek admitted, quietly.

Personally, he wasn't sure if some would ever get over the ingrained prejudice each felt for the other race. Too many years of conflict with the *Na'Reish* tainted their history. Learning that they'd once shared the same territory and the origins of their Gifts were the result of interracial breeding with the demons had shocked them all.

But no more so than discovering his grandfather and others, all revered figureheads on the Blade Council, had kept this information secret for decades. Then to find out Annika was his *Na'Chi* half sister—he shook his head—they were all issues he still struggled with, so he could understand why others were having trouble adjusting.

"As I was saying, find their tracks and where Varian and Kymora went over the edge." Arek grimaced at the thought of Kymora in the water. "Then hunt down the two missing renegades. Once we have them, we can organize a search for Varian and Kymora."

Zaune's hand gripped his shoulder. An unusual gesture for the young scout as he tended to avoid physical contact unless engaged in battle. "Varian will keep her safe."

Would Varian be able to elude the rebels hunting them? "I hope so." He peered up at the sky. "You better get going, Zaune. There's only a half hour until sunset."

"You're forgetting something, Light Blade."

"What?"

The young scout raised one dark brow. "Darkness won't stop us."

For a moment, Arek was almost jealous of the *Na'Chi* and their ability to see in the dark. "At least you're all good for something, then."

One corner of Zaune's mouth curled in response. "I'd take Rystin with me but I suspect he'll refuse, so I'll take Taybor and send Jinnae to get some of the others to help you with the prisoners."

Arek nodded and the *Na'Chi* scout headed off.

"Tell the Handmaiden I'm sorry. . . ."

The whispered plea drew his attention back to the Light Blade warrior lying against the house. He'd slumped farther down the wall. The hand gripping Arek's arm released him and pulled at the leather thong around his neck until his amulet slipped free. The man's fingers curled around the small disc, his eyes closed.

"*Mother of Mercy* . . ." His voice trailed off but his lips continued moving, praying. Arek inhaled deeply. The man wouldn't be the first Light Blade warrior he'd seen die, but this was the first who'd forsaken his vows, defied Kalan's order, and attacked those granted sanctuary. What had driven him to do so?

His last words indicated he regretted his actions. The *Lady* might ease his Final Journey if his repentant attitude was sincere. As the man's lips stopped moving, his hand relaxed and slid slowly to the ground.

Arek reached out to press his fingers against his neck. No pulse. Another warrior lost in terrible circumstances. He rubbed tired eyes and sent a brief prayer to the *Lady* asking for *Her* to judge him fairly and for *Her* protection for Kymora and Varian.

Pushing to his feet, Arek stared around the village. With the onset of evening, the odor of smoke hung like a pall in the air, acrid and heavy, the haze low and thick. Half the houses had succumbed to the flames, another three were charred, still standing but uninhabitable. During the search for Kymora, he'd seen the wanton destruction wrought by the renegades inside the houses.

Blackened ash and tendrils of smoke were all that remained of the crops he and his warriors had helped the *Na'Chi* put in three months ago. The vegetable gardens cared for by both races of children were destroyed, the plants trampled or uprooted and flung around the enclosure. And only a handful of bleaters had survived the slaughter. Their plaintive mewls as they called to flock-mates who would never answer were a somber accompaniment to the quiet stillness of the evening.

Arek grimaced. What other casualties would the cleanup bring?

KYMORA shuddered, unable to shake the icy cold afflicting her limbs. Her teeth were chattering so hard the sound echoed back off the walls. It didn't help that she was seated on a rock floor in the middle of a cave in a dress that continued to drip water.

Mustering what little energy she possessed, she wrapped her arms around her upraised knees and tucked her toes under the sodden hem, hoping that would help. Walking around, stamping her feet, movement of any sort would help generate body heat, but she didn't know the layout of the cave. Her staff was gone. And so was Varian.

Rubbing the goose bumps on her arms, she listened for his footsteps. How long had it been since he'd left her? Would he come back? Her shivering increased.

What would she do if he didn't? What if Veren and the other renegade ambushed and killed him? How would she make her way to safety when she didn't even know where she was? Icy tendrils sprouted from the cold knot in her stomach, wrapped around her chest, and squeezed.

Shallow, uneven breathing rasped in her ears. Hers. *Merciful Mother*, she'd made enough of a fool of herself today already without imagining things like Varian's demise or being abandoned in a strange place. She swallowed against the tightness in her throat.

"*Lady, You* are my heart. *You* give me the strength to face my fears and harness them." The mantra was barely a whisper, a familiar distraction; one she hoped would help her regain control. "Peace and harmony come from a disciplined and calm mind."

She inhaled a shuddering breath and released it slowly, but every muscle in her body remained locked tight.

"Kymora, I'm back!"

Varian's soft call triggered an overwhelming wave of relief. A whimper escaped her lips before she could stop it. She scrubbed at the tears burning behind her eyes, denying them leave to fall, not wanting Varian to see just how close she'd come to losing control. Again.

A strange rasping sound filled the cave.

"What are you dragging?" Her voice shook, much to her dismay.

"I found the perfect bedding . . . forest needles. I had to break off a whole branch and bring it back. . . . Didn't have enough hands to carry an armful of twigs and the wood." The deep resonance of his voice stroked her raw nerves, taking the edge off them. "But don't worry, it's all just outside. I made several trips before coming in. Won't be long before we have a fire."

Varian kept talking even as he left the cave and all she could hear was the intonation of it rather than individual words. It didn't matter. She was no longer alone. He was there, a steady, reassuring presence that warmed her more than the fire he built. The wood crackled and snapped, until she felt the air within the cave begin to warm.

"Kymora, you'll catch a chill in that wet dress." When his hand touched the nape of her neck, she shivered but finally began to relax. He cleared his throat. "You need to take it off. I'll spread it out over the other side of the cave. By morning it should dry."

Heat flooded her face, almost as hot as the hand resting at the base of her neck. He wanted her to unclothe? *Lady's Breath*, she felt vulnerable enough without being stripped to bare skin.

She shifted a little closer to the warmth of the flames. "I'll be fine now that the fire's going."

He moved away. "Kymora, you're shivering. We both need to get dry and warm." The slick sound of material being peeled from skin accompanied his statement, then she heard him squeezing water out of cloth. It splashed against the stone floor. Two thumps, one after the other, then more water splattered against the ground. "I'll be lucky if my boots aren't ruined by morning."

Varian was undressing? Awareness zapped her as if she'd touched the flames of the fire with her bare hand. Her pulse picked up speed. For one long heartbeat she almost wished for the gift of sight. She'd felt the solid strength of his body beneath her hands. Muscles as hard as blade steel, smooth, sculpted by a life spent outdoors, honed by the need to survive.

Her lips parted, the temptation to ask warring with her more cautious side. Asking if she could touch him, to trace and shape his body with her fingertips so she could "see" him in his entire masculine splendor was out of the question. Varian rarely allowed anyone that privilege, but the desire to possess that freedom flared inside her.

What was she thinking? He'd want to know why, and that was something she wasn't even sure she could answer. More warmth rushed into her cheeks.

"Kymora?" His question drew her from her thoughts. "Do you need help?"

"No!"

Silence greeted her outburst. Closing her eyes, she regretted her sharp reply. She twisted a piece of her dress with her fingers. What must he think of her falling apart like this?

"Is there some holy rule about disrobing in front of others I don't know about? Are *Her* Servants forbidden to do this?" His drawled queries weren't quite the response she'd expected. "*Lady* forgive me if I've offended you again, but you know how ignorant I am about these sorts of things."

The gentle humor coloring his voice reminded her of the time she'd discovered him on the walkway to the Temple, leaning against the cenotaph stones of the Light Blades who'd died in battle against the *Na'Reish*. Unable to read the inscriptions, he hadn't realized the significance of the memorial. When she'd enlightened him to the true source of the disgruntled looks he'd been receiving from the humans passing by, he'd been mortified.

"Ignorant?" She huffed, a small smile tugging at her lips. "I think *irreverent* would be a word more suited to you."

"You and Lisella are so much alike. No wonder you get on well together." His soft chuckle caressed her senses, but then his tone sobered. "Truly though, have I upset you?"

To spare herself embarrassment Kymora was almost persuaded to agree, but too many years as a Servant where the truth of her word was held in high esteem curbed the action.

"The only offense inflicted would be to my modesty." She averted her head, too aware that the blush staining her face would easily be visible in the firelight. "Being naked in front of someone isn't a comfortable thought."

"And you think I feel differently?"

"Varian, I can't see you."

"When I sit down behind you to help you get warm we're going to be skin to skin." Her heart skipped a beat. "You read other people through touch, much more astutely than anyone gives you credit." His voice dropped to a murmur. "Vulnerability doesn't just come through lack of sight."

Each word was stilted, his tone reluctant. Others claimed he was distant, cold, reclusive, and there were times Varian reinforced that impression with his solitary behavior, but now, with her, she savored his consideration. His honesty struck close to her heart and it swelled with grateful affection.

Before she could change her mind, she stood and, in one motion, pulled the saturated material off her body and held it out to him. Without a word, it was taken from her outstretched fingers. As she settled back into her huddled pose, the heat flushing her body had little to do with the fire.

She listened to Varian wringing and laying out her dress. His bare feet scuffed the floor as he took his time preparing the bed of forest needles. Was the noise deliberate? Usually he was so silent she had to strain to find his location.

"It's not the sleeping pad or clean linens you're used to"—his fingers closed around her wrist and he tugged her arm to the right—"but it's better than hard rock."

She smiled as the fronds tickled the palm of her hand. "They're soft and warm." They'd been piled into a mound thick enough to stave off any cold or dampness rising from the cavern floor. "They'll make a fine bed."

Varian drew in a silent breath. The gentle expression on Kymora's face proved a thousand times more preferable to the stark lines of fear that had pinched her face when he'd walked into the small cave. He was almost tempted to thank the *Lady* for giving him the right words to say, enough to distract Kymora from whatever dark thoughts she'd been contemplating.

Reaching for another branch of forest needles, Varian stripped the stem and added them to the bedding, then fed the stick into the fire.

"Aren't you going to join me?"

He couldn't detect anything in the tone of her voice, but he caught her scent, that light hint of summer flowers, but this time with a subtle minty freshness. Nervousness.

Unable to resist, his gaze strayed to the graceful curve of her naked back, so pale compared to the long strands of black hair that fell to just above her hips. Lithe muscles proportionally suited to her slender form, from the plump hint of her breast tucked against a raised leg to the flare of her hips and tender fleshiness of her buttocks, made her all woman.

Her skin was free of the spotted, uneven body markings that every *Na'Chi* and *Na'Reish* possessed. The absence of the natural tattoos fascinated him. His fingers itched to touch her. Was her skin as smooth as it looked?

In the flickering firelight, he could see every hollow and dip of her form, and what the shadows concealed, his imagination more than made up for. Enough that the lower part of his body began to burn with a deeper need, one he recognized and shouldn't be feeling. Uneasiness spiraled through him.

She was naked. He was just reacting like any other male would. Nothing else.

*"Why would any woman want Varian when there are other, unscarred males to choose from?"*

He winced as the memory ran through his mind.

The group of young *Na'Chi* women hadn't realized he'd been coming through the shrubbery near their latest camp, a cave at the foot of a rocky hillside in the forest.

*"It's a shame his face is scarred."*

The pity-filled comment was the last thing Varian had expected from his peers. His fingers stopped short of touching the jagged wound on his cheek.

The same female voice spoke again. *"Rystin says Varian thinks it's a badge of honor."*

*"Don't be too hard on him,"* another voice chimed in. *"He's a worthy scout."*

*"What, because he killed the* Na'Reish *warrior who followed Hesia to our camp?"*

*"Well, no scout has ever done that before. And if he hadn't, the* Na'Reish *would have found out about all of us."*

*"He can fight to protect me . . . us, but don't expect me to mate with him."*

The small group laughed. To a fourteen-year-old, the mocking sound was enough to heat his cheeks with shame and anger. Their behavior reminded him of the *Na'Reish*. How many times had he seen the *Na'Reishi* upper caste mock their underlings or others because of their physical imperfections?

He ground his teeth together. Why did a scar bother them so

much? They'd grown up together. They knew he was more than his looks, didn't they? He was about to step forward and berate them when the first female spoke again.

*"Have you seen the look in Varian's eyes when he kills?"*

*"What? The crimson hue? All the scouts show that color when they're fighting."*

*"No, not that. His are so cold and empty, but there's something else."* Her voice dropped to a whisper but Varian could still hear her. *"It's almost like he enjoys it. Another reason I won't be choosing him when it comes time to mate. Who wants an ice-cold killer sharing their bed?"*

Her rank disgust and horror left Varian reeling, too shocked to think or breathe. Devastated by their collective rejection, he'd stumbled away from the cave, not because her comments had hurt him, that had come later, but because she'd been right.

He didn't like calling on his *Na'Reish* half to help protect them. The aggression and violence he was capable of frightened him, but once that part of him took over, the battle rush consumed him. He did crave the victory, but wasn't that assurance the result of knowing the threat has been eliminated? Instinct and necessity motivated him and every other scout in the group. Without that double-edged blade, none of them would survive.

The dual conflict tormented him even now.

In the months that followed, he'd paid more attention to the way his peers treated him, particularly the young women. No longer so naïve, he watched them cement friendships, enter relationships, and experiment. Their behavior toward him showed a distinct lack of warmth and acceptance they showed the other males.

Never one to accept defeat, it took him another five years to accept the lesson learned from the humiliating incident. His value to the group was measured solely through the strength of his arm. His worth came from his skill with the blade. Nothing else.

They tolerated him but their message was clear. No one loved a killer, especially not one who rode the high of the carnage afterward.

Looking back, if it hadn't been for Hesia's love and encouragement acting as a counterbalance, he might have given in to his darker half and become the demon everyone feared. Instead he'd channeled all his efforts into ensuring her dream to see the *Na'Chi* safe succeeded. Without that driving him, what else was there to hold on to?

Varian sucked in a deep breath. His nostrils flared as Kymora's delicate scent filled his lungs and drew him back to the present. The friendship she'd instigated filled a hole inside him, one he'd never realized existed until recently.

He rubbed at the ache in the center of his chest. The growing tangle of emotions he felt when he was around her were becoming more intense. They scared him. Adrenaline-pumping, chest-squeezing, heart-stopping fear he could accept, it was something he'd dealt with on a daily basis all his life, but this fear burrowed deeper, sensitizing every nerve ending in his body and turned it inside out.

He wasn't sure what it meant, but one thing he knew for certain: Friends were all he and Kymora could ever be. There was no way he was going to leave himself wide open for rejection again.

"Varian?" His name stuttered on her lips and she hugged herself harder. A fresh ripple of goose bumps decorated her skin.

His decision to share body warmth now seemed like a bad idea. The pain of reliving a childhood memory hadn't lessened his arousal. There'd been no exaggerating when he'd complimented Kymora for her skill at reading people. She was going to get a very clear idea just what he was feeling for her once he sat down. But he couldn't let her continue to freeze.

Shaking his head, he tried to control his erection and quell the need feeding it. It took a few minutes of disciplined concentration, and while sweat beaded his skin and his hands shook, he felt confident that he wouldn't frighten her or disgrace himself.

"Sometimes, in the deep of winter, the *Na'Reish* patrols came close to where we lived, and we couldn't risk lighting a fire. Not even one for cooking." He sat down behind Kymora, stretching his long legs to either side of her. Curling his arms around her, he covered her smaller hands with his, keeping his hold loose as she tensed. He cradled her against him in almost the same position he'd used by the river. "We'd huddle together like this for hours to avoid succumbing to the cold."

Where she was pressed against his chest and abdomen, her skin was cold. He rubbed her fingers, massaging each digit to get her circulation flowing again.

"Is this why the children are always so quiet?" she asked. "I remember the healers' apprentice, Rissa, telling me that the first time she played a game of tag ball with them, they were appalled by the amount of noise the human children made. Did the patrols ever find you?"

"Noise always carried the risk of discovery. Keeping quiet was learnt at a very young age, and, yes, there were times when a patrol found us."

"What happened?"

Deep inside him, something flinched. A chill broke out across his skin. "You really don't want to know, Kymora." He couldn't help the gruffness in his voice. The less she knew about his other half, the better.

She was quiet a moment, then her fingers tangled with his and squeezed. "You killed them?" Her voice was soft, gentle, and not at all accusatory.

Varian sat frozen as her question triggered brutal, painful memories. The sight of *Na'Reish* and *Na'Chi* locked together in combat.

The faint sound of war cries.

The raw prick of animal-like rage.

Of bodies littering the forest floor. Some with their throats slashed.

Their blood a stark contrast against the myriad greens.

The rich, iron odor of it assaulting his nostrils . . .

He and six other scouts had killed a full *Na'Reish* patrol who'd ventured too close to their hidden camp. That had been their first successful ambush, the first of many. Heart pounding hard beneath his ribs, he stole a quick glance at his hands to assure himself the hot stickiness of blood didn't coat his skin. He grimaced, hating the vivid details that still haunted him almost as much as the actions he'd taken to survive.

He supposed it didn't take much to connect the facts. Not when Kymora already knew the *Na'Reish* killed on sight those they considered a bloodborn disgrace, but he was sure Kalan would never share the gory stories of his battles with her, so neither would he. She should be sheltered from such harsh violence. Instead he clenched his teeth and remained silent.

"Lisella told me you all moved your location every couple of weeks. That must have been hard. I've lived in Sacred Lake all my life. My parents were Guild-traders so we lived in Bartertown." Just like that, she changed the subject, and for that he was grateful. It gave him something to focus on other than his shortcomings. "When Kalan was appointed as the *Lady's Chosen*, we shared the apartment he and Annika live in now. After I became *Temple Elect*, the Temple dormitory became my home." Her tone grew wistful. "Sometimes I wish I'd been appointed as a Traveller."

"What's that?"

"A Handmaiden or Manservant who goes from village to town, ministering or teaching." He heard the smile in her voice. "They get to see and experience so much of the world. Sometimes I wish I'd chosen a different path for my life."

The ability to call one place home was something he'd longed for all his life. Living hand to mouth, driven to move every few weeks, every shelter just a place to eat, sleep, hide, never a home, always afraid of discovery, of being tracked and hunted down, then slaughtered. The differences between their lifestyles were stark, and the irony of each of them wanting what the other had didn't escape him.

"As *Temple Elect*, don't you oversee all the territory?"

"I instruct and oversee *Her* Servants." Her head turned to one side. "Do you remember the Councilors' shock when I announced that I would be living with you and the other *Na'Chi*?"

"I thought it was because of who we were."

Kymora squeezed his hand. "Well, that might have been some of it," she replied, dryly, "but mostly it's because the *Temple Elect's* responsibilities encompass everything within the walls of Sacred Lake. Travellers are appointed to cover everything else."

No wonder her decision to live with them in the village had unsettled the Blade Council and the rest of the human race. Defying convention took a lot of courage, but then he already knew Kymora was a woman of strong convictions.

"Did Kalan and you ever expect this alliance to cause so much trouble?"

"You're asking would I change what I've done if I'd known what would happen?" A small smile curved the edge of her mouth. "No. Not at all."

His admiration and respect for her decision to stand firm increased. "Why not? It's split your people. Now it's Light Blade against Light Blade. Surely it's not worth the strife this has caused you."

Kymora made a small sound of protest. Turning in his hold, she laid a hand on his chest. "Do you think Hesia regrets what she went through to make sure the *Na'Chi* survived? And what about Kalan? Do you believe he regrets his imprisonment in the *Na'Rei's* dungeon when it brought him and Annika together? Do you regret asking for sanctuary so your people could live a better life?"

Regret, no. His gaze strayed to the swelling and bruising on her jaw. With people being hurt by the dissension, it left him wondering if the price of the alliance was too high. "Hesia and Kalan saw their dreams reach fruition."

"Not without a struggle. Nothing good is ever achieved without one. This alliance is worth that, Varian."

"Kymora, the last time we visited Sacred Lake, your people hid in their houses and slammed their doors on us as we walked past. And unless we have a human with us in the markets, no one will trade with us. Surely you haven't forgotten that?"

Despite Hesia's dream, maybe there was no safe place for them to call home.

"Change is never easy, you know that," she reminded him. "The *Na'Chi* will find acceptance and humans will come to realize the blessing the *Lady* has bestowed upon us."

"A blessing?" He tried to regulate the amount of sarcasm in his tone and failed. Her faith reminded him so much of Hesia and Lisella. "You think the *Na'Chi* are a blessing?"

"Of course I do." A frown marred her brow. "At a time when we most needed each other *She* brought you to us."

He shook his head, astounded at her devotion to an unseen deity he refused to acknowledge. She hesitated a moment, probably having felt his negative response, indecision flashing across her features before she drew in a slow breath.

"Varian, *She* brought you to me. I can think of no greater gift than that."

# Chapter 5

"AREK, look." Lisella paused in helping him drag one of the slaughtered bleaters toward the trench he'd dug earlier. It already held several of the animals. Keeping his breath shallow to filter out the overwhelming stink of blood wasn't easy when the animals weighed as much as a full-grown person. Twenty-three beasts dead. What a senseless waste.

Arek glanced up and she nodded to something over his shoulder. Turning, he squinted, then shielded his eyes against the dying rays of the sunset. He couldn't quite make out the silhouette coming toward them across the field.

"It's one of the scouts." Lisella pushed a strand of hair that had escaped her ponytail from her face. "Zaune, I think."

Releasing the bleater and glad of the respite, he wiped his sleeve over his sweaty brow. "He went after the rebels and Kymora and Varian a little less than an hour ago."

"Maybe he's found something."

"Good news would be welcome right about now."

Lisella grunted in agreement. Arek lifted a hand in greeting as the young scout reached them. Violet eyes, calm and controlled, and the solemn aura surrounding the scout were usual. There were times he reminded Arek of what Varian might have been like at a younger age, the traits the two men exhibited were so similar.

"We've been unable to find the two rebels." Short and to the point, very typical. "Their tracks disappeared near the lower end of the escarpment. Their scent remained strong for a short distance but then vanished."

Arek cursed softly. Both Veren and Torant had to be experienced warriors to escape the detection of the *Na'Chi*. Kalan would need to know what had happened here as soon as possible.

"And what of Varian and Kymora?" he asked.

"We found Kymora's staff at the edge of the village. At the cliff face, clear prints lead to the edge. Taybor and one of your warriors went farther downstream to cross where the river is shallower. They're working their way back upstream on the opposite bank. Naylan and I will stay on this side. If we find nothing, we'll assume they drifted farther downstream. We'll keep searching. I just thought you should know about the renegades so you can post guards tonight."

Arek nodded.

"Zaune, before you head back out, call in at the village." Lisella's smile took the edge off the tension they were all feeling. "Barvi should have put together a small pack of food and water for you from the meal we were supposed to be celebrating with this evening. No sense in going hungry when we have all that food to spare."

"I was looking forward to some honey bread. . . ." Gratitude lit the scout's face. "Thanks, Lisella."

Arek watched Zaune head for the village. While steady, his gait was heavy. The younger man was tired, not that he'd ever admit to it. *Merciful Mother*, they all were. The events of the day were enough to age anyone a decade.

Weariness crept deeper into his soul as he considered all the things that needed to be done. Thankfully, burying the dead livestock was almost complete. The charred huts were unsafe and needed to be knocked down. A last check on the burned crops had to be done to make sure all the embers were out. The missing *Na'Chi* lookouts were yet to be found. A message informing Kalan of what had happened needed to be sent. And those were the most urgent tasks on his mental list. Arek let out a sharp breath.

Lisella's small hand grasped his and squeezed. Surprised, he glanced at her to find her observing him as intently as he'd been watching Zaune.

"We'll take it one hour at a time, Light Blade. That's all we can do." Her quiet words bolstered his weary confidence. "*Lady* willing, we'll all find solace and peace in a night's worth of sleep once the chores are done."

"Amen to that," he murmured.

BENEATH her hand, Kymora felt Varian still, even his breathing stopped. The crackling of the flames consuming the wood in the fire seemed amplified in the silence that stretched between them. Had her admission shocked him?

Her heart ached at the scorn and contempt in his voice when he'd refuted her claim that the *Na'Chi* were a blessing. His aversion to religion made for some awkward moments, but most times with her he'd kept such conversations light, often giving her more latitude when it came to remonstrating him for his behavior. She wasn't sure why she allowed that. Perhaps this time he'd lost patience.

Giving him a more personal slant had been the right thing to do. Deep down she knew it, even if she'd erred in her timing. Ready to accept whatever his response might be, she lifted her chin. Her insides quivered as she struggled to keep her anxiety from showing on her face.

"How am I a blessing?" Varian asked.

Derision coated every word, the timbre of his voice harsh, but beneath it she detected the smallest quaver of hope. Against her fingertips, his heart pounded in his chest. Hers beat just as hard and fast as she tried to decide how to best answer his question. She exhaled, slowly and deeply.

*You're my friend* hovered on her lips. She shook her head. Too shallow. He was a friend, but the connection between them was deepening. Other explanations flitted through her mind. None of those were appropriate, either. He deserved more than platitudes.

*Walk the path you start and discover the reward you seek at the end.*

The passage of scripture surfaced amidst her thoughts. *Lady of Light*, how many times had she advised petitioners to speak the truth in their hearts when faced with a difficult situation?

But should she? Her friendship with Varian was evolving; into what, she wasn't sure. Certainly there was a growing empathy and respect for each another; it'd been there from their first meeting in the Temple. Now her feelings for him were becoming more complex, more profound, more sensual in nature.

A small spark of excitement flared in her stomach. Was *this* the reason for her Fourth Journey? Many of her previous Journeys had focused on events in her life as the *Temple Elect*, so when the *Lady* had warned her to prepare for a change, she'd assumed this latest one would relate to it, too.

Kymora reached for her amulet. She traced the wavy lines of the sun symbol. What if this Journey turned out to be more intimate in nature? What if her attraction to Varian resulted in something more than friendship?

Should that happen, her actions would have wider implications beyond what unfolded between them. Her role as *Temple Elect* was so interwoven with her personal life, and vice versa, that sometimes separating the two wasn't possible.

Deep inside her, resentment flared.

As a young acolyte, she'd taken on the position in ignorance. Time had shown her the delicate and often difficult juggling act that accompanied her role. *Mother* forgive her, but it proved a burden she still struggled with.

*"Handmaiden, your Fourth Journey begins soon. Don't be afraid to take the path I've chosen for you."*

The *Lady* had spoken those words to her just before she'd met Varian and he'd asked for sanctuary on behalf of the *Na'Chi*. Very rarely did *She* speak to a Handmaiden or Servant about their future. At the time, she'd believed the *Lady* had been warning her about the existence of the *Na'Chi*, certainly an unprecedented circumstance in human history.

Had *She* been preparing her for this more personal experience instead? Kymora worried the edge of the amulet with her fingertips. Just once she wished she could make a decision based purely on what she wanted and not have to worry about how it would affect everyone else, yet in good conscience she couldn't. Could she?

Frustration burned in her stomach. *Lady* help her, indecisiveness and hesitancy were so unlike her. Lips thinning, she dropped her amulet and lifted her head in Varian's direction. For the first time, she was going to heed her heart. Taking a deep breath, she prayed her choice would be the right one.

Only one question remained: Was Varian ready to hear what she had to say? Unease churned in her stomach like a meal of spoiled stew, but Kymora dug deep for the courage to share her truths.

"Do you remember the first time we met?" she asked.

"Yes, in the Temple, you were praying at the altar after your duties for the day were concluded." Varian's tone was cautious, as if he was wondering what direction their conversation would take.

"I was unprepared for your swift attack. Pinning me to the wall frightened me."

Varian cleared his throat. "I'm not proud of how I handled that situation."

"I'm not berating you, just making a point." A small smile curved her lips at the memory. "You could have retaliated when I struck out at you. Instead you used your strength to contain the blows. You threatened me with words, you threatened my life with a knife in the Council chamber when the warriors drew their weapons, but not once did you ever follow through or hurt me."

"I'm a blessing because I threatened but didn't hurt you?"

She poked his chest at his obtuse statement, too aware of the warmth of his bare skin under her fingertip. It was a strange conversation to be having while sitting naked on the floor of a cave.

"I'm not finished. Just listen to what I have to say without interrupting." A grunt was his only response. "I've talked to Lisella, Zaune, some of the other scouts. . . . They've told me how you spent days looking for another safe place for them to live so the Na'Reish wouldn't discover you, about how hard you drove yourself and pushed them when you fled Na'Reish territory, following Annika and Kalan to Sacred Lake.

"I've listened to you play with the children, teach them to hide and track, instruct and discipline them when they argue. In meetings your opinions are measured, logical, sometimes impassioned, but not once have I witnessed a careless response.

"My point to all this—" A part of her registered the hard slab of muscle beneath her palm as she spread her fingers across his chest. She'd expected to feel a soft mat of hair, but his skin was bare and smooth. Another trait shared with the Na'Reish. Blinking, it took a moment to recall what she'd been saying. "Looking from the outside in, I see a compassionate man who knows the meaning of honor and duty, a protector with a generous soul."

"I'm not a saint. . . ." His hard-edged reply came as no surprise.

She shook her head. "I know that. You're surly, abrupt, antisocial most days, you speak your mind so plainly sometimes it offends. You're hard on your scouts, you demand the best from them, you drive them into giving more than they believe possible, you're sparing in your compliments. . . ." Beneath her hand his muscles tightened. Knowing her point was made, she halted her catalogue of flaws.

Trailing her fingers from his chest to his shoulder, she searched for and found the raised *Na'Chi* markings along the side of his neck. They continued up the side of his face, curved over his brow and into his hairline, the spots varied in size and shape, a pattern unique to each *Na'Chi*. The tactile sensation of them thrilled her, made her wish she could spend more time exploring all the places they adorned his body.

"These don't interfere with my getting to know someone, not like everyone else," she stated, unable to hide the huskiness of her voice. "I sense your heart. It's in your voice, against my skin; I analyze your actions and words."

She took another deep breath, her stomach churning as if she stood on the edge of the escarpment again ready to jump into the river, wondering at the wisdom of sharing all her truths with him.

With a swift prayer to the *Lady*, she leapt.

"Varian, it's what attracts me to you. Other than my brother, you're the only person who sees me as Kymora. Not the *Temple Elect*, the *Lady's* Handmaiden, or the blind priestess.

"You might call me those names, but they don't mean the same thing to you as they do to others." Her mouth twisted into a rueful smile. "Do you realize how much of a blessing that is?"

He didn't respond to her humor. As the silence between them lengthened, the aching hollow deep in her gut gnawed at her courage like a scurrier consumed carrion. Ducking her head, she withdrew her fingers from his hair and curled them in her lap.

Heat rushed to her cheeks and spread to the tips of her ears. *Merciful Mother*, had she just made a huge error in judgment?

# Chapter 6

"*DO you realize how much of a blessing that is?*"

Kymora's bold declaration echoed in Varian's mind. His breath caught. He should have expected it. She was every bit as forthright in her opinion as he tended to be; only she was much better at expressing herself than he was.

He'd never heard anyone describe him the way she just had. Sure, his people acquiesced to his orders and most respected the decisions he made because they knew their survival depended upon it. As their leader, it was his duty to ensure their well-being. But Kymora had recognized the lengths to which he'd gone to keep his people safe, and she'd made his actions sound worthy of admiration and acknowledgment. Her words warmed him, and the novelty of the sensation made his heart pound.

He licked his lips. Every instinct demanded he refute her words, deny her impression of him, deny that she could feel an attraction for him, deny he was a blessing to anyone, but he couldn't ignore the raw, earthy odor emanating from her, the truth of her claim under-scored by the knowledge that a person's scent never lied.

The prospect held him speechless for a long minute. He hated to admit just how deeply her belief in what she thought was the truth touched him. Calling her on a lie would have been so easy. He'd have cut her off without a qualm, but the scent lingering in his nostrils prevented him.

Yet he couldn't let go of the thought that she was attracted to him. Something buried deeply inside him stirred to cautious life. A shiver prickled his neck.

He wanted to believe her.

He *needed* to believe her.

Instead, sourness flooded the back of his throat. He wished he could claim the man she described was him, but he knew better. She hadn't felt the darkness inside him or seen the part of him he hated, and he prayed she never would.

It still didn't stop him wondering though what it would be like to kiss her. How many times had he fantasized about placing his lips on hers? Of holding her face in his hands and angling his mouth over hers and tasting her with his tongue? What would it feel like? Taste like?

The images filling his mind exploded like a fireball and resur-rected the erection he thought he had under control. Shuddering, he shifted away from her, hoping he'd relocated quickly enough.

Kymora moved within his arms. A heady combination of soured fruit and crushed spices filled his nostrils. Her head dipped and her fingers fisted so tightly in her lap her knuckles whitened. His con-tinued silence was hurting her.

He grimaced, her scent effectively dampening some of his desire. Her honesty and courage were so much greater than his. It made what he was about to do more difficult. His hands curled into fists.

"Your perspective of me is flawed." He kept his voice flat and hard. "You know nothing about me or what I'm like."

Kymora might be worldly wise in her role as *Temple Elect*—she would have to be—but her experiences were so different from his. She had a gentle softness, an innocence he refused to spoil.

"And you have no intention of enlightening me, do you?" Varian closed his eyes. Her skill at reading others was nothing short of phenomenal. She poked him with her finger. "That's the coward's way out, *Na'Chi*."

Her taunt sparked his temper, but a growing admiration for her bravery in confronting him replaced it. "Sharing my past with you is pointless."

Strands of her hair brushed his chest as she gave a quick shake of her head, tiny caresses over already sensitive nerves.

"*Lady's Breath*, Varian, you don't have the marketplace of personal demons cornered, you know." Her lips thinned, then pulled down at the corners a moment before she tensed, almost like she was bracing herself. "My fear of the water almost killed us both. Do you think I wanted you to see that side of me?"

"You have nothing to be ashamed of."

She ignored his protest. "Don't you want our friendship to evolve into something more?"

Longing stabbed him hard in the gut, but a rush of panic quickly overwhelmed it. She had no idea what she was asking. How could anyone find something like him attractive?

"Kymora, friendship is the only thing I can offer you." Even to his own ears, his voice sounded harsh.

"So I should count myself lucky and leave it at that?"

Her tongue was as sharp as Lisella's, but the sight of her chin trembling stabbed at his gut like a blade. His jaw tightened. She deserved somebody better than him. "If that's how you want to interpret it."

When her head lifted, the resolute expression on her face was a familiar one. "Varian, lying doesn't suit you."

Her fingers trailed across his inner thigh, featherlight, and the back of them brushed against his erection. The fleeting touch seared him from head to toe. He jerked back from her, a hoarse curse ripping from his throat. Her brash action stained his cheeks and hers with color.

"You can claim that's the result of seeing me naked if you want"— her voice shook but she forged on—"but I'm hoping you'll be the man I know you're capable of being." Her sightless green gaze almost met his. "The one to whom honesty and honor mean something."

Her words twisted the knife in his gut. Struggling to find an answer, he watched her confidence fade the longer he remained silent. But what could he say to her? His first duty was to his people, and with their alliance still on shaky ground, the possibility existed where the Na'Chi might have to leave.

Circumstances had already dictated he abandon one person he cared about. Hesia should have come with them when they'd fled Na'Reish territory, but she'd refused, claiming she'd only slow them down.

Disregarding the demon lurking inside him, if he and Kymora began some sort of relationship, he couldn't see her giving up her responsibilities, nor would he ask her to, so that meant leaving her behind.

His heart clenched at the thought. He could rail at the unfairness of life all he wanted to, but in the end, he knew his place. And it wasn't with a woman like Kymora. She deserved someone as decent and beautiful as she was, a man who could give her everything of himself— heart, body, and soul.

He wasn't willing to risk a relationship with her. It was best if they remained friends. It was that simple.

Kymora ducked out from under his arms and inched her way to

the bed of forest needles. He didn't stop her. Couldn't. He hated that his actions had hurt her, but she had no idea what she was asking of him.

"Whatever your decision, I'll still be your friend. Nothing will change that." She burrowed deep, making herself comfortable among the heat-soaked layers. The smile on her face seemed strained. "*Lady* bless your sleep."

Her soft words turned the blade again. Where was the anger for rejecting her? Why continue to offer him friendship when he'd hurt her?

Varian shook his head as he considered her words. The intimacy she offered him burned as brightly as the coals in the fire and combined with the desire feeding his erection. He wanted to hold her again, to feel her hands touching him skin to skin, to let her scent fill him and warm him from the inside out.

Kymora's sad sigh made him flinch and glance her way. Her eyes closed, shutting him out as effectively as if she'd turned her back on him, and left him feeling more than just cold sitting alone in front of a dying fire.

Despite only being an arm's length away, the space between them felt like the width of a gorge. Isolating and impossible to cross. An all too familiar ache settled in his chest. Rubbing it with the heel of his hand, he stared into the flames of the fire, knowing where the blame for his pain squarely lay.

He picked up a stick and stabbed it into the dirt at his feet, gouging out a deep furrow. Hadn't the past taught him anything?

He didn't *need* Kymora's friendship.

He didn't *want* a relationship.

He didn't *like* the strange feelings she was stirring inside him.

*Liar, liar, liar . . .*

He ignored the small voice in the back of his mind. Eventually Kymora was going to realize he had no place in her world and that he was barely tolerated in his. He waited for the voice to argue and was rewarded with a resounding silence. He issued a silent grunt.

But the words to tell her *his* truth stuck in his throat, trapped there by the yearning to maintain the illusion that he was worthy of more than being just her friend.

Kymora was right; he was a coward, and weak. Flicking the stick into the fire, he watched the flames lick the edges, heating the bark until it ignited with a fury similar to the one burning inside of him.

His lip curled. It seemed he was also a slow learner.

"THEY'RE back!"

Arek glanced up from his meal at the child's cry. In the firelight cast by the cooking fires, half a dozen *Na'Chi* emerged from the darkness between several houses. Two of them carried blanket-wrapped bundles over their shoulders. The woven wool bore ominous, dark stains. He swapped an uneasy look with the Light Blade beside him.

"Bodies." Jole's muttered comment carried a mournful edge. His blue gaze, normally sparkling and jovial, was somber. "But whose, Second? Human, *Na'Chi*, or renegades?"

Several *Na'Chi* adults rose from where they congregated with children and humans around the fires and converged on the returning group. Putting aside his bowl, Arek pushed to his feet as the scouts carefully placed their bundles on the ground.

The first to meet them, Lisella flicked her long braid over her shoulder and knelt beside one of the scouts. She placed a hand on his bowed head.

"Rystin?"

The scout shuddered at her quiet question.

"We found them. . . ." His gravelly voice broke and he fisted a wad of blanket in his hand. "Geanna and Eyan . . ." He flipped the edge open at the end of the bundle he'd carried.

Lisella's gasp ended in a moan, sudden grief transforming her expression and she fell to her knees next to the dark-haired scout. Claws of ice raked Arek's back as, beside him, Jole whispered a soft invocation for the *Lady's* mercy. The two missing watchers had been found.

Another woman rushed forward, blocking his view of which young *Na'Chi* lay wrapped in the blanket. Her high-pitched wail broke the night air, the noise so eerily out of place within the village it sent a vicious chill tearing along his spine.

"Their throats were cut and I can't even determine how many stab wounds were inflicted." Rystin's head lifted, his angular face etched with exhausted anguish. As his gaze latched onto Arek's, color suffused his cheeks and his lips pulled back from his teeth in a furious grimace. "They were butchered by Light Blades!"

The roar that erupted from the scout's throat was wild, raw. Every tendon and muscle in his throat bulged and flexed; his powerful body shook with rage. His black-flecked gaze locked with Arek's again, all traces of civility gone. Arek shifted his stance to one of preparedness as the *Na'Chi* took a step toward him.

Lisella's grip on his arm tightened. "This isn't Arek's fault, Rystin." Tears tracked down her cheeks.

"Give us the renegades. . . ." The growled demand barely sounded human.

The hairs on Arek's arms lifted. Adrenaline surged through him as several people, human crafters and children, backed away from the scout.

"What? So you can kill them?"

"They slaughtered Eyan and Geanna like animals! They deserve to die!"

A rumble of agreement came from some of the members of Rystin's party. Arek sensed the other Light Blades drawing level with him, their tension radiating like a physical wave.

His gaze swept over the gathered humans. Half a dozen crafters and child apprentices were scattered around the campsite. Only three other Light Blades stood with him; another two guarded the renegades in one of the houses.

Not all the *Na'Chi* agreed with Rystin. Several wore anxious expressions and glanced toward Lisella for guidance. But those around the scout were as angry as him, and with their superior physical strength, there was no way he and the other Light Blades were going to be able to stop them if it came down to a fight.

Even though his heart thudded like a fist on a drum, he kept his tone calm. "Kalan will deal with them."

"*Human* justice?" Rystin spat on the ground. "I think not."

"Second?" The terse whisper came from his left.

"Be at ease, Jole," he murmured, never taking his gaze from the *Na'Chi* scout.

"Varian wouldn't advocate revenge, Rystin." Lisella's soft reasoning earned her a hiss as he shook off her hold.

"Varian's decision to side with the *humans* was weak." The *Na'Chi* warrior flipped open the blanket covering the body at his feet. "All of you, look at the consequences of his action and tell me I'm wrong!"

Arek looked and his breath caught. *"Mother of Mercy!"*

He'd seen some horrific injuries in his time fighting the *Na'Reish*, but this turned his stomach. The teenage girl's head was nearly decapitated, so deep was the gash on her bloody neck. He could see only the top half of her blood-soaked torso, but through the ragged remains of her shirt, multiple wounds scored her body, too numerous to identify individual entry sites.

How could any Light Blade have done this to a girl barely out of childhood? He took several deep breaths through his nose and swallowed hard to stop his recent meal from rising from his stomach.

"Except for the rebels, you'll take all the *humans* and leave tonight. Go back to your city and tell your *Chosen* we no longer welcome his help." Rystin avoided Lisella as she tried to touch him. "We'll find our own place to live. By ourselves. Any *human* who comes near us does so at their own risk!"

"Rystin, no!" Lisella moved in front of the scout. "You have no right to decide this for all of us. Only Varian can do that. Ask him when he gets back. . . . We need to discuss this in a meeting."

"All we've done in the last few months is talk! It's a *human* custom!" He gestured to the bodies. "Look where it's got us!"

"Hesia warned us there would be opposition, but she also told us we would make friends."

"She might have been right once, but things have obviously changed since then."

"These humans here are our friends." Lisella gestured to those behind her. "You've taught Uwel how to track. You told me the other day he was one of your best students. Chelle shares your love of music. How many hours have you spent singing together by the campfire?"

The woman in question took a step toward Rystin, a trembling smile on her face. Arek admired her bravery, considering she stood much closer to the enraged warrior than many others. "I never imagined finding a friend whose passion equaled mine. It'd be sad to leave the village and end our friendship because of this."

"Not everyone shares your feelings, Rystin," another *Na'Chi* scout stated. A few near him nodded in support. "We should wait for Varian's return."

"What would Hesia advise us to do?" Lisella asked, her voice soft with compassion.

Longing mixed with regret flashed across Rystin's face, the expression so fleeting Arek almost missed it. He held his breath. Whatever Rystin thought of humans, he hoped the memory of the human-slave who'd risked her life to save the *Na'Chi* would influence his actions. A physical confrontation wouldn't help any of them.

"Very well. We'll wait for Varian to return." The grudging reply still shook with anger, but the *Na'Chi* turned on his heel and crouched to gather the young lookout into his arms. "I'll prepare them for burial."

"We can help." Arek steeled himself as that black gaze pierced him again. "Geanna and Eyan were our friends, too."

A contemptuous sneer twisted Rystin's lips. "We don't need or want your help, *Light Blade*."

He and his small group of *Na'Chi* disappeared with the bodies into the darkness beyond the firelight.

"Leave them be, Arek." Lisella joined him, her violet eyes flecked with dark purple. She smoothed a hand along his arm to ease her warning. "I know you all feel as grieved by this as we do but, for now, it's best if you and your warriors guard the rebels." A worried frown creased her brow. "And pray Zaune or the others find Varian and Kymora by tomorrow."

# Chapter 7

THE high-pitched trilling of a songbird woke Kymora. The sound strengthened, then faded, as if carried on a breeze. She inhaled deeply, the odor of wood smoke pleasant in the cool morning air. Soft fronds brushed her cheek, and for half a heartbeat, she wondered where her pillow was, then remembered she lay on the floor of a cavern on a makeshift bed of forest needles.

She frowned, expecting to be chilled by the morning air. Instead her front was warm, the reassuring sounds of a fire crackling and popping echoing off the cave walls, while the heated length of a body curled around hers staved off the cold along her back.

*Varian.*

She shivered as she felt his warm breath against her neck, the soft exhalations only one of many sensations assaulting her. *Lady's Breath,* every strong, well-toned inch of him was pressed against her.

From his bare chest, which she could feel rising and falling against her back, to the heavy hand resting on her waist, to his hips that cradled hers so intimately that his maleness lay in the cleft of her buttocks. Even his long legs were bent to mimic her posture.

Her whole body flushed. Her breasts drew tight as a burning ache began in them and wound its way south. The sensation made her squirm. Varian's manhood stirred, hardened. She froze. While she had very little experience with men, even semierect he seemed . . . amply endowed.

*Mother of Mercy*, she'd never been this close to a naked man in her life. The summers she'd spent as a child skinny-dipping with Kalan and Arek on the shores of Sacred Lake certainly didn't count. Waking up in the arms of a naked man was a whole new sort of experience, one she'd never indulged in, not even as an acolyte in the Temple.

Serving the *Lady* didn't condemn her followers to a life of celibacy. *Her* teachings encouraged living life in the fullest sense, but as a student and then as *Temple Elect*, her studies and duties had taken precedence over any intimate relationship.

Kymora's lips twisted in a wry smile. Maybe she should have . . . indulged. She could certainly use a little insight on what to do now. Especially after the conversation they'd had the previous evening.

And hadn't that gone well? A shiver worked its way across her scalp. Varian had shut down faster than a trader during a market brawl. He'd rejected her overture with such steely coldness she'd almost been convinced of his sincerity. If she hadn't felt the erratic flaring of his aura after she'd retreated from him, she'd have never been aware of his conflicting emotions. He hadn't been as uncaring or as unaffected as he'd wanted her to believe.

She sighed softly. *Merciful Mother*, she'd been right to tell him the truth, but he hadn't been ready to hear it, and pushing him wasn't going to work. How many times had Kalan or her tutors warned her about being too direct? She grimaced.

What was he afraid of? His past had something to do with it, yet he wasn't likely to enlighten her. Would asking Lisella or Zaune help? Meanwhile, acting on Varian's interest would require subtlety. He offered her friendship. So there was something she could work with, and work with it she would.

Varian's fingers tightened on her waist. "Kymora, are you awake?" His sleep-roughened whisper sent thousands of needlelike chills over her body and reminded her just how intimate a position they shared.

She swallowed. "Yes."

How long had he been conscious? Would he mention anything about the beginnings of an erection she'd felt pressing against her a moment ago?

"It's just after dawn."

It seemed not. She sighed softly. Instead he moved away from her, and the absence of his body warmth had her biting her lip. Forest needles crunched as he pushed to his feet.

"If you feel up to it, we need to get back to the village."

Why was he ignoring what he felt? She sat up, too, grimacing as her muscles protested. "I'm a little sore from the swim yesterday but I'll be fine once I get moving again." *Lady of Light*, awkwardness and hesitancy shouldn't dictate the discussion of something as beautiful and natural as attraction. "How are you?"

"Fine."

His short answer had her tilting her head, trying to gauge his disposition, but his monotone gave her little to go on. Nor could she sense anything from his aura.

Drawing her knees up to her chest, she wrapped her arms around them. "Is my dress dry?" Half a heartbeat later, the smooth knap of material brushed against her skin. "Thank you."

She fumbled with it a little figuring out where the front was, then slipped it on. She heard Varian dressing as she laced the neckline. With a layer of clothing on, she felt a lot less vulnerable and more able to tackle the conversation she knew they had to have. Whether it would be a one-sided exchange remained to be seen.

She cleared her throat. "Varian, about last night . . ."

"Kymora, just leave it be."

The hardness in his voice was like an iron grate closing solidly in her face. She fiddled with the hem of her dress.

"I'm sorry if I pressured you when I shouldn't have. Much like you, I tend to speak rather plainly." She laced her fingers together to hide their shaking. "I'm not apologizing for speaking my heart, but I didn't mean to make you uncomfortable."

As expected, Varian didn't respond. After a long moment, the warmth from the fire on her skin was cut off. The leather of his breeches creaked as he crouched between her and the flames. His familiar earthy scent filled her nostrils.

"You never know when to leave well enough alone, do you?" His soft whisper held an underlying thread of danger. Dark tendrils writhed at the edges of his aura; the harsh texture of them rasped against her mind.

Unbidden, a shiver raced up her spine. Her mouth dried. She started when his hand cupped her jaw. His thumb smoothed over her skin. Heat tingled where he touched her.

"Varian?" Even to her own ears, she sounded breathless.

"Shh." He inhaled, then released the breath in a deep sigh. "The bruise on your face is as black as root moss." He inhaled twice more before he spoke again. "If those renegades had crossed our path yesterday, I'd have killed them for doing this to you. No guilt. No second thoughts. No remorse."

His voice had gone hard again, only this time with an anger so deep and menacing she'd have wet herself had it been directed at her. Again his thumb stroked her jaw with featherlightness, such a contrast. Her heart pounded so hard she wasn't sure if it was in reaction to his admission or with arousal from his touch.

"That's who I am, Kymora."

Each word came saturated with a rawness that tore at her. Her thoughts jerked to a halt. Did he think she abhorred killing because of her religious views?

"Varian, protecting someone from harm isn't wrong," she assured him. "The *Lady* advises us to seek alternatives, but *She* doesn't condemn deadly force, not when it means protecting the weak or innocent or helping someone in need."

"Altruism wouldn't be my intent for killing them."

She fisted her fingers in the folds of her dress. Did he believe her a total innocent?

"I'm under no illusion you'd kill them with hatred in your heart." Through his touch on her skin, she felt him start. "*Lady* forgive me, but if someone I cared about was hurt, my motives would be just as base." She shrugged and gentled her tone. "I certainly don't fault you for admitting this about yourself. That's a part of being human."

She used the phrase only as a figure of speech, but being referred to as human shook Varian to the core. If only it were true, then he'd be free to lean forward and brush his lips against hers, in thanks and with the desire rushing through his veins with every beat of his heart.

He stared at her moist, full lips, wanting to taste her so badly his innards burned. She tempted him as he'd never been tempted before. Shifting his weight from one leg to the other, he grimaced at the lack of give in his breeches. She made him so hard, and without even being aware of it.

Long after she'd fallen asleep last night, he'd spent hours reminding himself to keep her at arm's length. She was the *Lady's* Handmaiden, an advocate of peace, a minister of tolerance and harmony, the light of her people.

His complete opposite.

Any relationship with her demanded trust and an openness he couldn't afford to indulge in. It would expose her to the darkness inside him, the part of him he couldn't live without. Not if he wanted to keep his people safe. But now, with the light of day, and her courage in the face of his opposition, his resolve crumbled like a bank of soil under flood.

He withdrew his hand, unsurprised to see his fingers trembling. She elicited that kind of reaction from him so easily it scared him. Her apology came from the misconception she'd caused his discomfort. He shook his head. He was his own worst enemy.

A strange scraping sound outside the mouth of the cave caught his hearing. Pivoting, he surged to his feet and took a step forward, placing himself between her and whatever threat lurked outside. He bit back a deep-throated growl, knowing the emotion originated from the half of him that relished the thought of killing the intruder.

"Varian?" Kymora's query was barely a whisper. Her fingertips brushed his lower back before latching on to his shirt.

"Shh, there's someone outside." He guided her to the wall of the cave and placed her hand against it. "Stay here while I take a look."

Watching where he put his feet, he crept toward the entrance. Bare hands wouldn't be much of a weapon against an armed rebel. He found a fist-sized rock and hefted it. The lack of finesse in using such a weapon wouldn't negate its intent. He'd done it before. Though vicious and messy, his goal would be achieved.

Carefully, he peered around the jagged edge, keeping to the darker side. The first light of the day glowed through the canopy, but the trees grew close together and blocked out most of the light. Shadows of differing shades cloaked the forest floor.

Disregarding the distraction of the leaves fluttering in the gentle morning breeze, he scanned the forest, lingering where the trunks were thickest and offered the most cover. The absence of bird and wildlife in the vicinity betrayed the presence of someone. His nostrils flared as he detected not only the fresh scent of water from the river but one much more familiar.

Placing his weapon aside, he stepped into plain view. "Zaune?"

"Varian?" The hushed voice came from his left. The *Na'Chi* scout emerged from a thicket of bushes. The dark colors of his shirt and breeches were hard to distinguish from the shadows. He glanced over his shoulder. "Seralla, over here."

A shorter, slender form emerged from the forest and picked her way around boulders and shrubs, covering the distance on silent feet. Zaune waited for the female Light Blade to draw level with him before they both made their way toward him.

"Are you all right, Varian?" Zaune asked. "We found where you and the *Temple Elect* went off the escarpment."

"We're both fine." He raised his voice. "Kymora, it's Zaune and Seralla."

The two scouts scrambled up the small ridge as Kymora joined him at the entrance. Knowing she'd feel the absence of her staff, he caught her hand and tucked it into the crook of his arm.

"Thank the *Lady* you're both safe." Seralla smiled as she seated herself on a rock. "We've been searching for you all night."

"What of the village? The renegades?" Varian asked.

"The village is secure. We captured ten rebels. Arek is guarding them. He sent us to track the two pursuing you." Zaune's grimace told him all he needed to know. "We lost their trail."

"Arek will probably have sent a messenger to the city, to Kalan," Kymora murmured. "He'll send help."

Varian placed a hand on top of Kymora's and squeezed in acknowledgment.

"How did you both cross the river?" Kymora asked.

Seralla pointed back through the forest. "There's a submerged bank downriver. We waded over."

Varian nodded; that was one problem taken care of. Putting Kymora through another stressful swim was the last thing he wanted to do. Her soft sigh was barely audible.

"Then let's get moving." His thoughts turned to the attack on the village. The anger from a minute ago seethed to the surface, and he knew it edged his voice as he spoke. "I want to get back to the village as soon as possible."

# Chapter 8

"THERE'S nothing salvageable in here." Arek shook his head as he scanned the interior from the charred doorway of the third fire-damaged house.

Sunlight filtered through the uneven holes in the thatched roof, spotlighting blackened furniture and shattered pottery. Some objects were burned beyond recognition. Something in the debris hit his boot. Bending over, he plucked a child's straw doll from the ash. Three limbs were missing; the fourth had been partially eaten away by flames. Rubbing a gloved finger over the blackened face, he watched the brittle surface crumble to dust.

The heavy odor of smoke and smoldering embers filled his nostrils, the acrid scent tinged by loss, heartache, and grief. Shaking his head, he dropped the doll back into the ash. No one was going to forget the smell of this tragedy in a hurry.

"Second Barial!"

The urgent shout was accompanied by the pounding of boots along the pathway. He turned to see a young girl in a healers' green tunic and pants running toward him, her dark curly hair bouncing against her shoulders.

"Check out the next dwelling," Arek told the *Na'Chi* woman beside him. "I'll be there in a minute." He stepped away from the damaged house as the healers' apprentice skidded to a stop. Her freckled face was flushed with exertion, her expression pinched by tension. "Rissa, what's wrong?"

"Lisella said to come quickly!" The gasped reply was accompanied by a tug to his sleeve. Wide, brown eyes peered up at him. "Rystin and some of the others are outside the house where you imprisoned the rebel Light Blades. They're demanding your warriors hand them over. . . ."

Arek cursed and took off for the center of the village. He'd sent more scouts out at dawn to help Zaune locate Varian and Kymora. The sun was barely three hours into the sky. Why wasn't Rystin waiting for their return? What had changed his mind?

Ahead he heard raised voices and shouting. Putting on a burst of speed, he took the last turn and almost barreled into a group of people clustered at the head of the pathway. Several adults, human and *Na'Chi*, were herding young children away from a commotion in the middle of the communal area.

"You're outnumbered, Light Blades. Move aside. . . ."

Three Light Blade warriors stood shoulder to shoulder in front of the closed door of a house. All were alert, their stances wide, their weight balanced on the balls of their feet.

Jole took half a pace forward. "This isn't a wise move, my friend." He gestured to his left. "Listen to Lisella."

"Rystin, you promised to wait until Varian returned." Through the press of bodies, Lisella moved in front of him. "Give the scouts more time to find him and Kymora."

"We've waited long enough. He's not here." The warrior nodded to one of the half dozen other *Na'Chi* standing with him. Lisella was gently but firmly drawn away from the brewing confrontation. "Someone has to take charge."

Arek moved to intercept Rystin, his thumbs hooked in the belt at his waist, relaxed, unthreatening.

"Back off, Rystin." He kept his voice calm. "These rebels remain under our protection."

"I told you they'd protect their own." The scout's lip curled. "They're not interested in justice."

An uneasy murmur swept through the gathered crowd, and three other *Na'Chi* moved forward to join the group with Rystin. Arek's gaze narrowed. Ten against four and the *Na'Chi* possessed superior strength. Not good odds.

"Last time I'm going to ask . . ." Rystin growled. Sunlight caught the edge of a blade in the *Na'Chi's* fist. "Your move."

"No, Rystin!" Lisella tried to break free of the scout who held her.

Jole stepped forward and Arek flung out an arm to stop him taking the offensive. "Hold!"

Another voice echoed his order, the deep voice coming from his left. The *Na'Chi* spun on their heels as Varian and a small party of six, including Kymora, emerged from between two houses.

Arek released a silent breath. *Thank the Lady.* He and Lisella shared a relieved glance before he homed in on Kymora. Other than an ugly bruise on her jaw and looking a little tired, she seemed fine.

Varian strode into the village center. What was going on here? His nostrils flared at the combined odors eddying around the gathering. Anger, fear, bitterness, and resentment, the strength of each clearing the tiredness from his body and charging it with adrenaline. The rush was enough to wake the beast within.

It was hard to tell what emotion came from which person. Varying degrees of unease and tautness etched everyone's faces. Rystin was the only one with a blade drawn, yet hands rested close to the hilts of daggers or on belts close to their weapons. The crawling sensation on the nape of his neck said they'd all been only moments away from conflict.

"Put away your weapon." Varian issued the command in a quiet but hard voice.

Rystin's black-flecked gaze darted from Jole to Arek, then to Varian, then he turned his back on them and dropped into a half crouch to face off with Varian, the move an offensive one. The scout had a temper, but surely he wouldn't attack?

Arek's soft, sharp inhalation registered. Varian kept his gaze on Rystin, but from the corner of his eye, some within the crowd exchanged uneasy glances. Lisella's expression went from concern to raw fear.

"Unless you're challenging my leadership, I'd sheath that dagger, Rystin"—his gaze dropped to the warrior's weapon, then lifted, one eyebrow arching—"and tell me what's going on."

"Someone has to look out for our people," Rystin snarled, fingers flexing around the hilt of his weapon before tightening again. "Your *leadership* killed two of our own."

Varian's frown deepened and he glanced to Lisella.

"Eyan and Geanna were murdered by the rebels," she explained, her chin trembling. "We buried them this morning."

Grief stabbed like a jagged splinter of metal into Varian's gut. The faces of both young scouts flashed through his mind. He'd taken them on many outings to test their tracking skills. Eyan's improvement during their last foray had earned him a compliment. It'd brought a shy but proud smile to the boy's face.

Rystin's actions now made sense.

Varian swallowed hard. "You have proof which rebels did this?"

"When have we discriminated between aggressors?" The scout stabbed a finger toward the house. "They attacked us! Eyan and Geanna were butchered. They deserve to die! All of them!"

"Our alliance with the humans—"

"Was a mistake!" Rystin's furious shout had those standing with the scout voicing their agreement. "Since when have we delayed meting out justice or defending ourselves against those who would see us dead?"

"Since we asked for sanctuary." His tone was as uncompromising. "We all agreed to the alliance when Kalan proposed it. With it went our cooperation. Justice may not be swift but it will be handed out in time."

"We can dispense it now," one of the other *Na'Chi* argued.

"Yes, we could, but what impression will it leave on the humans who don't understand us?"

Rystin snorted. "Very few want to understand us! We'd have been better off remaining in *Na'Reish* territory. At least there we knew who our enemies were. Here we have no idea!"

Varian nodded solemnly. "Granted, knowing who to trust here isn't easy, but it's going to take time to show the humans we're different from the *Na'Reish*." He locked gazes with Rystin. "The accusations leveled by Davyn and his supporters will be proved right if we kill the rebels now. Is that what you want?"

Around them bodies shifted. Varian inhaled deeply, testing the scents in the air. A clear divide existed. He hid a grimace.

"These rebels broke human law," he continued. "They have a right to be judged by their own people."

Rystin's shoulders bunched with tension. "You don't think we have a right to judge them?"

"Of course I do. Nothing would satisfy my heart more than ending the lives of those warriors one by one."

Varian glanced over Rystin's shoulder toward the house where the rebels resided. Beyond the closed door, the Light Blades awaited their fate. Taking a blade to their throats would satisfy the anger inside him.

Their lives for the ones they'd taken.

Protect and avenge.

*Na'Chi* justice.

Several months ago, he'd have thought nothing of that sort of behavior, from any of them. Their survival had demanded such a cold, ruthless approach. But circumstances had changed. There was more at stake now—an infant alliance that deserved a chance to succeed.

At the edge of his vision, Varian caught Arek shifting his weight onto the balls of his feet. The Second hooked his fingers in his belt, close to his blade. His team also shuffled uneasily beside him.

Varian sighed softly at the swift loss of trust between their peoples.

"But we no longer live in *Na'Reish* territory." He resorted to a more persuasive tone. "If we're to make new lives here living with the humans, we're going to need to change some of our ways."

"You should hear yourself." Rystin shook his head. "*Human* law. *Human* justice. *Human* ways." His bark of laughter was bitter. "We're *Na'Chi*. I say we remain true to our ways. If the humans can't accept us for who we are, then we're better off without them as our allies."

Lisella's gasp was the only sound in the tense silence that followed Rystin's announcement. Varian ground his teeth together at the scout's stubborn arrogance.

Patience gone, he pinned Rystin with his stare. "So, this is your justification for breaking my order?" he asked, words deceptively soft. "Is this a challenge for leadership, then? Be clear on this, Rystin. You know the possible consequences of issuing one."

# Chapter 9

A SHIVER skittered up Kymora's back. Few humans would have recognized the dangerous edge in Varian's voice, but she did. Apparently so did her guide, Zaune. Where her hand lay on his forearm, his muscles bulged and pulled tight, like he was forming a fist. What about the challenge had the young scout so concerned?

"Why is Rystin challenging Varian?" Kymora asked, keeping her voice low.

"Rystin's a fool!" Zaune's voice shook with equal amounts of anger and apprehension. "Now's not the time for this!"

She squeezed his arm. "What's going on Zaune?"

"Rystin is challenging Varian for the leadership of the *Na'Chi*." His breath hissed out from between his teeth. "When we lived in *Na'Reish* territory, decisions had to be made and followed without question. Any hesitation and we risked discovery and death."

She blinked, astonished. "A dictatorship?"

"It's how we've stayed alive and safe for so long."

"I meant no criticism; it's just that I've heard Varian ask for opinions and ideas, many times, before making a decision."

"When he can, he does that. It's what makes him such a good leader, but he won't hesitate to enforce his decisions. Any one of us can issue a challenge for leadership, but we have to be prepared to fight him for it. In the past, Rystin has come close but always backed down." He placed a hand over hers and his tone gentled. "If he confirms his challenge, they'll fight. Only one of them will survive."

"This is a fight to the death?"

"Yes."

"*Mother of Mercy!*" Her heart began to pound. "No one should have to die. Take me over to them, Zaune."

"You can't interfere."

"This can be settled by talking not fighting!"

"What do you think Varian's been trying to do in the last few minutes?" Zaune's harsh question had her biting her lip. "Rystin doesn't want to listen."

*But a fight to the death? Lady of Light!* The Light Blades spoke highly of the *Na'Chi's* fierce skills in training. Both warriors were evenly matched. Her heart contracted. She couldn't lose Varian. The selfish thought made her cheeks burn with shame, but she couldn't take it back.

"The *Na'Chi* need Varian and Rystin," she whispered. Her voice trailed off as her throat closed over. She swallowed hard. "*Mother of Mercy*, help us."

"This is our way, *Temple Elect.*" The young scout's voice was firm. "Would you weaken Varian's position by interfering? Because that's what will happen if you do. Rystin will gain support. You heard him. He believes we've made a mistake in coming here. If he wins the challenge, he'll take us back to *Na'Reish* territory."

"That's suicide!"

Zaune grunted in agreement. "Then let Varian do what he has to."

Blood drained from her face. "Are the children here?" she asked. "After all they've been through, they don't need to see this."

"Shella and Rahni took them away a few moments ago."

*Lady's Breath*, she felt sick. Kymora swallowed against the nausea rolling in her stomach. How could she stand by and listen to the two men fight to the death?

VARIAN locked his gaze on Rystin, waiting for the scout to decide the next move. His tense stance and the grip on the hilt of his blade declared his defiance. His expression was set, harder than he'd ever seen it before, the lines bracketing his mouth etched and determined.

"The *Na'Chi* need a stronger leader. With these people as witnesses, I challenge you." Rystin's statement was loud and clear.

In the air between them, the spicy odor of righteous anger strengthened. Varian took a slow deep breath, hoping to detect any hint of hesitancy or wavering resolution, determined to use any advantage to get the warrior to back down.

While he and Rystin had never really seen eye to eye on various issues, a shared love for their people had always united them. Of all the scouts, he was the one who'd tested him the most, during training and at meetings, but that tenacity and drive was what made him such an excellent warrior.

Varian inhaled again. Rystin's scent hadn't altered one iota. The *Na'Chi* needed every scout they had, especially with the alliance with the humans still in its infancy. But Rystin already believed his leadership was weak; arguing further would reinforce that impression with everyone else. He just wished the timing could have been different.

"So be it." His sharp nod served two purposes: to accept Rystin's decision and to shake the memories of growing up with someone he viewed as family. He had to if he wanted any chance of winning this fight. "Challenge accepted."

The crowd murmured and shifted back, giving them plenty of room. From the corner of his eye, Lisella moved toward Arek and the other Light Blades, and in a terse whisper, explained what was about to happen.

Varian didn't dare look Kymora's way. Couldn't. He'd have preferred any other outcome rather than her observing this fight. If he survived, she'd discover firsthand what he was, what his past had made him into.

For the fraction of a heartbeat he considered letting Rystin prevail.

*"Varian, it's too dangerous to stay here. The* Na'Chi *need to leave* Na'Reish *territory. But they need a leader, one strong enough to guide them away from here. You're the eldest, they'll follow you."*

Words from the woman he loved like a mother. Imparted on the day the *Na'Reish* warrior had followed her to their camp and he'd saved them all from him. From the moment she'd found him scavenging for food on a waste pile outside Savyr's fortress, Hesia had treated him like her own child, helping him learn the skills he needed to survive outside the fortress, teaching him the meaning of words like *love*, *tolerance*, *responsibility*, *duty*, and *loyalty*, all in preparation for the day he took on the mantle of leadership. Her dream of helping the *Na'Chi* survive became his.

*"The time has come for the* Na'Chi *to leave, Varian."* He'd never heard Hesia sound so excited yet look so sad. *"There's a Light Blade warrior within Savyr's dungeon. Once I take Annika to see him, we're going to help him escape. The* Na'Chi *must be ready to move and follow them."*

Varian scanned the faces of those she'd charged him with protecting so many years ago. They'd trusted her and now they trusted him. Letting Rystin defeat him in the challenge would damn them all, and that was something his conscience could never abide.

Whatever the result, the fight would resolve one problem. At least he wouldn't have to worry about Kymora being attracted to or wanting any sort of relationship with him. It might even end their friendship.

He pushed away the ache writhing in his gut. If terminating his friendship with Kymora proved the price of this challenge, then he'd pay it to see his people safe. They had to come first.

"No weapons." Varian pulled his blade from its sheath and threw it to the edge of the circle, watching to make sure Rystin complied before stripping his shirt from his body. "Hand to hand only."

He'd barely flung it aside when Rystin launched himself across the distance separating them. The scout's arms closed around his waist. Varian went with the momentum, falling backward. His back slammed into the ground. Dirt and debris dug into him as Rystin swung his fist.

Varian blocked the first blow but others made it through. Two to his chest, a couple to his ribs, even one to his jaw. All bruising but his adrenaline-charged system eliminated the pain. For now.

He wound a leg around Rystin's waist, twisted, and threw the younger man onto his back. More blows were exchanged as he tried to pin him. A fist hit close to Varian's kidney. A spike of agony lanced through his lower back. He grunted and jerked back. Releasing Rystin, he rolled to his feet.

The scout did the same, mirroring his wide-legged stance, circling with him. "You're holding back, Varian. I wonder why?" His lips twisted, more of a sneer than a smile. "We're not in training now."

*No, they weren't.*

Rystin's eyes turned the color of congealed blood, the only warning given before he charged. Opening his arms wide, Varian barely braced himself in time. Skin met skin in a sharp slap. Fueled by his full *Na'Chi* strength, Rystin locked his arms in the small of his back and squeezed.

"You're going to have to let go if you want to defeat me." Rystin's growled taunt was close to his ear, so low and distorted it was barely human. "But if you do, the humans will see what we're really capable of, won't they?"

A leg wrapped around his and swept his feet out from under him. With no way to roll or lessen the impact of the fall, Varian took the full force of it. His ribs flared in agony and he fought to breathe.

"Not allowing your *Na'Reish* half to rise is a weakness!"

Half a dozen bone-cracking punches pummeled his face. The iron scent of blood filled Varian's nostrils; the metallic taste of it coated his tongue.

"When I kill you, our people will have a leader capable of making the right decisions."

Another strike caught Varian's jaw. His vision blurred. Rystin was right. He was going to have to let his *Na'Reish* half consume him. Everything inside him railed at the idea, but what other choice did he have? They were too equally matched.

Varian heaved, all his frustration, all his anger, all his fear for what he had to do pouring through him as his body arched. Reaching deep, he tapped the dark half of his soul, the part of him he wished didn't exist, and gave it permission to rise.

Like a predator sensing freedom, it surged, and the darkness that came with it erupted into his veins, charging him with more adrenaline, greater strength, and cold intent.

Rystin's gaze widened as if he couldn't believe what he was seeing a moment before his hold loosened. With a throat-shredding roar, Varian grasped handfuls of Rystin's shirt and threw his whole weight to one side, forcing the warrior off balance, sending them both into a dizzying roll across the ground in a bid for dominance.

At the edge of his vision, he was aware of people scrambling to get out of their way. Unwilling to hurt a bystander, he flung himself clear. Rystin scrambled as quickly to his feet as he did, and they resumed grappling with one another.

A fast block allowed him to catch Rystin's arms. The hot scent of sweat and faltering resolve filled his nostrils. The predator inside him savored the weakness. Between one blink and the next, redness tinged his vision. After so many years, he knew Rystin's every move, every skill, every strength and flaw.

His heart pounded in his chest. Hauling Rystin around, he slid an arm around the scout's neck. Muscles bunching, bulging, he applied pressure to his throat, stopping only when Rystin's breath wheezed in through his mouth.

"No!" Rystin's choked cry was furious. Adrenaline spiked with the hoarse sound.

Varian grunted as Rystin's fingernails raked deep bloody furrows along his arm. Ignoring the stinging pain, he jabbed the back of Rystin's thigh hard with his and took the warrior to his knees. Rystin grunted, his labored gasps rapid, frantic. He swung an elbow once, twice into his ribs. The force behind the blows was weaker.

The sour odor of fear filled Varian's lungs, stroked his senses in a sinister caress. He leaned back farther, felt every muscle in Rystin's body strain and stretch, heard the hitch in his breathing as the extra pressure tormented already overwhelmed nerves.

How easy would it be to break Rystin's neck now and listen to the satisfying crunch of bone shattering? His blood rushed hard and hot through his veins. The redness in his vision brightened.

Varian blinked, a small part of him realizing just how close the beast within was to taking Rystin's life. He struggled against the urge, searching his thoughts for a memory, one to remind him Rystin was a friend not prey. He found one, of a time when he'd taught the younger man how to track, but it was like wading through sucking mud to access it.

He wasn't an animal.

Varian pressed his mouth close to Rystin's ear. "Withdraw your challenge," he hissed. "I'll spare your life."

Rystin issued a strangled denial, the fiery spiciness of his anger heavy in Varian's nostrils. Blood pounded harder in his ears, and he viewed everything through a veil of red.

*He challenged you! He knew the consequences! Kill him and be done with it!*

Varian's muscles ached as he controlled the deadly impulse.

"The *Na'Chi* need you," he growled. Sweat dripped from his brow into his eyes. He ignored the sting. "They need us both!"

"End it now. . . . Execute me. . . ." Rystin sucked in a rasping breath. "Or give up . . . the leadership!"

His fingers pried at Varian's forearm, continuing his bid for freedom. *Stubborn fool!* Couldn't he see past his fear? The futility of returning to live in *Na'Reish* territory?

Bitterness rising in his throat, Varian shifted his weight onto his back leg and grasped Rystin's head. Several warriors' braids caught among his fingers. The beaded ends bit into the palm of his hand. He'd threaded many of them into Rystin's hair himself. All tokens of events in his life as a scout.

Protector of their people.

"You're my brother, Rystin." The tightness in his throat distorted his voice so much the words were barely more than hoarse syllables. "You always will be."

He jerked the scout's head at an angle.

Hard.

Neck bones snapped.

Loud.

Even as part of him howled in exultation, each sharp crack stabbed like a knife into his body. Rystin twitched once, and then collapsed in his arms, ominously lax.

The sound of shuddering breaths rasped in Varian's ears. Harsh, rough, broken.

His.

He closed his eyes, swamped by the sickening high of victory as it rushed through him. The iron tang of blood coated his tongue. The warm weight of Rystin in his arms made him shudder.

He'd killed his brother.

Grief clawed at his heart and sucked the air from his lungs.

*Rystin knew the consequences!*

Ignoring the voice coming from the darkest corner of his mind, Varian replayed his every word and action, searching for something he could have done differently.

Rystin had deserved to die at the point of an enemy's blade, his duty as a protector justified. Honored.

Not like this.

"Varian?" Lisella's voice was soft, full of empathy, accompanied by a gentle hand on his bare shoulder.

He shrugged her off, her compassion grating on nerves too raw to cope. He opened his eyes, relieved to see the world in color again instead of hues of red.

"Varian, there was nothing else you could do." She came around in front of him; her violet gaze met his. Tears glistened on her lashes. She didn't try to touch him again. "Rystin gave you no choice."

He flinched. "Don't . . ." He barely recognized the gravelly voice as his own. "Rystin is dead." He swallowed hard, leashing his anger before sweeping the crowd with his gaze. "Does anyone else wish to challenge me?"

The *Na'Chi* who'd stood with Rystin averted their gazes. He disregarded the shocked and horrified expressions of the humans, unable to deal with the impression on them just yet. He'd deal with the consequences when he had better control of himself.

No one moved or spoke up.

"Then I remain leader. The alliance with the humans stands." Releasing one arm from around Rystin's body, he stabbed a finger in the direction of Arek. "The Light Blades protect the rebels within that house as they await judgment by the *Chosen* and his Blade Council." No emotion except cold intent carried in his voice. "My word is law. Break it and I will kill you."

Around the circle, *Na'Chi* heads bowed in assent, acknowledging his declaration.

"Rystin needs to be buried," Lisella said, quietly.

Varian clenched his jaw until his teeth ached. "I killed him." He gathered the body in his arms and pushed to his feet. His *Na'Chi* strength made lifting a full-grown warrior little problem. In the silence, the beads in Rystin's hair chinked softly against one another. "I'll do it."

She opened her mouth like she was going to protest.

"See to the humans," he growled. "They need your consolation and comfort. Not me."

She flinched at his tone. Invisible bands wrapped around his chest and squeezed, making it hard for him to breathe. Why was he destined to hurt everyone he cared about?

People parted as he neared the edge of the circle. Two dozen gazes created a burn between his shoulder blades as he walked past, his boot steps heavy in the hush that surrounded them. Ignoring them, he headed for the open field beyond the village, toward the two fresh mounds of dirt on a small rise.

He had a body to bury and a brother to mourn.

# Chapter 10

"*HOLY Mother of Light!*" Jole's astonished whisper reached Arek's ears. "He killed Rystin!"

Nodding, but unable to look away from Varian's retreating figure, a mixture of awe and trepidation churned in Arek's gut. The expression on Varian's face, or more appropriately, the lack of one, was etched into his mind. The warrior was made of ice. Only his gaze had held any emotion. His eyes had glowed with cold purpose.

Arek ran a hand through his hair, his body still tingling with the aftereffects of his own adrenaline rush. The raw power and strength exhibited during the fight was equal to any *Na'Reish* demon, their moves fast, vicious, and savage as they'd fought. Some of the blows exchanged should have shattered bones and paralyzed muscles.

"Did you see the color of their eyes? What did we just witness, Second?" Jole's brows dipped into a deep V. "I've never seen the *Na'Chi* do anything like that before."

No, none of them had, not in all the weeks they'd trained with them. Had any of the moves they'd just witnessed been used on them in training, they'd have been killed on contact. And the deep crimson in both warriors' gazes hadn't been a figment of his imagination, not with Jole mentioning it, too.

"Doesn't the *Lady* Gift humans with a variety of powers?" Lisella's softly worded question came from behind them. Arek rounded on his heel. She stood less than an arm's length from them, her deep violet gaze locked on them. "The abilities you saw—their enhanced strength, speed, agility, even the ferocity—they're all Gifts *She's* given to us."

"You label them as Gifts?" Arek regretted his comment the moment it left his mouth.

The flecks in Lisella's eyes blackened. "Then what would you call them, Light Blade?" She folded her arms. "You've fought the *Na'Hord*. You know how dangerous they are. If it hadn't been for our Gifts, we'd never have survived so long within their territory."

"But they fought like—" He bit off his reply, his cheeks burning, and he glanced away from her piercing stare.

"They fought like what?" she demanded, her tone sharp. "Animals?"

Inwardly he squirmed. How many times had his grandfather called the *Na'Reish* animals, then by association, because of the inherited characteristics, the *Na'Chi*? And hadn't he just implied the term animalistic to describe the fight?

To some extent, his grandfather had been right, the *Na'Chi* were more like the *Na'Reish* than any of them realized. He doubted Kalan or any of the Blade Council had been privy to this information. Even Annika might not have known, having grown up in isolation from her people.

"Why didn't you tell us about them before now?" he asked, jaw tight.

"Because we knew this would be your reaction."

Beside him, Jole spoke up. "Do all of the *Na'Chi* possess those Gifts?"

"Yes, although the scouts have had to hone their skills more than the rest of us. They've had to." Lisella's chin lifted. "Does this change the friendship we share?"

"Of course not!" Kymora's vehement response saved Arek from having to reply.

He released a slow breath. Any reserve on his part wouldn't have done a lot to calm the situation. With Zaune as her guide, the *Temple Elect* joined them.

Kymora gripped his arm tightly, and her cheeks were washed of all color. "Forgive us, Lisella, but we're all shocked by what's happened."

Shocked, awed, anxious, and if Arek was honest with himself, a little afraid of the new side he'd seen of the *Na'Chi*. What had Kymora sensed during the challenge? Now wasn't the time to ask her, but he needed to know the risk these Gifts presented.

How well could the *Na'Chi* control them? Reading their emotions was as easy as watching the changing colors in their eyes. That was true of most *Na'Chi*, but Varian possessed the strictest self-discipline he'd ever seen in any warrior, and he managed to hide what he felt more successfully than everyone else. Defeating Rystin proved he could call on his deadly Gift with very little warning.

*Not a comforting thought.*

Lisella's gaze swept over them all, wary, assessing, then her features softened somewhat. "I suppose your reactions are understandable." She glanced to him. "We've made a mistake in keeping this information from you. I'm sorry." Her shoulders slumped. "*Lady's Breath*, the last couple of days have turned into one huge, tragic mess."

Her apology went a long way to easing Arek's worry, but how would the other humans respond, particularly the crafters?

"We need to hold a meeting." He scrubbed a hand over his face. "It would be best to imply the Light Blades knew about these Gifts."

"Lie to the other humans?" Zaune asked, startled.

Arek glanced at Kymora. Her expression was thoughtful. Her mouth flattened as she nodded slowly. "A necessary deception; *Mother* forgive us. It will only take one crafter to mention the Light Blades didn't know about your Gifts during a Guild meeting. The Masters will complain to the Blade Council that Kalan put lives in danger by sending them to live with you. It'll undo months of progress and put the alliance at risk."

Arek released a heavy sigh. "As it is, the leadership challenge is going to be hard enough to digest."

"Rystin was given a choice." Zaune's voice was as hard and ice cold as Varian's had been. "He could have backed down. Against all convention, he was offered life again at the end."

It didn't make his death any more palatable.

"Where is Varian?" Kymora asked. "Can you see him, Arek?"

He turned in the direction Varian had gone. Out in the field beyond the edge of the village, he spotted the *Na'Chi* leader. "He's near the two mounds, where Eyan and Geanna were buried this morning, digging a third grave."

"He shouldn't have to bear that burden alone." Zaune's quiet statement had Lisella nodding in agreement.

Arek frowned. "Then don't let him."

"He'd never accept my help." A muscle flexed in the young scout's cheek. "He sees this as his responsibility."

"Then he's stubborn and pig-headed!"

Kymora's fervent outburst caught them all by surprise.

"What?" she asked, as if she sensed their astonishment. Her eyebrows rose. "Just because he bears the title of leader, you allow him to isolate himself?"

"He'll reject any offer of help."

She tilted her head, her exasperated expression emphasized as she propped a hand on her hip. "Then don't offer it to him. Give it to him."

"And risk his temper?" Lisella shook her head. "You're a braver woman than me."

Kymora squeezed the scout's arm. "Zaune, please take me out to see him."

"*Temple Elect*, wait until he finishes burying Rystin." The warrior looked torn between his loyalty to Varian and her compassion for his leader. "Rystin and Varian may have seemed like adversaries, but each would have given their life to save the other. The bond is as close as any you have with family. Give him time to mourn privately."

Zaune's description sounded very much like the connection the Light Blades shared, particularly within the smaller teams formed under each commander.

"He'll be dealing with a lot of guilt." Kymora's insight seemed accurate if the worry creasing Lisella's brow was any indication. Even Zaune's usual stoic expression reflected a hint of apprehension. After a moment, she inclined her head. "All right, I'll wait."

"He'll probably spend the night away from the village," Lisella added, a sad smile curving her lips. "Let me find you some food and water to take with you." As she passed Kymora, the *Na'Chi* woman reached out to touch her shoulder. "I haven't had the chance to say it's good to see you're safe. When Tovie arrived at the caverns and told me you'd stayed behind in the village, I was so worried."

A weary smile curved Kymora's mouth. "Thank the *Lady* one of the rebels had a conscience." She nodded toward the open field. "May the *Lady* also bless Varian for his timely arrival and skill at swimming."

Arek shifted his weight from one boot to the other. That was a story worth exploring, but the details would have to wait. "Kymora . . ."

Her head turned in his direction and she held up a hand. "I know what you're going to say. I'm going to see Varian."

"Even the people who know him better than either of us do are reluctant to approach him," he protested. Her jaw angled in a familiar, stubborn jut. "Confronting him isn't wise. He's still riding a battle rush. He's dangerous."

"Varian isn't a danger to anyone but himself." She faced him squarely. "Do you honestly believe he would hurt me?"

"Not intentionally."

"As for confronting him, I'm not that insensitive. He's grieving. I won't ignore that." The light touch to her amulet reminded him helping those in need was her job. "If he doesn't want to talk, then I'll just be there with him. Sometimes another's presence is all the comfort needed."

Letting her near Varian while he was in a volatile mood went against every instinct. Old prejudices were hard to shake, thanks to his grandfather's indoctrination. Arek scuffed the toe of his boot in the dirt.

Four months ago he'd have killed every *Na'Chi* on sight, including Annika, his half sister. Now, after living with them, he'd fight alongside them against the *Na'Reish* should the occasion arise. It didn't mean he still wasn't wary of them, but what a difference a few months had made.

Ironically, one thing stopping him from voicing his reservations was the trait that concerned him the most about Varian. His amazing self-control. The other was the friendship between the two of them. Of all the humans, Kymora was the only one Varian voluntarily sought out and spent time with.

"I don't like this idea but I won't stop you from doing your job." He sighed. "Go with the *Lady's* blessing." He shrugged as the other Light Blades shot him questioning looks.

Once Kymora's mind was made up, she wouldn't be swayed. Letting her go didn't mean he'd abdicate his responsibility of protecting her. He'd promised Kalan he'd watch out for her. This once though, he would trust in Kymora's judgment and the *Lady's* wisdom to see her safe.

"And may *She* also bless Varian," he added, dryly. "I suspect he's going to need *Her* patience and guidance in the coming hours."

HER sweet sunshine and flowers scent reached Varian before the sound of footsteps. He dug his fingers deep into the freshly turned soil beneath his hands, the moist warmth no longer mindlessly soothing. Shifting, he grimaced as every muscle in his body ached in silent protest at the enforced hours of stillness sitting at Rystin's graveside.

He refused to turn around. Why was Kymora here? Did she want to talk about the challenge? What he'd done? What did she think of him now? Every nerve in his body cringed and he shied away from looking into that dark pit.

Was she fulfilling her role as the *Temple Elect*? As skeptical as he was of the *Lady*, even he knew *She'd* disapprove of the taking of another's life, no matter what justification was offered. So, that ruled out offering him forgiveness.

Perhaps Kymora was here to administer solace? He tensed. Guilt gouged at his heart like a blunt spoon.

He didn't want it.

He certainly didn't merit it.

Sheltering in the caverns, building the village, adjusting to living with the humans, training with the Light Blades, all of this and more had demanded his attention over the last few months. If he'd been a better leader, he'd have made the time to talk to Rystin, soothed his dissatisfaction. Perhaps then the challenge could have been avoided and he wouldn't be kneeling at the foot of a burial mound mourning his loss.

Chest tight, Varian fought to suck in a breath. The pain was nothing more than he deserved, penance for taking the life of a brother. All he wanted was to be left alone. Was that too much to ask?

The urge to snap at Kymora and Zaune for intruding ached at the back of his throat. His lip curled. Giving in to his temper . . . now that was just the impression he wanted to reinforce after weakening and offering Rystin his life during the challenge. Varian clenched his jaw closed, determined to choke on his ire rather than voice it.

He didn't bother to control or mask his scent as the interlopers approached. Kymora mightn't detect his anger, but the *Na'Chi* scout would. Zaune should have known better than to bring her. The scout's familiar musky scent grew stronger, the piquant odor of trepidation accompanied by a bittersweetness.

The younger warrior was determined to protect her. From him. *Wise man.*

"Go away, Zaune," he growled. "And take her with you. I'm in no mood for company."

"And I'm in no mood to be led about like some pet *lira*, but we all have to live with things we don't like." Kymora's tart reply had him baring his teeth. "Thank you for bringing me here, Zaune."

The scout's flagrant disregard for his order as he left Kymora with him intensified the burn deep in his gut. He fisted his hands until every knuckle cracked and every muscle shook.

From the corner of his eye, the hem of Kymora's dress brushed the grass. The tip of her staff swept across the ground, grazing the mound of dirt next to him. She stopped at the foot of the grave and placed a small bag down on the ground.

"Whether Eyan, Geanna, or Rystin believed in the *Lady* or not"— lowering herself to her knees, she set her staff to one side, then arranged the skirt of her dress until she was comfortable—"they're deserving of a prayer to guide their passing, don't you think?"

Her question brought him up short. "You're here to pray for them?" He also turned to look at her.

*A mistake.*

In profile, she was so feminine and beautiful. The early-afternoon sun lit her face, her expression so calm and serene it reminded him of a lake at dawn, the epitome of tranquility. Even though she'd witnessed him killing Rystin, she still possessed an untouched sort of innocence, one he envied right to the darkest corner of his soul.

What would it feel like to know such peace? He swallowed hard and glanced down at his hands. They were filthy from digging the grave, coated in dirt that had mixed with his sweat and turned to mud. Rubbing his fingers together, the dried soil crumbled away and he wished his heart were so easily cleaned.

"They're *Her* children, too, no matter what they believed." Kymora clasped her amulet in her hands. "Prayer is a powerful medium. *She'll* listen if you're sincere."

Her words sparked an ache deep inside him.

"Even if you're a nonbeliever?" He wasn't sure if he'd voiced that question aloud until she replied.

"Yes."

Her simple answer made him blink. He'd assumed since he'd always rejected *Her* that the *Lady* would do the same to him.

"*She* walks beside us whether we choose a personal Journey with *Her* or not. *Her* love for us is unwavering and *She* welcomes our prayers or thoughts." Her thumbs traced the thin metal rays of the sun. "If you're not sure what to say, the *Lady* knows your heart and what you feel. It's what I rely on when words fail me."

He frowned. How could she ever be at a loss for words? Surely in her role as the *Lady's* Handmaiden she'd prayed many times over those who'd died?

"When you know the people you're praying for, the words become tangled with your emotions." She closed her eyes and fell silent.

Familiar enough with her role as priestess, Varian knew her thoughts were focused on the dead and their Final Journey. The awkwardness he usually experienced witnessing a religious rite was strangely absent. Instead it felt right the three *Na'Chi* were honored in such a way. Perhaps knowing they believed in the *Lady* helped.

Breathing deeply, the pungent odor of freshly dug soil washed through him. He stared down at the three graves, his gaze resting on each. The heat of the midday sun rippled and danced like a master musician's fingers over her instrument.

A corner of his mouth lifted. The comparison would have pleased Rystin. Tonight the humans would sing a death-song in memory of the three *Na'Chi*, a ritual he never quite understood. Why sing of something that caused you pain? But it was their way, and he'd respect it.

Varian rolled his shoulders, glad for the quiet. Death had come too soon for all three, and he hoped that if the *Lady* truly cared, then their faith in *Her* would see them safely to whatever afterlife *She* granted them.

Did wishing them protection and peace constitute a prayer? He felt foolish enough just thinking about petitioning a deity he hadn't prayed to in over fifteen years. Perhaps *She'd* listen since he hadn't asked anything for himself.

He waited until Kymora's head lifted and her eyes opened before he spoke again.

"Hesia made sure each of us knew about her faith. Eyan and Geanna followed the *Lady's* teachings. Rystin may not have been as devout as the younger ones, but he also believed in *Her*." He took a slow, deep breath. "They would have appreciated you praying for them."

Kymora closed her eyes briefly, Varian's words easing much of the tension between them. Silently she thanked the *Lady* for her guidance and for the wisdom to employ the strategy she had in approaching him.

The animosity in his opening greeting had been as fiery as the sun beating down on them. Zaune's faltering stride and squeeze of warning on her forearm made her question her judgment. Had she not sensed the raw pain behind the anger in Varian's voice, she'd have been forced to concede that Arek was correct in his assumption.

During the challenge, she hadn't been able to distinguish between either Rystin or Varian's auras, the intensity of their emotions so strong it'd been like staring into the sun. The aftermath had left her frightened and shaken, and battered by the fear of what they'd witnessed coming from the other humans around her.

Combined, the grief and guilt marking Varian's soul felt like a livid bruise scoring her senses. Now with barely an arm's length between them, his aura pulsed with a heaviness that concerned her. It was shockingly raw, like an open wound that wouldn't heal, almost tangible in its intensity.

*Mother of Mercy*, how long had he carried this around with him? Blinking fast, Kymora fought the sting of tears behind her eyes. Varian would mistake them for pity, shut down, and her chance to help him would be lost.

Resting back on her heels, she folded her hands in her lap. "I'll include them in my prayers tonight." She hoped the tremor in her voice would be mistaken for sorrow for the dead rather than her reaction to his pain. A small smile curved her lips as a recent memory surfaced. "I'm going to miss Eyan's mischievous pranks. Geanna was usually mixed up in them with him. I don't think I can remember a day going by when they didn't play one on someone."

Varian's grunt was noncommittal. Even as focused on him as she was, all she could detect was his incredible pain. Did he want to talk?

"Many of the crafters spoke highly of Rystin, particularly Chelle." Her voice trailed off as Varian's aura flared, slashed at her like the claws of a *lira*, as if the scout's name were a catalyst. It took everything she possessed not to flinch and betray her reaction. Then she sensed nothing. The void that remained was cold, empty, and rock hard, like a barrier slammed down between them.

Mouth dry, she licked her lips. "Arek says Rystin was a skilled scout and Lisella told me he liked teaching the young scouts in training to track." She held her breath, waiting for some response. Would he open up about Rystin? "I wish I'd known him as well as they had."

# Chapter 11

As the silence between them grew longer, all Kymora could hear was the rush of blood in her ears and the hum of insects enjoying the midday heat.

"Varian?" She clenched her fingers together, hoping to hide how much they shook.

"I'm sorry I robbed you of the chance to know Rystin." Varian's hollow-voiced statement raised goose bumps over her entire body. "But I won't apologize for what needed to be done."

The declaration held a hint of ice-cold fury. Kymora winced. Surely he didn't believe she blamed him for what had happened? *Lady's Breath*, she'd only wanted to give him an opening into the conversation.

Turning, she reached out toward him. Her hand was knocked away.

"Don't touch me!" he snarled.

Air swirled against the skin of her arm as he rose to his feet. Dirt crunched under boots, and he sounded farther away from her when he spoke again.

"Rystin challenged me. I killed him. I did what I had to, to ensure my people's survival. If that makes me a monster in your eyes, then so be it. I am what I am and what I'm needed to be."

Blood rushed from Kymora's face. *Mother of Mercy*, his voice sounded so desolate, so lifeless.

So alone.

Did he truly think she saw him like that?

Gathering her staff and the bag Lisella had given her, she rose. Touch was the fastest way to connect, and it would help her read him, but she had little doubt he'd pull away again if she tried.

"Varian, I didn't mean to sound like I was judging you." She swallowed, wishing she knew what words to say to convince him. "I thought . . . if you wanted to talk about Rystin, I could listen. . . ."

Inwardly she cringed. Her explanation sounded lame even to her.

"Ever the good priestess . . ." He snorted. "Hesia always said confession was good for the soul." He issued a sour laugh. "Conserve your effort; mine isn't worth saving, *Temple Elect*."

His bitter anger and dark sincerity buffeted her. The barrier around his aura burst and anguish bled out like a heart's vessel sliced open.

Kymora took a step back, overwhelmed. Did he truly think he wasn't worthy of forgiveness? From the *Lady* or anyone else? Or was it that he couldn't accept redemption, no matter who offered it? She suspected the latter.

As if he could no longer stand being in her company, Varian walked off, his boot steps hard and rapid as he left her standing alone by the burial mounds. His departure made it clear her presence was no longer welcome.

Kymora twisted the strap of the bag hanging over her shoulder.

*Merciful Mother*, what had given him the notion she'd been there in her capacity as the *Lady's* Handmaiden instead of as a friend? The prayer and discussion about the *Lady* had just been talk guided by what she'd sensed in his aura. Hadn't he ever had anyone to open up to when faced with times of hardship, like now?

Her thoughts stalled as something Zaune said in an earlier conversation surfaced and coupled with her past memories of Varian's behavior. Her lips parted on a shocked breath.

*Varian had never had a friend.*

No, that wasn't quite right. Zaune and Lisella would claim to be his friends without hesitation.

Varian didn't *believe* anyone saw him as anything other than their leader.

From previous conversations with Lisella, Varian had just turned fifteen when he'd taken on the role. Given their precarious circumstances and what she now knew about the *Na'Chi*, the obligation he had to have felt to go it alone so as not to seem incompetent or weak must have been strong.

A self-destructive assumption, one she knew well. Kymora's heart picked up speed as she smoothed her fingertips over the leather stitches along the edge of the bag. Leadership came with certain expectations, ones that set you apart from everyone else, and it made forming true friendships hard.

Never had she and Varian been more alike or so different in their personal experiences.

Kymora held her amulet to her lips a moment. "*Lady of Mercy*, how do I aid a man who doesn't want my help?"

Leaving him to go through this alone went against every instinct. Giving up on him would accomplish nothing. While she didn't fault them, that's exactly what Lisella and Zaune had done earlier. She drew in a deep breath.

The first time they'd met, Varian had reached out to her, established a connection, and from it their tentative friendship had been born.

*"It's not easy letting others in, Kymora. I'm not a people person. Circumstances have never fostered the level of trust needed to form that sort of bond. I let very few people close to me, but with you, I'm willing to try."*

He'd said those words to her just before joining a roomful of Councilors and their families for the midday meal. She'd asked him to accompany her and he'd made the effort, a difficult step for him. Just how difficult, she was only now beginning to appreciate.

She pursed her lips. Letting a misunderstanding ruin their friendship wasn't something she was willing to accept. Even though her insides quivered at the thought of facing his anger, she braced herself to follow him and correct the error. A lot of it was self-directed; she recognized that now. Getting him to see past that was going to be the challenge.

Flexing her fingers around her staff, she recalled the direction his footsteps had gone and went after him.

THE trees in the forest provided instant relief from the sun. Varian slowed his pace as a faint breeze rustled through the leaves. It cooled the sweat on his body.

Halting in a small clearing, he tilted his head back and allowed the sounds of the forest to fill him, desperate for a modicum of peace from the fury burning inside him.

Who had decided he needed the *Temple Elect's* intervention? Lisella? Arek? Perhaps one of the other *Na'Chi* unhappy with his leadership? Maybe Fannis. Had they played on Kymora's sense of responsibility, knowing she'd put aside her personal feelings to help him as the *Lady's* Handmaiden? Was that why she'd approached him?

A frustrated growl erupted from deep in his chest. Half a dozen strides later, he reached the edge of the clearing. Spinning on his heel, he paced back. His *Na'Reish* half was so close to rising again he could feel that part of him straining, pushing against his control, like an animal clawing at his innards, ripping and tearing, seeking a way out.

His hand closed around a branch on a nearby tree. With a flick of his wrist, he snapped it free and hurled it as hard as he could over a clump of bushes. The urge to destroy every tree and plant within arm's reach itched beneath his skin.

"Varian?"

He froze as Kymora's call came from behind him from the very edge of the forest. Her familiar scent wafted on the breeze, filled his nostrils, and wound its way inside him, kick-starting an adrenaline rush that left him shaking.

*Don't answer.*

He didn't but he looked. Glancing over his shoulder, he saw her making her way through the trees, sweeping her staff in front of her, her stride strong and determined.

"Varian?" The bag over her shoulder snagged on a low bush and jerked her off balance. She stumbled before regaining her footing and freeing herself of the entanglement.

His brows lowered. What was she doing here? Didn't she have any sense of self-preservation at all? She should have stayed by the gravesides where she was safe.

Free of the bush, her head cocked to one side, the concentration on her face absolute as she listened, trying to pinpoint his location. So he remained motionless, even resorting to holding his breath to avoid discovery.

Biting her lip, Kymora started forward again, her pace slower, more cautious, as she moved deeper into the forest, only this time away from where he was standing.

*Let her go.*

*If she gets lost it's her own fault. She should have known better.*

A vision of her tripping and hurting herself played out in his mind. It was swiftly followed by the knowledge that two renegade Light Blades were still unaccounted for. Alone she was helpless.

He clenched his fists. Allowing her to walk into danger or come to harm would be wrong. Not only that, but he'd given his word to her brother to protect her all those months ago.

Cursing under his breath Varian went after her. She yelped in surprise as he seized her arm and jerked her around to face him.

"You lack the sense of any sane person, you know that?" he snarled.

Wide-eyed and pale cheeked, but with relief visible on her face, she squared her shoulders.

"I thought I'd lost you." Her hand lifted toward him and he tensed, but at the last moment she dropped it to her side. "I didn't want you being out here alone."

"Did you even consider the risks of following me?" He kept his tone scathing. "There are still two rebel Light Blades roaming the countryside. Given the chance, I'm sure they'd attempt to kill you again."

Her cheeks lost more of their color but her jaw remained tilted at a defiant angle. "Don't you care that the same applies to you?"

"Actually, I don't." And that was the truth, plain and simple. Red leeched into the edges of his sight. Should their paths cross, nothing would stop him from killing them. The *Na'Chi* inside of him looked forward to the encounter.

"Well, I do."

Her declaration shocked him into silence for a full dozen heartbeats. He'd anticipated some sort of angry retort, not such impassioned honesty. There was no mistaking the heavy incenselike scent saturating the air around her. It was enough to make the red edging his vision fade.

"It's your job to care." He let her go.

Her hand shot out and grabbed his arm. "Yes, it is, but I'm not here as the *Temple Elect*. I didn't ask Zaune to bring me out to the burial site so I could comfort you as the *Lady's* Handmaiden. I'm sorry if I gave you that impression. My faith is so much a part of who I am, I can see how you'd think otherwise, but I came as me—Kymora—because I knew you needed a friend." Her voice softened. "I care about you!"

Varian stood there feeling peculiar, an uncertain warmth curling in his gut even as he shook his head. A part of him wanted to laugh in disdain at the idea, but another, more selfish part coveted every word.

The yearning made him ache. Made him crave with a hunger so powerful it terrified him. He wanted to pull away, break the physical connection so he could unravel the thread tying her words to his soul.

He couldn't. He ground his teeth together, hating that he could be so weak.

"Well, there's a first." Varian issued a harsh laugh and jerked out of her hold. "Who'd have thought a priestess could lie so convincingly?"

# Chapter 12

KYMORA sucked in a shocked breath at the deliberate insult. Derision saturated every word. Her throat tightened at the emotions pouring from his aura. They were all twisted and tangled: fear, disbelief, hope, confusion, anger. All wrestled for dominance.

"I know you don't mean that." Half expecting him to block her, she dropped her staff and reached up with both hands to touch the sides of his face, surprised when he let her. Her palms brushed several thin, tight braids of hair on either side of his head.

Among the *Na'Chi*, they were the symbols of his scout status. The small, hard, handmade beads tied at the ends were warm to the touch. Her fingers grazed his ears, moved lower to his jaw. Stubble prickled her skin. Beneath her fingers, the muscles in his jaw flexed, hard with contained anger.

The raised *Na'Chi* markings at his temples were smooth but irregular in size and shape. She traced one hiding in his hairline. They were so much a part of who and what he was.

Unique. Fascinating.

He caught her wrists and just held them still, his grip firm, a good reminder not to test his patience.

"Have I ever told you how I was appointed the *Temple Elect*?" she asked.

This close, she felt his surprise at her change of topic.

"No." Varian's reply was barely a hoarse rumble.

"I discovered my Gift when I was six years old." A small smile hitched the corners of her mouth upward. "My father was finalizing travel arrangements of a shipment of woven rugs for a client. The crafter delivered them on a hand-pushed cart, all rolled up and carefully covered with waterproof hides. He unwrapped one to show my father. The bleater fur was incredibly soft, like the pelt of a newborn *lira* cub. There were so many beautiful colors woven into the patterns. . . ."

Beneath her fingers, Varian's jaw twitched. "You were able to see?"

"For the first six years of my life."

"How did you lose your sight?"

"I'm getting to that. As traders, my parents would deliver goods all over the provinces. Mother returned from the Eastern Crags Province a few days before she fell ill. What we didn't know then was that animals in a village she'd visited were infected with Claret-rash, a sickness that can transfer to humans."

"I remember Hesia telling me once how *Na'Rei* Savyr ordered the slaughter of a caravan of new slaves infected with Claret-rash so they wouldn't pass it on to those in his fortress." Varian's quiet recount was somber. "Despite her pleas to isolate and treat them, he deemed the effort a waste of resources. He wanted her remedies and supplies used on the *Na'Hord*, his army. Slaves were easily replaced; his soldiers were not."

Untreated, Claret-rash was a painful way to die. Kymora closed her eyes, her heart aching for the pain the healer must have felt being unable to even try and help those who'd suffered.

She cleared her throat. "By the time the healers in the Eastern Crags realized what was happening and reported it to the Master Healer at Sacred Lake, half the province had become infected."

"What about your mother?"

She acknowledged his question with a nod. All she sensed from him was curiosity, as if his anger had been put on hold, for the moment.

"Kalan and I were playing in the yard next to my father's workshop. He was still negotiating with the crafter when I felt a strange explosion of sadness. It was so strong I burst into tears. My father came over and all I could tell him was that mother was hurting." Kymora took a deep breath. "She'd just discovered the rash covering her body. Her emotional reaction triggered my Gift."

"Did she have Claret-rash?"

"Oh, yes. Our whole family ended up in isolation. Kalan and father escaped infection—" She cleared her throat to ease the huskiness from her voice. "Mother died from it a week later but not before passing it on to me.

"I don't remember much of that time. Just snatches of memories, of the hospice, of a healer talking to my father, then nothing. I'd succumbed to the fever. When I woke up, I asked why it was so dark."

The heavy mint scent of *Vaa'jahn* permeated her memories of that time. The strong herb had been used to wash all the hospice linens and her clothes, the medicinal brews tasted of it, they'd even rubbed the thick unguent over her body, all in an effort to combat the infection. She couldn't smell it now without remembering that time.

"Very few survived, and those who did woke up blind," she said, quietly. "One of the less severe consequences of the fever."

"Less severe?" Varian sounded aghast.

"There were . . . additional problems. Some people woke but weren't there in mind or spirit, others were afflicted with paralysis or speech problems, a few had poor or no memory of their lives before

getting Claret-rash. Several even had a combination of these mala-
dies." She gave a half shrug. "The loss of my sight seemed merciful
compared to what happened to others. While I didn't appreciate it
as a child, I grew to understand just how blessed I'd been."

Kymora slid one hand from Varian's face to touch the amulet lying
on her chest.

"Four years later, Kalan and I were found on a search. He went
straight to the Light Blade barracks to begin his training as a warrior.
I started my studies at the Temple not long after. My Gift was most
suited to serving the *Lady*. By then I'd learnt how to use a staff and
all my other senses to compensate for my lack of sight."

She'd honed her Gift so well the *Temple Elect* at that time had
chosen her to help the senior Servants with dispute settlements. Being
able to read people's auras during times of high emotion helped with
counseling.

"In a class full of sighted acolytes, book learning and the challenge
of performing the required rituals or duties were difficult." She
cringed inwardly at the memories of how her peers disliked being
assigned to read the lessons to her so she could memorize them but
spoke about it anyway. "Very few wanted to help someone who was . . .
different."

"Children can be cruel."

Varian's voice trailed off as she traced the raised ridge of scar
tissue along his cheek. "How old were you when you received that?"

"Fourteen. A *Na'Reish* warrior followed Hesia one day when she
brought food to us. As one of the oldest, I was on watch outside the
cavern where we were living. Surprise was my only advantage."

She didn't have to ask him if he'd killed the warrior. *Na'Reish*
demons, of any class, valued the purity of bloodlines to the point of
obsession. Had Varian not killed him, Hesia would have died, too,
for helping them.

The *Na'Chi* had inherited the prejudice for physical deformities from their *Na'Reish* parentage.

"Your story?" Varian prompted. "How did you end up as *Temple Elect*?"

The knot hardening in her stomach made her consider editing her answer. Not even Kalan knew the full details of what happened after she was appointed as *Temple Elect*, but Varian needed to understand her past to understand his. She moved a few paces away.

"When my predecessor died in his sleep, the Temple Servants and Blade Council considered many of my teachers as his replacement." Smoothing her thumb over her amulet, she continued. "The *Lady Herself* appeared to the most senior Servant declaring *Her* choice. Me. I hadn't even achieved Handmaiden status, just went straight from acolyte to *Temple Elect* in one night."

"That didn't usually happen?"

She shook her head. "It's only occurred one other time in recorded history. Then, the acolyte was in her thirties, much more educated in the teachings of the *Lady*, and with years of life experience." Kymora turned so Varian could see her face as she continued. "Can you imagine the Blade Council's response to my being appointed? Keep in mind many of the Councilors were those you met the day you claimed sanctuary from me—Benth, Corvas, Davyn, and Yance."

"All seasoned Light Blade warriors."

She ticked off her fingers as she went. "I was twenty-one . . . an acolyte completing my studies . . . still discovering the limitations of my Gift . . . and blind." She licked her lips, her mouth dry. "Suddenly, I was expected to lead as the head of our order. The position demanded I make decisions about religious affairs and give opinions to Councilors who were twice my age."

"Wasn't Kalan your *Chosen* then?"

"Not for another two years."

"All of them were followers of the *Lady*, surely they had faith in *Her* decision?"

"While they couldn't refuse *Her* choice, the Council debated it for three weeks." Her pulse throbbed so hard her whole body tingled. She stroked her amulet, lips thinning. "They agreed that the skill involved with my Gift and the insights that came from it would off-set the issue of appointing one so young to the position of *Temple Elect*."

"They needed an excuse to accept your appointment? Condes-cending idiots!"

His outrage on her behalf heartened Kymora, but still she ducked her head.

"Kymora?" Varian's hand covered hers, inhibiting her action. "What's wrong?"

"They might have needed an excuse to value my appointment"— her voice wavered and she cleared her throat twice before being able to continue—"but so did I. I needed them to accept me so badly it was easier to let them believe what they wanted. Although by doing that, everyone assumed I could cope.

"For a while I even convinced myself I could. Eventually the complexities of the issues were way beyond my expertise." A strangled laugh escaped from her before she could stop it. "I realized too late I couldn't confide or turn to any of my teachers or other Servants for advice."

"They wanted a confident leader, not one who had doubts or concerns as real as their own."

Kymora nodded. "My own desires isolated me."

"Why do you blame yourself when their lack of faith contributed to the mess as well?"

She gave a half shrug. "I turned to Kalan and Arek for help, but I let them believe they were two of several people I asked for counsel. We talked over problems, made lists of solutions. I spent hours in the Temple in meditation and prayer. With the *Lady's* patience and their guidance, I struggled through the two years until Kalan became *Chosen*.

"I'm sure the *Lady* meant it as a lesson in humility, and I took it as such, but that time of my life isn't something I'm proud of so I've kept it to myself."

Until now, although she didn't voice those words aloud. For a long moment Varian said nothing; he even stopped rubbing her knuckles. Nothing in his aura hinted at his thoughts; it was as if he'd locked down every emotion. Did he believe her?

"We're more alike than you think." Heart beating hard in her chest, Kymora laced her fingers through his. "There's no need for you to be alone anymore, Varian. Can't you see that?"

# Chapter 13

*T*HERE'S *no need for you to be alone anymore.*

Varian's heart twisted as Kymora's declaration played over in his mind. How could nine simple words have the power to breathe life so quickly into a desire long suppressed?

How many nights had he stared up at the sky and wished for a life where enduring loneliness wasn't a daily struggle? And how many times had he denied any of it even mattered because he knew the impossibility of his dreams, instead forging on, ignoring the longing, burying the emotion so deep he'd thought it'd died in the darkness?

Kymora understood.

Varian let her go and sank to his knees on the leaf-littered ground, head bowed, hands clenched on his thighs so hard his knuckles turned white. He shuddered, throat so tight he could barely breathe.

While their upbringing had been entirely different, some of the events in her life mirrored his own. Some good, more than a little of it ugly, and she'd refrained from censoring any of it.

She. Really. *Understood.*

Her hand brushed the crown of his head.

"It's all right. I'm here." Her hand squeezed his shoulder. "You don't have to be alone anymore."

The bag on her shoulder slid to the ground a heartbeat before she knelt in front of him. She stroked his bowed head; the simple gesture and warmth of her touch provoked a peculiar yet strangely familiar feeling within him. What was it?

Trawling through his memories, it took going back over a decade to discover the answer.

*"Why don't our mothers want us, Hesia?"* The echo of his own voice as he saw a younger version of Hesia's care-worn face in his mind. *"Why are the* Na'Reish *trying to kill us?"*

Beyond the darkened entrance to the cave where they sheltered and hid from the patrols, the winter wind carried the cold breath of first snow. Huddled around a small fire, he and half a dozen other *Na'Chi* children waited for the healer to answer.

A tiny cry came from inside the small basket sitting beside Hesia. She reached in to comfort the newest member of their small group.

*"The why isn't important, Varian."* The newborn settled, and she placed her arm around six-year-old Fannis. *"You need to remember the Lady considers each of you as precious as any* Na'Reish *or human child. She loves all of you."*

Her gentle blue gaze linked with his and her smile warmed him more than the flames of the fire between them.

*"She loves your markings"*—she ran a finger over Fannis's temple— *"the color of your eyes, even your need to drink blood."* Her expression became more serious. *"The bond you all share is unique. You might have different mothers and fathers, but you're like a family now. You need to be there and care for one another. Don't forget that."*

Varian shared a look with the others seated in the circle, the significance of Hesia's words sinking into his ten-year-old mind. The children around him, and those Hesia would bring to live with them, were his brothers and sisters.

Lisella's hand crept into his and squeezed, then she'd reached to take the hand of the person who sat beside her, until eventually each of them were linked together. They were bound by blood and had to look out for one another. They accepted one another. That was all that mattered.

The connection between them then was the same sensation warming Varian now. For the first time in a very long while, he felt a sense of belonging.

Of recognition and acceptance.

Every part of him fed on the sensation, savoring it until he floated like he was on a blood-high. He had trouble swallowing. The muted greens and dappled shadows on the leaves beneath his knees blurred.

Varian sucked in another uneven breath, the scent of spring flowers and sunshine filling his lungs. Blinking against the burning in his eyes, he lifted his head. While Kymora's deep green eyes were unfocused and fixed to the left of him, they sparkled with life and a quiet strength very few probably recognized. The peaceful expression on her face was compelling, exquisite.

The ache in his chest to feel even a fraction of what she was feeling stabbed so hard he winced. How did a person find such calm? He couldn't remember a time when he hadn't worried about the future or fought for everything he'd ever needed. He felt lost, unsure of himself, and hated it. He scrubbed a hand over his face, so tired of trying to understand his fluctuating emotions.

"Talking could help." Kymora's words were soft, hesitant, and her pale pink lips curved at the corners in a small, nervous smile. Varian frowned. She was reading his aura. He stiffened. Her smile faltered. "Or not. We can just sit here if that's what you want."

*What he wanted . . .*

Fisting his hands on his thighs, Varian stared at her, his gaze drifting to her lips. They looked soft. Her mouth parted and her teeth caught the flesh of her bottom lip and gnawed at it. Desire rushed through him, making him hard.

Just once he wanted to taste her. To know what it would be like to kiss a woman who cared for him.

In front of him, Kymora stilled. "Varian?"

His heart kicked in his chest. She was using her skill again. If she couldn't figure it out, there was no way he was going to tell her what he was feeling.

Her hand skimmed along his arm as she reached up to touch his face. The feel of her fingers as she trailed them over his jaw, his chin, his mouth, ignited a burn deep inside him. She cupped his face in her hands.

Instinct warned him it would be foolish to let her continue, but no one had ever touched him like she did, like she saw something good in him. For an instant, he felt as if he were whatever she imagined him to be.

Not the leader.

Not the warrior.

Not the killer.

Something else, something more, and even though it frightened him, he liked what he felt. A groan welled from deep inside his chest.

"Varian, it's all right." A flush stained her cheeks. Her fingers tangled in his hair. He shuddered. "I think I understand."

Varian gripped his thighs hard to stop himself from closing the distance between them. He had little doubt that Kymora would allow him such intimacy. That she would, filled him with tentative hope, something he hadn't felt in a very long time, but she didn't know the real him. Acting on what he felt would be wrong.

He grasped her arms, but before he could move her away from him, she tugged his head downward and laid her lips against his.

# Chapter 14

KYMORA'S head spun at her audacity, but kissing Varian seemed right. His emotions were swinging wildly enough, yet the one she sensed strongest was desire. She pressed her mouth to his lightly, careful not to crowd him or push him into backing off.

Varian's lips were incredibly soft, warm, and edged with the delicious friction of stubble. Hot, shocking, delicious. During her younger years, she'd heard her classmates talk about the pleasure involved in a first kiss, but she'd never imagined it would be like this. Sweet and addictive.

She hovered over his mouth, her breath mingling with his, her lungs filled with his woodsy, outdoors scent. *Merciful Mother*, why wasn't he responding? Wasn't she doing it right?

Varian grasped her upper arms. With a growl that came from the back of his throat, he pushed her away from him as his aura flared again. She gasped, her senses overwhelmed. This time even her skin felt flame burned. The sensation fanned over her body and spread through her limbs until the heat pooled low between her thighs. She arched toward him.

"What are you doing?" His voice was so deep it was guttural.

The flush on her cheeks deepened and spread down her neck, but she kept her head high. "I thought that would be obvious."

His fingers tightened on her arms. "Why?"

She placed a hand on his chest. His desire was so strong there was no misinterpreting it. Her mouth went dry anyway.

"Because I thought you . . . we . . . we would enjoy it."

The emotions pouring from him cut off so fast she swayed. With a hissed curse, he released her. Kymora bit her lip as she listened to him scramble away from her. His rejection felt like a slap in the face.

The awful truth was she'd brought it on herself. Acting on impulse had been a stupid thing to do. She'd promised Lisella and Zaune she wouldn't push him, and what had she done?

More slowly, she rose to her feet, reaching out for any nearby tree. Her forearm brushed a sapling and she used it to lean against. "I'm sorry. . . . I'm so sorry." She squeezed the trunk until her fingers ached. "I felt your desire. . . ." What could she say to him to make it right? "I acted on instinct—"

Still no response.

Kymora bit her lip. She was only making the situation worse. Where had she dropped her staff? One step to the right, then another, and her boot connected with something soft. The bag. She scooped it up.

"I know I don't have a lot of experience in kissing someone but I thought you—" She ducked her head, throat closing over. More heat burned her cheeks. She swept the ground with her boot. Where was her staff?

She wasn't expecting Varian's hands to lock around her biceps, nor the speed with which he propelled her backward. He wasn't rough but neither was he gentle as he pressed her back against the trunk of a tree. She let out a startled cry followed by a gasp when he pinned her there with his body.

The man was a wall of sleek, rigid muscle. His hips rested slightly above hers while his firm, taut stomach leaned against her in a way that brought another rush of heat, this one deep inside her. His bare torso wasn't the only part of his body that was rock hard and unyielding. Her breasts drew tight and the heavy, throbbing ache between her legs reignited.

"Not experienced?" Varian's words were so close to her mouth his warm breath scorched her lips. His voice vibrated through her like the sound of distant thunder. "Your claim is untrue."

"No . . . that was my first kiss." Her voice hitched as his fingers tightened their grip. In disbelief or surprise she wasn't sure. "When would I have had the time to have a relationship? And with whom? My peers? The ones who resented my presence?"

The tension arcing between them held her motionless. Instinct warned her Varian was poised on the edge. Of what, she couldn't fathom. He'd shut himself off from her again and all she had to go on was her sense of touch.

"That was your first kiss?" he rasped.

"Yes."

His body relaxed the tiniest bit. It gave her hope.

"Why would you waste it on someone like me?" The anguished anger in his question helped her push aside her doubt. She hated the shame in his voice.

"How can you say that?" she countered. "Kissing you is not a waste. I'd like to do it again. . . ."

His erection pushed against her abdomen, thickened. Did that mean he liked the idea or was it just an automatic reaction to her words?

"Kymora—" His breathing was harsh and uneven like he was

trying to control himself. "I don't know. . . ." He swallowed hard, the sound loud in the quiet between them.

Common sense warned her to back off and give him some space. Her heart urged her to try to reach him, to show him it was all right to care, to trust someone. To trust her.

"Where's the harm in sharing pleasure, Varian?" she asked, softly. "Especially as we both want it?"

A long moment passed, then, "I don't know how."

"You don't know how?"

"To kiss." His admission was low pitched, hoarse. "To give you pleasure."

Kymora stopped breathing. He'd just experienced his first kiss, too? What were the chances of that?

"Now who's the disbeliever?" Varian's dry sarcasm made her flush. "You're blind so you don't have a visual reminder of my imperfection."

"It's just one scar!"

"One scar too many."

She blinked. "The *Na'Chi* women told you that?"

"They talk. . . . I see it in their faces."

He bit off his words as if he realized what he'd just said. Kymora's temper sparked. Since living with the *Na'Chi*, she'd heard them speak in whispers about her disability. During the first few weeks, everyone except Varian had smothered her with assistance, treating her like a child.

Sure she'd needed their help to orient herself to a new environment, but there was a lot of difference between being dependent on someone as opposed to getting used to a change in circumstances. Their assumption she belonged in the former category grated. Some, like Lisella and Zaune, had since learned otherwise, but most still viewed her as helpless, so she could relate to what Varian was feeling.

"There are qualities much uglier than a scar." Needing to touch him, to reassure him, Kymora slid her hand up along his arm, aware that the flesh under her hand felt like steel, all striated, hard-cut muscle and tendons. "Perhaps they should take a look inside themselves before condemning someone for how they look!"

With a decade of overhearing conversations about your less than desirable qualities, reinforced by a lifestyle you had no choice in living, it was no wonder Varian saw himself the way he did. No one deserved that sort of life.

The injustice of it ate at Kymora's soul. "Do you think your scar matters to me?" she asked, cupping her hand against his jaw. The muscles there flexed, but he didn't pull away from her. Her fingers found the hard ridge of flesh bisecting his cheek. She went on tiptoe to press a kiss over it, then laid her cheek against his so her lips brushed his earlobe. "You could have a dozen and I wouldn't care. Don't use it as an excuse to push me away, Varian. I'm not them."

Her heart pounded beneath her ribs. His aura was still closed down tight. He wasn't reacting in any way. She was truly blind and disliked it. A lot.

Then he turned his head, just a fraction, and his lips brushed hers. Slow, featherlight, but Kymora felt it all the way to her core. She gasped, unable to stop the breathy sound.

He was so tentative, tracing his way across her mouth, tasting of salt and male spice. Though hesitant and unsure, the gentle caress of his lips made her ache. When he shifted away from her, she felt the tiniest crack in his aura. Desire, thick and heavy, licked at her senses.

"I don't know what I'm doing." Varian's voice shook and his fingers flexed where he grasped her arms.

"And you think I do?" Kymora couldn't help the nervous laugh that spilled from her. "Varian, we can learn together. There's no benchmark measuring what we do except how we feel."

"I shouldn't be doing this." He stepped back from her. "But it seems I'm weak."

"Not weak. Human." Kymora smoothed her hand down his arm. "Desire should be shared and enjoyed."

Varian laced his fingers with hers, marveling at the delicate length of them and lighter hue of her skin against his. The smallest of touches from her made him vulnerable, no matter what she claimed, and only the *Lady* knew why she affected him so profoundly, but a small part of him craved every tingle, every prickle of awareness, every shiver of pleasure, to the point where he ignored common sense.

Uneasiness curled in the pit of his stomach. Violence and Kymora didn't belong anywhere near each other. Hesia had never revealed the specific details of his conception, but all *Na'Chi* were the products of rape. Brutality incarnate. The legacy of his birth was as much a part of him as the traits that gave him dark hair and violet-colored eyes.

He used violence to survive. How many times as a child had he stolen food and clothing from human-slaves who had little enough themselves, breaking or destroying what few belongings they had to make it look like a *Na'Reish* warrior had ransacked their hovel so as not to betray his presence?

He couldn't count the number of *Na'Reish* he'd killed, whether it was in defense to ensure his own or others' survival, or deliberate, bloody murder when the smallest chance of discovery outweighed his preference to spare a life. And he knew, even if he had the choice, he'd kill again if it meant saving others.

He and violence were brothers of the same womb. And yet he still wanted to be with her. He wanted to do more than that. He wanted to do everything the others had hinted at in ribald conversations around their watch campfire.

Stroking. Licking.

Teasing. Sucking.

Mating.

But what sort of future could it lead to?

He shook his head. What did Kymora want from him? Did she think he would change if she worked with him long enough? He wanted to, wished for it so many times, but nothing could alter what he was.

"You've retreated to that dark place inside you. . . ." Kymora's quiet accusation drew him back to the present.

She closed the distance between them, her other hand coming to rest in the center of his chest, directly over his heart, and tucked her head beneath his chin. He tried not to notice the softness and curves resting against him nor how well she seemed to fit, like she belonged there.

Her fingers squeezed his. "Sometimes all you need is a little faith to overcome fear. I'm here, Varian, and if you let me, I want to help you."

Her offer warmed a small part of the darkness within him. How did she do that? Make him believe in the impossible?

A heaviness settled in his gut. Kymora's life was so different from his despite the surprising commonalities they shared as leaders. When it came down to it, he had little to offer her in return and she had so much to lose. She was better off without him.

He pulled away from her, this time holding her at arm's length before releasing her. "I won't live up to your expectations, Kymora." Surprise lit her face a heartbeat before she frowned, her lips parting. He cut her off before she could speak. "You're wasting your time trying to help me."

Bending down, he picked up her staff. When he rose, she was standing in front of him, a speculative look on her face.

"Believing in you isn't a waste of time, Varian," she said softly, a familiar stubborn tilt to her chin.

Something remarkably like panic shivered up his spine and wrapped around his neck. She'd worn that same look the night they'd sheltered in the cave, like she didn't credit what he was saying. He grimaced. The distinct advantage in being able to read his aura worked in her favor, especially since he lacked any sort of control when he was around her. He felt like he was fourteen years old again.

Vulnerable.

He *hated* that feeling.

The expression on her face gentled. Had she felt *that*, too? He tensed, not needing her pity.

"I'll take you back to the village." He thrust her staff into her hands, cutting off whatever she'd been about to say. "You shouldn't be out here."

At least there she'd be safe and he'd be able to put some more distance between them. Something he should have done the moment she'd approached him at the burial site.

# Chapter 15

"WHEN were you going to inform me of the *Chosen's* arrival?"
The terse question stalled all conversation around the communal area in the village center until all anyone could hear was the pop and crackle of the fire in the middle of the large area.

Arek glanced toward the couple emerging from the twilight shadows between two houses. Both were silhouetted by the purple-hued sky.

At Varian's side, Kymora's expression lit up, a wide smile splitting her face. "Kalan's here?"

Varian's dark gaze swept the gathering of *Na'Chi*, humans, and Light Blades, his brow furrowed, the tightness around his eyes and mouth grooved deeply. Arek had little doubt he'd noted and counted the number of extra Light Blade warriors seated in the circle.

"I'm here, Kym." Dressed in full battle leathers, her brother rose from where he'd been sitting with Lisella and Zaune. He stripped off his gloves and tucked them into his belt as he crossed the circle to engulf Kymora in a tight hug. "Arek's messenger arrived late last night. We've ridden hard to get here."

Bringing him up to date on the aftermath of the attack and attempt on Kymora's life had taken the best part of an hour. Arek had never seen Kalan so furious as he had been during their visit to the house where the renegades were being held. The chill in his green-eyed gaze as he'd stripped them of their amulets, then questioned them reminded Arek of the day the Blade Council had passed judgment on Davyn, his grandfather, for trying to kill Annika.

Arek shifted his weight from one foot to the other. Having a *Na'Chi* half sister still made the skin on his scalp crawl, thanks to a lifetime of his grandfather's influence, but training with the scouts had helped somewhat.

The memory of their first terrible meeting haunted his thoughts. He'd wanted to kill Annika. The shame of his own actions weighed like a millstone around his soul, but a lifetime of beliefs were harder to shake than he ever thought possible.

A shiver worked its way along his spine. That he'd allowed himself to be blinded by Davyn's brand of hatred turned his stomach. A part of him still loved the man he remembered as a young boy, but the way he'd betrayed the Blade Council by hiding the origins of human and *Na'Reish* history left a hollow ache inside him.

"How is Annika?" Kymora asked.

Her question drew Arek back to the present. She'd released her brother from their embrace. Excusing himself from the group he sat with, he joined Varian, Kalan, and Kymora. Kalan nodded a greeting.

"Busy." Kalan's gaze flickered from the *Na'Chi* leader to his sister, lingering on her as if he was making sure she was all right. Reassured, the tense expression on his face eased. "Since she began working at the hospice, Master Healer Candra has her collating all her herbal remedies and recipes into a single journal. She sends everyone her greetings."

Kymora's head tilted. "Annika didn't come with you?"

"She wanted to." His lips thinned. "But I didn't know what to expect when we arrived here." He turned toward Varian. "I'm sorry to hear Geanna, Eyan, and Rystin have completed their Final Journey." His deep voice was quiet as he held out his arm to the *Na'Chi* leader. The scout gripped his forearm after a momentary hesitation. "*Lady* bless them and your people as they mourn their passing."

"Thank you." Varian's response was short, terse. The lines around his mouth deepened as he tilted his chin toward the crowd. "Why the large contingent of Light Blades?"

"Your people's safety is important to me, Varian," Kalan said, softly. His brow creased a moment before clearing. "There is another reason I brought them with me, although that news can wait awhile. Lisella informed me everyone was about to sit down to a meal when we arrived."

Varian's jaw flexed and his dark eyes flashed black. So used to the scout's calm composure, Arek was caught off guard by the uncharacteristic display of temper. He tensed, prepared to step between the two men. The *Na'Chi's* gaze flickered to him, his nostrils flaring. Arek cursed that his scent gave away his intentions.

"I'm sure that's Ginn's cooking I can smell." Kymora leaned closer to Varian. "And I bet the children are all hungry. I know I am."

The intense expression on Varian's face eased to one of tolerant resignation. Just like that, her interference calmed him. Arek's eyebrows rose at the swift change, and he exchanged a glance with Kalan. They'd seen Kymora work her magic numerous times, usually on pig-headed Councilors.

"I'll go help Lisella and the others." Varian transferred Kymora's hand to her brother's arm, then excused himself.

As if his agreement were a silent signal, the hum of conversation resumed behind them.

"Lisella was adamant we wouldn't see Varian until tomorrow

morning." Kalan's comment was low, carrying no farther than their small group. "She and Arek told me about Rystin's challenge."

Kymora's eyes closed a moment and her hand tightened on her brother's arm. "Varian might not show it, but he blames himself for all three deaths."

"Why?" Arek asked. "The rebels killed the two watchers, and while Rystin's death came as a shock, Varian was following *Na'Chi* custom."

"In hindsight I suspect he feels he should have made different choices." Her statement made Arek shake his head. "I don't presume to understand the life they led hiding in *Na'Reish* territory, but their safety dictates his every action and decision." Her smile was sad. "His people's lives rely on his skill as a leader."

"No one person should have to bear that amount of responsibility." Kalan's soft statement held a thread of anger. "There's no such thing as perfect choices, Kym."

"We all know that," she replied, just as quietly. "But Varian's the one who has to accept there was nothing else he could have done to prevent those deaths. All we can do is reassure and support him."

"You seem to have had some success doing that this evening." Arek glanced across the circle. "Varian returned to the village and he's now helping with the evening meal."

Kymora chewed on her bottom lip a heartbeat before speaking. "I haven't suggested it to him yet, the timing has never been right, but he needs to do more of that. Socialize with his people, with ours." She sighed. "Having the crafters and their children live with them has helped, but the longer the *Na'Chi* remain isolated, the harder it will be for everyone else to accept them."

Kalan grunted. "Lead by example."

"Exactly." Her nod was somber. "At the moment, his reticence influences others."

"Perhaps I can assist."

Arek raised an eyebrow. "How, Kalan? We agreed to give the *Na'Chi* the time and space they needed to acclimatize to living with us."

The warrior's jaw tightened. "Let's eat first. The news I have to share should be told to everyone."

"But . . ."

"After the last couple of days you've all had, a warm meal, good company, and a chance to relax is something you could all use." His friend's green-eyed gaze slashed to him. "Besides, this meeting could take a while."

"You know what Kalan's like when he's made up his mind, Second." Kymora tucked her hand into his elbow. "Let's go get our meal. I'm hungry."

Reminded she probably hadn't eaten since breakfast yesterday, well before the attack on the village, Arek placed his hand on top of hers and squeezed. "My apologies, Kymora."

With him on one side and Kalan on the other, they headed over to the line forming before the servers. During the next half hour, conversation was minimal or light as everyone ate in small groups scattered around the open area.

Arek caught Kalan's eye and tilted his head to his right. Bowl in hand, Varian stood alone near the wall of a house. While his sto-icism and shuttered stare were enough to deter anyone from joining him, after several minutes of observation, not one *Na'Chi* made the effort to include or invite him into their group. They all avoided or ignored him.

"Varian's by himself again, isn't he?" Kymora's question was tinged with quiet pain.

Arek shared another more startled glance with Kalan. "You're reading our auras?"

"Not yours," she murmured. "His."

"Across this distance? You're able to pick his out from among so many others?" Kalan asked, voice reflecting his surprise.

She put aside her bowl, her brow furrowing. "If you could feel him the way I do, Kalan, you'd understand why I can identify him so clearly. He shouldn't be alone."

As she reached for her staff, Kalan placed a hand on her shoulder. "I'll go."

Indecision flitted across her face a heartbeat before she acquiesced. Kalan collected two cups and a skin of water before heading to where Varian leaned against the side of the house.

Arek finished the last of his meal. Kymora picked at hers. He reached across to tug on a lock of her black hair as he used to do when they were younger.

"They'll be fine," he commented. Her pensive expression didn't ease. "We've a few minutes to spare before the meeting. Why don't you tell me how Varian convinced you to go swimming in that river, eh?"

That drew a small smile. "Convincing me had nothing to do with it, and I'm sure someone's filled you in on the facts."

"Humor me."

She did and Arek was satisfied when it diverted her attention from her thoughts. His respect for Varian grew when he discovered he'd chosen Kymora's safety over confronting the two rebels. By the end of her recount, Arek found himself staring across the circle at the scout.

The bond between the warrior and Kymora came as no surprise. He'd seen her calm explosive situations before, using just her voice and skillful words, and Varian was volatile. His behavior and reactions that afternoon during the challenge and when he'd watched them by the graves was proof.

Some resented Kymora's complete honesty, and there were times she offended those she spoke to, but no one could claim her as lacking in generosity or that her compassion was insincere.

In fact, if anything, she was giving to a fault. She served their *Lady* very well, more than anyone he'd ever known, embodying the qualities of a true Handmaiden. This instilled confidence in those whose lives she touched, and Varian it seemed was no exception.

The warmth and excitement in her voice as she spoke about him made him wonder if there was more to their friendship than anyone expected. An unlikely pairing, one he didn't believe would work. But then he'd assumed the same about Kalan and Annika.

He shook his head. Whether or not Kymora and Varian shared something other than friendship really was none of his business. Besides, his feeling was based on nothing more than instinct. For now, it would be best for all if he kept his thoughts to himself.

# Chapter 16

"OVER the last three weeks, *Na'Hord* patrols have attacked villages along the border."

Kalan's somber announcement started a murmuring among the humans. The musty odor of unease coming from them wafted on the evening breeze and prickled the hair on the back of Varian's neck. His gaze swept the circle of those gathered for the meeting. Raids were common along the border. What had them so upset?

"The *Na'Reish* are taking slaves but only the healthy and fit." In the flickering firelight, the furrows in Kalan's brow were pronounced, the angles of his face more severe. "They're leaving no survivors."

Across the circle, Kymora's head jerked up, her features slack with shock. "They're massacring everyone else?"

Varian's nostrils filled with the piquant scent of fear.

Her brother nodded. "By the time our outriders came across the attacks, the *Na'Hord* had moved on or retreated back across the border."

"This isn't usual?" Varian asked.

"No. In the past they'd raid, capture as many as they could, then leave." Kalan's jaw flexed and the hand resting on his knee curled into a tight fist. "Their patrols have also attacked towns near Whitewater River—Tianda, Nan Pirto, and Crosso Falls."

"They're all a day's ride inside our border!" This came from one of the crafters. The woman glanced at the man beside her. "My sister and her family live in Tianda. . . ."

"There were wounded and more people taken."

The woman gave a small cry and reached out to the man for comfort. Kalan's words were little reassurance for the ones who'd lost family members in the raids, although Varian kept that thought to himself. Other humans began talking amongst themselves; a few rose to their feet, too upset to remain seated.

"Why were they attacked?" Varian had to raise his voice to be heard.

Kalan raised a hand for quiet, then spoke. "We suspect the *Na'Hord* are testing our defenses. That, combined with the raids, suggests they're stockpiling blood-slaves and gathering information for a larger incursion."

Varian grunted. "Savyr's reputed for going to war when he perceives a threat, whether it's against other *Na'Reish* clans or humans."

"How are we a threat to him now?" asked another crafter.

"Annika believes he's learned about our alliance."

"The *Na'Reish* have never denied our existence." Lisella's brow creased, her slow tone thoughtful. "They've just killed us on sight. I don't think they ever expected we'd find sanctuary here, and now that we have . . ."

"Exactly." Kalan's grin was more of a grimace than a smile. "While you are few in number, your scouts' Gifts would benefit us in any conflict with the *Na'Reish*."

The *Chosen's* gaze locked with Varian's, level and steady. The knowledge of the enhanced abilities of the scouts was there in the green depths. Who'd informed him? Arek? One of the other Light Blades?

"A scout in each patrol along the border would help even the odds in any confrontation," Kalan continued. "It would give the Blade Council time to call in all off-duty Light Blades from across the provinces and to conduct searches for new warriors to join our ranks. We can no longer ignore the danger signs that suggest Savyr is preparing for war."

"War?" someone cried. "*Mother of Mercy*, surely not!"

The musky odor hovering in the air thickened to almost overwhelming proportions. Varian's heart began to pound. He drew in a deep, calming breath. Several *Na'Chi* shifted restlessly as they too reacted to the increased level of the humans' distress.

He traced the lip of his cup with his thumb. So, the reason for Kalan's visit to their village was dual purposed? To deal with the rebels and request their help? To date, the *Na'Chi* had been offered sanctuary and an alliance. They'd trained a handful of Light Blades in covert techniques but had yet to contribute in any significant way.

He gestured to the houses among the shadows. "Joining your patrols would mean leaving this village."

"True." The human leader gave a brief nod. "With the threat of more rebels, either renegade Light Blades or others who support the ex-Councilors, you'd all be safer back at Sacred Lake."

Several *Na'Chi* grumbled at the suggestion. Varian kept his tone neutral. "And if we wished to remain here?"

"That's your choice"—Kalan's gaze never wavered—"but I would ask that you let me assign more Light Blades and others to live with you. You're going to need help rebuilding your houses and planting more crops in time for winter."

The *Na'Chi* didn't have the manpower to rebuild and replant, not in the time left before the seasons changed, and to forsake one for the other would leave them homeless or hungry come winter.

Varian glanced around the circle, his gaze lingering on the younger members of their group. Hardship was a way of life for all of them, even the little ones.

"You're going to need every warrior for this coming war." He was sure Kalan knew that. "We've made do before with living in caverns, we can do so again."

"Rebuilding here or living in the caverns, I'd still like more Light Blades living among you." The hard-edged steel in Kalan's voice reinforced the promise he'd made to them months ago. "I won't compromise on your safety."

Varian inclined his head, impressed that the *Lady's Chosen* continued to be a man of his word. Kalan wanted this alliance to work as much as he did.

"Whether we live here or there, there's still the chance we'll be attacked." Taybor, one of Rystin's strongest supporters, spoke up, a deep frown on his brow. "We're not going to know who the rebels are."

They had enemies within and without. Varian raised an eyebrow, curious as to how the human leader would respond.

Kalan acknowledged the statement with a nod. "The Blade Council has imposed sanctions on the families of these renegades. They'll also be enforced on anyone who supports them. Trade, services, supplies, labor, travel." He raised a finger for every area he listed. "Restrictions or bans will be placed on accessing or utilizing them."

"*Chosen*, some of the families might be ignorant of what's happening." Kymora bit her lip. "Is it fair to punish them as well?"

"The decision wasn't made lightly. These families can petition to have the sanctions lifted. An aura-Gifted will be present in the meeting to validate the sincerity of those who appeal."

"Aura-Gifted?" Varian glanced across the circle. "This skill is like yours, Kymora?"

She nodded. "Yes, although it's much more finely tuned to

thoughts and emotion. A rare Gift, extremely reliable, but one that makes it hard for these people to live among others."

"So, the sanctions are a deterrent." Varian speared Kalan with his gaze. One more issue needed to be dealt with before he made any decision. "But what of the renegade Light Blades?"

"They've already been stripped of that title and they'll be imprisoned alongside the ex-Councilors."

"We would have killed them." There was little warmth in his tone.

Kalan barely blinked. "You had every right to defend yourselves, but capturing the rebels has helped."

"How so?"

"When the Blade Council received Arek's message, your restraint was seen as an act of mercy by the Councilors. You've proven yourselves different from the *Na'Reish*." Kalan's gaze never wavered and Varian appreciated his bluntness. "By assisting us to defend the border, others will see you cooperating with us against the *Na'Reish*. There's nothing more convincing than seeing an alliance in action."

"A common cause to offset anxieties?"

"And to establish a bond." Kalan inclined his head in agreement. "I'm not dismissing your concerns about being attacked or the problems we're all experiencing adjusting to one another, but time is a luxury we can no longer afford. I'm expecting as much of my own people as I am of yours."

The promise Kalan had made to the Blade Council a few months ago involved him stepping down as the *Lady's Chosen* if the alliance proved a failure. He was risking his future as much as the *Na'Chi*.

"Hesia warned us many times of Savyr's unwavering desire to see the human territories conquered and enslaved." A familiar pang of loss pricked close to Varian's heart as he thought of her. "She knew we'd stand a better chance working together."

"So, you're saying we really don't have a choice about staying here in the village." Taybor's terse declaration brought about a flurry of remarks.

Varian ran a hand through his hair and zeroed in on the small group of *Na'Chi* sitting around Taybor. Even without scenting them, their tense gestures and terse whispering betrayed their fear. His soul ached to see them so affected. Trusting others would never come easily, not with the life they'd led up until now.

But retreating and hiding from the humans and *Na'Reish* wasn't the answer. They'd be living half a life, spending every day looking over their shoulders, confined by restrictions to ensure their safety, never allowed to enjoy the pleasure of true freedom. What sort of leader would he be to condemn them to that style of life? They all deserved something better, but forcing the reluctant would do more damage than good.

"It's a time of compromise." Kalan's voice rose over the others. He waited until all discussion ceased, then leaned forward. "There's a wing of apartments in the Light Blade compound I've made available to you. The rooms are in a much more private area than the storage building-cum-dormitory we constructed for you last time. That space would be yours, strictly off-limits to everyone else, unless invited."

A thoughtful and generous gesture. Varian's estimation of the human leader lifted several notches.

Taybor rose to his feet, his jaw clenched at a stubborn angle. "This needs to be said, but you may not like what I have to say."

"You're free to express your opinion." Varian kept his tone level. "You know I value everyone's thoughts."

"It's no secret some of us think the alliance with the humans isn't going to work. . . ." His voice trailed off and he glanced at those seated on the ground beside him and received several nods of encouragement. "And your word is law, Varian. We know if you agree to the

*Chosen's* plans, we'll have to cooperate." His gaze flickered to Kalan and he dipped his head. "We appreciate the compromise, but the simple fact is there are those of us not comfortable with total inclusion. Not yet."

Varian inhaled a deep breath. A faint bitterness tainted the air. How was he to balance the needs of those who were afraid and the demands of living up to their part of the alliance?

"Safety overrules anyone's unease, Taybor." His hard tone had the younger man's brows dipping low.

"Varian, may I make a suggestion?" Kymora's question stalled his response. "What if the *Na'Chi* return to Sacred Lake, but only those who volunteered would work with the crafters who've lived here with us, or go on patrol, or help with the searches?"

The flames consuming the wood in the central campfire popped and crackled in the quiet that followed her question. Almost every pair of eyes turned to him. Relief flooded through Varian with Kymora's proposal. Had she sensed his concern? He didn't care if she had, not this time. He released a slow, soft breath. This was something he could work with.

"We'll return to Sacred Lake," he stated, then fixed his gaze on the scout. "And the *Temple Elect's* suggestion is an acceptable alternative for those who need more time to adjust."

Taybor nodded once and retook his seat among the others.

Kalan lifted his cup in salute, the corners of his mouth curling upward. "To the success of our alliance."

Varian raised his and others followed their example. Much of the tension of the last several minutes eased with the toast.

"With the decision made, perhaps we can end the meeting and spend some time catching up with friends?" Kymora asked.

"A good idea," Kalan agreed. "But there's one more thing I'd like to discuss with you, Arek, and Varian privately."

A frown creased Kymora's brow. Varian met Arek's gaze, one eyebrow lifting. The warrior shrugged. The *Chosen* hadn't informed his Second of the topic to be discussed.

Varian pushed to his feet. "Let's go for a walk." He gestured toward a pathway leading into the darkness beyond the firelight. "This way."

# Chapter 17

BENEATH Kymora's fingertips, the muscles in Kalan's forearm were tight and hard, much like the heaviness saturating his aura. She smoothed her hand over the coarse weave of his shirtsleeve until she could lace her fingers through his.

"What haven't you told us, Kalan?" she asked. "Is there more bad news?"

Her brother squeezed her hand. He continued walking in silence until the sound of voices faded and were replaced by the soft chirruping of night insects and distant mewls of bleaters settling down for the night. Underfoot the ground changed from hard-packed earth to the softness of grass. If she had to guess, they were walking just outside the perimeter of the village.

"I didn't want to share this back there. It isn't common knowledge yet. The Council will make these details known but in a controlled fashion to avert panic." Kalan drew her to a halt, his thumb smoothing over her knuckles. His voice dropped and deepened. "Seven villages and another three towns, other than the ones I named, have been attacked by the *Na'Reish*."

Kymora stiffened as Arek's aura flared. His shock matched hers.

"You said the *Na'Hord* massacred those they didn't take." The Second's voice shook. "How many people—"

"Close to two thousand dead." Kalan's tone was grim. "And as far as we can estimate, almost four hundred and seventy taken in the raids."

*"Merciful Mother."* Kymora swallowed hard as tears burned behind her eyes.

"Outriders have reported that crofters along the border are leaving their farms. They're afraid to stay."

To her right, Varian grunted. "Word of the attacks will spread as they move farther inland. Your people will soon know the truth, *Chosen*."

"Arrangements are being made for their arrival. The first of them will reach Sacred Lake in the next few days. Guild-leaders and certain members of the community have been informed about the attacks, and the Councilors are working with them on how to best disseminate the details as well as prepare for the influx of refugees." Kalan issued a heavy sigh. "Kymora, I've asked your most senior Servants to brief every Traveller. For the last week, they've been warning the towns and villages they journey through as well as preparing them for the searches."

"And what about border patrols?" Arek asked.

"I've assigned twenty different patrols to various strategic locations. What I need to know, Varian, is how many scouts can the *Na'Chi* provide?"

"Discounting the Light Blades I've trained over the last few months, there are eighteen warriors ready to join your patrols."

Kymora sucked in a sharp breath and turned toward him. "Varian, some of your scouts are only in their teens."

"They might be young, Kymora, but this is something they've

done all their lives," he replied. "They have years of experience fighting the *Na'Hord*."

Kymora's heart ached with the reminder that none of the *Na'Chi* had ever experienced a normal childhood. Kalan slid an arm around her shoulder and she leaned into him, needing his mute comfort.

"If we can get everyone ready to move by early morning tomorrow, we'll return to Sacred Lake before midafternoon," Kalan outlined. "After that things need to move fast. Arek, assign the *Na'Chi* scouts and warriors who've trained with you evenly into new patrols. I've spoken to all the commanders and informed them you and Varian have two weeks to get them used to working together and familiar with the *Na'Chi* scouting techniques before the ones on the border rotate back. Not ideal, I know—"

"—But we'll do the best we can." Arek's rejoinder held a hint of dry humor. "Kymora, a few prayers wouldn't go astray about now."

A small smile curved her lips as Kalan huffed a laugh.

"I expect the Temple and *Her* Servants are going to find their workload increased in the coming weeks," he surmised. "I was hoping Savyr would hold off just a few more months . . . but we tread the Journey *She* sets us and deal with the obstacles we come across."

He paused and the lighthearted moment passed. His soft sigh was Kymora's only warning just before he released her from his hug and placed his hands on her shoulders.

"Kymora, I'm assigning two Light Blades to you once we return to Sacred Lake."

His quiet words sent a prickle of unease crawling up her neck. "No. If they're what I think they're for . . . no!"

"After the attempt on your life, the Blade Council wants to ensure your safety."

His aura flared for half a heartbeat. A gritty sensation scraped across the edge of her mind, then cut off so quickly Kymora knew he was controlling his reaction. She frowned.

"The Blade Council?" So they'd instigated this motion? She shrugged off his hold. "They can't sanction something like that without your agreement."

"I happen to concur with their opinion."

His answer set her teeth on edge. That might be part of the reason, but his aura hinted at something else.

"With you, I know you're just being protective of me." She swallowed hard, trying to ignore the hard knot forming in her stomach. "With some of the Councilors . . . they're worried about my being blind, aren't they?"

A second of silence gave her the answer she needed. As much as she loved him for wanting to safeguard her, the idea that he'd let the Councilors use her blindness as the reason for foisting two guards on her grated.

"Kymora, we can't afford to lose you."

She tilted her head upward, lips thinning. "So says my brother, or the *Lady's Chosen*?"

"Both!" The word exploded from him in a rare show of temper. "*By the Light*, Kymora, right now civil war is the last thing we need. You know that's what would happen if the *Temple Elect* was killed by renegades." He blew out a sharp breath. "And how can you expect me to remain impartial? You're my sister! I love you. I'm worried about your safety."

"Kymora, you know he only has the best of intentions," Arek intervened, his tone placating.

"I don't need you siding with him, too, Arek." She'd spent too many years learning how to be independent to let them use emotion to sway her. "Kalan, you're going to need every Light Blade defending the border, not tasked with minding me."

Kalan released a frustrated growl. "I knew you'd react this way. Sometimes you're stubborn to the point of ignoring common sense, Kym." Uttering a curse, he strode away from her. Gravel crunched under the heel of his boot as he turned back. "I didn't want to do this; I thought you might see reason. . . . This edict is not negotiable, *Temple Elect*."

She sucked in a shocked breath at his steel-hard tone. He'd also used her title, a huge indication of how serious he was.

"You're not giving me a choice?" He *knew* how she felt about being a burden to anyone.

"Kalan, Arek, would you mind giving me a moment alone with Kymora?" Varian's calm request and his hand touching her shoulder stopped her from losing her temper entirely.

She listened to her brother and Arek move away, the grass crunching under their boots with each footstep. Kalan's aura remained unreadable, but she could easily imagine his thoughts seething beneath it. Well, at the moment, so were hers.

Varian remained silent long after they'd gone, as if he was giving her time to cool down. He was watching her. She knew by the way her skin tingled that he was.

"So . . ." She flexed her fingers around her staff to relieve the cramps from gripping the shaft too hard. "Do you agree with them?"

"Do I need to? Put aside your anger and think clearly about this," came his calm reply. "Would you leave your people without their spiritual guide? Is Kalan the sort of leader to arbitrarily impose his will on others? Is he wrong about the risk of civil war?"

"Just because I'm blind doesn't mean I'm helpless." She winced. Why did that have to come out sounding so defensive?

"I would never accuse you of that and you know Kalan wouldn't, either." Varian's declaration prodded at her conscience. "But we all have limitations."

She didn't want to hear his logic. "I know not being able to see poses a greater risk, but I've worked hard to overcome that. Don't you see that by accepting the Council's edict, it will only reinforce the message that my blindness is a liability?"

"And that bothers you."

She threw her hands in the air. "Of course it does!"

The respect of others and confidence in her abilities had taken years of work. Presenting a poised facade in the face of doubt and discrimination hadn't been easy, but she'd done it. *Lady of Light*, being assigned two watchers would undermine all she'd achieved. Couldn't he see that?

"Those who know you won't view it that way. And for those who don't, does it really matter what they believe?"

Kymora dug her nails into the wooden shaft of her staff. "I was hoping for a little understanding."

"I do." Sincerity pulsed from his aura. "But you're the head of your order, Kymora. All motivations aside, the *Lady's Chosen* and the Blade Council need their *Temple Elect*." His tone gentled. "This time your personal feelings don't matter."

That stung. She swallowed hard and folded her arms. "I can look after myself. I don't need guards."

*Merciful Mother*, what an asinine response. Her cheeks heated. The silence stretched and she shifted from one foot to the other.

"Compromise is never easy."

Varian's reply wasn't quite what she expected. In his blunt fashion, she'd expected to be berated for her childish attitude. *Lady* knew Kalan and Arek's patience would have worn out by now.

She chewed her lip. Varian was waiting for her to concede his point. How many times in the past had she ignored other's perceptions and forged onward? More heat infused her cheeks. *Lady's Breath*, when would she learn to curb her pride and accept some things were beyond her control?

His hand curled around hers. "Come on, Kymora, if I can agree to reintegrate the *Na'Chi* into your world, then you can put up with two bodyguards."

The inevitable left her feeling nauseated. "I still don't like it."

"I know." His fingers stroked hers. "We can struggle through our less than satisfactory situations together."

His dry attempt at humor extinguished the last of her anger.

"I'm going to hold you to that."

"I suspect you will." Varian grunted. "And I'll probably live to regret it."

His response brought a small smile to her lips. Banter wasn't something he engaged in all that often. It warmed her that he made the effort.

She grasped his forearm and squared her shoulders. "Let's get this over with and go tell Kalan."

# Chapter 18

THE familiar odor of lemon-scented candles and earthy incense filled Kymora's lungs as she knelt at the foot of the *Lady's* altar. The coolness of stone penetrated through the light robes of her station, but it was welcome relief from the heat of the day outside the *Lady's* Temple where she'd spent a greater portion of the day mixing with those who'd attended the Summer's End service, then headed into the city for the People's Market.

Since returning to Sacred Lake, she'd been swamped with official duties and so many meetings she'd barely found time to meditate. Had it been only a week since she'd walked into her office with Sartor, her most senior Servant, to discuss what had happened in her absence? To be fair, he'd handled everything he possibly could and sent missives for the most urgent matters, but there'd still been a long list of issues needing her attention.

Kymora's shoulders sagged. Seven days, and it already felt like she'd been back a month. Reaching for the amulet around her neck, she smoothed her fingers over the sun etching, then bowed her head, trying to clear her thoughts. Even a few moments of calm and quiet would rejuvenate her.

The ever-present auras of her two bodyguards indicated they waited a respectful distance about halfway down the center aisle of the Temple. They'd followed her around all week, attending meetings or services or remaining unobtrusive as she'd spoken with worshippers on personal matters.

Fuzziness blurred the edges of their auras, indicating boredom. She sighed and wished she could dismiss them back to their regular duties, but Kalan's orders had been quite specific. Unless she was in her personal quarters, where they were to take up position outside her door, they went with her everywhere regardless of who she met with or what function she attended. Her mouth tightened. Keeping his distance all week was a wise move on her brother's part, as she was still tempted to give him a piece of her mind.

Her frustration lasted all of three heartbeats before she let it go. It wasn't justified. Meetings had occupied him, too, most revolving around strategic planning or organizing provincial searches. Like her, at the moment, his time was at a premium.

Which reminded her to take advantage of the midafternoon break. Refocusing, she recalled her favorite passages of scripture to clear her mind, then spent the next several minutes in prayer. She ended with the customary ritual of burning incense.

As she dusted her hands and felt along the altar for her staff, soft boot steps sounded behind her. Being so deep in prayer, she hadn't registered the presence of two new auras. One like sunshine and fresh air, the other more reserved, even a little wary, both familiar.

"Annika! Kalan!" Kymora turned. "I missed you both at the Summer's End service."

"We planned to come." The wavy softness of Annika's hair

brushed against her chin and cheek as the shorter woman enclosed her in a warm hug. The faint odor of *Vaa'jahn* clung to her. Kymora smiled. It wouldn't surprise her if Sacred Lake's newest healer had spent the morning in the marketplace hospice. "Unfortunately, a messenger arrived from the Lower Crags Province and the Council had to convene to hear it. I hope we aren't disturbing you."

"Of course not. I've finished my meditation." Kymora drew back. "It's good to see you. This week has been so hectic. Is this visit our chance to catch up?"

Annika's light laughter filled the air. "Well, I guess it serves two purposes. I wanted to see you earlier in the week. Kalan thought it best to give you a few days to settle back into your duties, especially as you've been helping resettle the refugees with families here in the city."

"My senior Servants have coordinated most of that." She gave credit where credit was due.

"Today I had to drag Kalan here. He's under the impression you mightn't be on speaking terms with him."

Kymora pursed her lips. So that explained her brother's aura.

"So, am I forgiven, Kym?" Kalan's somber question held a hint of uncertainty.

Her knee-jerk reaction to his edict hadn't been her finest moment. "While I'm still not happy, there's nothing to forgive." She reached out a hand, glad when he took it and pulled her close.

"I considered a thousand other ideas, Kym," he murmured, and pressed a kiss to her forehead. "If there'd been a better one, I would have suggested it instead."

"I know." She rested her cheek against the coarse knap of his shirt and wrapped her arms around his waist. "I'm sorry I gave you such a difficult time."

"If it's any consolation, a pair of Light Blades follow me around everywhere as well," Annika informed her. "And for good measure, every Councilor has that privilege, too."

"Really?" Kymora ducked her head to hide a smile.

"If the rebels would try to kill our *Temple Elect*, then it stood to reason they might try to disrupt the Blade Council," Kalan commented.

Dark satisfaction bloomed inside her. *Lady* forgive her that emotion, but it made her feel a whole lot better. "I bet they were so thankful for your concern for their welfare."

"Conceit doesn't suit you, *Temple Elect*."

His dry response drew a delicate snort from Annika. Kymora decided to let the subject drop and gestured toward the congregational pews. "Let's take a seat. You said you were here for another reason?"

The front pew creaked as they sat on it. Smooth with age and use, the cool wood held the faint scent of beeswax, the care and maintenance provided by one of her oldest Servants. He performed the chore daily, without fail. Next time she saw Nemtar, she needed to thank him for his efforts.

"The outrider who arrived this morning brought word that eighty-seven potentials were found on their search." Kalan's voice held quiet hope.

"That is good news. The result bodes well for the searches in the other Provinces." Kymora smoothed the skirt of her robe over her legs. "Are those discovered all potential warriors?"

"Yes, they're the only sort I asked to be sent back to the city. Anyone else found with a *Lady's* Gift, their names were to be recorded, along with their location, for future reference." Kalan paused, his aura dulled by a roiling heaviness. "But amongst those arriving, there will be some as young as fifteen."

Kymora reached for and clasped her brother's hand. "So, you

believe *Na'Rei* Savyr is preparing for war, then?" It would be the only reason Kalan called for searches to include potential Light Blade warriors so young.

"We can't risk being caught unprepared, Kym." His hand squeezed hers. "The *Na'Reish* outnumber us, even with the *Na'Chi*. If we don't start training new warriors, and young ones at that, we may not last in an extended conflict."

How many sleepless nights had he experienced, particularly since making that decision? Probably quite a few.

She mustered a small smile. "I'll pray to the *Lady* for strength and mercy. Perhaps *She'll* find it within *Her* wisdom to intervene and avert the darkness of war."

After a short silence, Annika spoke up. "There's a celebration at the lakeside this afternoon. . . ."

Kymora's smile widened. "Yes, the Summer's End Festival."

"Kalan and I asked the *Na'Chi* if they'd like to go. Lisella, some others, and the children are coming. . . ."

"I hear a *but* in there."

The younger woman chuckled softly. "I'd forgotten how well you read people's voices." Her chuckle petered off into a sigh. "Not everyone wanted to go. . . ."

Again her voice trailed off. Her aura reflected the heavy concern threading Kalan's.

"Let me guess: Varian's one of them?"

"Many of the scouts have declined to attend." Kalan's somber tone held genuine concern. "Arek tells me while training has gone well, the last few days have been hard. There's still tension. He had to break up a fight between Zaune and one of the warriors in his patrol yesterday. Apparently there was some reference made to the scout being a freak of nature."

Kymora gasped. "Oh, *Mother of Light!*"

"Attending the festival is the last thing many of them feel like doing at the moment," Kalan continued. "Not that I blame them, but the whole idea of mixing socially, in a setting away from training, might help relations."

Annika cleared her throat. "Perhaps if you approached Varian, he might change his mind and maybe it would encourage others, too."

"Turning the other cheek is easier said than done." Experience had taught Kymora that. "And Varian can be incredibly stubborn."

"Sounds like another person I know," Kalan teased. She scowled in his direction. Then his tone became more serious. "Would you try, Kym?"

Knowing how important this was, for all of them, she nodded. "All right, I will, but we're going to need some *Na'Chi* friendly supporters with us, brother. The last thing we need is for another altercation to break out while everyone's down there."

"I'm already ahead of you there." She could hear the smile in his voice. "Candra and most of the healers' Guild will be attending. Arek is rounding up the warriors and crafters who've lived with the *Na'Chi* in the last few months."

"You know, if Lisella is taking the children, perhaps some playmates would be in order."

"Rissa has a host of friends at the city orphanage," Annika commented. "She and I might pay them a visit this afternoon."

Kymora nodded, then grinned. "And visiting Varian and the scouts is a great excuse to cancel my appointment with Councilor Elamm. It won't hurt to reschedule for another day."

"Then we'll see you this afternoon on the lakeshore," Annika said, excited. "Hopefully with Varian and some of the scouts."

"*Lady* willing." Annika's confidence in her was a little daunting. She could only ask and see what happened, but first she needed to visit her room.

Her priestess robes were going to remain behind, hanging on the hook on her wall, while Kymora Tayn visited Varian in the *Na'Chi* apartments. It'd been a long time since she'd worn anything other than her robes, but this time she didn't want there to be any mistake about who was approaching him.


"VARIAN. Kymora Tayn is outside requesting to see you."

Varian paused in cleaning the blade of his dagger. *Kymora Tayn?* Brows lifting, he glanced up at Zaune, who stood just inside the archway to the common room where several *Na'Chi*, including himself, were tending to repairs of various personal items.

"That's what she said." The young scout wore a bemused expression. "I greeted her as *Temple Elect*. She's not here in her official role and insisted I call her Kymora."

Curious.

With care, Varian placed the newly sharpened dagger on the table in front of him and wiped his hands with the rag. "Show her in."

With a nod, Zaune disappeared back through the archway. Glancing toward the only window in the room, the angle of the sunlight pouring in on the woven floor rug indicated it was late afternoon.

Varian grunted. With the morning spent training with the Light Blades, the rest of the day had been theirs to do whatever they wanted. The humans, from Guild-members to Light Blades to those in the city, all celebrated something called the Summer's End Festival. From midday the Light Blade compound had been pretty much deserted. It was a reprieve of sorts from the heavy schedule of training and constant presence of others.

In the relative silence of the apartments, Kymora's lighter-pitched voice echoed along the corridor outside the common room as she chatted with Zaune. Varian's pulse raced a little faster, and one corner of his mouth curved upward. Almost a week had passed since he'd last seen her.

The familiar hollow *tap-tap-tap* of her staff as she made her way from place to place, her cheerful tone as she greeted those around her, her soft laughter. She'd woven her way into the daily life of the *Na'Chi* during her time with them. Funny how a person could become used to certain things.

He rose as she and Zaune appeared in the archway. At first glance, she wore a forest green dress, nothing as elaborate as those worn by the Councilors or Guild-wives. The simpler style complimented her slender form. Unable to look away, and so used to seeing her in the neutral-colored robes of her calling, the difference was mesmerizing. The color of this dress reminded him of rug-moss, the sort that grew around the base of a tree. It drew out the deep green of her eyes. The material flowed around her body, from her shoulders to her hips, while the skirt brushed the toes of her boots.

Her long black hair had been pulled back into a ponytail, the end of it brushing the curved swell of her buttocks, and around her neck, the familiar sun amulet glinted in the afternoon light.

She looked elegant, beautiful.

As Zaune escorted her to the table, her scent reached him. His nostrils flared. Fresh honey and nectar. The smell of her hit him hard and streaked southward, igniting every nerve in his body on the way.

She tasted just as sweet, too. He almost groaned at that thought. The memory of her kissing him surfaced quickly, only adding to the raw pleasure rushing through him. His gaze dropped to her lips, shocked at the intensity of his arousal.

He sucked in a slow breath, trying to control it. Zaune's gaze linked with his, a sparkle of surprised amusement in the violet depths, an effective reminder that those who could read scents as easily as him surrounded him.

"Blessed Eve to you all." Kymora's greeting carried to everyone in the room, and it gave him time to gather his scattered senses. She looked left, her warm smile directed at the small group sitting on cushions on the floor in front of the unlit fireplace. "Fannis, Taybor, Yari . . . and Jinnae . . ."

The four scouts exchanged startled looks with one another before each murmured a reply.

Zaune grunted. "Amazing how you do that. That's a handy skill you have, *Temple* . . . um, Kymora."

Her smile widened. "It's certainly proved useful living with all of you, especially as you're so quiet. Even with my hearing, you all speak so softly it's hard to work out who's talking."

The young scout pulled out a chair and helped her to sit, then excused himself. He retreated to the other side of the room where he'd been tending his own weapons when he'd heard the bell announcing a visitor to the apartments.

Kymora laid her staff aside, resting it against the chair beside her. "Cleaning weapons?" she asked.

Varian glanced to the table. While he'd sealed the small jug to her right, the tang of blade oil lingered.

"Just some routine maintenance." He moved the various blades and equipment there to the far side. She didn't need a stain or tear in her dress.

"You should be outside enjoying the weather while it holds." Kymora tucked a fold of her skirt under her thigh. "You do know about the Summer's End Festival down on the lakeshore?"

"It's been mentioned once or twice today." Varian sat down and leaned back in his chair. While her pleasant expression remained, the faint odor of bitter herbs settled in his nostrils, and she smoothed her fingers over the edge of the table. "What are you so nervous about, Kymora?"

Her cheeks flushed a delicate pink. "I came to ask if you, or any of the others, would like to accompany me to the festival." Her smile took on a wry twist. "I'd like to say I came up with the idea on my own, but I'd be lying. Kalan and Annika came to see me. . . . They mentioned Lisella and some others were going. . . ."

"And that we weren't." A coldness curled, then settled in his gut. So, once again others had enlisted her to help him. First Kalan and Annika, then Lisella several times during the day. She'd even sent some of the children in to ask him. Did they think that if enough people asked him, he'd change his mind?

Rubbing shoulders with several hundred people, knowing many of them would be staring and whispering about them, was an experience he could do without. Been there, done that last time they'd lived in the city.

Whether the *Na'Chi* had gone together or in small groups to visit the Guild-halls or to explore the streets and People's Market, he'd felt like an oddity with the humans constantly peering at him, some with outright fear, others with blatant hostility, most with varying degrees of trepidation. Not a lot had changed since their return.

He wasn't going to go through something like that again at the lakeshore. "Kalan explained that the event attracts many. People even travel in from the farmlands nearby."

She sat a little straighter in the chair, anticipation tugging at the corners of her lips. "It's one of our much-anticipated festivals. Many don't get to meet and mix like this until after harvest. There's always too much to do in the next few months."

"Lisella, all the children, and several others left half an hour ago. Annika mentioned setting up a spot somewhere near the grove of needle-trees. They should be there by now."

"The clearing in the grove is a great place for a group. Close enough to participate in the festivities but far enough away to be out of the main area." Her hands stilled on the edge of the table. "Rissa's probably organized them all by now into teams for a game of flutter-tag. I bet she's even convinced some of the adults to join in." She issued a husky laugh. "There's a lot of fun to be had trying to steal a length of ribbon from someone's belt."

Rissa. Thanks to the young human, the *Na'Chi* children had learned quite a few games since they'd arrived at Sacred Lake. They'd drop whatever they were doing when she arrived to greet her with hugs and smiles, something she returned with genuine compassion. The children had had so little to celebrate living in *Na'Reish* territory. At least some of them would grow up knowing what it was like to live as a child instead of a hunted animal.

"Then you're missing out on everything by being here." He folded his arms, ignoring the glances of the others in the room.

Kymora's smile faded a little. Her chin lifted. "If tag isn't your thing, we could always sit and watch. . . . Oh, and then there's the most mouth-watering rock-oven-cooked bleater on offer at the food stall, not to mention the sweet-treasures, a pastry that dissolves on your tongue. They have so much honey in them, but once you taste them, you can't stop at just one. . . . I don't know how many times as children Kalan and I would stuff ourselves full of them and then go home feeling sick. . . ."

Excitement, pleasure, and wistful longing flickered across her face as she recounted the happenings at the festival.

Varian shook his head. Why would you want to steal a ribbon from someone's belt? And eat something until it made you sick? Where was the sense in that? Some of the things humans did were just plain . . . strange.

But then, when had any of the *Na'Chi* ever indulged in something that even resembled the pleasure she described? Sharing a meal that left each one of them with a full belly was as close as they'd ever come. In an environment where violence and survival dominated every action, relaxation and fun tended to rank low on a list of priorities.

If he were honest, her enthusiasm made him crave a slice of her life. The human side of him yearned for it. But to experience it meant being a part of the crowd. That left him feeling queasy. It was hard enough working with Arek to train the other Light Blades. Every hour was a trial of his endurance, every bitter scent of tension a test of his patience, every slight a temptation to live up to their fears.

Kalan's and Kymora's hearts might be in the right place, and their actions to include the *Na'Chi* were sincere, but tolerance and acceptance from humans as a whole race seemed an impossible dream. Especially when so many of them denied the truth of their origins.

Varian made a fist beneath the table. Disappointment was one bedfellow he could do without, and today he had little patience for it.

His earlier uneasiness gnawed away at him. With her skill at reading auras, surely she'd felt his reluctance? Was she ignoring her senses? Or did she have another motive for coming here?

"Are you expecting me to fulfill the promise I made to you that last time back in the village?" he asked. Her brows dipped in confusion. "The night your brother assigned you two Light Blade warriors as guards I said we'd struggle through our less than satisfactory situations together. Are you calling in that favor?"

Her mouth dropped open. "No! I'd never do that."

"Are you sure?" He kept his voice low and a tight rein on his thoughts. He didn't need her sensing anything other than what she could hear in his voice.

"Varian, I knew then you were just joking to lighten the mood."

In the short silence that followed, her head cocked to one side as if she were trying to read him. Her brows dipped; the skin around her eyes tightened. He tensed, expecting to bear the brunt of her temper, but then her teeth clamped on her bottom lip.

She stood, the chair scraping on the stone floor in her haste to rise. "I shouldn't have come here." She reached for her staff, her smile strained. "I know how much you value your solitude. I'm sorry I disturbed you."

Letting her believe the error was hers twisted his insides.

*If she'd taken the hint, she could've avoided this.* The reasoning did little to ease his conscience.

From across the room, a blade hissed as it was shoved into a sheath. Zaune rose from his seat and strode over to them.

The young scout's mouth flattened. Violet eyes flecked with black locked with his. His scathing look stated quite clearly what he thought of Varian's behavior toward her.

"I'll go with you, Kymora." Zaune's voice held none of the spicy anger coming off him in waves. "I don't know what a sweet-treasure is, but I think I'd like to try one."

He helped her from her chair, all the while challenging Varian with his gaze. Varian stiffened, jaw clenching. Part of him demanded he put the young scout in his place; another part of him knew the discipline would be undeserved. So he held his seat.

"I mightn't be able to stay long," Zaune warned her. "You know what I'm like in crowds."

She placed her hand on his arm. "I understand."

Varian's cheeks heated. Of all the *Na'Chi*, Zaune had the least incentive to want to attend the festival.

"If you're going, I might, too." Jinnae put aside her mending and pushed to her feet.

Kymora's smile returned. "Anyone else?"

The others declined. She hesitated, her head turning in his direction as if giving him the option to say something. Why would she, considering how he'd treated her? What did she see in him that moved her to give him a second chance?

Insides knotted, Varian wavered, tempted by her compassion, the words to accept her offer on his lips. Why, only the *Lady* knew. Understanding his weakness could wait until later. Instead, with fingers that felt wooden and stiff, he reached for the dagger and cloth he'd set aside and began cleaning the blade again.

Kymora's shoulders sagged. "Enjoy Summer's End, then, and may the *Lady* bless you."

Tucking her hand in Zaune's elbow, she and the two young scouts left the room.

Some of the tension left his body, but after a few minutes, Varian set the blade down again, his concentration no longer on the task. Rising from the chair, he strode to the window. Outside, the compound was as empty as the hollow feeling growing inside him.

Kymora's injured expression remained burned into his brain. Why? He turned his head aside.

*Don't be a coward. Face the truth!*

He'd pushed her away just to avoid being hurt. That was why. Better to reject someone first before they rebuffed you. He wasn't proud of the attitude, but it'd helped him survive when he'd needed it most.

He stood there staring out at the dirt-packed compound, his gaze finding the stone-inlaid pathway that edged the Memorial Garden. It'd been there, the day Kymora had invited him to lunch with the Councilors and their families, that he'd first realized just how much he valued the budding friendship they shared. Her manner was as forthright as his, but she never used that bond to her advantage, and yet he'd accused her of that this evening.

His lip curled in disgust. At himself, not her. She hadn't deserved his surliness any more than his cruel behavior. Kymora had come to him as a friend and he'd treated her with disrespect. Zaune's anger was justified.

*I'm such a beast.*

He flinched, unable to deny the accusation. He stared down at his hands resting on the windowsill. All his knuckles were white. They shook when he released his hold.

*Walking the difficult path takes courage. . . .* Words of scripture from the past, whispered in Hesia's voice.

He wished she were here to hold him and tell him everything would be all right, like she used to when he was a child. But she wasn't. And she didn't need to be for him to know the path his conscience demanded.

Taking it would leave him vulnerable. Varian closed his eyes, hating the acrid taste coating the back of his throat. *Fear.* How many times had he faced it down and refused to let it master him? Letting it win now wasn't an option.

He could watch the crowd from a distance, at least until he spotted Kymora, then he'd ignore them as he made his way to her. Inhaling an uneven breath, he straightened away from the window.

As he passed by the table, he picked up the dagger and fastened it to his belt. He was responsible for his actions. Apologizing to a friend would be a way to start making amends.

Would Kymora accept it?

# Chapter 19

"TEMPLE Elect! Temple Elect! *Help me . . . he's going to get me!*"

Tovie's excited cry rose above the chaos of the festival. Amidst the cacophony of singing and musical instruments, the hum of hundreds of voices and other unidentifiable noises, Kymora grinned as his giggling turned to a squeal. Two sets of footsteps pounded toward where she leaned up against the solid trunk of a tree at the edge of the clearing.

"Ha! Got you!"

Something peppered Kymora's legs and side as Arek's triumphant cry rang out. The fresh minty odor belonged to needle-leaves. Crushed underfoot, like during a vigorous game of flutter-tag, they released their pleasant scent. She brushed the thin, segmented fronds from her dress, listening to the scuffle going on in front of her.

"That ribbon is mine!"

"No, no, it's not." The young *Na'Chi* boy's laughter almost made his words unintelligible.

"You wriggle like a dirt-burrower."

A small body rolled against her foot. Kymora reached out and a small hand grabbed hers. She hauled the six-year-old onto her lap, feeling the flutter of his ribbon against the inside of her arm.

"He's safe, Second," she declared. "This young warrior made it all away across the clearing to me. He deserves a second chance."

"Hey, those aren't Rissa's rules!" Arek's complaint drew another giggle from Tovie. The Light Blade warrior issued a deep sigh. "I guess you did outrun me."

Tovie scrambled from her lap. "Thanks, *Temple Elect*." With that, he was off, his boots crunching over the soft ground.

"You know, the Light Blades should play a game of tag with kids once a week as a part of their training." Bark scraped as Arek slid down the tree trunk onto the ground beside her. The scent of hot sweat mingled with the minty odor of crushed needle-leaves. Through the sleeves of their clothes, the heat of his arm warmed hers. "Chasing them for an hour is enough to keep up your fitness level."

She laughed. "I dare you to raise that at the next Commanders meeting."

"You know how dangerous it is to dare me, Kymora!" He snorted. "I can just see Yevni's face—" His comment cut short with a grunt. "Well, now, that's something I wasn't expecting. . . ."

"What?" The tone of his voice tempted her to reach out and try to read the auras closest to her, but prudence won out. There were far too many people around and she was too close to them to risk being bombarded by their emotions. "Arek? What do you see?"

"I thought you said Varian wasn't coming to the festival."

Kymora tried to keep her expression smooth. She hadn't told anyone about the scene with him back at the *Na'Chi* apartments. If Kalan or Annika heard about it, they'd feel guilty for asking her to approach him.

"I did," she replied.

"Well, he's standing by the jugglers on the foreshore."

Her face heated with the memory of his cold rejection. She stiffened. What was he doing here?

Arek shifted beside her. Kymora snagged a handful of his breeches. "Where are you going?"

"To get him. There's a large group of people between where we are and him, so he can't see us."

Before she could say anything, he was gone. Kymora dropped her hand and dug her fingers into the soft layer of debris on the ground next to her. Why had Varian come down to the lake? In their conversation, he'd given every indication of a man reluctant to accompany her.

Trying to tempt him with her recollections of festivals past had backfired. Pushing him only left him feeling cornered. So he'd lashed out. It didn't excuse him for his rudeness, and accusing her of using their friendship had hurt.

With relations between the *Na'Chi* and humans strained enough, she'd taken the passive option and left rather than confronting him in a room full of scouts.

Kymora pressed a hand to her cheek, aware that it felt hot while her fingers were cold. She blinked fiercely, nursing her temper. *Lady* help her, they'd have a reckoning, but not now, not while the sting of his allegation and the burn of his refusal remained fresh in her mind.

Reaching for her staff, she pushed to her feet. "Ehrinne?" she called.

The scuff of a boot step sounded behind her as one of the two Light Blade's assigned to her stepped closer. "Yes, *Temple Elect?*"

For the first time, she was grateful for their presence. If Varian was coming from where the entertainers were located, then she needed to go in the opposite direction.

"Where are the food stalls?"

"To your right about seventy paces. There's a gentle downward slope to the ground here in the grove before it changes to pebbles. Once you feel them under your feet you'll be on the lakeside."

The odor of cooking food would guide her from there. With mealtime approaching, the crowd gathering around the serving tables would be growing. Varian's aversion would serve her well. A spiteful thought, but she had little patience for him now.

"Thank you." Anger gave each swing of her staff extra momentum as she headed for the food stalls. Keeping to a steady pace wasn't possible over the uneven ground, especially in the grove of trees. The tip of her staff kept striking raised roots, and it took time to step over or go around them. The lack of speed added frustration to her ire.

"Kymora!"

She ignored Arek's hail, hoping he'd think she hadn't heard him over the growing noise of the festival. Musicians nearby were playing a popular folk ballad and many sang along. Neither of the Light Blades said anything, but she was sure they wondered what she was doing.

The change of terrain occurred the same time as hurried footsteps approached her from behind.

"Kymora, wait!" Varian's voice. "Please."

*Merciful Mother*, she couldn't face him now, but her steps faltered, her parents' teachings regarding good manners too ingrained to blatantly ignore him.

*"Temple Elect?"* Ehrinne's soft query came from her left. The older woman's hand touched her elbow. "Is everything all right?"

She only had to give the word and both Light Blades would intercept Varian. Temptation parted her lips but, knowing him, he wouldn't be turned aside easily, so she closed them and shook her head.

"It's all right, Ehrinne, thank you." With a soft sigh, she turned in his direction. The air stirred in front of her. She smelled the familiar tang of blade oil and heated male. Keeping her expression neutral, she waited for him to speak.

"Kymora . . ." His voice was deep, gravelly, and hesitant. "I need to talk to you." Pebbles clicked against one another, like a boot was being scuffed against them. "But not here. Can we walk along the shore?"

She arched an eyebrow. "What more could you have to say to me than what you've already said, Varian?" She made a deliberate effort to moderate her tone, but it was still clipped, controlled, and infused with just enough heat to warn him how close she was to giving in to her temper.

"Kymora, I came to apologize." Low pitched, his voice resonated with emotion. "I'm sorry I treated you the way I did. . . ."

Her breath froze in her chest. He was apologizing to her? Here? Intense curiosity burred against the edge of her mind and broke through her shock. They were attracting attention from those nearby.

Surprised by the strength of the intrusion, especially considering she'd closed herself off from reading auras, Kymora cocked her head toward Ehrinne. This wasn't a conversation that needed to be over-heard. "Which direction is the inlet?"

"Turn directly left, *Temple Elect*."

"Let me know when we've cleared the crowds."

"Yes, *Temple Elect*."

It would've been easier to let Varian guide and inform her, but her mood was less than conciliatory. Varian remained silent as they walked farther away from the festival, but he was so close to her she could feel the heat of his body, feel the heavy presence of his aura brushing hers.

But the farther away from the noisy crowd they went, the more she began to question the wisdom of her decision. Dealing with him now wouldn't be peaceful or easy, her emotions were nowhere near steady enough, and that was something she'd always prided herself on when dealing with others. This time her usual caution and control seemed nonexistent.

"We're two minutes' walk from the last group of people, *Temple Elect*."

"Thank you, Ehrinne." Kymora slowed her pace. "Would you both mind giving us some privacy?"

"We'll drop back to a distance of thirty paces, no more."

She waited until the sound of footsteps receded. And even then she delayed a few more seconds, not liking the cold uncertainty curling in her stomach. Being unable to use her skill to read Varian's aura left her feeling helpless. Was this confrontation a part of her Journey? What if neither of them were ready for it?

*Blessed Mother*, how was she to know if this was the right pathway? She inhaled an uneven breath.

"Why didn't you just say no to my invitation, Varian?" Her voice shook as she kept a leash on her temper. "The *Lady* knows I tend to get pushy, but I'd have accepted your decision if you'd just come out and told me."

The pain in Kymora's voice slashed at Varian like a dull-edged blade. His hands fisted at his sides as she struggled with her emotions. Anger, disappointment, doubt, sadness, they all flickered across her face, some lingering longer than others.

"Kymora, I'm sorry." His stomach knotted so badly it felt like a whole coil of rope tangled in there. He ran a hand through his hair. "I overreacted."

"I didn't deserve to be treated like that."

He winced at the contained fury in her voice but took the criticism rather than defend himself. "I know."

"I understand you find it hard to trust others, Varian." Her fingers flexed around her staff. "Surely you've known me long enough to realize I won't take advantage of you?" She widened her stance, almost as if bracing herself. "If you truly think I'd do that, then our friendship ends here."

Varian stilled. Her announcement should have brought relief.

This was the excuse he'd been waiting for, the ultimatum that would give him a reason to cut free of any entanglements with her.

And yet, the hollow ache inside him seemed to get only worse. His gaze lifted to her face. She stared over his shoulder, the sunlight turning the green depths of her eyes hazel. A frown marred her brow; her hair tumbled over her shoulders like a black waterfall. Needle-leaves lay tangled in some of the strands. There was such strength in the lines and angles of her face.

She faced him with an elegant dignity. He'd never imagined anyone like her would ever call him a friend. She talked and listened to him. She made him feel warm in places he'd thought permanently frozen. She made him feel more than what he was.

Deep down he hungered for more of Kymora's brand of friendship. She was like a piece of sweet-nut, addictive and hard to relinquish once tasted. He liked being treated as somebody of worth.

Another swift glance at her face and he knew her statement was no idle declaration. For someone as generous and giving as Kymora, even she'd reached her limit with him. And considering his behavior of late, he didn't blame her. But the thought of giving up everything they'd shared ate at his soul like acid.

"I was afraid." Even to his own ears he sounded gruff, surly, but Kymora didn't reprimand or criticize him. He dragged in an unsteady breath. "Yes, you pushed and I used that as an excuse to hurt you so I wouldn't have to face my fear."

He cringed on hearing himself admit that aloud. The skin across his shoulder blades prickled and crawled.

"Varian, I know you don't like mixing in large crowds. That's why Annika and Kalan chose the grove as the site for our group." Her voice softened. "And if that was still too overwhelming for you, I would've been happy to move farther away with you to watch everything from a distance."

Her compassion humbled him. "You're too forgiving."

Kymora tilted her head down, the frown on her forehead thoughtful, her expression intense. When she looked up again, her mouth was set in a firm line. "Varian, you have to learn to reach out to people, to trust them. Living a life in fear is no life at all." Sincerity resonated in her voice. "I understand that better than most. And I think you do, too."

He issued a silent grunt. Her strength and vision astounded him. How many times had he demanded the very best of his scouts, pushed them to what they thought were their limits and then watched them fill with satisfaction as they achieved more than they believed possible?

Kymora worked in much the same way. If she could face her fears with such honesty and dignity, then he could make the effort, even if it felt like walking over hot coals.

He wiped a hand along the length of his breech-clad thigh. "I value our friendship very much."

Some of the tension left Kymora's expression. "Then let's be open and truthful with one another. No matter how much it frightens us."

"I'll try."

She nodded once, accepting his response. "*Lady* knows it won't always be easy, but if we want this to work, then we can always find a way." She gestured back along the shoreline. "Would you like to watch the festivities with me?"

The longing to experience what she had as a child returned. "What, here?"

"Yes, if there's somewhere to sit down, or we can return to the grove if you'd like."

Her suggestion had him glancing over her shoulder at the crowded strip of lakeside. Torches and fires were being lit to compensate for the descending twilight. They dotted the shoreline like glow-flies. Groups of figures still gathered around the various entertainers and stalls lined along the outer city wall and shoreline. The noise level, even at this distance, was constant.

With the workday over, more people were coming through the wide-open double gates to join those already there. His skin prickled at the thought of going anywhere near that crowd. He'd almost suffocated searching for her before Arek had found him.

"Well, your silence tells me going back isn't a good idea."

Guilt prodded him at interrupting her celebrations. "But you were with the others. . . ."

"And now I'm with you." Her simple answer touched his heart. The hand she held out to him was accompanied by a smile.

Varian stared at her hand. She trusted so easily he was frightened, for her, for his lack of understanding in how she could give it so freely.

He blinked and focused on her fingers. They were long, graceful, and unsteady.

They *trembled*.

His gaze snapped to her face. Her lips were parted, just barely, the bottom one caught between her teeth. Two small signs of vulnerability, each powerful enough to make his heart seize.

Together they felt like a blow to his gut.

Her uncertainty at how he'd perceive her gesture left him dry mouthed. Couldn't she feel how much he admired and respected her boldness? How he marveled that she seemed to take his surliness and reticence in her stride, then make him feel as if none of his flaws mattered?

Something warm and tender expanded in his chest. It hurt and it didn't. He swallowed hard.

Her courage gave him the impetus to lace his fingers with hers. Against his darker skin, hers seemed pale, and incredibly delicate. He ran a thumb over the softness of her palm, so different than his calloused skin, then traced the slender width of the back of her hand.

Did she know how good he felt to be touching her? Would she

notice how his hand shook, too? Did she feel the same tingly warmth working its way down along her arm to other places deep inside her?

The sensation was more a connection than something sexual, although there was a thread of desire woven through it. He didn't feel the urge to act on it though. The tension between them was gone, and for now it was enough to just take pleasure in what they shared.

Varian cleared his throat. "There's a spot on the bank behind you."

He made sure Kymora was comfortable on the grassy knoll before sitting beside her. Stretching his legs out across the fine-pebbled down slope, he stared out across the lake. The gently rippling surface had changed in color from the time he'd first come through the lake-gates from the city. It'd gone from a beautiful deep blue to a blue-shadowed ebony with the onset of night.

Its serene quality reminded him of Kymora. Both were nature's gifts, with natural beauty on the surface and in their hidden depths. Both were to be enjoyed and savored. And, as the silence between them lengthened, the sense of peace inside him at just being there with her was relaxing. No awkwardness. No pressure. No discontent.

*Soul comfort.* Hesia's words to describe the rare things that made you forget any hardship or problem and reminded you of the joy of just existing.

Until this moment, he'd never really understood the term. For now he was content to take it minute by minute. Regret, doubt, and uncertainty could wait until tomorrow. He'd deal with the fallout then. He released a slow breath.

Kymora folded her legs sideways and leaned in so that her body pressed against his, then tucked her hand into his larger one. He glanced to where the two bodyguards stood farther along the shore. Neither faced them directly, but the older woman's gaze flickered over them every so often. Nothing in her expression reflected any response to their intimate position and that surprised him.

"Ehrinne or Nendal are seasoned warriors, too well trained for gossip." Kymora's soft comment eased some of his concern. Was she using her skill or had she guessed his concern? He still wasn't sure he liked her being able to read him, if that's what she was doing. Her thumb stroked over his knuckles. "The sun's set behind the mountains."

Her comment drew him away from observing the guards. He grunted. The sun had sunk below the ragged mountain range. Several minutes ago.

His enhanced vision compensated for the lack of light so he hadn't actually noticed. A wispy bank of clouds hung low over the silhouetted range, one or two obscuring the snow-tipped caps. Varying shades of gold, orange, and deep burgundy trimmed their underbellies, contrasting sharply with the violet-hued backdrop of twilight. The landscape was a little dulled, like a washed-out, overcast day, but he could still see everything clearly.

"How did you know?" he asked.

"The air is cooler and I can hear the Night-lark's song coming from where they nest on the ramparts of the city wall." Sensory details, the sort most underutilized. Him included. "The dusk-parrots have also settled in the upper branches of the needle-trees. If you tune out the music from the festival, and listen really carefully, you can hear them squabbling over the best positions. They must sort it all out because by the time full dark comes, they're silent."

Varian snorted gently, his lips twitching at her description. "You make them sound like children arguing over being put to bed."

"They do, don't they?" She chuckled, then her head tipped toward him. "Are you smiling?"

He stiffened as she reached up to touch his face.

She hesitated. "Varian, I can't read your aura with the crowd so close by. Too many thoughts and emotions."

He cursed the instinctive reaction. Without her Gift, she was truly blind. Taking her hand, he placed it on his cheek and let her feel his smile, needing the connection of her skin on his more than he wanted to pull away.

Her voice dropped to a whisper. "You can smile, you know. It's not like anyone can see you and ruin your intimidating I'm-your-leader image. Especially me."

It took a moment to realize she was teasing him. None of the other *Na'Chi* felt comfortable enough with him to attempt it. More amazing though was that Kymora had the capacity to make fun of herself and her disability.

Her fingertips trailed over his lips, whisper gentle. "I like knowing I've made you happy, Varian. It makes me content."

Her words were another blow to his gut. She made expressing her feelings sound so easy. Too used to holding on to and hiding his, he recognized a soul-deep weariness that came from denying them and dared to speak freely.

"Then I will try to smile more often when I'm with you."

Her smile was his reward. His eyes stung and he blinked hard several times. What he wouldn't give to freeze this moment in time. He didn't want to go back to the grove to the others or contend with the horde of people swarming along the shoreline like pollen-eaters.

"Then we won't." Kymora caressed his jaw, drawing him back to the present.

"What?" he asked.

"I heard you whisper something about not wanting to return to the festival." He hadn't realized he'd spoken his inner thoughts aloud. "Summer's End is a night to enjoy. We can do that just as easily here as over there."

Varian relaxed and his fingers tightened around hers. Tonight wishes did come true and every minute would remain in his memory. Revered.

Cherished.

# Chapter 20

"WORK as a team!" Varian shouted, then ground his teeth together as Taybor took advantage of the two Light Blade warriors' lack of collaboration.

The *Na'Chi* scout feinted one way and, as the younger human moved to block him, he dodged in the opposite direction. He then hooked an arm around the human's neck and shoulders and under his thigh, and body-slammed him to the ground. Dust billowed up to join the haze already coating the training area. Varian slapped his breech-clad thigh in frustration.

"Stop!" He stepped over the line carved into the dirt and into the arena. A cheer came from the next one over but he ignored the noise. Their area was one of twelve scattered around the exercise compound being used for training this morning.

The two warriors still on their feet halted training. The young man on the ground remained there, sucking in huge breaths of air, his sweaty face now smeared with a layer of dirt.

"Aelois, Drascan, the timing of your moves are out. The aim is to keep Taybor's attention split between you, wondering which one of you will attack first. Even one step out of sync and you give him the chance to anticipate. And once on the ground, you're as good as dead."

With a grunt, Aelois sat up and wiped his face with his sleeve, a grimace creasing his features. Against the more heavily framed *Na'Reish* demons, both humans needed speed, and their lean, wiry builds gave them that advantage.

"Aelois, you have the skills, you're fast and agile, you know how to fight, it's just that you're used to battling one-on-one." Varian held his hand out to the man. After a moment's hesitation, the Light Blade took it, accepting his help to rise. Varian clapped him on the shoulder. "Go from the beginning again. Stalk your opponent, time the moves, and take Taybor out."

From the corner of his eye, two figures standing at the edge of the arena caught his attention. Varian nodded to his scout to begin the training session again and backtracked his steps.

Kalan and Arek waited for him, decked out not in training leathers but full battle gear, their hair pulled back into tight ponytails. Black leather breeches, boots, body armor, weapons belts. Carved into their leather chest plates was the *Lady's* sun symbol, a striking piece of workmanship brought out by the morning sunlight. Both also wore somber expressions.

"What's wrong?" he asked.

"An outrider arrived an hour ago. A *Na'Reish* patrol has been spotted half a day's ride from here." Kalan's mouth flattened into a hard line. "We don't know if it's just scouting or intending some sort of attack. I need five of your most experienced scouts and five Light Blades who you feel will work best together. We leave as soon as they can get their armor and weapons."

"Do we chase or kill the *Na'Reish* patrol?" he asked, adrenaline already surging through him at the thought of a confrontation.

The *Chosen's* emerald gaze locked with his. "I have no intention of leaving any survivors to report back to Savyr."

Varian glanced to Arek. "I can think of three Light Blades. . . ."

With the Second's input, they had a team chosen in a few minutes.

"Inform them." Kalan bared his teeth in a grim smile. "May the *Lady* bless us on our venture. Its success could be a much-needed morale boost."

Within half an hour, the party of a dozen Light Blades and *Na'Chi* scouts, Varian included, congregated outside the stables. The human warriors all wore their armor and weapons. Glancing at his own scouts, he made sure each had their thick leather vests on. Unused to the humans' stiff armor after years of fighting in just the clothes on their backs, they'd all opted to wear the more supple leather vests. They wouldn't stop a blade as well as the harder armor, but they had their Gift and wits to compensate.

Each Light Blade began saddling the war-beasts used by outriders, although these were larger than the ones he'd seen previously.

Zaune sauntered over, one eyebrow lifting as he watched the proceedings. "Are we expected to ride them?"

"Looks like it." Varian pointed his chin to the left. "Arek's ordered each to be double saddled."

Six of the behemoths stood shoulder to shoulder, their tri-horned snouts tethered to the hitching post. Fur coated their hides in coarse waves, but in winter it grew into tightly curled ringlets, giving them a shaggy appearance but one that kept them warm and dry and was able to stand up to the worst the mountains could throw at them. This close to them, the musty oil secreted by the beasts that gave their hides waterproofing was quite strong.

Thick muscles rippled beneath their hides, from shoulder to haunch, their broad backs well accustomed to bearing the weight of two riders. Large brown eyes gave them a docile appearance, but they were hardy animals and their endurance over distances more than made up for their lack of speed.

Arek wasn't a small man, but next to his beast he looked like a stripling youth. He crouched down beside his mount and unfettered its front legs, then lifted each clawed hoof, checking between the segmented toes for debris. It took two to lift the double-seated saddle onto its back, but in less than a minute, the straps were secured around its body.

The *Chosen's* Second threw his saddle-pouch over the handle-grip between the two seats, then turned toward them. "Choose your beast and mount up."

Varian headed for the blond warrior. "You realize none of us have ridden before."

"Won't take long to learn, *Na'Chi*." His mischievous grin didn't reassure him. "Just hang on to the handle-grip until you get the feel of their gait, and use your thighs to steady yourself. Rely on your shoulders and they'll be sore in an hour."

Instructions delivered, the human placed a booted foot against a large calloused pad of skin behind the beast's knee and gripped the edge of the saddle. With a half hop, he sprang upward, and in one twisting movement, ended up seated in the front saddle.

He leaned down to offer Varian his hand. "Use his back knee, just like I did."

Varian clasped Arek's forearm and within a few seconds was seated behind the warrior. The saddle proved quite comfortable, the seat more padded than he'd first expected, and the handle-grip between them helped balance him while he settled. It was an odd feeling sitting a man's height off the ground.

"Ready?" Kalan called. Each Light Blade replied with an affirmative. "Move out. Double-time once we clear Southgate."

Once outside the city, the pace picked up to a ground-eating gait.

For the first quarter hour, Varian struggled with the intricacies of balance and rhythm. He ignored the first half-dozen amused looks Arek shot over his broad shoulder.

"Just let the rocking motion of the animal become your own!" the Light Blade warrior advised.

"You're enjoying this, aren't you?" The growl in his tone just made the warrior laugh.

"Come on, Varian, after all those weeks you goaded me in scout training?" The human's grin matched the brightness of the midday sun. "Welcome to my world, *Na'Chi*."

That deserved a jab in the ribs, but he was too busy trying to follow the advice and avoid bruising his buttocks any more than he had to. Eventually though he worked out the rhythm and was able to focus on the countryside.

From the city, they headed in a southwesterly direction, following the valley plateau. The terrain was mostly tundra scattered with patches of tufty grass and open stretches of hard-packed ground. Ahead the plateau petered off into undulating plains covered in more varied vegetation. The Lower Crags curved away from them to the west.

"Where are we headed?" He had to raise his voice to be heard over the drumming thud of clawed hooves.

"Toward a little village called Ostare." Arek pointed to a wooded area on the plains. "That forest extends all the way to the border. The *Na'Reish* use it as cover to get into three Provinces undetected."

Varian shaded his eyes from the glare of the midday sun. A white haze hung low over the green-tinged grassland to the left of the forest. "Arek, there's smoke ahead."

The warrior straightened, his thighs clamping tightly around the thick body of his mount as he rose from the saddle to peer into the distance. After a moment's observation, he let out a piercing whistle that attracted Kalan's attention. He signaled the patrol to a walk and passed on the information.

"If Ostare's been attacked, then it's only been in the last half hour. There's so little wind today, we should have seen plumes of smoke if it'd happened any earlier." Kalan's expression hardened. "We pick up the pace. Arek and Varian, you're scouts. The rest of us will stay mounted when we reach the village."

A quarter hour more and they could see black smoke beginning to billow into the sky as whatever fire had been started began consuming denser materials. By the time they reached the village, a score of thatched crofts, there was little doubt it'd been raided.

Debris spilled out of the huts: smashed tables, scattered clothing and blankets, shattered pottery. Animal pen gates lay ajar, some broken, others ripped from their hinges. Stock lay slaughtered inside; very few wandered free.

A cold shiver went down Varian's spine as he scanned their surroundings. Other than the hungry crackling of flames consuming several of the houses, and the acrid scent of smoke saturating the air, the place was ominously silent. Seemingly empty.

Arek drew their beast to a halt and slid from the saddle. Varian dropped down beside him, landing lightly. The change in the human warrior was startling. The mischievous glint and lighthearted visage were gone, replaced by something more glacial, harder, and much fiercer. Deadly. His scent was spicy sharp, underscored with an ice-cold bite.

Passing the reins to the warrior closest, Arek caught his eye, pointed to the hut directly ahead of them, then arced his finger to the right. Varian nodded as he drew his dagger and took the lead.

Rounding the first mud-walled hut, Varian halted and threw up an arm, his fist clenched. Arek halted. A thin, barefooted leg lay sticking out of the doorway. Another stride and he crouched close to the doorway and peered inside. His gaze narrowed as he inhaled the heavy, metallic stench of blood and other bodily fluids. The odor stung his nostrils.

"Three dead, a woman and two young children," he stated, voice low, expressionless. He ducked under the low frame. It took a moment for his eyes to adjust to the dimly lit interior. Keeping his breathing shallow, he knelt next to the first body.

No matter how many times he witnessed death, particularly those who were innocent or unable to defend themselves like this crofter family, each left a dry ashlike taste in his mouth.

He tilted the young boy's head back with his finger. His heart started to pound. The *Na'Reish* had been here. Even in the dimmer light of the hut's interior, nothing could hide the bloody holes on his neck.

"This child has teeth marks on his neck."

Arek entered the hut, his expression bleak, his mouth set in a grim line. He stepped past him and searched the other two bodies, another young boy, possibly only two or three years of age, and an older woman, most likely their maternal elder.

"These two have been drained as well," the human said.

Varian knew then any others they found would most likely be of similar ages and share the same fate as these three. The *Na'Hord* patrol the outrider had spotted was a raiding party, and those taken alive from Ostare would be fit, healthy, and able to maintain the fast pace the raiders set in their retreat to the border. Breath hissed between his teeth.

Arek's tone was brusque. "Let's check the rest of the village and report back to Kalan."

The rest of their search turned up fourteen more bodies, all elderly or very young, all bearing the same teeth marks on their throats or wrists.

Returning to the others, Arek related what they'd found. As he finished, Varian surveyed the ground to their left.

"The *Na'Hord* patrol went this way," he announced, and pointed out the faint tracks pressed into the dirt on a worn trail that led away from the village to the nearby forest. "There's fresh *Vorc* scat and human footprints, maybe a dozen people. Shall I track them?"

"Go with him, Arek," Kalan ordered. "We'll follow. This is one *Na'Hord* patrol that won't be making it back to the border."

# Chapter 21

VARIAN ghosted through the forest just ahead of him, slipping from one form of cover to another with such skill Arek lost track of him more than once. While his scouting skills had improved since training with the *Na'Chi*, this display just raised his respect for them several notches. No wonder they'd survived for so long in *Na'Reish* territory undetected.

Crouching behind a moss-covered tree stump, Arek scanned the trail ahead. The temperature beneath the thick canopy of mature trees provided welcome relief from being out in the sun. The lack of heat meant the ground retained its moisture, so the tracks they were following were easy to detect in the spongy soil.

Puzzling though, the *Na'Hord* patrol had made no effort to cover their passing. Pulling his dagger from its sheath, Arek carved an arrow on the western side of the stump. A marker for Kalan and the others who followed a hundred paces behind.

Movement from the corner of his eye halted his actions. Varian stepped from behind a thicket of thorny-woods and covered the remaining distance between them on silent feet.

"There's a clearing ahead." He kept his voice low. "The *Na'Hord* are camped there. A full unit. And nineteen humans." His lip curled. "After scouting around the clearing, I was able to get within a dozen strides of the one warrior they'd posted as a lookout. With such complacency, we should be able to ambush them."

Arek's gut tightened. Why were the *Na'Reish* being so careless? Their behavior just didn't make sense. Now would be a good time to strike though, while they were stationary. On the move, there were other variables like mounted *Vorc-Riders* to consider. Camped as they were, the deadly *Na'Reish* mounts would be muzzled and tethered. One less risk to contend with.

"Mark out a map while I get the others." Arek tapped the ground with the tip of his dagger, then sheathed it. "We're going to need to leave the war-beasts behind while we carry out the ambush."

He returned with the others several minutes later. All twelve of them crouched around Varian's map, and the *Na'Chi* warrior filled them in on what lay ahead.

"As your people have more experience in this sort of operation, it's yours to lead, Varian," Kalan declared. Arek lifted an eyebrow while the other Light Blades made sounds of surprise, earning themselves a glare from the *Chosen*. "I want those farmers rescued, and the *Na'Chi* clearly have the advantage in this sort of environment."

Bending once more over the map, Varian issued his orders to each pair of Light Blades and *Na'Chi*.

"The two extra warriors"—and here he pointed at Arek and Kalan—"will be free to assist where needed after Zaune takes out the sentry. All clear?"

Adrenaline surged through Arek as each of them checked their weapons and armor. This time, just like every other occasion he'd faced the *Na'Reish*, he thought of his parents. Had they felt the thrill of the rush in the minutes before battle? The sense of rightness knowing what you were involved in was what you were born to do?

His memories of them had dulled over the passage of time. Occasionally a scent or a sensation would trigger a memory of them, but he recalled little of their physical features. Savyr's vengeful machinations left him without a mother from three years of age, and he'd lost his father to grief over her death not long after. He'd grown up hearing deeds of their service from others who'd known them, although many bitter reminders from his grandfather on how the *Na'Reish* had destroyed both their lives had balanced them.

So while serving as a Light Blade warrior was his calling, his life's ambition involved killing every *Na'Reish* demon he could sink his blade into.

Threading his way through the mature forest to the clearing and *Na'Hord* patrol, Arek touched the amulet around his neck. Lady, *protect* Your *children and bring us safely home.* A ritual prayer he always recited before a skirmish.

The group slowed once they were in sight of the clearing, going to their bellies to take advantage of the cover provided by the uneven ground or fallen or dead tree debris. Every so often the murmur of conversation or raucous laughter drifted toward them on the gentle breeze.

Varian signaled a halt and they all waited as Zaune disappeared into the undergrowth. A short time later he returned, his eyes reflecting the crimson glow of his Gift, and he nodded to Varian. The sentry had been taken care of.

Varian gestured in several directions, and each Light Blade/*Na'Chi* pair split off to take up their position. Heart thumping double-time, Arek peered through the underbrush where he and Kalan crouched behind a thick stand of young saplings.

In the small clearing, nine *Na'Reish* demons lounged around in various poses of relaxation. Some sat on dead logs pulled into a rough semicircle; others reclined on the leaf-littered ground.

Arek frowned. Their relaxed demeanor said they weren't in any hurry to leave human territory. Raids for blood-slaves were usually exercises in stealth and speed. Why weren't they fleeing for the border? Surely they weren't so confident they thought they'd managed an invasion without being detected?

His innards grew cold as one of the *Na'Reish* ambled toward the group of men and women huddled around the base of a needle-tree. The demon was at least seven feet tall, all brawny muscle from his thick shoulders right down to his long, powerful legs.

His heavily boned face was broad, rugged, but with an aristocratic flare to his cheekbones. Deep purple eyes surveyed everything around him with the arrogance of an upper-born Lordling. As his gaze settled on the crofters, his black lips peeled back into a malevolent smile, revealing pointed teeth sharp enough to shred flesh.

How many humans had the demon killed to feed his hunger for blood? Arek's gut heaved as he fisted his hands. He controlled it with the thought that by the time the sun set, this *Na'Reish* warrior would never feed on any human again.

Black-mottled markings ran down either side of the demon's face, matching the color of his long hair, and disappeared beneath the edge of his body armor. The same mottled effect covered his bare arms. The segmented sections of his chest plate fit together in a pattern that reminded Arek of the leathery hide of a ground-burrower. A sheathed sword lay strapped to his hip.

As the only one wearing armor of such fine quality, this demon had to be the *Na'Hord* leader, a *Na'Reishi*, one of the upper class. The others wore a collection of mismatching pieces and were most likely members from the *Na'Reishu* and *Na'Reisha* castes in the Lordling's Clan.

The *Na'Reishi* leader stopped a few steps from the crofters, hands hooked into his sword belt, his legs braced wide as he surveyed them all. He pointed at one of the younger women.

"You, female, come to me." The deep, gravelly command drew frightened cries from some in the group. The woman in question curled in on herself, her arms wrapping around her head in a protective manner.

Cold fury ripped up Arek's spine. The *Na'Reishi* wanted her for one of two reasons, and by the way he was unbuckling his armor, it wasn't for use as a blood-slave. Arek reached for the hilt of his sword.

A hand clamped down over his.

"Easy, Second," Kalan murmured.

"He's going to rape her." His reply came from between clenched teeth.

"Wait for Varian's signal. Give the others a chance to get into place."

The demon peeled the segmented chest plate over his head and dropped it to the ground. His vambraces followed.

Arek's mouth flattened. Fury ignited in his blood. "We can't let him hurt her. . . ."

An undulating war cry split the air. Cold, furious anticipation blasted through Arek as he drew his sword. Kalan was right beside him as they tore through the undergrowth, and the others exploded into the clearing, homing in on their targets.

Caught unprepared, the *Na'Reish* scrambled to meet their attack.

Arek watched astounded as each *Na'Chi* warrior launched into a barehanded assault on their intended victim. What each lacked in height and brawn as compared to their opponent, they made up for in speed, agility, and guile. Every move, every feint was designed to distract so their Light Blade partner could approach from behind.

"Arek! Kalan!" Varian yelled and pointed.

The *Na'Reishi* commander grappled with Jinnae, one of the

younger *Na'Chi* scouts. His arm lay wrapped around her throat. Lifting her off her feet, he used her as a shield against her partner.

Kalan went left, and he went right as they converged to help. The demon threw the young *Na'Chi* woman across the clearing with a roar. With a scraping hiss, he pulled his sword from its sheath.

Arek kept his attention on the demon, unable to check if Jinnae was all right.

"Light Blades!" The snarl was accompanied by a deadly grin. "Your blood will sate my hunger tonight."

Kalan's grin was just as cold. "You can try, demon."

Arek called on his Gift as the *Na'Reishi* engaged his friend. He and Jole, the other Light Blade, provided distraction as the sound of metal meeting metal and the cries of battle rang throughout the clearing.

Peripherally, Arek tracked his surroundings. To his right, *Vorc* growled and tore at their tethers, but the chain-lines held. Thank the *Lady* for that, as the *Na'Reish* trained their beasts to attack humans on sight.

Arek feinted with his sword. The *Na'Reishi* turned away from Jole. The demon's parry sent vicious vibrations up the length of his arm. The familiar power of Kalan's Gift surged. He lunged under the demon's guard, his sword piercing beneath his left ribcage.

Violet eyes bulged. One large hand seized Kalan's wrist. Arek thrust. His blade bit into the demon's abdomen. Jole came in low, slashing across the *Na'Reishi's* back.

With a pained howl, the demon sank to the ground, releasing his sword. The fall drove both his and Kalan's weapons deeper. The *Na'Reishi* threw back his head and roared. His hand groped along his waist. Light caught on a bare blade.

"Kalan, watch out!"

The dagger bit into Kalan's side until only the hilt could be seen. Arek sucked in a shocked breath. He drove his power, his Gift, into the demon's body.

The *Na'Reishi* fell, but the thrill of victory was absent. Arek dropped his sword as Kalan collapsed, and caught him just before he hit the ground.

"*Merciful Mother!*" His friend gasped, pain carving deep grooves in his face. He pressed a hand to his side.

"Easy, my friend, easy." Arek's voice shook as he peeled Kalan's bloody fingers away from his wound. "Let me see how bad it is."

His mouth dried. One of the thick leather straps cinching Kalan's armor to his body was partially cut. After striking the buckle, the blade had deflected into the gap between that one and the next.

More war cries filled the air. The cadence wasn't *Na'Chi*. An icy chill ripped through Arek.

"*Lady's Breath!*" Jole's invective matched his paling face, and his wide-eyed gaze was fixed on something behind them.

Arek twisted to look. Through the forest, figures darted and wove their way toward them. More *Na'Reish* demons. The dappled shadowing made it hard to count how many. "Another patrol!"

Outnumbered and already down at least one warrior, the odds had just gone from good to potentially devastating.

Kalan's hand squeezed his. Urgency blazed in the pained depths of his gaze. "Take. It. Out. Now!"

"I need his shirt, Jole." Arek pointed with his chin at the dead demon. "Pad and bandage."

Field dressing at best whereas Kalan needed a healer. A swift glance at the advancing *Na'Reish*; they had a minute, maybe two at the most.

Arek curled his hand around the dagger hilt. "Ready?"

Kalan swallowed hard and nodded.

Arek yanked the blade from his side. Through gritted teeth, Kalan screamed. His body arched, then collapsed again, half conscious. Jole packed the makeshift bandage against the wound and tied it tight with another strip of material.

While he did this, Arek scanned the clearing. The fighting still raged on. Relief flooded him to see every other Light Blade and *Na'Chi* still standing.

Another demon fell and a dark-clad figure dumped the body to the ground.

"Varian!"

The *Na'Chi* leader's head snapped up, his gaze glowing almost red. Arek knew he'd spotted the new patrol when he bared his teeth in a feral grimace. He covered the distance between them in seconds.

"Kalan's wounded. He needs a healer." Arek grasped the *Na'Chi's* arm, gaze locking with his. "Retreat with the others. You're still in charge. Jole will back you if the other Light Blades protest. You must get the *Chosen* back to Sacred Lake. Understand?"

"You're his Second." Varian's brow dipped low. The words were guttural, deep, not quite human. "Why aren't you going to lead them?"

A scream of rage jerked them around. Varian launched himself at the *Na'Reish* warrior charging them from the edge of the clearing. A blur of movement, he kept low, and took his opponent down in a bone-crushing tackle. The two of them rolled across the ground.

More *Na'Reish* entered the clearing, each issuing a battle cry. Terrified into action, the farmers scattered in all directions. Their bid for escape stalled the demons for a few precious seconds.

*Merciful Mother*, they were all going to be slaughtered if they stayed. Not even the extra skills and strength of the *Na'Chi* would help them. And the Blade Council couldn't afford to lose the *Lady's Chosen*. Not now.

Arek snatched up his sword. They were going to need a distraction. It wasn't exactly how he'd imagined his Final Journey, but at least he'd get to take out as many *Na'Reish* as he could before he fell.

"Jole, take Kalan." Heart pounding, he couldn't look at his best friend as he rose. He did share a steady look with Jole. Had to. Someone needed to understand his decision, and despite their friendship . . . no, *because* of their friendship, Kalan wouldn't.

"Get him out of here," he rasped. "I'll help Varian."

Jole's eyes widened with shock, with disbelief and astonishment, then finally acceptance. Jaw flexing, the warrior nodded slowly and pressed his own sword into his hands. Arek grinned. Two weapons were better than one.

"*Lady* protect you, Second."

"Arek . . . no!" Kalan's hoarse protest made Arek's throat tighten. *Lady's Breath*, he knew. Reluctantly he met his friend's glazed gaze. "This is the only way, my friend. Tell Annika . . . I should've made the time to get to know her. . . ." The agony in Kalan's emerald eyes pierced him. Arek stood, wishing he had time to say a proper farewell. "*Lady* bless you."

Insides churning, he ignored Kalan's repeated hails. He hurried around them to Varian. The *Na'Chi* leader had his opponent in a headlock. With a deep-throated growl, and a vicious twist, he snapped his neck and dropped the body to the ground. Arek grasped a handful of his leather vest and pulled him to his feet.

"Get everyone out of here. Now, before it's too late." He reinforced the order with a shove, then dodged in front of him, sword already swinging to block the *Na'Reish* warrior bearing down on them.

Arek widened his stance as their swords clashed and grunted as the blow jarred his shoulder. He swept the other sword blade in low, felt it bite deep into the demon's leg. The seven-foot warrior howled, knee buckling. One large fist lashed out. The blow caught the side of his head. Arek staggered. He lost his grip on one sword.

A *Na'Chi* war cry rang out.

The one indicating retreat.

Head ringing, he forced himself upright. Another *Na'Reish* warrior came at him. A huge broadsword arced overhead. He leapt back to avoid being cleft in two, then caught sight of Varian. The *Na'Chi* finished off another opponent on the opposite side of the clearing. The warrior disappeared into a shadowed stand of saplings, the last to leave.

Lady *protect them*. A deep-seated calmness filled Arek. *And guide me on my Final Journey.* The second *Na'Hord* unit was seconds from overrunning the clearing.

"Don't let them escape!" The roared order came from somewhere to his left.

Arek pivoted to face yet another adversary. He blocked one more arm-numbing blow. Something slammed into him from behind. The impact of hitting the ground drove the breath from his lungs. Another massive fist swung at him.

It hit.

Everything exploded in a ball of light. He lost his grip on his sword.

Darkness overwhelmed him.

# Chapter 22

"COUNCILOR Elamm, welcome." Kymora held open the wooden door to her apartment. She pasted on a polite smile.

*Lady* forgive her the lack of a genuine response, but a frisson of disapproval mixed with self-importance already radiated from the older woman's aura. What irked her more was that the Councilor made no effort to hide it.

Since being appointed to the Blade Council, Elamm'd taken to meeting weekly with her to discuss the Temple's involvement with community projects. All well and fine if the Councilor's intentions were sincere, but there was an element of political ambition souring her deeds. And during Council business, the woman seemed to take a perverse pleasure in pointing out the negative of any issue.

A potent and off-putting combination that tested Kymora's patience every time she had to deal with the woman.

"Please come in." She kept her smile firmly in place. "I've prepared a pot of tea. Would you like a cup before we begin our meeting?"

"*Temple Elect*, that sounds like a wonderful idea." The older woman's voice was deep, full bodied, the vowels in her words heavily rounded by a provincial drawl. "It's been a hectic day visiting with the refugee families. Most of them had to leave their belongings behind when they abandoned their homes. They just didn't have the means to transport everything. So I've approached the Weavers Guild to organize a schedule for making and supplying necessities such as blankets and clothes to these families."

"With winter approaching, they're going to need those essential items," Kymora agreed.

As the Councilor moved into the room Kymora used for official private meetings, a light floral scent tickled Kymora's nose.

"Have you also been chatting with Master Gardener Pel?"

Rich laughter accompanied the sound of her guest's footsteps to the table in the middle of the room. "He and I have a mutual interest in propagating Keri-blossoms. I've asked him to grow several dozen for my private garden."

Several dozen? A little self-indulgent on her part, and more than a little time consuming for the Master Gardner, especially now, considering the number of crops he needed to plant and care for that would help feed the refugee families the Councilor professed to have such concern for. But she resisted pointing that out.

"The blossoms do have the sweetest scent." Kymora joined her and reached for the small metal kettle she'd set there earlier. "The incense he makes from the petals for the Temple is one of the most popular used by the worshippers as an offering to the *Lady*."

With a careful hand, she poured two cups of tea. The heat from the steam rising from the water helped her gauge when to stop.

"I thought you'd appreciate *Yasri*-tea. It's a blend of sweet citrus combined with an aftertaste of mint." She pushed one cup toward the older woman, then took a seat before cradling her own. "Quite refreshing for this time of day."

After a delicate sniff, the Councilor's sigh was appreciative. Kymora masked her smile behind the edge of her cup, knowing she'd made the right choice. Elamm's love of fine teas originated from her home province. The farmers there were suppliers for the best-quality herbs traded and sold within human territory.

"It's nice to have someone else appreciate a good tea and the right time to drink it." A quiet sip, then the cup knocked against the wood as she placed it on the table. "*Temple Elect*, as much as I'm enjoying this, I'm aware that your time is precious, so perhaps we could discuss the reason for my visit?"

Her aura was sharper, humming with resolve and determination.

"Please, call me Kymora, Councilor."

"Then call me Jho." She affected a soft sigh. "I'm not sure how to broach this. . . ."

*Lady of Light*, she sounded so sincere in her concern. It set her teeth on edge, but Kymora waited, gripping the sides of her teacup tightly, and tried to savor the steamy aroma.

"There's some concern . . . from a number of parties . . . that you seem to be neglecting your duties as Sacred Lake's priestess," she murmured.

"Neglecting my duties?"

"That's the impression." The woman's tone was heavier, her drawl more pronounced. "Rest assured, I don't think that for a moment. But I thought it important you know I've been approached by . . . some . . . who've expressed these concerns. On several occasions, and in . . . shall we say . . . an increasingly vocal fashion."

Kymora resisted rolling her eyes and instead searched her memories for whom the Councilor mixed with socially. She enjoyed the company of several influential city leaders, some of the minor Guildmasters, and the other Blade Councilors.

"In what areas have I been tardy, did they tell you?" she asked.

"Well, they're concerned that in your absence you delegated almost all of your duties to your head Servant, Sartor."

The woman's aura pulsed with a tightness Kymora recognized.

"He's more than capable of handling those responsibilities." She set her cup aside and leaned forward. It was time to get to the heart of the matter. "I'd appreciate your honest opinion, Jho. Was it the delegation of responsibility or because I was living with the *Na'Chi* for almost four months?"

"The latter."

"Thank you." She reached for the kettle and topped up her cup. "Another?"

"Yes. This conversation merits at least two cups."

"It's more like a four or five, I'd say," she replied, unable to disguise her dry tone. Again, *Lady* forgive her lack of tolerance.

The Councilor's laughter seemed forced. "Indeed." She inhaled a deeper breath. "You're taking this well, considering."

"I'm not dismissing your concerns, Jho, or those held by those you've mentioned." Kymora tapped her fingernail on the edge of her cup while keeping her tone modulated. Reason not emotion was the wiser path. "The truth is I don't know that there's much I can do to allay them. I'm back in Sacred Lake, and with the *Na'Chi* now among us, there's no need to delegate. I've taken over the majority of my responsibilities again. Sartor has returned to his tutoring position with the acolytes." She splayed one hand outward in a half gesture. "Perhaps given a little more time, these people will see I continue to honor my oath to the *Lady*."

The older woman cleared her throat. "Maybe if you spend a little less time among the *Na'Chi* . . ."

Kymora sat back in her seat, frowning. "Jho, the *Lady* has claimed the *Na'Chi* as her own. They're as much a part of my realm of responsibility as any human." Another sip of tea didn't help calm her temper.

She took a slow breath. "My suggestion would be to remind those concerned of the *Lady's* words. No offense intended, Councilor, but while I know bringing their concerns to me is part of your work, I'd encourage them to talk with me."

"I did inform them of that option," the woman hastened to assure her. "But if the occasion arises, I'll certainly remind them again. Thank you for your understanding and guidance, *Temple Elect*. At least now you're aware of the concerns going around and can address them appropriately." Again her aura thrummed with self-importance, as if satisfied that she'd reminded Kymora of her duty and moral obligations. "Now, with that little bit of unpleasantness over, shall we enjoy another cup of tea?"

*Turn the other cheek . . . tolerance and patience bring their own rewards.*

Kymora recited the verse of scripture over and over as she poured them both another cup, and while the discussion moved on to a more neutral topic, the recent Summer's End Festival, her attention turned inward.

Why hadn't she been approached directly by these friends of the Councilor? Of greater concern, how many others considered her absence a dereliction of duty? The unprecedented decision to live with the *Na'Chi* had been taken to alleviate concerns not create them. Were the comments genuine or just Elamm and her close circle of friends taking advantage of their status with her?

Or could these concerns be generated by those sympathetic to Davyn and the renegade movement? Were they manipulating Elamm for their own purposes? What were they hoping to achieve?

An icy shiver worked its way up Kymora's spine as she swallowed the last of her tea. The last supposition didn't bear thinking about, but after the attack on the *Na'Chi* village, nothing could be dismissed or assumed as impossible.

A visit to the Temple was in order. It was time to seek the *Lady's* guidance.


VARIAN pulled on the reins of his war-beast, slowing its pace until it came to a stop, then he swiveled in the saddle to peer along their back trail. He ignored the rivulet of sweat trickling down the side of his face, more concerned with the possibility of being followed than any minor discomfort.

The other five mounts with their riders and passengers drew alongside. The few crofters who'd escaped with them sat down underneath the tree nearest them. With their village destroyed, they would join the refugees being billeted at Sacred Lake. What had happened to the others, no one knew, but it was very likely they'd been recaptured.

Taybor cradled a semiconscious Kalan in front of him. His strength alone kept the human leader in the saddle. No one spoke; their tense expressions mirrored his.

No snapping of bushes, no thud of pursuing footsteps, no battle cries. Other than the irritated chatter of a winged-*hobaan* scolding them for intruding in its territory, the forest remained peaceful and quiet. All its odors natural and clean.

His gambit of retreating through the forest had paid off. With Kalan's wound so deep, bleeding out had been a certainty in a prolonged run across the open plains. Blood needed time to clot. He'd sacrificed speed for stealth to save the *Chosen's* life.

"Zaune, Jinnae, check our back trail," he murmured. The two scouts slid from their beasts. "Go as far as the last creek, then cover our tracks."

With a nod, the scouts disappeared into the shadows.

Retreat, rest, camouflage. A process they'd repeated for the past two hours.

"We'll let the war-beasts take a break for a few minutes." Varian dared to glance at the second saddle behind him. The empty space ate at his gut. The image of Arek taking on and falling beneath a wave of *Na'Reish* warriors was burned in his mind like a slave-tattoo. He couldn't shake it or the guilt of having left him behind. He squeezed the reins until the leather squeaked in protest.

Beneath his skin, from deep within, the darkness of his other half fought to emerge, a predator straining to get free. With the amount of adrenaline still coursing through his veins, he had little doubt his eyes still glowed with battle rage. A silent growl vibrated in his chest.

"How's the *Chosen*?" His voice was so gravelly and deep each word came out distorted.

"Stable." Taybor's violet gaze met his. "The scent of his blood isn't fresh. The ride hasn't reopened the wound."

"I'll live." The hoarse statement vibrated with raw pain. How much of it came from the wound or with dealing with the loss of his best friend, Varian could only guess.

"Commander." One of the Light Blade warriors leaned forward in the saddle. "Let me go back and search for Arek."

Varian flinched, his gut coiling and writhing like a night-winder caught out in the midday sun. The dark beast inside him roared in favor of the suggestion. It wanted to return to the clearing and seek vengeance for the loss of a good warrior.

"I'll go with Larn." The lone female Light Blade's voice shook. "The Second may still be alive."

The odds were slim. He resisted voicing the thought. They all knew the chances. Acknowledging it aloud would only antagonize the humans and add to their pain.

And his.

"You honor the Second with your loyalty." Again his words came out warped.

The Light Blades shifted in their saddle along with the crofters;

all shared uncertain glances among themselves. He wrestled to control his darker emotions, but it was like trying to trap a wild *lira*. They kept slipping and darting through his mind, avoiding any leash he cast out to contain them.

"My orders stand. Our priority is the safety of the *Chosen*."

"Varian." Kalan's call drew his gaze. Emerald eyes locked with his, blazed with empathy and understanding. Varian gritted his teeth. *Merciful Mother*, he couldn't deal with this. Not now. "No one could have predicted this outcome."

The darkness within surged. The forest, the ground, the other warriors, even the air between them all bled of color except one. Red stained his vision.

The burning, the pain, the guilt chased each other around and around inside his head. Every turn became smaller, tighter, more vicious. Each sharp enough that it felt like he was being skinned from the inside out.

The war-beast beneath his thighs shifted and snorted as if sensing the predator in him. He drew the reins taut.

"Varian." Kalan's voice sounded tinny, distant. "*Na'Chi*, look at me. I need you."

The meaning of his words penetrated. The tension receded so fast it left Varian swaying in the saddle. He gripped the hard leather edge to steady himself.

Slowly he lifted his head. His nostrils flared at the sour stench tainting the air. He blinked at the mix of raw fear and blatant concern on the faces around him, human and *Na'Chi* alike.

He shuddered. *Lady of Light*, how close had he come to losing it? To letting his *Na'Chi* half consume him? He only allowed that to happen during battle, never any other time. Nausea churned in his gut.

"Varian?" Kalan's hard tone steadied him. Once again their gazes locked. The human leader straightened in the saddle, his hand pressed against his injured side. "I'm relying on you to get us all home. Larn, Forence, when we return you can organize a search. For now, you follow Varian's orders."

Neither Light Blade looked happy but they assented.

"Can I rely on you to get us home, *Na'Chi*?"

Kalan's question focused him. The human knew. He knew of the struggle going on inside him. It was there in the depths of his gaze.

Varian nodded, unable to vocalize his agreement. He grasped on to the task, needing it like a ship needed an anchor in the storm.

*Tomorrow.*

Tomorrow he'd deal with what had just happened. Right now their survival depended on him.

That he could do.

# Chapter 23

THE hospice proved almost as chaotic as the Temple's tutoring hall. The strong antiseptic odor of *Vaa'jahn* hit Kymora as she and Lisella pushed their way through the crowd congregating outside the building. She hesitated in the doorway, wincing as dozens of emotions bombarded her, all varying in intensity. They were so tangled she couldn't tell one person from another.

Fear underscored every impression though. News of the patrol's return had spread like a brushfire, particularly when there were rumors of the *Chosen* being wounded. Of all the emotions hitting her, this one was focused. The tightest knot came from a huddle of auras somewhere inside the building and to her right.

Was Kalan there? Was he all right?

Too many voices. Too much noise.

Kymora sucked in an unsteady breath, her heart pounding. Her fingers squeezed Lisella's forearm. Mother of Light, *let him be all right*.

The *Na'Chi* woman's hand closed over hers. "Ehrinne, Ashah, would you wait here? Stop these people from coming in and disturbing the healers? I'll take the *Temple Elect* into the hall." The two Light Blade bodyguards murmured their assent. "This way, Kymora."

Some of the chatter from the crowd dimmed as they made their way through the reception area, then into the hall. Their boots clicked on the stone floor, mingling with the murmur of voices coming from somewhere ahead.

The odor of *Vaa'jahn* strengthened. Childhood memories stirred and Kymora shivered. So many negative feelings belonged with her past inside this building.

Death had taken her mother within these walls.

She'd lost her sight.

And now Kalan was here.

Before her illness, she'd visited the hospice with her mother many times, delivering packages for patients from loved ones who lived in the villages her mother visited while trading.

From memory, she knew individual cots lined either side of the hall. One between each window. A small cupboard sat next to each to store the patient's belongings and to provide a table for their medications or a preparation area for treatments. A single stool resided under the end of the bed along with a chamber pot. The area around each bed would be conspicuously clean and neat.

The most serious illnesses or injuries were treated at the far end of the hall, in a curtained-off area. Her heart picked up speed as Lisella continued walking along the hall. Were they headed for that corner?

"What can you see?" She couldn't voice her question any louder than a whisper. "Do you see Kalan?"

"Yes." A wealth of emotion saturated the affirmation.

Kymora's knees threatened to buckle. Her throat squeezed shut. "Is he all right?"

"Candra and Annika are with him," Lisella assured her. Would

Annika be able to use her healing Gift to help him? "I can't see a lot. Many of the patrol are here, too, gathered around. Taybor, Jinnae, Jole, Varian, Larn . . ."

Kymora searched the tangle of emotions for her brother's aura. The quagmire of emotions were still too intense to sift through, and the beginnings of a headache throbbed behind her eyes.

Lisella slowed. "We're here."

"Ahh, Kymora . . ." Master Healer Candra's husky voice came from in front of them. "Lisella found you."

Fabric rasped against fabric, then a pair of cool hands grasped hers. As soon as the elderly healer touched her, Kymora could feel her aura. It hummed with energy and vitality. Calmness also radiated from her. The Master Healer's Gift stroked against her aura, a subtle warming sensation that soothed her and eased the headache.

Kymora squeezed her hands in thanks. "What's going on, Candra?"

"Kalan was wounded while on patrol."

She swayed. Candra's grip tightened on her. "How badly?"

The older woman led her off to one side and helped her sit. By the softness under her and the way Candra's wiry body pressed close to hers, they sat on the end of a cot.

"A dagger in his side. Deep, but the blade missed all his innards, thank the *Light*." The healer's tone was concise but compassionate. "He's lost a lot of blood, but Annika's healing the wound now. Once it's sealed and smeared with *Vaa'jahn*, he'll begin to recover. He'll be weak for a few days. He'll spend the next couple of weeks in bed to make sure everything mends properly and he regains his strength."

"Kalan won't like that." Even to her, her voice sounded faint. "He's never been one for bed rest."

Candra's chuckle was rich and full. "True, but I'll do my best to keep him there."

The resolve in her promise held reassurance. Much of the tension in Kymora eased. She sucked in a shuddering breath.

"I've done as much as I can for now." Kymora turned toward Annika's voice. A wave of weariness mingled with relief and love brushed against Kymora's mind. "He'll sleep the night through. I'll stay with him."

A collective sigh whispered around the room. Several people began talking at once.

"Now that you know Kalan will be all right, I suggest all of you go and rest." Candra's order brooked no argument. "Bathe, eat, sleep. You can visit tomorrow, after breakfast. No sooner."

Kymora made to rise, but the healer's arm tightened around her shoulders, holding her in place. Footsteps and voices moved away down the hall, someone retreating faster than the others. From Annika's direction there came a wooden scraping sound, like she was dragging a stool across the floor.

Air whispered past Kymora's cheek, and the soft swish of skirts caressed her leg as Annika sat down on the other side of her. A smaller hand took hers. Annika's skin was slightly damp as if she'd just washed her hands.

"There's something else you need to know, Kymora." Candra's tone shook and her aura flared. A slash of pain scored her mind. Kymora stiffened. "I'm sorry you felt that. . . ." Her words grew thicker, more unsteady.

"What's wrong?" A prickle of unease wound its way along her spine. "Is there something you haven't told me about Kalan?"

"No, he's fine," Annika reassured her. The strength of her love for him came through clearly. "He'll be well in time."

"Then what?"

"One in the patrol didn't make it back." Beside her Candra inhaled a shuddering breath. "Arek's gone, Kymora."

"Arek?" Heat followed by an icy coldness flushed through her body. "What do you mean . . . gone?"

"The *Na'Reish* attacked Ostare and took the villagers. Kalan and the others pursued the *Na'Hord* patrol, intending to rescue them. It seems there were two patrols in the same area. They don't know why." Annika recounted the facts in a soft voice. "When Kalan was wounded, Arek ordered Varian to retreat with the others. He then stayed behind to provide a distraction to give them time to escape."

"He stayed behind?" Her question came out as a hoarse whisper. The pain welling in her chest left her gasping for breath. "He didn't come back with them?"

"No."

"He's dead? Are you sure?"

"Varian saw him fall." Grief roughened Candra's reply.

Kymora swallowed against a tight throat. Light Blades captured by the *Na'Reish* suffered an agonizing death. They were seen as a food source, not slave material. Her eyes burned.

*Arek's gone.*

The words echoed in her mind. They bounced around, chasing each another in an endless loop. Her nose tingled.

*Arek's gone. Arek's gone.*

Something warm trickled down one cheek. So many memories of the boy she'd grown up with . . . the man . . . the warrior. Kymora closed her eyes, unable to stop the memories once they began pouring through her. The loss of Arek, his loyalty, his passion, his charm, even his irreverent sense of humor, would strike deep. He'd been a friend to many.

*Her childhood friend . . . Kalan's best friend . . . the man they both loved like a brother was . . .*

*. . . dead.*

She shuddered and pressed a hand to her chest, between her

breasts. Her heart ached. Heat scalded her cheeks again. The memories replayed faster.

She didn't want to remember. She didn't want to feel.

Someone was crying, sobbing, like their heart had been torn from their chest. Had one of the Light Blades remained behind?

She should find them. Offer them comfort. A prayer to ease their pain.

Her legs wouldn't work. The strength had gone out of them.

Why was it so hard to breathe?

Arms wrapped tightly around her. "Ahh, Kymora. I'm so sorry." Candra's soft voice crooned in her ear.

She lifted a hand to her cheeks. The moisture there belonged to tears. Hers. The keening came from her throat. The grief she felt was hers. Not another's.

All numbness fled. Anguish rolled over her like a wave, reaching so deep it swamped her soul. She rocked back and forth, sobbing until exhaustion stole her tears and her voice and then she grieved in silence.

How long she remained lost like that she didn't know, but eventually she became aware that she rested against the soft warmth of someone's body, her head pressed against a shoulder. Wetness soaked the material beneath her cheek. She felt hot and prickly all over. Drained.

"Does Kalan know?" Her voice grated, cracked.

"He knows." Annika's soft reply provoked more tears.

Her soul ached for him, for both of them.

Candra hugged her. "You should rest but not here. Go home."

Returning to her apartment in the Temple dormitory turned Kymora's stomach. Once there she'd be alone, confined by the silence and hollow emptiness of the rooms. Usually a haven, they felt more like a cell tonight. She shivered, the cold working its way into her.

"Lisella, would you accompany her?"

"Of course."

Kymora wiped her face on her sleeve. "The Council . . . the other Light Blades . . . someone needs to tell them about Kalan"—her voice wavered—"and Arek. . . ." Her throat closed over for several heartbeats. "Davyn should be told. Arek is . . . was . . . his grandson. Someone—"

"Let me worry about that, Kymora." Candra's no-nonsense tone relieved her of all responsibility. The sense of relief was profound. The healer's voice gentled. "Go with Lisella."

"Come on, Kymora." She allowed the *Na'Chi* woman to help her to her feet. "I know Kalan's asleep, but would you like to say good night to him before we go?"

Her brother's skin was cool to the touch. His hand and fingers limp when she laced hers through his. Skimming her fingertips upward, over his shoulder, neck, and then head, she traced his brow, then trailed them over the side of his face. A day-old beard rasped against her skin.

She pressed two fingers to the hollow just beneath his ear, felt the beat of his pulse, weak but steady. A little farther down his neck she encountered the chain of his amulet. Bowing her head, she prayed with her heart, unable to form the words in her mind.

Taking a deep breath, she lifted her head. After smoothing out the blanket covering him, she rose. "I'm ready."

Lisella took her hand. Neither of them spoke as they left the hospice. Her Light Blade guards followed at a respectful distance. They were halfway to her apartment before Kymora realized she hadn't asked after the others in Kalan's unit.

"Lisella, was anyone else hurt?"

"No. Just a few bruises and scrapes."

Amidst all the voices, she didn't recall hearing Varian's. "Is Varian all right?" Lisella's aura vibrated, her worry a dark stain that flared, then abruptly cut off. "He's not, is he? I can feel your concern."

"Now's not the time to worry about anyone else," she said, gently. "Let's take care of you. A night's rest will help."

"I don't need my apartment, Lisella." Kymora stopped walking. Her throat closed over. Swallowing hard, she shook her head. "The silence will drive me mad. I'd much rather be around other people."

Lisella's aura burred with confusion. "You don't wish to grieve by yourself?"

"Not at the moment." Alone, the pain in her heart would be too much to face. Too raw. Too ugly.

Kalan needed to heal. Annika remained with him there. Her relationships with her Servants were more professional than personal. *Mother* forgive her, but not even meditating or praying to the *Lady* was going to comfort her. Not tonight.

Being with the *Na'Chi*, with Varian, would help her cope with the worst of it. There was no one else she felt more comfortable with.

She took a steadying breath. "I'd like to return to the *Na'Chi* apartments with you."

For a long moment, Lisella said nothing, as if contemplating her request. "All right. But first, there's something you need to know about Varian. Something Taybor mentioned . . ."

# Chapter 24

VARIAN stalked across the main room of his apartment, every step filled with the same restless, angry energy as the last hundred. He glared down at the rug beneath his feet. Perhaps he'd feel better if he could actually hear the satisfying thump of his boots on the hard floor.

He shook his head. Who was he fooling? Battle-rage still rode him hours after the conflict. *Nine* hours. A first. Like a hearth full of embers, the sensation burned deep inside him, smoldering and hungry. Demanding he do something to feed the craving.

Beyond the walls of his room, outside in the corridor, the muffled laughter of children and the slap of bare feet on stone darkened his already foul mood. Usually the sound of them playing games brought him peace, but tonight the noise only added to his aggravation.

His fingers flexed. He could *feel* the sweat-slick skin of his last victim's head on his palms. The vibrations of vertebrae grating together as he snapped the demon's neck remained imprinted in his hands. The bitter stench of fear still lingered in his nostrils. Four

*Na'Reish* demons lay dead in the clearing, thanks to him, and each fed into the darkness inside him.

*Not good enough. Not this time.*

*A good warrior had fallen.*

Adrenaline surged through him again, fueling the hunger, nourishing the anger, changing them into something deeper, hotter, and gut-rippingly painful. Growling, he stalked back past the table in the center of the room. The candles in the candelabra flickered with the breeze of his passing. Light glinted off two flagons, a single cup, and the covered plate of a meal long since gone cold.

Another pass. This time he scooped up the cup perched on the edge. He gripped the glazed side tightly and stared at the dark crimson liquid contained within. Mouth thinning, he drank what was left in it, savoring the rich iron tang of *geefan* blood as it slid down his throat. He picked up the flagon to refill the cup and found it empty.

Varian eyed the depleted containers. Two were usually enough to sate his blood-hunger and lull the beast within an hour after consuming his fill. The physical hunger was gone, but the other still remained.

Beneath his skin his muscles twitched. The urge to hurl the cup against the wall and listen to it smash beat as hard as his pulse. His hand shook as he placed the cup down again.

Why wasn't that part of him submerging? Returning to the darkness where it belonged? He sucked in several deep breaths.

Issuing another growl, he scrubbed both hands over his face, then grimaced at the itchy feeling of dried blood and sweat that still remained on him from the battle.

*Mother of Light*, a bath wouldn't go astray, if only to get rid of the *Na'Reish* stink from his skin. He plucked at the ties on the thick leather vest. Maybe that would settle his other half.

A quiet knock at the door came as he flung the heavy vest over the back of a chair. He ignored it and unbuckled his weapons belt.

The knock occurred again, a little harder. "Varian? It's me, Zaune."

After hearing Kalan would be all right, he'd returned to the *Na'Chi* apartments, declining the younger scout's invitation to join them in the common room to eat and feed, preferring the solitude of his own room, too wired to risk remaining among company.

"Go away." Words whispered through gritted teeth. "Not. Now." If Zaune thought he'd changed his mind, then the scout would find out he was mistaken. It was tempting to send him away, but he couldn't ignore the possibility that Zaune might be here for another reason. Raising his voice, he called, "What?"

The latch on the wooden door lifted and it swung open. The young scout peered into the room, his expression wary. "There's someone here to see you."

Varian tensed. The last thing he wanted right now was a visitor.

"Varian, may I come in?" Kymora's soft, melodic voice came from behind the scout.

The sound of it wound its way through him until it pooled in his gut. Everything in him went tight, alert. The feeling it evoked was primal.

*Wild.*

He froze. The last thing he needed was Kymora sensing him like this. He backed away from the door and put the table between them. The edge of the leather belt bit into the palms of his hands as he squeezed it.

Zaune's gaze dipped, noting his movement, then it narrowed. When Kymora started through the door, he held an arm out to block her from entering. The protective gesture provoked the beast in him while his human half lauded the scout.

"Now's probably not the best time," Zaune murmured.

"Varian?" The slight hoarseness in her voice made it crack as she spoke his name. His gaze snapped to her face. She looked pale, tired;

dark smudges ringed her eyes. The wildness inside him clawed to get free. Every instinct screamed that he go to her.

He *couldn't*.

She should go. He didn't want her here.

*Liar.* The word exploded from the darkness in his mind.

He threw the belt on the table, harder than necessary, and it clattered against the wood.

Kymora flinched. A fine tremor ran through her body; her fingers flexed around her staff. She stood firm.

*You need her.*

*Invite her in. She needs you.*

He frowned, then inhaled. Her scent filled his lungs, a familiar combination of sunshine and sweet flowers, but there was a darker undertone, slightly soured.

Grief. Sorrow. Sharp and raw.

And it reminded him why he couldn't deal with her now. She needed comfort, but he was the last person she should be relying on to provide it.

"You should listen to Zaune, Kymora." His gruff reply earned him a glare from Zaune. Varian ignored it and turned away from them, not waiting to see them leave.

Instead he headed for the archway that led to the bathing room. His muscles hadn't stopped twitching, and the edges of his vision were beginning to wash out. Reaching for the collar of his shirt, he pulled it over his head. In his haste, the material tore. He peeled off the rest of his clothes and left them where they fell, scattered in a haphazard trail across the floor. His lack of control was unnerving.

Padding to the edge of the rectangular pool set into the floor, he untied the leather strip holding back his hair. Steam rose from the bath in lazy spirals. Beneath the steam, the surface of the water rippled, moving across the pool where it trickled into a trough set at water level.

The steady sound of it washing away into pipes built into the floor reminded him of the waterfalls he used to wash under in the forest. The only difference being the heated water, a luxury he appreciated since coming to live among the humans.

For half a second, he considered lighting one of the braziers but couldn't see the point. He could see just as well without it. Besides, soaking in the semidarkness suited his mood anyway.

Sinking into the water, he closed his eyes and submerged, glad the pool was large enough to fit his long frame. All sight and sound cut off as he stayed there, holding his breath. The heat soaked into him. The utter darkness and silence was as close to peaceful as he was going to get. Pity he had to breathe.

Surfacing, he slicked his hair back off his face, then leaned against the side. He stared up at the shadowed ceiling, willing himself to think of nothing to do with the events of the day.

The faint clack of wood on stone whipped his head around. A shadow crossed the archway in the other room.

"Kymora?"

"Yes?"

Disbelief racked him. "What are you doing here?"

There was silence after his question. Perhaps the angry growl in his voice was making her reconsider her decision of intruding on him. He hoped so.

"I didn't want to be alone tonight." Her reply was quiet, barely above a whisper.

The emotion in her voice hit him low in the gut, tugged at him like hooks in a fin-swimmer. The image of her standing in his apartment doorway, her face strained by grief, remained vivid.

His fingernails clawed at the bottom of the pool. "There's a room full of *Na'Chi* down the corridor."

Again there was silence, then the hollow *tap-tap-tap* came toward the room. Kymora appeared silhouetted in the archway, her mouth a flat line, her face pinched with raw emotion.

"Do you know how worried the others are about you?" A fine tremor of anger laced her question. "Stop isolating yourself from those who care." She hesitated, blinking rapidly. She swallowed hard. "I need you."

Varian clenched his jaw at the shine of tears in her eyes. As much as he wanted to deny her, the promise he'd made to her the night of the Summer's End Festival bound him. Rather than deflect her, he tried to warn her.

"You have no idea what you're asking of me right now, Kymora." His voice was so deep it grated. Just a few minutes in the water had restored some of his color vision, but it washed away again with her words.

She stepped farther into the room, a familiar jut to her chin. Beneath the water, his hands clenched. *Mother of Light*, she was as stubborn and contrary as him. Just how far would she push him?

"I can feel your need, too, Varian."

The beast inside him reacted, almost as if it'd been waiting for her to challenge him. Varian surged from the pool. Water sluiced off him in sheets. He headed straight for her.

Kymora retreated half a step, her expression morphing into shock at whatever she sensed coming from him. Reaching out, he yanked the wooden staff from her hands and flung it away. It cracked against the wall, then bounced away across the floor, the staccato beat loud, discordant.

Crimson hues outlined everything. She wanted honesty? He'd give it to her. He grabbed her shoulders and propelled her toward the wall behind her. Pinning her there, he leaned in close.

His lips brushed the shell of her ear. "What need can you sense in me, Kymora? Because I'm struggling with more than one," he growled.

She shivered beneath his touch. Her natural scent changed. Became the faintest mix of spices and acidic sourness. *Desire laced with unease.*

His pulse quickened. Fire licked beneath his skin. One heartbeat and predatory instinct morphed into raw sexual arousal. The intensity stole his breath. Kymora's rapid breaths puffed against his cheek. Her scent curled its way through him.

Varian shook with the effort to stop himself leaning into her and taking her mouth with his. One kiss. One simple kiss and he'd lose control. Kymora wasn't ready for what that would unleash.

*Lady of Light*, he wasn't ready.

Kymora swallowed dryly, frozen in place by Varian's voice. It didn't sound like him at all. It was hard and rough and so deep it vibrated right through her. The volatile energy emanating from him made her breath catch. She pulled away but had nowhere to go with the wall at her back.

"Well, Kymora?" The earlier coldness was gone, altered into a gravelly rumble that stroked her senses.

His hand skimmed along the side of her neck, and his thumb pressed under her jaw, tilting her head toward him until she could feel his breath against her lips. His touch was gentle, almost tender.

His thumb stroked the tendon in her neck. Heat flushed through her and her heart pounded faster. She tried to calm herself and focus on his aura, but it pulsed and beat against hers. This close to him, she could no longer distinguish what his emotions were.

There'd been pain, like she'd sensed before as he'd knelt at the foot of Rystin's grave. Guilt. Anger. Denial. Helplessness. Exhaustion. Fear. Each poured from him, raw and unchecked, like pus from a wound.

Yet she'd also felt his need for comfort and a flicker of desire in the wildness threading all these emotions together before he'd leapt from the pool and closed in on her. Now they were all so intense they blended together into one searing ball. She couldn't tell which one dominated. The swift changes in his moods left her confused. And apprehensive.

Lisella had tried to warn her. Perhaps she should have listened.

Wet skin dampened the palm of her hand as she tried to push him away, but he was a hard wall of sleek muscle, impossible to budge. "Varian, you're scaring me."

"Now you exhibit some self-preservation?" She flinched at his sarcasm, but he moved half a step back from her. "Get out of here, Kymora, before I lose what little control I have left."

He released her, his touch gone so swiftly she swayed and had to press her hands to the wall to steady herself. Instinct warned her to leave while she could. But the tiniest waver in his voice made her pause.

Without her Gift, reading his voice was all she had to rely on.

Mother of Light, *guide me so I can help him. So I can help us both.*

Heart pounding in her chest, she stayed where she was. She licked dry lips. "Would that really be such a bad thing?"

# Chapter 25

"LEAVE, Kymora!" Varian's voice never rose above a hoarse rumble, but anger edged each word. "Can't you feel how close I am to losing it?"

Kymora shivered but didn't back down. "Your emotions are so strong they're blinding me. I can't tell one from the other. If you'd talk to me—"

Varian's curse cut her off. The air stirred in front of her. She started as his hands grabbed her shoulders. Her temper ignited. She brought her arms up, elbows out, and broke his hold on her. She thrust both palms forward. They slapped against the bare flesh of his chest. He grunted but it didn't push him away from her like it should have. He was just too strong.

"Don't manhandle me, Varian," she warned him. "Just tell me what you want!"

Breath hissed from him. "Tell you?" he rasped. "How can I when I don't even know?"

The muscles beneath her hands shifted, flexed. Two thuds close to her head made her flinch, his arms caging her in against the wall. Pure strength surrounded her. Hot. Dangerous.

The air between them vibrated with tension, and with something else that started a warm flutter in her stomach. Temper and desire warred inside her. Why wouldn't he open up? How could she be aroused at a time like this?

His mouth covered hers in a kiss. Hard. Savage. The power of it poured into her, so intense it broke through her shields. It left her stunned. But it was the heat behind it that overwhelmed her. Fire consumed her, racing along every nerve ending, sinking beneath her skin, spiraling past muscle and bone until it reached her center, and once there it exploded, searing her from the inside out. She had no control over what she felt, no sense of time, no thought outside the all-consuming kiss.

Varian's fingers threaded through her hair, tangling, tightening, tilting her head back, breaking their kiss. Kymora sucked in a desperate breath. Sometime during it, she'd wrapped her arms around his waist. Her hands lay on the flat planes of his back, her fingers tracing the muscled ridges on either side of his spine. Only his body pressing against hers kept her upright.

Varian shuddered against her, his soft groan vibrating through his chest, then into her. The sound rolled through the length of her body. She arched against him, absorbing the sensation.

His lips claimed hers again, just as hungry, just as hard, but only for a heartbeat. Then they began to soften; his hands cradled, then cupped the back of her head. His mouth parted and his tongue tasted her, just the barest lick across her bottom lip. She moaned, her fingers digging into his back, needing more. Craving it.

Another tortured groan came from deep inside his chest. "I can't control myself." His gravelly voice rasped against her senses. "I'll hurt you."

This close to him, touching him skin to skin, his fear jolted like a shock against her heart. Kymora suppressed her elation over the revelation. A few weeks ago, he'd never have revealed any sort of weakness, to anyone.

"You won't." She sounded breathless, and in truth she was. *Merciful Mother*, she hadn't expected his kiss or the intensity of it. Hand shaking, she felt for his face, his cheek. Stubble abraded her palm. His head turned into it. "I liked your kiss." She ran her fingers over his lips, enjoying their soft texture, the moist remnants of the unexpected kiss. "I trust you."

His hot breath dampened the skin on her wrist. She gasped as his teeth bit into the fleshy part of her thumb, just hard enough to sting. Pure pleasure streaked through her, first to her breasts, tightening her nipples, then hard downward, straight to her core.

He released her thumb, and his damp forehead pressed against hers. "You shouldn't."

He shifted closer, wedging himself against her from hip to shoulder. All lean muscle. Steamy heat and hardness. His escalating hunger a fiery caress against her mind, threatening to burn out of control and take her with him. Again.

"This is dangerous. I have very little control over this side of me, Kymora."

His admission sounded torn, like it had been ripped from somewhere deep inside him, but *Lady's Light*, he was finally talking to her. She tried to focus on that and put aside the pleasure, for the moment.

Easier said than done as she placed her hands at his waist and the temptation to trace the jut of his hip bones beckoned. If she reached around, she'd find his body markings trailing down his back and over the sides of his buttocks. "You're talking about the battle rush?"

"This isn't me. . . ."

The more she thought about how the *Na'Chi* treated Varian, and that included Lisella and Zaune, the angrier she became on his behalf. Allowing such a generous, giving man to doubt himself to the point he abhorred the very essence of what he was, whether through thoughtless comments or resignation . . . they were all complicit.

*Blessed Mother*, if only he could see himself through her eyes.

"Varian, it is you." There was a swift intake of breath and he stiffened beneath her touch. She didn't let him vocalize his protest. "You're demon. You're also human. You're tough, ruthless, and harsh when you need to be. But you worry, you care, and you're dedicated to seeing to the safety of your people." She spread her fingers against his chest, over his heart. "You have the qualities and the flaws of both. You're as the *Lady* made you. You can't value one above the other. Human, *Na'Reish*, *Na'Chi* . . . you're each of these. And I want you . . . as . . . you . . . are."

He stilled. The silence lengthened. Would he believe her truths? His aura trembled, the rawness of his pain vying with a sensation of lightness. That gave her hope. And it made her next decision easier.

"I didn't mean to interrupt your bath." She ducked under one arm and slid her hand along the other to pull him away from the wall. Her boots splashed in the puddles of water Varian had made getting out. "Get back in and I'll join you."

Without waiting to see if he entered the pool or not, she made her way to the wall where the hooks for towels and hanging clothes were located. She hung her *Lady's* amulet on one, then toed off her boots.

Varian's lack of response had her biting her lip. Was she doing the right thing? Twice before, despite his obvious desire for her, he'd pushed her away. Would he do that now? Had she read him wrong?

Kymora reached for the tie at the back of her Temple robe and began unlacing it. Her skin felt almost too sensitive. Her breasts ached and her nipples remained taut from their kiss. The heat lingered, too, banked low, the evidence in the wetness between her thighs. No sound came from behind her, yet her shoulder blades itched.

Varian *was* watching her.

Her body flushed as she shrugged out of the robe and let it fall to the floor, clad in nothing but her skin and her need for him. Hands shaking, she hung it on the same hook as her amulet. His continued silence sent a shiver along her spine. She bit her lip and remained facing the wall.

Then water splashed behind her.

"Be careful crossing the floor." Varian's voice was slightly muffled, like he'd turned away from her. "It's slippery."

Kymora took a slow, deep breath. The note of wary acceptance in his voice allowed her to turn and make her way to the pool.

Varian lifted his gaze only once Kymora entered the water, then slid to the opposite side. To remain any closer would be too much of a lure. He'd kissed her. Twice. And the second time he had been barely able to pull away.

As it was, he'd acted like an animal, wild and uncontrolled. His cheeks burned with the memory, in shame but also in confusion. Kymora's arousal, her hot, sweet scent, had filled his lungs, and even now it carried across the distance separating them.

She'd *enjoyed* the kiss. When he'd been terrified of the darkness and violence driving him, she'd confronted that part of him, unafraid. She'd accepted it, taken it, and now she shared his bath, beautifully naked, a delicate flush coloring her cheeks.

Color had returned to his vision. The significance of that detail drew a grunt from him. She'd calmed him, evidence of her power to tame that side of him. Her strength and incredible Gift shook him to the core.

And he wanted more. Seeing her hesitate after undressing, and knowing the courage her bold move demanded from her, the hunger to see what she planned for them prompted him to invite her to join him in the bath. Just this once, he wanted to explore what was between them and damn the consequences.

Kymora lowered herself into the water. While it covered her shoulders, he caught tantalizing glimpses of her body through the floating curtain of her long hair. The curve of a pale breast, the hardened tip of a nipple, the shadowed dip of her waist, the lean length of a leg. The show heightened the tension thrumming through his body.

It rode him hard. Even now he could feel her hands on his waist, burning their shape into his skin, and the softness of her body where she'd pressed against him. It was on the tip of his tongue to ask her to touch him again. Instead, he lay back against the side and gripped the cool tiles along the edge to stop himself from going to her.

The next move would be hers.

"Varian, is there soap-sand?" Kymora's lilting voice caressed his senses.

"To your left, in a small rectangular box."

She felt along the edge of the pool until she found the cleanser and a cloth next to it. Using the tiles of the bath as a guide, she worked her way around it toward him. When her hand brushed against his, she stopped.

"It's not easy deciphering strong emotions," she murmured. Removing the lid of the soap-sand container, she dipped her fingers in and sprinkled some on the wet cloth. "Yours are so intense it's like a blinding light shone directly in my eyes."

Linking fingers with him, she smoothed the cloth along his forearm. He tensed. What was she doing?

Kymora paused, head tilting to one side. "Skin-to-skin contact offers a clearer impression, but there's still only so much I can interpret through touch. I thought after that kiss . . ." She hesitated. "Every muscle in your arm just tightened, but I'm having trouble reading you. . . . Don't you like what I'm doing?"

Oh, he liked it. What he wasn't sure about was being the focus of her scrutiny. Not now. Not when he didn't fully understand the unusual changes in his behavior or what was happening between them. She claimed his emotions were so extreme she had no idea what he was feeling yet had managed to read him pretty well.

Kymora sighed softly and released his hand. "Not being able to use my Gift leaves me feeling helpless, like I've gone blind all over again. When that happens, I try to take control of the situation." She issued a strangled laugh. "It seems when it comes to you, I have very poor judgment, Varian. I don't mean to keep provoking you or make you feel uncomfortable. I'm sorry."

She backed away from him then, the strained expression on her face becoming more drawn. Kymora was demanding, too, like him in some ways, but she gave so much more, her soul generous in ways he knew he'd never match.

"Wait." His tone was rough, and he hated how she flinched.

He probably should have expected the reaction, considering all he'd done so far was growl and snap at her. He didn't want to reveal anything more about himself to her. He hated the vulnerability that came with it. Yet despite that, he found himself powerless to deny her.

When that had happened, he wasn't entirely certain. Perhaps during the time in the clearing, after he'd killed Rystin. Something had changed between them then, something irrevocable. He ran a hand through his hair.

"You haven't made an error in judgment." Varian grimaced at the way his voice closed up on him, and swallowed hard. Kymora deserved more than silence or halfhearted attempts to explain what he was feeling, but the words he wanted to say lodged like shards of glass inside his throat. "Having someone care about you . . . the way you care about me, is humbling, Kymora. You worry about what I feel. It matters to you and I guess that's something I'm just not used to. . . ." He took a deeper breath. "When I kissed you, all I could think about was wanting more."

He shuddered, the rawness of the memory abrading already sen-

sitive nerves. He could still taste the sweetness of her lips. Just
remembering it made him hard now. He shoved the memory aside
and forced himself to face the more grievous issue.

"Do you know how close I came to just taking what I wanted?"

"But you didn't."

Three simple words. Compelling. Guilt relieving. How did she
do that? Varian shook his head.

A small smile curved Kymora's lips as she started back in his direction. "So, assuming you liked kissing me, can I also presume you
liked me washing you?"

The thought of her touching him again didn't bear thinking
about.

"Kymora . . ."

"What?" Her fingers laced with his again, ignoring his warning
growl. Heat shot up his arm. "You think you're the only one worried
about losing control? *Blessed Mother*, Varian, join the Guild! That kiss
almost killed me."

The cloth scrubbed along his arm with more force, but he barely
noticed. Her admission about his kiss had him riveted. She'd really
liked it? The flush on her cheeks deepened, as if she was still thinking about it.

"Do you know how hard it was to focus on our conversation after
that? You're not the only one who wanted more." She poked his
shoulder. "Whatever happens between us, I'm sure we'll cope with
it." Her temper hadn't yet reached full steam, but damned if he didn't
like to see her riled. "Right now, I want you to lay back and enjoy
this."

The order, reinforced by another rough swipe, this time along
his chest, made his lips twitch. The swing in mood eased the last of
the tension inside of him.

Pure sensation and vulnerability. She gave him both. Gifts he
never thought to experience with any woman.

Varian caught her wrist on the next pass and pulled her closer to him. She landed against his chest with a surprised grunt.

"Use your bare hand," he suggested. "It'll feel better."

*For him or for her?* Kymora nearly asked the question, surprise almost startling it out of her. Was he really inviting her to touch him? She released the cloth. It hit the water with a soft plop, then she laid her hand flat on his chest. The heat coming from his skin wasn't all generated by the water or steam.

"This is the first real chance I've had to see you," she murmured, her throat tightening. Who had he let touch him before now? Very few people, if any.

Leaving her hand resting on his chest, she tried to sort through the numerous emotions flicking through his aura. The lightness was still there, although it felt slightly forced, as if Varian were fighting to hold on to it. There was a tinge of apprehension mixed with confusion, but the emotion growing stronger by the second was desire. She didn't want to rush their time together, so she focused on something a little less intense.

"Would you mind wetting your head? I want to wash your hair."

As Varian ducked beneath the surface of the water, she scooped up a generous handful of soap-sand. He ended up with his back to her, kneeling, resting back on his heels so she could reach. It made combing and rubbing the suds through his hair easier.

"You have three braids on one temple and two on the other." They were longer than the rest of his hair. Small wooden beads tied off each at the end. "This bead's round. The one next to it is elongated."

"They each represent an event in my life." Varian's stilted tone indicated reluctance, but he kept talking. "The round one signifies the first time I trapped and slew a wild *Vorc*."

Kymora fingered a small ribbed one. "And the others?"

"The longer bead signifies the first *Na'Reish* warrior I killed."

"The one who followed Hesia to your camp?"

"Yes. She made it for me. I also asked her to make the triangular one. That's her bead, to honor everything she's done for me in my life. The fourth one indicates I'm a scout." The last braid had several small beads threaded through it. Varian's fingers covered hers as she felt them. "Lisella made these for me when I became leader of the *Na'Chi*. They're all the same shape, but each are the colors of the forest."

"They're like a journal of your life." She rinsed his hair, then lathered up more soap-sand.

Starting at his neck, she ran slick hands over his broad shoulders, moving slowly, following the line of muscles. They weren't thick, not like some warriors, but they were hard, toned by years of outdoor living. Spreading her fingers, she kneaded them and worked her way down his back. The raised trail of natural body markings guided her down his shoulder blades, over his rib cage, to the top of his hips. Every so often she came across a hard, uneven edge of flesh, perhaps a scar, although she refrained from asking him about them.

"What color are your markings?" She lingered over the larger ones decorating the flesh on either side of his waist. The muscles beneath her fingertips twitched.

"Brown." It was only one word, but Varian's voice was both deep and hoarse.

Kymora blinked. Had her touch aroused him so quickly? The idea made her smile. "Dark like the bark of a needle-tree or light like the spots on a *lira*-pelt?"

"Both. Those on my face and going down my back are dark. The ones on the back of my legs are lighter."

She splashed water over his skin, cleaning the suds from it, then found the markings on his shoulders. "These ones are larger, not as closely grouped together." She pressed a kiss to the first she found and used her tongue to trace the uneven edge. His skin tasted of heat and citrus. His shoulder jerked. "You know, I'd like to do this to every one of them."

Varian's body went tight, much like his voice. "Kymora . . ." A protest, but one with very little heat.

"If you don't like something I'm doing, Varian, you'll have to tell me."

Moving onto her knees behind him, Kymora curled her arms around his ribs to reach his chest. She brought herself flush up against him and stifled a moan. His back felt like hot steel against the softness of her breasts and belly. The water lapping against them teased her senses.

Her cheek brushed the cool lobe of his ear. "I'm not exactly paying attention to your aura." All her attention was on the physical plane. She stroked his chest, discovering more solid lines and curves. More heat. More hardness. Inhaling, she savored his scent and the tangy steam. "What I'm touching is distracting me. A lot."

She dipped her hand in the soap-sand box and spread the granules over his chest. The foam tingled against her skin. Every contour, every texture, every inch of skin impressed itself into a tactile map inside her brain. As her fingertips skimmed over the flat disc of his male nipple, it hardened. The flesh around it raised and prickled into goose bumps.

Varian's breath hitched. The sound wound its way inside her where it found the heat banked since their kiss and fanned it. "I have no objection to what you're doing." That came from between gritted teeth.

"Good." She rested her chin on his shoulder and let him feel her smile against his skin. "Because your pleasure is mine."

And it was. Any reserve she felt about being so bold was absent. The more he responded to what she was doing to him, the more incentive she felt to discover what excited him. She was entirely focused on him, his body, his enjoyment.

She remained still, letting him think about her last words a few moments longer before gliding her hand lower, over his ridged abdomen. The rasp of his breath elevated; his stomach sucked in at her touch. His desire flared, strong enough that she felt it through her shields. Her heart lurched in response.

"Too fast?" She hesitated, her fingers resting above his navel.

His ribs expanded. "Unexpected."

"I want to go farther"—her voice dropped to a husky whisper—"and curl my hand around you . . . touch you. . . ."

"*Lady's Breath*, Kymora." Varian shifted in her hold, his curse a grated growl. He gripped her wrists, his long fingers wrapping around them firmly but not tight enough to hurt, as if he was going to stop her. The strength in him vibrated along the length of her arms. Against her cheek, his throat worked as he swallowed. "I have very little control left. . . ."

Fear darkened his aura like a stain. Even without sensing the emotion, she knew he still worried about exposing her to his other half, the part of him he believed to be the darker, evil half. Her heart ached.

"Trust me." She pressed a kiss to the soft skin of his neck. "Let me do this . . . for both of us. . . ."

He might outmatch her physically, but she hoped he wouldn't refuse her. She wanted him to believe in what she'd told him earlier. That she wanted him—all of him—not just what he wanted the world to see.

Kymora held her breath. Would he trust her enough to see to his pleasure?

# Chapter 26

KYMORA'S lilting plea wrapped around Varian and tugged hard, yet he kept his grip firmly around her wrists, needing time to think. It was difficult when every nerve in his body was centered on where her hand lay, just over his navel, her fingers stretched wide. Heat coiled in his lower belly and drew into a tight knot until all he could feel was his blood pounding there. Throbbing. Aching.

Needing.

He wanted to continue but balked at the risk to her.

"Varian, please"—the husky softness of her voice seemed to beg and caress his senses at the same time—"just this once, and if you don't like it, then I won't touch you again."

She would keep her promise, of that he had no doubt. Slowly, he released her wrists and gave a jerky nod, unable to voice his consent. His need outweighed his fear. This time.

"Thank you," she whispered and pressed an open-mouthed kiss to his jaw.

His breath left him in a hiss as her hand slid the remaining distance and closed around his erection. She held him gently, but her touch burned. In less than a second, he went from hard to harder and breathless.

"I don't know how you like to be touched. . . ." Her voice wavered. "Would you show me what you like?"

Hunger sizzled through him, from head to toe. Groaning, he let his head fall back onto her shoulder but wrapped his hand around hers.

"Tighter, like this." The words were guttural. "Slow to begin with . . ."

The residual soap on her hand made the first smooth stroke feel like a lick of fire. He shuddered.

"Again . . ." He groaned as her fingers played over him. "Harder this time . . ."

He thrust forward as he drew her hand back along his length. The friction seared him again.

"Oh . . ." Her gasp sounded in his ear. ". . . *Blessed Mother* . . ."

Varian didn't have the breath to agree with her. A few more strokes and he let her go. The tight points of her nipples poked into him, an erotic caress that left him dizzy and a little light-headed. Having her pressed against his back, moving with him, feeling what he did, added an intimate element that made the whole situation more intense.

Reaching back with his hands to grip the outside of her thighs, he knew he'd need something to hold on to as she continued to work him, discovering what made his breath catch and what wrenched a groan from deep within. And she succeeded in accomplishing both. More than once.

The light sweat covering her skin smelled of honey and spice. The slap and surging of water against his skin. Her uneven breathing, hot against the damp skin of his neck. Her arousal fed his, an invisible hand that stoked the fire beginning to blaze out of control.

His gaze flooded with crimson so rapidly it left him reeling; the darkness within rose fierce and fast, taking advantage of his weakness.

"*Merciful Mother*, no!" His breath labored hard as he struggled to hold it back, but the fire sweeping through him had him completely at its mercy. He couldn't find the restraint he needed. Panic slashed through his gut.

"I'm here, Varian." Kymora's arms tightened around him. "*Mother*, your aura . . . your pleasure burns me"—her breath caught on a ragged moan—"inside and out."

He focused on her voice, bucking against her hand.

"So hot, like a branding iron against my skin . . ."

The friction, the rhythm, the sensory intensity; everything in him grew tight, imploding fast. The molten sensation she was coaxing from him now was more powerful than anything he'd ever experienced before.

"Help me feel it, Varian. Let go."

As if her words were a command, the heat exploded. He stiffened in shock. A hoarse cry came from his throat. His hips lifted, his body arched. Exquisite pleasure surged, searing every nerve ending as it released. Each wave increased twofold and ripped through him, leaving him writhing. Heart, mind, and soul.

How long he rode the shockwaves, he had no idea, but when he regained some sense of his surroundings, everything around him had reclaimed its rightful color even though it was hazy and blurred. He had to blink to bring it back into focus.

Kymora still held him close, her arms locked around his body, one hand splayed over his hammering heart, her cheek pressed to his back. His lungs worked like a set of bellows. Water splashed against the sides of the pool, a soft accompaniment to the pounding of his heart in his chest.

"*Mother of Light*, that was . . . I felt you peak." She kissed his shoulder, sounding as shaken as he was. Reverent. Awed by the moment. "There are no words to describe it. . . . It was like I was inside you, Varian . . . so amazing. Just . . . incredible."

Her voice centered him, as it had at the moment he'd feared losing control. He had, but not in the way he'd expected. Everything inside him felt shattered, weak, but deep inside there resided a stillness he'd never felt before.

*Peace.* A deep, restful peace.

Turning in her hold, Varian pulled her in against him and buried his head in the crook of her neck. "Kymora . . ." His voice broke, but he didn't care.

Her strength gave him an anchor. She stroked his hair, her touch so gentle it made his eyes burn.

"I know." Her lips pressed against his temple. Her courage astounded him. "I know, Varian. I sense it. . . . I'll hold you. I won't let you go."

Closing his eyes, Varian relaxed with a shuddering sigh. And believed.

"LIGHT Blade . . ." The voice came from a long way off, as if from the end of a very long tunnel. "Light Blade . . . you have to wake up. . . ."

This time the voice came with a shaking motion that made the pounding in Arek's head worse. He groaned and rolled onto his side. An earthy odor filled his nostril as his cheek pressed against something prickly but cool and damp. Hands helped him to sit. His shoulder scraped against a rough, fibrous surface. A tree?

"Come on, Light Blade." The cajoling voice was edged with tension. "Our time is short. . . . Can you hear me?"

Arek forced open eyes that wanted to stay shut. Dim light and shadows danced around him. He blinked several times, trying to make sense of what he saw. Was that moonlight or had his head been hit so hard he could no longer see clearly? Gazing upward, a half crescent moon silhouetted branches swaying in the darkness. A breeze rustled the leaves overhead.

"Is he awake?" A feminine voice, soft, filled with fear.

Arek worked his tongue around his dry mouth and tasted the lingering iron tang of blood on his lips. "Where am I?"

The broad-shouldered shadow crouched in front of him turned from surveying the darkened woods. "You're in the Crag Forest. West of Ostare."

The last thing he remembered was a *Na'Reish* gloved fist connecting with his head. He frowned, wincing as pain lanced through his head. The image of retreating figures pushed through the ache.

Varian. The others.

Had they escaped?

Arek shivered, and not because of the cool temperature. There'd been another dozen demons converging on the clearing. He'd fallen. Why wasn't he dead?

"How did I end up here?"

"The *Na'Hord* pursued your patrol. In the confusion, you were left for dead." The female voice moved closer. Moonlight lit the slender figure of a girl in her midteens. She huddled beside the older man. Their simple garb identified them as crofters. "Yenass and I dragged you away, then we carried you here."

A spine-chilling howl echoed through the forest.

Arek stiffened and jerked his head in the direction of the sound. The sudden movement blurred his vision. A wave of nausea rolled in his stomach.

*Vorc.*

Way too close.

The *Na'Hord* were using the beasts to track them.

The girl bit back a cry as the man's gaze locked with his. "We're being hunted."

"Run. . . . Leave me. . . ." Arek didn't even try to rise. His limbs felt heavier than they should, and with the light-headedness and nausea, he'd be sick before he took a dozen steps.

"You're our only hope, Light Blade." Sour sweat filled his nostrils as the crofter moved closer to him. "Unbuckle his armor, Senna."

"What?"

The man began yanking at the straps of his armor. "I'll trade clothes with him."

The jerky movements made the drum in Arek's head pound harder. He groaned. "No, you have to go . . . while you can. . . ."

"Yenass, you can't!" The girl grabbed the older man's arm.

He rounded on her, expression tight. "Listen to me, sister. He stands a better chance of freeing you than I do once you're recaptured, but not if they see him dressed as a Light Blade." He shoved her toward Arek. "Get his boots off. Hurry!"

Another howl pierced the stillness of the night. This one much too close for comfort.

Arek blinked the crofter into focus. "Run." The word felt thick in his mouth.

"How far do you think we'll get before being chased down?" the man hissed. "There's a gash on the side of your head as wide as my hand, and a lump to match. You're motion sick. If we run, you'll die. Senna and I will still be recaptured and in no better position than before when the *Na'Reish* took us from our village." Desperation strained his voice. "At least this way they won't know you're a Light Blade, and once you regain your strength, you might be able to help Senna or any others they recapture. The chance may be slim, but it's better than nothing."

Nausea rose to the back of his throat. "I can't let you sacrifice yourself. . . ."

With one swift motion, the crofter whipped his coarse-woven shirt over his head. "Put this on the Light Blade, Senna."

Sobbing, the young girl followed the order. The man tugged his chest plate free. Arek's vision faded in and out with the rough movement. His head dipped toward his chest; his eyes closed of their own accord. *Merciful Mother*, he couldn't lose consciousness now. He forced his head upright and sucked in a deep breath.

As he became aware of his surroundings again, he lay flat on his back on the forest floor. The crofter was lacing a pair of trews over his hips. The coarse material scratched against his skin as he tried to sit up. Cool air brushed the bare soles of his feet.

A savage growl filled the air. Senna screamed. Yenass spun to face the threat. Arek rolled onto his side, gritting his teeth. He reached out, too late, to grasp the farmer's leg, the one wearing his leather breeches and knee-high boots.

A large shadow launched itself from the darkness, straight at the crofter. The furred *Vorc* landed in front of him, the landing spraying dirt and debris over them all. With the beast came a pungent musky odor that made Arek gag. The hulking animal knocked Yenass to the ground with one swipe of its foreleg.

Sharp claws grated against the hard leather chest plate. The crofter cried out.

"No!" Senna scrambled toward her brother. "Yenass!"

Biting back his nausea, Arek grasped a handful of her dress. Her broken cry was drowned out by the vicious sounds of a predator executing its kill. Pulling the young woman back, he wrapped his arm around the girl, shielding her from the gruesome sight of her brother being torn apart, grateful the darkness obscured the worst of the attack.

*Lady's Breath*, the *Vorc* wasn't muzzled. Reins and a halter were buckled onto its pointed snout. The saddle cinching its thick body was empty. How close was its rider? Without the *Vorc-Master*, it would come for them once it finished with Yenass.

Fear sharpened Arek's senses, but his body refused to cooperate. Arms trembling, his head spinning, he tried to get to his knees.

His grip tightened on the girl's arm. "Senna, run . . ."

She remained on the ground, rocking, sobbing. The sound of bones crunching turned his stomach.

"*Shavesh ka ris!*" The deep-throated command came from somewhere beyond the death scene.

The *Vorc* lifted its head. Its jaws opened. The soft thud of something hitting the ground sent a shiver down Arek's spine. He didn't want to imagine what it might have been. An almost inaudible rumble came from the beast as it turned its head toward them, its green eyes glowing in the moonlight. Lips peeled back from teeth as long as a human hand.

"*Shavesh ka vaag!*"

The animal ceased growling and slowly lowered its barrel-like body to the ground, but it never took its gaze off them. If they tried to flee now, it would attack. The hot metallic scent of blood carried on the breeze. Arek dry heaved as the girl struggled to free herself from his hold. His head throbbed.

"Be still, Senna," he whispered, grimacing. "Don't let your brother's sacrifice be in vain."

"Well done, Eayash." From between two trees, the towering form of a *Na'Reish* warrior emerged. He strode up to the *Vorc* and slapped its shoulder with a gloved hand, then knelt to examine what was left of Yenass. Another two demons jogged from the darkness to join him. "Ha, Eayash discovered the Light Blade."

The shorter of the two spotted them and circled the carnage. "And we've found two more humans." He grinned. The show of teeth had Arek reaching toward his waist before he remembered he no longer wore a weapon. "That makes twelve."

The *Vorc-Master* pulled a length of rope from the saddle and flung it at him. "Bind them and let's get back to camp."

Arek's fists clenched as the *Na'Reish* closed in on them. He summoned his Gift. It thrummed through him as he searched for any sort of pointed weapon. A stick or branch would do. While the demon wore armor, nothing protected the vulnerable skin of his neck.

A soft whimper and a warm body pressed against his side. Senna.

*Merciful Mother*, he'd nearly forgotten all about her. Yenass's last words echoed in his head.

The demon with the rope made a gesture toward him. "This one's injured."

The *Vorc-Master* strode over to them, seized the front of his shirt, and hauled him to his feet. The sudden rise left him reeling. Arek grunted and grasped the hard leather vambrace encasing the demon's wrist, more to hold himself up than in defense. He could barely close his fingers around the thick wrist.

A large hand gripped his hair and jerked his head to one side. Arek groaned as pain shot through his head and down his neck.

A snort came from the *Vorc-Master*. "The gash has stopped bleeding. The human's healthy enough. He'll recover. Tie him and the female."

Arek was shoved toward the second demon. Coarse rope wrapped around his wrists. Senna cried out as she was dragged to her feet and bound beside him.

"If he doesn't keep up"—the *Vorc-Master* gripped the back of his neck; Arek swayed as his vision blurred again—"we can always drink his blood."

Taunting laughter accompanied the threat. He braced his feet wide. *Mother of Light*, he wasn't going to let that happen.

The *Lady* had postponed his Final Journey. *Her* reasoning remained a mystery. He'd die before serving any demon as their blood-slave, but for the moment, he was their captive. In human territory. And this patrol had a lot of ground to cover before making it back over the border.

He'd bide his time. He'd take the chance he'd been given and use it.

His lip curled.

By the *Light*, there was no way he'd call any demon *master*.

# Chapter 27

WHEN Varian woke, he did so with the instant knowledge that he wasn't alone in his bed. Flesh to flesh, curled under the blankets with him, Kymora still slumbered, her soft, even breathing tickling the bare skin of his chest. A blessing, because it gave him the time to look at her in the early-morning light coming through the window of his room.

While he couldn't see much of her with the blanket tucked up over her shoulders, he could certainly feel her. All warm, soft curves pressed against his side, a slender leg draped over his thigh, her knee resting on the skin of his hip. Her head lay on his shoulder, her long black hair spread over him and the pillow like a cloak.

One delicate hand lay relaxed over his heart. A gesture she seemed to favor whenever she was touching him, one he very much liked. The connection almost felt like a claiming. His lips curved as he gently placed his larger one over hers so he could feel her whole hand against his chest. She'd certainly claimed him last night.

"You're happy." Kymora's voice was husky and sleepy.

"Did I wake you?"

She rubbed her cheek against him, then lifted her head. Her eyes opened, the beautiful deep green color that reminded him of rug-moss, and stared past him. He lifted his hand to trace her brow, then smoothed his thumb down one cheek and across her full bottom lip.

"You were thinking, rather intently." She gave him a warm smile that lifted his heart rate. He dropped his hand to the shoulder peeking out from the blanket. The skin there was as soft as her cheek. "And there's a stillness inside you I haven't sensed before."

Her observations stopped him stroking her skin. Instinct wanted him to move away from her, put some distance between them. Kymora shifted onto one elbow and propped her chin against his ribs.

"Just say it, Varian," she whispered against his skin. "You trusted me last night. And with something more incredible than a few words."

"No one has ever touched or made me feel the way you do," he said, the words a low-pitched, stilted confession. "For the first time I can remember, I don't feel like I'm fighting with myself. You bring me peace."

The truth came from his heart. It made him uncomfortable saying it out loud, but the gut-freezing vulnerability that usually accompanied those sorts of thoughts was strangely distant. It was almost like her presence kept it at bay.

The smile Kymora gave him made his heart do a slow roll in his chest. Her affection, so spontaneous and freely given, warmed him. It was something he craved more of, and had ever since he'd first met her.

"See, that wasn't so hard, was it?" she asked, and pressed a kiss to his sternum.

Her hair slid against his skin in a silken caress. Heat licked his skin, spiraled deep. And just that quickly, he had an erection, one that nudged the arm she rested low over his abdomen.

Her mouth quirked upward. "Although I might know of something else that is."

Her gentle teasing drew a rusty laugh from him. Her face lit up with such pleasure he wished he'd indulged sooner.

"You're so beautiful," he murmured. Using one finger, he lifted and smoothed the long strands of her hair behind her ear. "Would you . . ."

"Would I what?" One thin eyebrow arched and her expression sobered. "Tell me, Varian."

"I've wondered . . . wanted . . ." He inhaled and her sweet scent mixed with citrus filled his lungs. "I need to kiss you."

Kymora tilted her head, sifting through his words. The pitch of his voice had altered just slightly after his hesitation. The prickly, burring sensation against her mind made her sigh. Varian's wariness shouldn't have surprised her. Last night had been precious. He'd let her in, but altering instinctual behavior would take time.

"That's not what you were going to say," she mused, keeping her tone neutral. He'd shut her out if she showed any censure or anger. "Not that I would refuse you a kiss." Heat filled her cheeks as she snorted quietly. "Actually, there's little I'd deny you if the truth be known."

A spasmodic quiver rippled across Varian's abdomen, then his muscles tightened beneath her arm. His breathing deepened, while a tension that hadn't been there before crackled between them. A fluttering invaded her stomach.

"Lay back." The tenor of his voice strengthened, deepened. She'd heard him use that tone on the training field.

Kymora smothered another smile as she did as he asked, their positions reversed. Now she lay on her back and he'd moved onto his side. She felt the blanket tugged down her body. The cooler air lifted goose bumps on her skin.

"What are you doing?"

"Looking at you." The soft woven blanket stopped moving at the crest of both her breasts. "A little bit at a time. Teasing myself." His voice lowered, became huskier. "Pleasuring you."

Her heart beat faster. "How—" She had to clear her throat before she could complete her question. "How will you do that?"

A wave of warmth washed over her, body heat, Varian leaning over her, then his mouth brushed hers. Not a quick press of flesh on flesh, but a lingering, sensual meeting of lips that lasted several heart-beats. She reached up to tangle her fingers in his hair, tugging, letting him feel her need, her desire for him.

A groan came from the back of his throat, muffled against her lips. She parted hers, wanting to taste him, the heat of his mouth. The tentative slide of his tongue against hers heated her blood and sent sensation racing through her to pool between her thighs.

Varian broke the kiss. Her moaned protest ended in a cry as his teeth scraped the side of her neck, then bit hard enough to smart but not break the skin.

"Varian!" she gasped.

"You do this to me." His growl vibrated against her throat. His tongue stroked the pinched flesh, then suckled it. The damp warmth of his mouth on her skin made her shudder. "Yet the mindless frenzy . . . the animalistic urge to take . . . it's still there but it no longer dominates me . . . not when I'm with you. You center me."

Kymora closed her eyes as he laid his forehead against hers. She cradled the back of his head, savoring the simple pleasures of the warmth of his skin against hers and the wild, earthy scent of his desire.

"This isn't about me though," he murmured. Her fingers tightened in his hair in mute protest, but she kept quiet, knowing he had more to say. "I just wanted you to know, in case you can't read my aura. Or you become too . . . distracted."

That made her laugh. She smoothed her hand across his face to find his lips and discover them curving upward. "I like to see you smile."

He kissed her fingertips, then he drew both her arms over her head and pressed them against the pillow. "Touching me isn't allowed from now on. If you do, I stop what I'm doing."

Her heart tripped in her chest. "And what will you be doing?"

"Experimenting." His mouth tickled the shell of her ear even as his voice dropped to a whisper. "Scouts talk. I want to try some of the things I've heard about but never experienced." His weight on the bed shifted and his voice came from a little farther away. "I also want to discover what pleases you."

Kymora bit her lip. She suspected anything he did would please her. It didn't stop her imagination taking flight though. Scouts weren't the only ones who talked. How many times had she overheard the Temple Servants sharing tales of their mutual exploits and wondered if she'd ever get to experience them for herself?

The soft touch of Varian's finger at the base of her throat claimed her attention. He traced a slow line straight down between her breasts, dragging the blanket to a point just below her ribs. The friction of the heavy weave and exposure to the air tightened her nipples into sensitive buds.

"*Mother of Light.*" His hissed curse was almost reverent. "I know you're naturally modest, so last night I didn't look at you all that closely, Kymora. Not even when you entered the water." His hands spanned the width of her rib cage, just touching the undersides of her breasts. "Now I wish I had."

Kymora drew in an unsteady breath, expecting him to touch her then. He did, but with only a single finger, one from each hand. He traced circles on her breasts, drawing them smaller and smaller, the speed slowing the closer he came to her nipples. The burning beneath her skin intensified the closer he came to her nipples. They throbbed with the concentrated sensation. She clenched her hands in the soft material of the pillow, needing the contact to ground her.

"You like that." Satisfaction and hunger laced Varian's words.

Her smile trembled as much as she did. "Yes."

His thumbs brushed over nipples. Pure pleasure speared from the point of contact to the heat coiled tightly between her thighs. Her back arched from the bed. Wet heat engulfed her left breast, a tongue swirling around the quickly peaking nub.

"*Varian!*" She choked on the fiery experience. He began to suckle.

Kymora remained breathless as Varian took his time pleasuring her breasts with his mouth, his tongue, and his lips, his entire attention concentrated on her and how she responded. His absolute regard, his focused intent pushed against her mind even as she spiraled higher and higher, swept away by what he was doing to her. Everything seemed to be moving too fast, yet every moment felt drawn out, like time had been dipped in treacle.

"I could spend the whole day doing this." Varian's voice was a low rumble against her hypersensitive skin.

Kymora sucked in an uneven breath. "By the *Light*, you'd kill me if you did!" Hot breath brushed over her dampened skin as he laughed. *Lady*, how she loved the deep, sensual sound of it. "Can I touch you yet?"

He issued a negative sound. "I won't be able to concentrate if you do." One hand smoothed down her side. The rough calluses on his palms and fingers lightly abraded her skin. The sensation made her shiver. "I want to see the rest of you."

He dragged the blanket all the way off her this time. At the long, drawn-out silence, Kymora swallowed against a dry throat. "Varian?"

"Hmm?" He sounded distracted. His weight shifted farther down the bed. One warm hand clasped her hip, then a bristled jaw scraped across her thigh and rested there. "Your scent makes my mouth water, Kymora. It's like honey and spice. Unique." He grunted. "You know,

now that I've memorized it, you won't be able to approach me without my knowing it anymore."

"But I'm aroused."

"Doesn't matter, aroused or not, I'll still know when you're near."

The idea held a certain appeal. "My aura-reading skills, your sense of smell. Now we're even."

Soft chuckling accompanied the slide of his hand on her hip. She felt the lightest of touches brush the curls on her mound, a soft downward stroke. First one side, then the other.

"Do all humans have hair here?"

Kymora smiled at the curious question. From firsthand experience, she now knew *Na'Chi* bodies were naturally hairless, a characteristic inherited from their demon parent.

"Yes."

His thumb parted her folds and brushed against her swollen core. Her breath hissed in through her teeth.

"So hot and wet."

Her laugh was more of a hiccup. "That's your fault, Varian."

"So it is." Lips nibbled the skin of her inner knee. "I want to see more."

Varian's heart pounded in his chest at the sight of her stretched out on his bed. He pushed her leg to the side, watching for any sign of reluctance or discomfort. That she'd allowed him the liberties he'd already taken astounded him.

The color in her cheeks darkened. Her teeth clamped on her bottom lip as he opened her to his gaze.

"Tell me if you don't like this, Kymora."

Her lips curved as he used her own words from last night.

"This is all new to me." The lilt in her voice was more pronounced. "It's the unknown, not you, that's making me anxious."

"It's new to me, too. Remember?" He stroked the soft skin on her thigh, then pressed a kiss there. "Comfortable?"

"Not yet, but if you get on with whatever you're doing, I'm sure I'll get there." The corners of her mouth twitched. "Eventually."

Varian bit the flesh so temptingly close to his mouth for her taunting. She yelped, then laughed. He let her feel his smile against her skin. "Be careful I don't consider that a challenge, Kymora."

She shivered with his warning. Her scent grew stronger. He drew it deeply into his lungs and let it wrap around him, like her hand had last night. The memory made him ache and throb now.

Kymora moaned softly. "I can feel that, Varian." Her husky voice drove like a spike through him.

His hands shook as he smoothed them along each of her thighs, up to where he finally allowed his gaze to settle. Her feminine folds glistened, so wet and swollen. "*Dear Mother* . . . you're beautiful."

He used two fingers this time to tease open her folds. Her soft, swift inhalation told him just how sensitive she was. He stroked, gently, learning the contours of her sex, watching how his touch made her respond. A gasp. A groan. Flesh flinching, then flushing with need.

Discovering what pleasured her most.

And what drove him to the fiery edge of insanity.

From conversations among his scouts, Varian knew a *Na'Chi* female could be stimulated to her peak with his fingers, but there was another way. One much more intimate. Anticipation unfurled in his gut. Since beginning this game of experimentation, he'd been aching to try it. But would a human woman . . . would Kymora like it?

"Yes!" Her hissed affirmation surprised him. Was he broadcasting his emotions that strongly? "Please, Varian!"

Rising up on his knees, he placed his mouth over her, wanting . . . needing to taste her. Her salt-sweet essence exploded on his tongue the same time she cried out and shuddered. Her hips pushed up, undulating. She worked herself against his mouth, muscles straining against him. Moving his tongue against her changed her cry to a moan, and the shudder became a convulsion. Her flavor intensified.

He held her tight, steadying her with his hands, drawing out her pleasure until the power of her need abated. She collapsed onto the bed in a loose tangle of limbs.

Varian drew back, her taste still coating his lips. Intense satisfaction at the sight of her so sated replaced his reluctance in letting her go. Moving up beside her, he enjoyed watching Kymora come down from her peak. Her breathing remained erratic. He could hear the heavy thumping of her heart as well as see it pulsing in her throat. Wetness sparkled on her closed eyelids.

His heart thudded hard. Once. Had he hurt her?

Tentatively, he touched her flushed face. "Are you all right?"

Kymora curled into him and wrapped her arms tightly around his waist. "I hope you're done experimenting, Varian." Her voice was a hoarse whisper. Her fingernails dug into the skin low on his back. "Not sure if I'll survive anything more right now."

The wide grin on his face felt unfamiliar, but he couldn't contain it. He released a slow breath and dared to savor the way she fit against him.

"Smugness doesn't become you, *Na'Chi*," she murmured against his chest.

He grunted and considered her statement. Sure, there was an element of conceit in what he'd done for her, but most of what he felt was satisfaction. Yet something else was there, another emotion, hidden beneath them. What was it? The heat reminded him of desire, but it was infinitely deeper, softer. Definitely unfamiliar.

His gut tightened as he tried to figure out what it was; frustration heated his blood when he couldn't. Not wanting to spoil the moment, he dismissed it with a shake of his head. Later. He'd worry about whatever it was later.

A faint knocking drew Varian from his thoughts.

Kymora stirred beside him. "Someone's at your door."

"Stay here." He pulled the blanket up over her as he slid out of the bed. A quick search in the chest at the foot of his bed produced a clean pair of breeches. "I'll see who it is."

As he left, he pulled the door to his room partway closed, not wanting anyone intruding on Kymora's privacy. His plans for the morning included spending time with her, so seeing who their visitor was and getting rid of them quickly took priority over anything else.

Lisella stood on the other side of his apartment door, an apologetic smile on her face. "I'm sorry to disturb you." She fiddled with the end of her plait, twisting the black strands around her fingers. Voices and laughter echoed down the corridor from the main living area. It seemed others were already up, even at this early hour. "Is Kymora with you?"

Varian raised an eyebrow. "You know she is, Lisella," he said, and folded his arms. "I can hear Ehrinne's voice in the common room. She wouldn't be here if Kymora wasn't."

Lisella's smile faded and her gaze searched his. After several moments, she took a deep breath, like she'd made up her mind about something.

"I've been worried about you, Varian," she said. His nostrils flared as he caught a sharp peppery scent coming from her. "We used to talk, but ever since we arrived in human territory, that hasn't happened much."

The truth in her statement prodded his conscience. Lisella had always sought him out as he'd never been one for mixing with others. Sometimes they'd talked, sometimes he'd just listened while Lisella filled him in on the goings-on of their group. With the alliance, something new always seemed to be cropping up. Establishing a new home, planting crops, meeting and living with Guild-families, training the Light Blades; all new issues and problems to cope with.

Still, guilt prodded him. "There's been a lot going on. We've both been busy, Lisella."

"True," she agreed, a sad smile curving her lips. "But perhaps we've both been remiss, letting that get in the way. I should've made more of an effort to spend time with you."

"You can't split yourself a hundred ways. I'm able to look after myself. There are others who need you more."

"But it helps to have a friend to share the load." Her gaze met his again, and the green flecks in them warned him she wasn't going to be deflected. "When Zaune came back to the common room alone last night, I was surprised. I didn't think Kymora would be able to reach you this time, not after what Taybor told me."

Varian's mouth flattened. Who else had he spoken to about what happened out on that patrol?

"I know you both don't always get on, Varian, but he was genuinely concerned about you. Don't forget you share the same Gift. You might be the strongest scout among us, but he knows the struggle of dealing with battle rush. His fears concerning it aren't all that different than yours."

His head jerked up. "He believes he'll end up like me?"

"You two are more alike than you think, Varian." Lisella's voice softened. "One thing I've noticed though is that the scouts who mingle with others seem to recover from it faster and cope with it better."

His thoughts turned inward. If what she'd observed was true, then it could explain why he was having difficulty dealing with battle rush. Since their arrival in human territory, he hadn't spent as much time with her or the children as he'd done in the past. Too many other things had taken precedence.

"I'll say just one thing more, then leave the subject alone. I don't know what sort of friendship you share with Kymora but I'm glad she visited you. And that you didn't turn her away." She reached out to lay a hand on his arm. "You needed her last night, as much as she needed you."

Lisella had to be curious about their relationship, but he was glad she didn't question him. He glanced toward his room.

"Kymora didn't actually take heed of my no, Lisella. I'm sure Zaune told you that." A small smile twitched on her lips. He grunted, suspicions confirmed. "She's too much like you."

"Scary, huh?" Her eyes sparkled. His narrow-eyed glare was ignored. "It's about time someone refused to put up with your stubbornness."

Leveling his gaze on her, he lifted an eyebrow. "So, why are you here, Lisella?"

She cleared her throat but thankfully said nothing else. Her expression sobered. "Rissa just arrived from the hospice with a message from Candra."

This early? Varian straightened. "What was the Master Healer's message?"

"Kalan's awake and asking to see both of you."

# Chapter 28

KALAN lay propped on a stack of pillows with Candra and Annika flanking him. He looked drawn, even after a night's rest, and his skin was pale, but the hard gleam in his gaze as he greeted everyone offset any physical weakness.

Except for the white bandage wrapped around his waist, the human leader was bare chested, and it made the bruising radiating from underneath it easy to see. The patch of skin above the top edge of the bandage was almost black. In close, *Na'Reish* fists could do a lot of damage. Had he not been wearing armor to absorb any impact during the battle, Varian suspected Kalan might have also sustained broken ribs. A shiver slithered down his back at how close they'd come to losing him.

"Against my advice, the *Chosen* has insisted on this Council meeting." The stern expression on Candra's face informed everyone gathered in the hospice that she had her Master Healer's pouch well and truly strapped around her waist. "Keep it short."

Her brown-eyed gaze strafed each Blade Council member and

him in clear warning that they heed her instruction before she settled herself on her seat next to Kalan's bed.

She placed her hand on his arm. "I don't care how strong you think you are, *Chosen*, if you tire I will call a halt to the proceedings."

Her words were murmured, too low for any human to hear, but Varian caught them. With a wry twist on his lips, Kalan inclined his head in acknowledgment.

"*Chosen*, I'm sure we can postpone this meeting a few days." The gray-haired woman sitting farthest away smoothed a hand over the folds of her dress. "At least until you're on your feet."

"This can't wait, Councilor Shellana," Kalan refuted. "Although I thank you for your concern."

Varian scanned the group, curious as to why he and Commander Yevni, the senior Light Blade trainer, had been invited to attend. Sitting next to Kymora, the barrel-chested warrior was easily the biggest man in the room, his silver gray hair and sun-weathered face more suited to the training fields than the sterile healers' hall.

Beneath the pervading odor of *Vaa'jahn*, Varian detected the aromatic scent of fresh-fallen rain. Even without the exchange of glances and inquisitive raised brows passing between them, it seemed the other Councilors were wondering the same thing.

"*Temple Elect*, would you mind opening this meeting with a prayer as well as a benediction for Second Barial?" Kalan asked. While the request had been made steadily enough, the tautness in his jaw betrayed his inner turmoil.

Varian grimaced, his gaze darting to Kymora in time to catch the flash of pain that crossed her face. There'd been no time to speak with her about Arek and what had happened during the patrol. Last night hadn't been an appropriate time and then the request had come from Candra to visit the hospice.

Yevni reached out to place his large hand over hers where it lay on her lap. "*Temple Elect*, if you don't mind, I'd like to do that." The warrior's bass tone, usually full and loud from shouting orders on the training fields, was subdued. His pale blue eyes were bright with unshed tears. "I knew Arek since he was a babe and a youngster pestering me for his first sword. It'd be an honor if you'd let me lead the prayers."

"Thank you, Yevni." Kymora placed her other hand on his, her voice husky. "I think Arek would have liked that."

The warrior glanced to Kalan and earned a nod of gratitude. The others bowed their heads. Varian dug his fingers into his thighs. As Yevni began speaking, familiar tendrils of guilt wrapped around him. He closed his eyes, not to pray, but to escape the memory of failing Arek the day of the battle. There was no escaping it though in the darkness.

*"With leadership comes responsibility."* Hesia's soft voice whispered in his head.

His hand trembled as he fisted it. He'd accepted that burden long ago, but the pain of a bad decision or loss of a life never hurt any less. When so many relied on you, there was always that niggle of doubt he could have done something differently.

"Thank you, Yevni." Kalan's voice brought him back to the moment. He allowed several moments of respectful silence, time for anyone who needed it to compose themselves.

Kymora used the sleeve of her dress to wipe her eyes. Varian resisted the urge to cross the circle and gather her into his arms.

Had it been just Candra, Kalan, and Annika present, he might have considered comforting her, but with nine others watching, his solace would cause only speculation that could harm her reputation, and he refused to do that.

"With Arek gone, I need a new Second." Kalan's statement drew several murmurs and nods of agreement. Yevni's presence now made sense. "Varian, will you accept the position?"

A frisson of shock ripped along Varian's spine. He stiffened.

"What?" Rellyn Nyon, one of the retired Light Blades on the Council, stood up from his seat. "*Chosen*, surely Yevni's the better choice."

The beefy warrior threw back his head and laughed, his teeth showing white against his dark tan. The booming sound startled them all.

"Councilors, Kalan knows better than to offer me the rank of Second. My strength lies in training and strategy, not leadership." The big man gestured across the circle. "Anyone with eyes knows Varian can fight and lead. Arek often spoke of his respect for him as a trainer." He leaned forward on one knee. "The *Na'Chi* is the more experienced warrior for what Kalan needs right now, especially in the situation we face with the *Na'Reish*."

Varian frowned as several gazes shifted to him. He straightened under their regard, but the man he focused on lay waiting on his bed for an answer. The *Chosen* couldn't be serious in his offer, could he? And Yevni . . . Varian swallowed hard. After working with the instructor during training, he knew the warrior didn't hand out praise very often, so his support shocked the breath right out of him.

"There is no one I trust more than Varian, Councilors."

Varian froze with Kalan's declaration. Questions and protests exploded from the Councilors. The human leader ignored them all, his gaze fixed on Varian. What was going on? The transition of living and training with the Light Blades was difficult enough, for both races. What was Kalan hoping to achieve by appointing him as his Second, someone who would outrank them all?

The man seated on the other side of Candra cleared his throat and scraped a hand through his salt-and-pepper hair. "You're wanting our warriors to take orders from a *Na'Chi*?"

Varian sucked in a sharp breath, but before he could respond, Yevni snorted.

"They already do, Orphesius." His tone held heavy censure. "If you'd come down to the training grounds this past week, you'd have seen Varian's skill for yourself."

"By overlooking them, you risk insulting every Light Blade warrior. . . ." Outrage shook in Nyon's voice.

"My choice isn't intended as an insult, Councilor." Kalan's calm response settled the meeting. "Nor should Yevni's recommendation be dismissed. He's been the backbone of the Light Blade training program for nearly thirty years. And I'm surprised more of you can't see why I've chosen Varian over any of the Light Blades."

The silver-haired man seated next to Varian grunted. "You need someone you can depend upon."

"What are you saying, Benth?" Nyon asked, the expression on his face incredulous. "There are any number of Light Blade warriors he could choose as Second. All reliable, all well skilled, with years of experience."

"But he doesn't know which ones support Davyn or the rebels." With her mouth pressed flat, Candra waved a finger at all of the Councilors. "As unpalatable as that is, we must face that fact. Can you imagine the damage that could be done if Kalan appointed the wrong person?"

Councilor Elamm cleared her throat, her frown as deep as Nyon's. "We've taken measures to ensure Davyn's supporters think twice about—"

"The *Na'Chi* don't want the alliance to fail; those among our own ranks do." The Master Healer shook her head. "Internal strife will put everyone's safety at risk. And as Varian and Annika have both pointed out in past meetings, *Na'Rei* Savyr will take advantage of that if he learns we're divided."

The human leader raised a hand. "Councilors, I informed you all as a matter of courtesy, not so you could debate my choice." Kalan's gaze returned to Varian. "Varian's the only one with the right to dispute the appointment."

Again all eyes focused on him. Varian shifted on his stool.

Jaw clenching, he suspected Kalan's move to be deliberate. Why hadn't the warrior asked him privately? He understood the logic of the arguments, yet not why he'd been chosen after the failure at Ostare. To decline the position now, in front of the Council, would weaken the human leader's position, and as Candra pointed out, put everyone's safety at risk.

Varian pushed back his anger at being manipulated. He met the *Chosen's* gaze. One dark eyebrow lifted in silent challenge.

No, the warrior hadn't manipulated him. That inferred some sort of deceitfulness. The only charge he could level at the human was that the man was determined to see their alliance succeed. The interests of both peoples drove him. Varian also couldn't deny the fact that the *Na'Chi* needed this alliance as much as the humans.

Kalan Tayn was a formidable strategist.

"I'll accept the position, *Chosen*." Varian kept all conflicting emotions out of his voice.

Relief flickered across Kalan's face. He blinked. The warrior hadn't been as confident of receiving a positive answer as he'd portrayed?

"We'll talk more later." Satisfaction swirled in the emerald depths of Kalan's gaze as he relaxed onto the pillows behind him. Candra leaned forward to check him. He gave her a reassuring smile. "For now, Yevni will continue to train the returning off-duty Light Blades. The potentials also need to learn the new patrol techniques. Varian, work with Yevni and decide which of the Light Blades you trained would make good instructors for this task. Once that's done, Jole will brief you on all the patrols we have out at the moment, their locations, and what information they've sent back to us. They're now yours to lead."

"Perhaps if I come over to the *Na'Chi* apartments after the meeting, we could discuss our plans then?" Yevni asked. Varian nodded.

The warrior rubbed his hands together. "Good. This evening we can inform the Commanders together."

"That's all I wanted to discuss for now, Councilors." Kalan's announcement drew a firm nod from Candra.

"*Chosen*, please, there's one other issue I believe needs to be addressed." Jho Elamm rose from her stool. "I'll try not to be long, Master Healer. My apologies, *Temple Elect*, but this concerns what we discussed the other day." The slender woman inclined her head in Kymora's direction. "I'm afraid there's been . . . further developments. . . ."

Kymora straightened in her seat, and while her expression didn't change, Varian sensed her trepidation. What issue was the smaller woman referring to? And what had Kymora so worried?

"Three of your senior tutors have approached me," Elamm continued. While her tone seemed appropriately apologetic, an overly sweet odor coming from her indicated otherwise. "And as the problem seems to have spilled into our Temple, I felt the Council should be made aware of the situation."

"What matter are you referring to, Councilor?" Kalan asked.

"Councilor Elamm approached me earlier this week, *Chosen*." Kymora's voice remained calm and low. "She informed me that there's some concern circulating within the community that I was neglecting my duties as *Temple Elect*."

Candra snorted. "That's absurd!"

"Nevertheless, their dissatisfaction is there, Candra, and it's growing," Elamm retorted. "Just yesterday I spoke to each of the Servants myself to ascertain their concerns."

The woman paused, wetting her lips, her gaze sweeping the group, as if gauging everyone's reactions. Several Councilors were shaking their heads, expressions somber.

The sickly sweet odor increased as Elamm took a breath. "All three are considering leaving the Temple."

Kymora's face lost color and her hands tightened in her lap. "Why haven't they discussed this with me?"

"Perhaps their confidence in you has been shaken."

The sickly sweet scent altered, took on a sour odor. Varian's gaze narrowed. Even being unfamiliar with the protocols involved with the Temple, a rift like this within the order couldn't be good. Especially not now.

"Councilor, the *Temple Elect* will need the names of these Servants. She can't be expected to address their issues by going through a third party such as yourself." Kalan raised his hand as Elamm made to speak. "You've brought the matter to the Council's attention, now leave her to resolve it."

Varian cocked his head, satisfied with how swiftly he'd cut the woman off. The politics within the group came as no surprise. He'd seen it at work the first time he'd sat in on a meeting. Only then, Davyn had driven the machinations that had corrupted the integrity of the Council.

Candra rose from her seat. "Kalan needs to rest now. Thank you all for coming."

Elamm glared at the Master Healer. She looked once around the circle for support, but everyone else had risen from their seats and were taking their leave. The ex-province leader's mouth turned downward, but she made no attempt to challenge Candra, a wise move considering the implacable expression on the Master Healer's face. After bidding Kalan a stilted good-bye, Elamm left with one of the other Councilors.

Varian pushed to his feet to watch her leave. Both Kalan and Candra had circumvented her before she'd been able to gain an audience. She'd proven to be no friend of Kymora's, but what had she thought to achieve by raising the issue in Council?

"Varian, perhaps we could begin our discussion. . . ." Yevni's request drew him from his thoughts. "Let's detour via the kitchens before we head to the apartments. I missed breakfast with the summons from Kalan, and I suspect we'll still be making plans come the midday meal. . . ."

After a glance toward Kymora and discovering her sitting on the edge of her brother's bed, Varian accompanied the older warrior along the center walkway in the healers' hall. Any speculation about Elamm's motives would have to wait. There were more urgent issues to deal with.

# Chapter 29

KYMORA slid the partitioning curtain across the prayer room archway, needing the privacy contained within the small room. Her hands shook as she threaded the securing tie over the hook set into the wall. No one would disturb her with the curtain shut. She pressed her forehead against the cool stone and concentrated on taking deep breaths.

Beyond the curtain, voices began singing. Usually the sound of the acolytes practicing their devotional hymns brought a smile to her face but not this evening. Eyes closed, she listened to several verses and almost wished for the return of her days as a student. After spending the last several hours in meetings with her senior Servants, her time as an acolyte almost seemed more appealing.

With a sigh, she straightened and made her way to the small offertory set into the wall. A minute later, three Keri-blossom incense sticks burned, their sweet scent filling the room. Remaining on her knees near the shelf, Kymora reached for her amulet and bowed her head.

"*Lady of Light, Mother of Mercy*, I ask humbly that you hear your Servant." Without warning, her throat closed tight and tears burned behind her eyes. She traced the lines etched into the amulet, trying to return to a meditative state, but the familiar action didn't help. "I desperately need your guidance and wisdom."

A soft breeze pushed against her robe, fluttering it against her legs, and a familiar energy pulsed against her mind. Kymora bit her lip to contain her cry of relief and tried to compose herself as the odor of incense was replaced with the lighter, refreshing scent of new-fallen rain.

"HANDMAIDEN, I HEAR YOUR PRAYER."

"You bless me with your presence, *Lady*." Her voice was thick with tears. "Thank you."

"I FEEL YOUR PAIN. YOUR SOUL IS TROUBLED."

"Forgive me, *Lady*, but I don't know what to do." Kymora tried to organize her thoughts, but they just kept chasing each other around in her head, tangling together and eluding any sort of order.

"PEACE, HANDMAIDEN." The warmth of a hand pressed against her bowed head. "CALM YOURSELF. CLEAR YOUR MIND AND SPEAK WHAT'S IN YOUR HEART."

Kymora blinked hard, her cheeks flushing with heat. *Merciful Mother*, she was behaving like a first-year acolyte. Tiredness wasn't an excuse, nor was impatience. She inhaled a slow, deep breath, concentrating on letting the sweet, floral scent of the incense spread through her. Several breaths later, she felt calmer but nowhere near as composed as she should be. It would have to do.

"*Lady*, have I failed you?"

Kymora cringed at the way she blurted the question. Where was the control and maturity fitting of a practiced Servant? One worthy of being in *Her* presence?

"WHY WOULD YOU ASK THAT?"

She took an uneven breath, calling on her strength to speak in a more modulated tone. "I believe I've neglected my responsibilities as *Your Temple Elect.*"

The hand stroking her head stopped. "IN WHAT WAY?"

"Today I met with all my senior Servants. There were several who expressed concerns that my absence from the Temple has affected my service. That my priorities threaten our ministry." Her chest and voice tightened. "The time I've spent and continue to spend with the *Na'Chi* troubles them greatly. There are some who wish to leave the Temple and be posted elsewhere because of this."

To hear three of her most senior tutors accuse her of putting the *Na'Chi* above the needs of their own people still made her heart ache. Perhaps she shouldn't have spent so much time away from Sacred Lake living with them.

Ever loyal, Sartor had argued on her behalf, claiming he'd handled the role in her absence, yet Kymora had sensed a general dissatisfaction with her actions from others in her order even though they hadn't spoken up. If she'd returned once a month to spend a few days dealing with matters, perhaps this problem could have been averted.

"DON'T LET THEIR LACK OF FAITH SOW THE SEED OF DOUBT IN YOURS, HANDMAIDEN." Reassurance brushed her mind. "YOU SERVE ME WELL."

The relief lifted a load from her shoulders. Tears forced themselves from between her lashes. "*Your* words comfort me, *Lady.*"

And they did.

Nothing mattered to her more than fulfilling *Her* will. Yet no matter how much she'd reassured the tutors of her intentions, their requests to be stationed elsewhere remained adamant.

The Temple would feel the loss of three experienced Servants. None of the acolytes were ready to take on their full-time responsibilities, and those already serving in that position had discovered their workload doubled since the *Na'Reish* raids on the border. She couldn't ask them to take on any more.

Nor could she recall any of the Travelers. They were still disseminating information to the Provinces for the Blade Council. But to deny the Servants their requests and keep them on until she could find replacements would only create tension, and at the moment the Temple needed to remain a source of strength and harmony.

"YOUR THOUGHTS REMAIN TROUBLED."

The soft-spoken words made her heart ache. "I don't mean to insult the confidence you've shown in me, *Lady*. . . ."

"DID I NOT SAY YOU WOULD BEGIN YOUR FOURTH JOURNEY?"

"Yes." She squeezed the amulet in her hand. "The day Varian asked for sanctuary for his people from me. My journey has begun. . . ."

"INDEED IT HAS. YOUR HEART, YOUR FAITH, YOUR DEDICATION HAS MADE YOUR LIFE-JOURNEY . . . UNIQUE." Satisfaction reinforced *Her* words. "THE PATH IS CHALLENGING, YET YOUR EFFORTS WILL REAP REWARDS."

And there lay her dilemma. "But how am I to fulfill *Your* mandate when I'm torn between serving our people and the needs of the *Na'Chi*?"

In the silence that followed, she could hear the thumping of her pulse in her ears. Her heart lurched as the scent of fresh-fallen rain faded and the warmth of the *Lady's* touch disappeared. Had she been too bold in her questioning?

Kymora grimaced. Did the *Lady* intend that she figure this out on her own? Perhaps that was part of her Journey. Was there someone else *She* wanted her to go to for guidance? But who?

Kalan? He needed time to heal. Causing him to worry would delay that process.

Arek was gone. Her chin trembled.

Candra? Favoring one Councilor above another would likely be seen as a conflict of interest. More internal bickering would do more harm than good.

Varian? He had his hands full dealing with the promotion to the *Chosen's* Second. She had barely seen him the last few days.

Shoulders sagging, she reached for her staff. Maybe sleeping on it would provide her with the answer she needed.

A breeze swirled around her; the scent of new-fallen rain once again teased her nostrils. Kymora's heart lifted. "Forgive my audacity, *Lady*. I didn't mean for my question to upset you—"

"BE AT EASE. YOUR QUESTION DID NOT OFFEND ME."

She sensed an aura of deliberation. It reminded her of the time just before the *Na'Chi* had arrived in Sacred Lake, when *She'd* revealed information to her about her Fourth Journey.

*Her* aura bled compassion. "KYMORA, YOU SERVE ME WHETHER YOU WEAR THE *TEMPLE ELECT* ROBES OR NOT."

Kymora froze and the breath rushed from her lungs as the meaning of *Her* words penetrated. Her head snapped up.

"*Lady?*" she whispered, her lips numb with shock. "You wish me to—to step down as the *Temple Elect?*"

No *Temple Elect* in the history of the order had ever resigned from the role. All had remained as head of the Temple until their deaths. Again Kymora sensed the *Lady's* hesitation.

"THE ANSWER LIES IN YOUR HEART."

Warmth flowed around her, heating her skin, then it sank deep inside her.

"YOUR COURAGE IS YOUR GREATEST STRENGTH AND WEAKNESS." *Her* scent began to fade. "FINISH YOUR FOURTH JOURNEY, HANDMAIDEN."

Within one heartbeat and the next, *She* was gone. Kymora remained on her knees, her senses reeling. She replayed every word spoken, every nuance uttered, every sensation bestowed upon her by the *Lady* in her mind.

". . . *you serve me whether you wear the* Temple Elect *robes or not.*"

Was *She* asking her to abandon the role of *Temple Elect* or give up the Temple entirely? If she were fulfilling her role, why leave? What would it achieve?

Stepping aside yet to remain as a Servant would mean following the directives of the new *Temple Elect*. She could be assigned to another Province. How could she serve the *Na'Chi* if that happened?

To follow *Her* will and continue helping the *Na'Chi*, the only other option available would be to relinquish her status as a Handmaiden. Kymora shook her head as an ache filled her chest. But serving in the Temple was her vocation; she'd spent years studying and training her skills and her Gift. She couldn't imagine doing anything else.

Without the robes of a priestess, how could she continue to serve *Her*, their people, or the *Na'Chi*? How could it benefit anyone?

*"Finish your Fourth Journey."*

Her hands shook so much that it took four strikers to light another stick of incense. Would resigning be the end of her Fourth Journey? What would she do without a vocation? Who would she be?

Kymora shuddered. She couldn't bring herself to leave the prayer room. Not yet.

Not when so much rode on interpreting the *Lady's* words correctly, and not when her final decision would impact so many in a time when they could least afford more unrest.

Who would replace her? Finding someone could take months. The Blade Council would be left without a spiritual advisor. And how would this affect the people? They needed the security and strength of strong spiritual leadership.

Kymora wrapped her arms around herself. With war with the

*Na'Reish* looming, the rebels threatening civil war, the *Chosen* almost dying, resigning now would only add to the turmoil.

*Lady's Breath*, how could she be responsible for doing that?

NODDING his thanks to the Light Blade holding open the door for him, Varian's step slowed as he entered the *Chosen's* apartment. The place appeared to be very similar to his: a main living area with an open archway and two wooden doors, a bathing room, and bedrooms. While his apartment remained spartanly furnished, there were more personal touches added here. A beautifully woven rug in shades of blue patterned with geometric circles lay on the floor while a variety of weapons and shields hung on the walls and several chests sat lined up beneath them.

The great fireplace to his left crackled and popped, and the scent of burning wood permeated the room. Annika crouched in front of it, stoking it with a poker. She smiled a greeting.

"Evening, Varian." Kalan sat at a large table in the middle of the room looking a lot healthier than the last time he'd seen him in the hospice over a week ago. "Thank you for responding to my message so quickly."

Master Healer Candra's influence was evident though in what the human wore—boots, a loose pair of breeches, and an untucked long-sleeved shirt. No belt, no weapon.

"Welcome to our home. Not quite what you were expecting?"

Varian raised an eyebrow, unaware that he'd given away his thoughts.

"When I first arrived here, and after seeing how the *Na'Reishi* lived, I thought the leader of the humans would live in more luxurious surroundings," Annika commented, dusting her hands on the sides of her dress. She pointed her chin in Kalan's direction. "He used to live in the barracks with the Light Blades before we met and claims he never got around to fancying up the *Chosen's* apartment."

"If you want to see luxurious, secure a dinner invitation from Councilor Elamm," Kalan said in a dry tone.

"Pass." Annika snorted. "That one time was enough, thank you very much." She motioned him to the table. "We were just about to sit down for a cup of tea. Will you join us?"

As Varian approached, Kalan rose slowly from his chair, one arm supporting his side, the other outstretched in greeting.

Varian wiped his hands on his breeches, grimacing at the dirt and dust staining his clothes before he took his arm. He'd been in the middle of training with Zaune when Kalan's message had arrived. "How are you?"

"Better." The warrior shared a look with Annika, a touch of amber fire in his emerald gaze, a grin curving his lips. "Thanks to my personal healer."

Annika's answering smile was gentle. Warm. Their gazes held a moment in an unspoken communication, a look that conveyed heat and something deeper.

Nearly six months ago, Varian had watched both of them make unconditional sacrifices to save the other. After being stabbed by Davyn, Annika nearly hadn't been found in time. Kalan had shared his blood with her, despite believing he'd become her blood-slave, something he'd long abhorred, to save her life.

Given what humans thought of the blood-addiction they suffered when the *Na'Reish* took a slave, Kalan's ready acceptance had caught Varian by surprise and earned the human a huge chunk of respect. Until he'd revealed that information to Kalan, the warrior hadn't realized the addiction would be Annika's, not his.

Then after the formation of the new Blade Council, Annika had walked out with the *Na'Chi* after realizing the humans weren't ready for an alliance with them. She'd given up her future with Kalan, deciding it wasn't fair to make him choose between her or his people.

*Love.* The emotion that empowered and sustained both of them. Witnessing it now, the connection sparked a touch of longing and envy in Varian. He glanced away, feeling like he was intruding on a private moment.

"You two talk. I'll pour the tea." Annika reached for the pot resting on the tray in the center of the table.

"I'm sorry I haven't had the chance to speak to you before now," Kalan began. He closed the book in front of him, then pushed it out of the way. Lines of tension creased the edges of his gaze. "I appreciate your patience, considering the circumstances."

Varian nodded his thanks as Annika pushed a steaming cup toward him. "The Master Healer made it very clear that we were to give you time to heal."

Kalan chuckled. "One of Annika's guards mentioned the threat of a pox infection."

"It was hard to tell if she was joking or not. *Vaa'jahn* masks her scent well." Varian sipped his tea, then set the cup down. "Besides, there's been plenty to keep me busy this week."

As much as Varian enjoyed the company of the human leader and Annika, Kalan didn't seem to be in any hurry to address the reason for inviting him here. And he wanted some answers they'd both been putting off addressing since his appointment.

"So, why have I been invited here, *Chosen?*" he asked, gaze direct. "Do you require a progress report on our patrols or are you going to tell me why you chose me as your Second?"

The warrior's eyebrows lifted high. "I'd forgotten how candid you could be." He shook his head. "The reasons I gave at the hospice stand, Varian." His lips thinned and his brow furrowed. "Not being able to trust my own people burns in my gut like acid. I just thank the *Lady* you accepted the position that day I put you on the spot."

The stark honesty in his voice was sobering. Varian decided to return the favor.

"You risked the future of your people." He couldn't keep the bite of anger out of his voice. "I very nearly decided you were manipulating me, and I don't take that from anyone."

Kalan inclined his head. "I gambled you'd see past your shock."

"Your choice proved unpopular with some."

For a long moment, the warrior was silent, his gaze thoughtful. "You're including yourself in that assessment."

He almost flinched at Kalan's accurate insight. A deep breath later, he met his gaze. "My carelessness lost you your best friend, *Chosen*."

There was no point honeycoating the truth or avoiding it. Grief darkened the depths of Kalan's gaze as it pulled the skin over his cheeks taut.

"How were you careless?"

Varian ground his teeth together. "I should have scouted farther beyond the perimeter of the clearing."

"How far did you go out?"

"A three-minute walk in all directions."

"That's twice what our scouts are trained to do."

Where was the anger or reprimand he'd been expecting with that admission? The human's scent remained neutral, unsoured by a lie.

"No one can anticipate all the risks, Varian. You deal with the situation as it's presented to you. You did. That second *Na'Hord* patrol acted out of character. We've never had two infiltrate our borders so close together. It's a new tactic. One we'll anticipate from now on."

"We needed to succeed that day. The mission failed."

"We might not have achieved our original goals, but seven villagers were rescued that day." Kalan's expression grew grim. He grunted. "Do you know how many people we've saved in the past once we've learned about a raid? None. Involving the *Na'Chi* in that mission was a positive move, regardless of the loss we suffered."

Varian stared into the tannin-colored depths of his tea. Kalan's responses were nothing like he'd imagined.

"*Lady* knows I've made my fair share of mistakes as a leader that I wished I hadn't." Looking up, he discovered a hard glint in the warrior's gaze. "You can't make perfect choices, *Na'Chi*. Learn from your mistakes, adapt, and move on."

The verbal slap upside the head caught him by surprise but also reminded him the *Chosen* could be just as forward as he was when he needed to be. Kalan's understanding and acceptance took the edge off his guilt.

He ran a finger around the edge of his tea cup. "Do you regret our alliance?"

"No." The adamant reply eased more of his anxiety. "I'm only more determined to see this work."

"Many here in the city are removed from what's happening on the border, but with the influx of refugees, the effects are just starting to be realized." Annika refilled their cups with fresh tea. "*Lady* willing, it won't be long before everyone understands the importance of this alliance."

Although he didn't voice it aloud, the question remained: Would they realize it in time?

"Kalan has many of the Councilors organizing the efforts to resettle or house the refugees." Annika placed her arms on the table and leaned forward, her violet gaze somber. "If the *Na'Reish* continue their raids or begin full-scale attacks, winter will be hard for many this year."

Varian drained his cup. "You're keeping the Council involved but also aware."

"If they see the effects, they can't ignore them." Kalan's every word held a hard edge. "Unlike the past, I won't let apathy or lack of empathy dictate this Council's actions. And as I said to you back in your village, we no longer have the time to let this alliance evolve naturally. We're going to have to forge it through battle, against the *Na'Reish*."

His respect for Kalan's strategy lifted another notch as he settled back in his chair. "Forge is a good word for it."

More than a little heat had been applied on the training field this week by Yevni to make the mixed patrols work together. On the older warrior's advice, he'd taken patrol after patrol out to test their cohesiveness and to solidify the bonds of familiarity and teamwork. While not every run brought them up against a *Na'Hord* patrol, he had seen some improvement in the way the warriors, human and *Na'Chi*, interacted.

"I believe we're beginning to accomplish something." The man offered a smile at his puzzled expression. "You'd be surprised what I overheard in conversations during the time I spent in the hospice. There were quite a few patients or people who visited the hospice who mentioned that they felt safer knowing that the frequency of patrols had been increased."

"The Guilders are appreciative of the extra help from the *Na'Chi* who have volunteered to work alongside them, especially now with the extra workload of supplying basic supplies to the refugees." Annika's warm smile brimmed with enthusiasm. "And Lisella's excursions with the children into the city are also attracting attention. The perception is that *Na'Chi* children aren't as threatening."

Varian cocked a brow at that statement. "Those *children* can incapacitate a full-grown human if they wanted to."

Kalan shrugged, then grinned. "What they don't know . . ."

Annika rolled her eyes. "This will work, Varian. Have faith."

He grunted but made no comment. "*Small steps, Varian.*" Lisella's words. How many times had he heard her utter them to other *Na'Chi* since they'd come to live in the city again? She had more patience and vision than all of them combined.

"So, fill me in on how the patrols are going." Kalan rubbed his hands together. The change in subject was a welcome one. "I haven't had a chance to catch up with Yevni or any of the other Commanders yet, but I've noticed you've had patrols coming and going from the border this past week. Not knowing how things are progressing is driving me insane."

"Kalan . . ." Annika's soft reprimand was accompanied by a resigned shake of her head. "Candra will have your head if she hears you've been talking work."

"Who says she's going to find out?" he asked, a mischievous glint in his eye. "None of us are going to risk the pox by telling her, are we?"

# Chapter 30

KYMORA bid farewell to the last visitor to the Temple with a soft sigh of relief. The sound of voices retreating down the steps and along the walkway between the Memorial and Temple Gardens was replaced by the distant hubbub of activity inside the Light Blade compound.

In the last week or so, all of the Servants had reported an increase in the number of people attending the services. As much as she enjoyed conducting prayer rituals, the personal petitions left her exhausted. They relied upon the judicious use of her Gift, and often the emotional stress in the minds of those who approached her made identifying their needs difficult. It was delicate work.

Kymora turned her face up to the sun and let the midafternoon warmth soak into her. In another month or so, standing outside, feeling the heat rising from the flagstones through the soles of her boots, wouldn't be possible. The winds from the mountains would descend and howl across the lake, pushing the chill from the first snows into the city.

"Are you communing or sun basking?"

Lisella's question brought a smile to Kymora's face. She turned toward the soft clunk of boots on hard stone.

"Sun basking," she replied. "I didn't realize you were waiting there. I'm sorry."

"You look tired." A lock of Lisella's hair brushed against Kymora's cheek as she enclosed her in a brief hug. "I sat in on your last service."

The strong odor of lanolin lingered in the soft fabric of her dress. The *Na'Chi* woman must have been helping the weavers at the Guildhall, perhaps carding or spinning bleater wool, prior to attending the service.

"I don't know how you handle so many requests," Lisella commented. "Do you always use your Gift during services?"

"Only if the petitioner gives their permission. Many in that last service were refugees from near Whitewater Crossing. A *Na'Reish* attack destroyed their village. They were seeking peace from the devastation of losing everything."

"I'm guessing you'll be seeing a lot more of that in the coming months." The *Na'Chi* woman's voice held a hint of sadness. "The numbers of refugees are growing by the day."

Kymora squeezed her hands. "Rissa tells me you offered to take in the children left homeless by the attacks."

"The orphanage in the city can't accommodate any more. They're sleeping two in each bed now. Besides, we have the room." Lisella chuckled. "Tovie and the other young ones think it's great. More friends to play with."

"How are the *Na'Chi* doing? Annika tells me those working with the Guilds are settling in well."

"I'm glad you asked. It's part of the reason why I've come to see you."

Kymora gestured to their right. "Shall we walk in the gardens?"

Lisella tucked her hand in the crook of her arm, and Kymora followed her lead as they headed down the steps. The heavy, sweet scent of Keri-blossoms carried on the faint breeze, growing stronger the closer they drew to the gardens.

"Almost all of the *Na'Chi* are involved in some sort of interaction within the Light Blade compound or out in the city," Lisella said. "Those working with the Guilds are finding it rewarding. The chance to learn new skills is keeping them occupied."

Kymora cocked her head at the somber inflection in her tone. "But?"

"The hardest to encourage are the scouts. They're spending a lot of hours training and out on patrol. Necessity dictates their schedule, but it's placed them under a lot of pressure."

Lisella drew her to a halt, her aura pulsing, prickling with concern. Cool air brushed against Kymora's cheeks and the intensity of the sun lessened, as if they stopped beneath a tree. Leaves rustled overhead as the breeze intensified, confirming her suspicions.

"Battle rush is something all of them deal with," the *Na'Chi* woman continued. "When we lived in *Na'Reish* territory, they dealt with every threat with deadly force. When they came back, they were all affected but able to deal with it. Each of them had their own circle of friends and those they'd mix with. Here the dynamics are a lot more complicated."

"There's also prejudice to deal with," Kymora added, quietly. "Outside your group, but also within it."

Lisella's sigh was heavy. "Yes. There's always been an element of fear in those who weren't scouts, but because the battle rush subsided much more quickly, it wasn't so bad. Here, and with all the other stresses of adapting, both situations are more pronounced."

"Varian's affected, but who else have you noticed?"

"Taybor, Zaune, and to a lesser extent, Yari." She was silent a moment. "It's the ones who don't socialize as much who seem to be suffering greater problems. It takes them more time to come down from their battle high."

"Have you never had a scout not recover? Do you know what happens if they don't?"

"No."

Kymora's gaze narrowed at the slight waver in her reply. "But you suspect something?"

Beneath her hand, every muscle in Lisella's arm tensed. "When the *Na'Reish* fight, they reach a similar battle high. It usually ends once they feed. That's why we always make sure there's plenty of sustenance around when the scouts return. But Hesia used to talk about how some *Na'Reish* warriors would go berserk from their highs. They'd kill everyone in sight."

An icy shiver worked its way along Kymora's spine. "And you think the same will happen with the scouts."

"We're all half *Na'Reish*, Kymora." Lisella no longer hid her anxiety. "We share so many traits. The scouts push themselves much more than most of us, so the risk is higher for them. And now, with them out on patrol so often and having to deal with other stresses, the effects are driving them to their limits."

"Do the other *Na'Chi* know all this?"

"Some."

"Everyone needs to be informed, Lisella." Kymora placed her hand on top of the younger woman's and squeezed. "If you care for these scouts and don't want to run the risk of losing them, then you're all going to have to work together to save them. Work out ways to keep them involved and socializing, even if it's just among yourselves."

"I wanted to let you know because I believe the only thing averting this from happening to Varian is the connection you share with him. The last few patrols have been the toughest. He retreats to his room because he senses the others' fear of him, and nothing either Zaune or I do can convince him to come out before the next day."

Varian had needed her? Kymora's insides tightened until it felt like she'd eaten a thorn-bush. "Why didn't you come and get me? I would've visited. . . ."

Why hadn't he come to her instead of retreating to his room? She bit her lip, already knowing the answer. It hurt to think he'd rather suffer alone than allow her to see him as he was. He still didn't trust her. His stubbornness frustrated her. Her heart thudded hard.

"You've been so busy and I'm aware of the pressure you're receiving from your Order to cut back on the time you're spending with us."

"Oh, Lisella." Her voice shook as her mouth pursed with anger. Not toward the Na'Chi woman but toward those who would dictate her actions. "If you think Varian needs me, I want you to promise to send for me. I'll come, no matter the time or what I'm doing."

Lisella released a shuddering breath. "*Lady* bless you, thank you, Kymora." Her aura shimmered with relief. "You do so much for us already. . . ."

"What I do for the Na'Chi is more personal than professional."

"I know." Her longer fingers gave hers a quick squeeze, strong and sure. "Varian's never said anything, but I'm glad you two are . . . friends. He won't tell you, but he wants you and he needs you."

The stress placed on the two verbs hinted that the woman knew more about their relationship than she'd let on.

"What I share with Varian is precious to me, Lisella," Kymora admitted, aware that her emotions were close to the surface and probably easy to scent.

"You care for him? I mean, as more than a friend?"

Kymora remained quiet for several heartbeats, unsure if she should elaborate any further.

"I understand if you don't want to talk about this now," Lisella murmured.

Kymora shook her head. "This is the first time I've had the chance to talk to anyone about it. I do care for him. Deeply." She issued a hard sigh. "But getting him to believe it is another hurdle."

Lisella responded with a dry grunt. "Varian's never let himself get close to anyone. That's half the problem."

"You do realize some of the women in your group can also be held accountable for that, too?" Her hands curled. "I'm sorry if I offend you by saying that, but they treat him like he has a contagion and all because he doesn't live up to their image of a desirable warrior. Their prejudice toward someone with a physical affliction is appalling."

"You experienced it when you lived with us." That was delivered as a statement rather than as a question. "That prejudice is inherent in the *Na'Reish*, and we've had the misfortune to inherit it." Her aura flared with a combination of joy and sympathy. "But you've gone past the surface and seen what's inside him. . . ."

"The Varian everyone sees is what you've all made him." Kymora didn't bother to soften her criticism. *Lady* forgive her for being so judgmental, but she couldn't stand by and not say something now that the opportunity had arisen. "He might come across as strong and hard and surly, but there's so much more to him than that. He's just like any of us, with fears and desires and dreams, but he only sees his worth in terms of what he can do for all of you. He's denied himself so he could be what you needed him to be. He'd do anything for your group. He loves you all that much!"

"I know." Lisella pulled her into a tight hug, her voice thicker and huskier. "And I thank the *Lady* he has you. I had hoped . . . but I wasn't sure whether you were trying to help him as a friend or priestess." She let her go but still gripped her arms. Her voice lowered. "Varian mightn't realize it yet, but he has a deeper bond with you than any of us. The day Zaune took you to see him at Rystin's grave, all of us expected you'd return with him. When you didn't, then brought Varian back to the village with you, his temper defused, it amazed us. Kymora, you reach him when no one else can. He responds to you, and as long as you can do that, then he can be saved."

Lisella's confidence in her was daunting. She might have made aiding people her life's work, but that didn't mean she was an expert. Nor did she want to just help Varian. She wanted there to be something more between them.

Friendship would be the foundation, yet what they shared now had gone past those boundaries. He desired her, and not knowing exactly where she fit in Varian's world, or whether he wanted her there, created a whole new level of anxiety. And being unsure and uncertain played on her deepest insecurities. She should have talked to Lisella well before now, but so much had happened in the last few weeks.

Kymora inhaled a deep breath, and let it out slowly. "Most times I have no idea what Varian is thinking. He won't talk to me and I'm unable to sense his aura. He shuts himself off or blinds me with the intensity of his emotions. I feel like I'm searching in the dark. Sometimes I wonder if I'm doing the right thing, whether I'm helping or just harming him. How do I know I'm reaching him?"

Lisella patted her hand once. "What does anyone do when they feel threatened emotionally? They try to push you away . . . get you to reject them any way they can."

Overhead the leaves in the tree rustled and mixed with the sound of flapping feathered wings. A squabble of twittering and chirruping broke out. The noise brought back the memory of Varian that night in his bathing room, when he'd surged from the pool and pinned her against the wall.

He'd tried to use not only his physical presence but also the other side of him to scare her, goading her to deny him out of fear. In the forest clearing he'd tried anger; before the Summer's End Festival he'd used insults.

"He mightn't tell you what he's thinking, but he'll show you," Lisella said, drawing her out of her thoughts. "I've learned to look for what he does more than what he says, or doesn't say. If he were the fearsome leader some believe he is, he wouldn't play with or talk to the children. He wouldn't have listened to Taybor and the others in his decision to come back to Sacred Lake. He wouldn't have given any of us a choice."

The sound of many voices chattering came from the direction of the Temple. Footsteps accompanied the wave of noise. Kymora drew Lisella off the pathway and onto the grassed area, searching for one of the bench seats she knew were scattered around the Temple Garden. The acolytes were emerging from their tutoring sessions for their lunch break.

They were well back from the pathway when the crowd descended, and by taking a seat, most would know not to interrupt them. The gardens were often used for private conversations or meditation.

"Kymora, *Lady* knows Varian can be stubborn, but don't give up on him, you're just what he needs. You see him and accept him for who he is," Lisella stated, hands tightening on hers. "I won't pry any more, but your courage is what will save him. You'll help him believe in himself, never doubt that."

A shiver trailed along Kymora's scalp, then down her back. Reassurance and apprehension both came with her friend's words. The *Lady* had said to her, her strength lay in her courage, and now Lisella had told her the same thing.

Her smile was wobbly. "I'm glad we had this chance to talk."

"So am I." A heartbeat of silence, then Lisella's tone altered and became more businesslike. "There are five patrols returning this evening. I thought we could have a communal dinner in the common room. Invite a few close to the *Na'Chi* . . . Kalan and Annika, some of the healers, a few from the orphanage, maybe Jole and Yevni."

She nodded. "Not too many or the scouts will retreat to their rooms."

"I'll go ahead and organize it for tonight. I'll also inform those coming of the reason behind the dinner." Lisella embraced her again. "Thank you for listening and understanding."

She returned the hug. "See you tonight, then."

# Chapter 31

"THIS is Sacred Lake, Johy." Varian tried his best to keep his tone soft, but there was nothing he could do about the guttural deepness. He focused on maintaining a gentle hold around the boy's thin waist and sifting through the many scents pouring off him rather than the uncontrollable energy churning inside of him.

Bitter fear coated the child; the strength of it hadn't abated since they'd found the small blond-headed boy near the burned ruins of his small farming croft. Other than the boy's parents, who'd died in the initial assault by the *Na'Hord* patrol, the half-dozen surviving family members had been left alone.

Croft destroyed but no slaves taken. And they'd discovered the same results at the next eight farms, a disturbing change in behavior by the *Na'Reish*, one that Kalan needed to know about.

"See the cluster of people dressed in green near the stables?" Varian motioned with the hand that held the reins. Candra headed the group of healers waiting with the stable hands. "They're going to check to make sure you're well."

If only they could help him as easily. This time his patrol hadn't even engaged the *Na'Hord*; just the evidence of their presence had been enough to draw out the beast in him, and nothing he'd done could push it back. He'd spent the last several hours seeing the world in crimson hues, the density of the color dependent on his fluctuating moods. A worrying new development since he'd last experienced battle rush.

Varian squeezed the reins, hoping the sharp bite of the leather would distract him from the heavy tension crawling beneath his skin. *Mother of Mercy*, it felt like his muscles were turning themselves inside out.

Reining in the war-beast, he eased its pace to a walk, then to a halt as they reached the stables. The Master Healer was already issuing orders to her crew. Healers threaded their way through the patrol, helping Johy's siblings and extended family dismount.

"Varian." Candra greeted him with a nod as she peered up at him and his passenger.

"Take the boy," he said, grimacing as the instruction came out more like an order. He lifted the child over the top edge of the saddle and leaned down to pass him to her. A second later he joined them on the ground. "This is Johy, his grand-elders, and siblings. His parents were killed."

His terse explanation drew an assessing look from the older woman. The voices, the rumbling calls of the war-beasts to those already stabled, the salutations of friends and family meeting the returning Light Blades were all starting to set him on edge again. Varian was grateful the child was Candra's primary concern for the moment. It would give him the time he needed to slip away and escape the crowd. Handing the reins to a stable hand, he grabbed his travel pouch and turned to leave.

"Second!" The hail came from Jole. The blond Light Blade warrior signaled him to wait.

Lightning-fast, his skin prickled with anger and frustration so intense his hands began to shake. His crimson vision altered to red, and what felt like a swarm of red-hot burrowers gnawed at his gut. He sucked in several deep breaths to stop himself doubling over.

His heart began to race. He heard it throbbing in his head. He reached out a hand and gripped the hitching post, unsure if what he felt was blood-hunger or the effects of battle rush. Or a combination of both.

Jole ducked under the neck of his mount, but as he drew nearer, his pace slowed and one eyebrow raised. Whatever he saw made him reassess what he was about to say. "I'll make the report to Kalan and Yevni." He nodded once. "You go take care of yourself. Feed. Rest. Sleep."

Nausea replaced the red-hot burrowers in his stomach. "Thank you." It was all he could manage.

Pivoting on his boot heel, Varian felt a tug on the sleeve of his arm. A pair of wide eyes in a pale face stared up at him.

"Johy," Candra said, her softly spoken words gentle and soothing. "Varian has to go now."

The small hand clutching his sleeve dug in tighter and the boy's fear scent strengthened. His reluctance to see him go surprised Varian, considering the boy hadn't said a word during the entire ride. It'd been a one-sided conversation all the way. Something must have reached him though.

Varian fisted both hands, torn between leaving the boy in Candra's capable care and his need to go before the darkness inside him consumed him. The shaking in his hands had moved to the rest of his body. Sweat beaded his brow and itched on his scalp. The irritation made him want to snap and break something. He ground his back teeth together.

*Lady's Breath*, he couldn't lose it. Not now. The boy didn't need to see him display any sort of violence. Not after the shock he'd suffered.

Sucking in a deep breath, he slowly crouched, meeting Johy's frightened gaze. He grazed a finger along his dirt-smudged cheek. He shuddered. Touching the child centered him for a moment; the intense sensations warring inside him eased a little, drove back the nausea. He let his hand drop to the boy's shoulder, wondering who needed the contact more. Him or Johy?

"You see that group of *Na'Chi* and humans over there?" he asked, amazed Johy didn't flinch at his gruff tone. "They're here to take you to your new home. Get you and your family settled. You'll be safe with them."

A small tremor vibrated through the boy. He shook his head and moved closer to him. Varian looked at Candra, not sure what else he could do for the child, not in the state he was in. He couldn't depend upon Johy's calming influence.

"Rissa." Candra's soft call brought the young apprentice over to them. "This is Johy."

The freckle-faced girl put her healers pouch aside and crouched to be on eye level with the young boy. "Hey, Johy. I'm Rissa." She placed a hand on the child's arm. Her dark brown eyes glazed over a moment as she used her Gift, then a crooked smile curved her lips. "It's all right to be afraid, but we aren't going to hurt you."

Varian watched the young ten-year-old healer work her magic on the child, chatting on about inconsequential things as Candra treated his scrapes and bruises. Varian stayed, not that he had much choice in the matter with Johy still holding on tight to his sleeve. But slowly Johy's grip eased and Rissa convinced Johy to take her hand instead.

Able to sense injuries on the emotional plane, Rissa's skill would prove invaluable as the boy was going to need her help after seeing his parents killed in front of him.

"I've some friends you should meet. They're just over there. . . ." She shared a conspiratorial smile with Johy. "They're just like Varian, only our age. You ever played flutter-tag?"

And just like that, she led the child away to meet those who would see them settled into their new homes. Varian ran a hand through his hair and let out an unsteady breath, hoping some sense of normalcy would restore the child.

"He'll be fine." Candra's soft comment drew his attention back to her. The healer's dark gaze fixed on him. Her brows drew down and he knew she'd spotted the way his hands shook. Without contact with Johy, the symptoms had returned. "Now, I'm more worried about you. The flecks in your eyes are enlarged and they're almost red."

Varian rose from his crouch to avoid her outstretched hand. He didn't think he could stand someone else touching him. "I'll be all right. I'm just hungry."

If it was possible, his voice sounded even more guttural. A figure broke away from the far group of people and came toward him. Lisella. Slung over one shoulder in a carry sling was a stoppered jug.

"Varian, don't ignore what your body's trying to tell you," Candra said, her expression changing to one of deep concern. "You're so restless I can feel the energy rippling off you. I don't need to touch you."

His stomach cramped, sudden and vicious. His skin felt hot, like he was burning with fever. *Mother of Mercy*, he was close to end-stage blood-fever. He pushed past Candra and headed straight for Lisella, knowing the flask would contain enough *geefan* blood to sate his immediate hunger, at least until he could get more from the kitchens.

"Varian!" Candra called. "Wait!"

He ignored her, wincing as everything went dark crimson. His head pounded and his hearing became hypersensitive. Conversations changed to garbled noise, like water rushing over a waterfall, every footstep sounded like a hammer, even the rattle of metal and rasping slide of straps on fur as the stable hands unsaddled the war-beasts felt like splinters being driven into his brain.

"Varian?" Lisella's scent reeked of uncertainty. "What's wrong?"

"The jug . . ." The words felt thick in his mouth. He snatched the ceramic container from her, but his hands were shaking so badly he couldn't pull the stopper. A growl rumbled deep in his chest.

"Let me help. . . ." She plucked the stopper free.

An rich iron odor filled his nostrils. He drained the jug in one go, hardly tasting the thick metallic-flavored liquid. The cramping eased but the itching beneath his skin and the red-hot sensation eating away at his insides returned, twice as bad. He groaned and doubled over, dropping the jug. Pottery smashed.

"Varian?" Lisella's scent morphed to fear.

He bit back a cry as his other half surged from the darkness like a predator emerging from the shadows, strong, with lethal intent. "Get away from me!"

Her hand gripped his shoulder. Redness saturated his vision. Heat flamed inside him. With a growl, he turned. His hand seized the arm that touched him, the other closed around her throat.

And squeezed.

Lisella's choked gasp fed the hunger inside him. The beast inside him savored the shocked expression on her face. Her fingers pried at his. The hoarse sound of every breath energized him. Her fear wound its way through him, nourished his satisfaction.

"Varian!" Her lips shaped his name but no sound came out.

"Varian, stop! You're hurting her!" Someone yanked at his arm. "Jole!"

Someone tackled him from the side. The collision broke his grip around Lisella's throat. He hit the ground hard. The impact drove the breath from his lungs and cracked his head back against the hard-packed dirt.

Head spinning, he blinked up at a bloodred sky that abruptly changed to blue. A forearm pressed against his chest. Jole's weather-tanned face stared down at him, his expression two parts steely resolve, one part concern.

Rasping gasps and coughing reached them. Varian turned toward the sound. Jole's weight shifted and the edge of a dagger was placed against his throat.

"Easy, *Na'Chi*," the Light Blade warned. Hypersensitive, Varian could feel the deadly hum of his Gift.

Collapsed on the ground, with Candra kneeling beside her, Lisella attempted to suck in deep breaths. Tears tracked down her cheeks. Around them the small crowd buzzed with whispers. Their bitter fear saturated the air. As the last few minutes crystallized in his mind, shock lanced through Varian.

"*Merciful Mother . . .*" His voice, hoarse and gravelly, broke. "Lisella? What have I done?" A shudder tore through him. Red finger marks ringed her throat, a violent tattoo that shook him to the core. Nausea rolled, and his stomach dry heaved. "Let me up, Jole. Candra, is she all right?"

The warrior on top of him pressed harder with his dagger. The elderly healer glanced up, the lines creasing her face white with tension.

"It's all right, Jole," she said, her tone low. "The energy inside him, he has it under control."

Controlled, a small mercy, but not banished. Jole slowly rose off him, sheathing his dagger. Varian pushed himself upright, every limb trembling, his heart tearing at the tears tracking down Lisella's face.

"Oh, *Lady of Light . . .* I'm sorry. . . ." He dropped his head into his hands as a groan welled from deep inside his chest. "I'm so sorry. . . ."

What had he done?

"Varian . . ." Lisella's harsh whisper lifted his head. Her gaze locked with his. With Candra's help, she climbed to her feet and came over to him. She reached out to touch him, hand shaking. "I'll be all right. But you won't . . . if you don't get help. . . ."

The painful rasp in her voice made him flinch. Throat tightening, he averted his gaze, no longer able to meet hers. He'd attacked her. If Candra and Jole hadn't stopped him, he'd have killed her. The darkness inside him writhed, but guilt choked it back.

"Don't let this beat you, Varian." Her hand tightened on his shoulder. "We can't lose you now." She made him look at her. The flecks in her gaze were a deep, solid green.

Not yellow.

*Fear.*

Or black.

*Anger.*

Pure green.

*Steely resolve.*

It gave him the strength to push to his feet even though every muscle felt like one of Candra's gelatinous salves. The pain eating away everything inside him hadn't disappeared. If he ignored it, the beast would return, eventually, and he doubted any interference would stop him until he killed someone.

Varian trembled. The shadow staining his soul would consume him. He wasn't supposed to hurt the ones he cared about. There'd never be any peace for him if he did that.

"Kymora . . ." he rasped. "Where's Kymora?"

"You're not going anywhere near—"

"He won't hurt her, Jole." Lisella pointed in the direction of the Temple. "Apartment . . . meditating . . ."

The gathered crowd backed away as he staggered in their direction. Varian grimaced at the heavy stench of fear rolling at him in waves but didn't let it stop him. His breath shortened as everything around him began leeching of color again. Beautiful blues, greens, browns, and yellows altered to the faintest of crimson hues.

*No, not again.*

His heart pounded fast and sweat bloomed all over him by the time he reached the end of the Memorial Garden walkway. He leapt up the Temple steps, taking three at a time, his boots cracking against the stone.

Varian stumbled to a halt in the open Temple doorway, catching himself on the wooden supports. He stood there, shaking, as two young acolytes looked up from cleaning the floor. Neither commented as he headed along the covered walkway paralleling the Temple. It led to the dormitories and Kymora's apartment.

Fear ate at him, hard and vivid, the closer he drew to her door. Her two Light Blade guards stood in the corridor, a short distance from her apartment. Lisella's abused throat flashed in his mind. Instinct screamed that he was putting Kymora in danger. In just a heartbeat, he could very well turn on her, too. He'd come too close once already to hurting her, and now he stood poised on the edge of a very high cliff. It wouldn't take much to make him tumble over.

*Mother of Mercy*, how he wished he could exorcise his darker half. Banish it, bury it, cut it out. He'd give up his colored eyes, his body markings, his enhanced senses and strength, everything he liked about being *Na'Chi*, if he could just be rid of it. All it seemed to do was grow stronger and hurt those he cared about.

As he passed the Light Blades, he nodded a response to their greetings, unable to voice a reply. He halted in front of the apartment door. He placed his hand, then his forehead on the rough panels. The odor of wood and Keri-blossom incense, Kymora's favorite scent, assailed his nostrils. It was wholesome, clean, much like her.

He breathed in deeply, trying to capture a little part of her for himself, trying to reconstruct the sense of peace he felt when with her. Just thinking about it sparked a craving as strong as the battle rush heating his veins.

His gut twisted. The truth was that peace would never be his.

1

Not permanently. Darkness held him. Now it almost controlled him. He feared himself and what he was capable of doing. How could he put Kymora at risk?

His heart constricted. He wanted her. It was that simple. She brought him happiness and light. She showered him with her smiles, addicted him to them like a blood-slave to his mistress's blood. She saw him as a friend, a companion, and lover. Unscarred. Whole. Desirable on so many levels. She made him feel complete. Worthy of so much more than he deserved.

More truths.

But despite that mutual attraction, what right did it give him to endanger her? How did he deserve her when that thing lived inside him?

Varian shut his eyes. The sound forced from his throat was too unpleasant to be a laugh and too abrasive to be a gasp. He dropped his hand to his side.

It didn't matter how much he wanted everything she offered him. He cared too much for her to take the risk. He'd rather die with Jole's dagger planted in his chest than jeopardize Kymora's life.

# Chapter 32

THE door to the apartment opened and Kymora stood there. Even dressed in her Temple robe, she took his breath away. Her expression was relaxed, calm, and the smallest of smiles curved her full lips. She smelled like a garden full of flowers, the floral fragrance light and sweet. Meditating. She'd been burning incense and meditating.

Varian frowned. Then how had she known someone was at her door? He fisted a hand, keeping his curse to himself. Had she sensed his emotions? *Lady* knew they had to be pouring off him. He was too rattled to care or feel frustrated by his lack of control.

"Varian?" Her soft, melodic voice sent a shudder through him. The warmth and welcome in it felt like a balm, soothing some of the rawness inside of him. "Come in."

She stepped back, opening the door wider, and motioned him into her apartment. He remained on the threshold. Her common room was simply furnished, a table and chairs sanded but not painted, a braided rug spread on the floor, a padded chair near the fireplace, a small prayer niche set into one wall. A stick of incense still burned there. Neat, full of textures and warmth. It suited her.

"I don't think that's such a good idea." The roughness in his tone should have been warning enough.

Her head cocked to one side, her expression contemplative half a heartbeat before she stepped toward him. He stiffened as her outstretched hand made contact with his side. Slender fingers skimmed his leather vest, then her arms slid under it and she embraced him.

His throat squeezed tight and he opened his mouth to warn her again, but all that came from him was a ragged gasp that quickly turned into a series of uneven, lung-shuddering breaths. He stood as she hugged him, not moving, fearing and waiting for the darkness to surge and take control.

But all he could feel was her. Her hold wasn't tight, but every soft curve she possessed pressed against his torso. Her arms looped loosely around his waist and her palms were flat against his lower back. As he looked down at her, she placed her cheek against his collarbone, and the top of her dark-haired head brushed against his jaw.

"Do you know this is the first time you've sought me out after coming back from patrol?" she asked. "I'd really like it if you'd come inside and visit."

With two simple sentences, a profound sense of comfort washed through him. Lightness and warmth. Until his body relaxed, he never even realized just how tense he was. He caught himself, one arm reaching out to lean against the door frame, the other wrapping around her.

Kymora tightened her hold on Varian as his body sagged, taking some of his weight even though he caught himself against the jam of the doorway. His every breath juddered in and out of his lungs, sounding like a winded war-beast, only she knew the force of his emotions drove him, not exhaustion. His muscles trembled and his whole body quaked with whatever was tearing him up inside.

The strength of them had alerted her to the fact he was outside her apartment to begin with. The raw blanket of pain that bled from him like hearts-blood, rich and thick and uncontrollable, covered a wealth of other emotions, ones so tangled and twisted she had no chance of sensing what they were. Not yet. He needed a little distance and time before dealing with what had brought him to her.

She was surprised to be able to identify any of what he was feeling. Was it because he'd come to her, needing her help? An active participant in a resolution session was easier to read than an uncooperative one. Whatever the case, this time she wouldn't be going in blind.

Kymora lifted her head from his shoulder. "Come inside, please, Varian."

With gentle coaxing, she brought him into her apartment, closed the door behind them, and headed straight for her bathing room. Nudging the arm she had wrapped around him, slung over his shoulder, was his travel pouch. Judging by the bulge, it had a change of clothes inside.

"If you're anything like Kalan, the first thing he likes to indulge in once he comes off patrol is a bath." She kept her tone deliberately light. "He swears that it takes a good hour of soaking to get rid of the musky odor of war-beasts on his skin. A poor excuse when I know he's always been partial to hot water and a long bath."

Varian said nothing, not even when she stopped at the edge of the pool and began unlacing his vest. His breathing had eased and he no longer trembled so violently. His aura held the dull edge of numbness, like he'd reached the end of his strength.

Or the eye of the storm.

As she slipped the vest from his arms, she grasped his hands. His skin was cold to the touch.

"Unbuckle your weapons belt and give it to me." She kept her voice soft but firm. "Just leave your clothes on the floor and get into the water."

As she hung his belt and vest on the wall, he complied with her instruction. For the next quarter of an hour, she talked about her day, alternating between just chatting and passing him a cleaning cloth and soap-sand. When he was ready, she handed him a towel, then rifled through his travel pouch to find clean clothes.

"While you're drying, I might send to the kitchen for some *geefan* blood." She pulled a rolled-up ball of material out of the pouch. A quick shake and she knew she held a shirt, the light scent of herbal wash lingering in the fabric. She held it out to him. "I'm assuming you're hungry?"

Varian's hand closed over hers, but he didn't take the shirt. A faint tremor shook his fingers as his aura flashed with dark heat. The intensity of it startled a gasp out of her.

"Kymora . . ." His voice broke on her name, a heart-wrenching half groan, half grating sob. "We shouldn't be doing this."

"Why not?"

"I attacked Lisella." His tone was flat, emotionless, but his aura lit up again like a log thrown on embers. Through the contact she had with his hand, a wave of guilt and regret closely followed by horror and disgust swamped her.

Her heart picked up speed with his admission as she fought to keep her reaction from showing on her face. "Is she all right?"

"I almost killed her." His voice sounded like gravel grinding against itself. "Jole stopped me but I hurt her."

His breath caught in a strangled hiccup as he pulled his hand away from hers and left her holding the shirt. "Varian?" He didn't reply. She tilted her head, listening. There it was again, the muffled hiccup. "Varian?"

Kymora moved toward the sound. Her foot nudged warm flesh.

She reached out and found the top of Varian's head at waist level. His head was bowed, the bare curve of one shoulder and arm cradling it.

She dropped to her knees beside his huddled form and wrapped her arms around him again. Silent now, his shoulders quivered in telling jerky movements.

*Merciful Mother*, he was crying.

Kymora's throat closed over and tears burned in her eyes. *Lady* knew what it cost him to open up to her like that, but his courage brought a shaky smile to her lips. She pressed her cheek against his damp hair and just held him.

If Jole had stopped him, he'd done enough to save Lisella and bring Varian out of the effects of battle rush. The exact details could wait.

"Lisella's all right," she murmured. "You wouldn't be here if she weren't." Thank the *Lady* for *Her* mercy as she had little doubt Varian would be in chains or dead if he'd killed her. "That's all that matters."

"I can't . . . control it . . . anymore." Every word sounded torn from his soul. "It's inside me . . . waiting . . . in the darkness. . . . It's like a parasite. . . . It just burrows deeper, growing bigger, poisoning me. . . . I can't stop it. . . . I tried. . . ."

Kymora hugged him harder. Like a dam bursting, the words just poured out of him. She wasn't sure if he realized what he was saying, but as she listened, much of what he revealed gave her a very clear picture of everything she'd ever felt or sensed in him.

He saw himself as two separate identities. Varian, leader of the *Na'Chi*, and the beast, the thing threatening to take over the man. Anger heated his words, his muscles tight with frustrated rage that he couldn't control that part of himself. Impotent fury rode beside the fear as he believed he'd succumb to the part of him he saw as dark and evil. Despair interlocked all of it because he thought himself beyond forgiveness or redemption. All for being who and what he was. For what he'd done and everything he feared he would do.

Warm tears tracked down her cheeks, but she refused to let go of him to wipe them from her face. His outpouring filled her with hope, as painful as it was to listen to. He'd come to her. He'd fought against everything from his past to share his fears with her, a dual gift of giving her his trust and baring his soul.

Kymora traced the bowed curve of his head, the soft dampness of his hair sliding over her fingers. He shifted under her touch, the muscles of his shoulders and arms bunching with tension. His aura was brittle with shock, and shame bled through the cracks. He tried to pull away from her, but she refused to release him.

"You'd deny me the pleasure of comforting a friend by pulling away," she said, softly. "Do you truly believe I'd let you face this alone?"

Did he expect her to abandon him when he needed her the most? The thought slashed at her heart like a blade. That it hurt so much drew her up short. Then she blinked, a slow, deliberate motion that gave her time to digest the impact of what it meant.

*She loved him.* Her heart beat harder. Part of her balked in surprise; another part accepted it with a sense of rightness and joy.

Varian made a small sound in the back of his throat, and something flickered through his aura. With her focus torn between her realization and him, she almost didn't catch it. As exciting as her insight was, analyzing what she felt would have to wait.

"You're not weak, Varian."

She moved so she was kneeling in front of him instead of beside, so he could see her face. This time she wanted him to see her expression. Water on the floor soaked into the folds of her dress, but she ignored it. She reached up to caress the side of his face.

*Lady of Light, be merciful and generous, steady my thoughts and guide me in my Journey.* A Journey perhaps now she understood more clearly.

"This jaw doesn't belong to a weak man." She trailed a hand over his shoulder and along his arm. "Nor does this strong arm, or these capable hands." She pressed her palm to the center of his bare chest.

"Beneath this warm flesh beats the heart of a compassionate man, one who's fought his whole life to fulfill his people's dream. Just because you feel the need to lean on someone, to accept someone else's strength for a little while, doesn't make you weak."

Varian's chest rose on a sharp breath. She placed her fingers over his lips.

"You've always looked out and cared for others. Even me when I needed it." The night spent in the cave after the rebel attack on the *Na'Chi* village was vivid. Kymora leaned forward and brushed her lips over his brow. "Please, I need to take care of you."

Kymora held her breath. She was asking for more of his trust, pushing him. She swallowed against a dry throat. The hand that stroked his stubble-rough cheek trembled.

The fierce tenderness on Kymora's face held Varian transfixed. While her lashes were wet with recently shed tears, the warmth in her emerald gaze wrapped around him like a blanket, soft and comforting. It was there, he could feel it, the tranquility he'd craved while standing outside her door.

Something stirred deep inside him, expanding, heating fast. His heart jolted and he stiffened, afraid that somehow he'd triggered the darkness to rise. But the rush never eventuated and the heat settled in his chest and infiltrated his heart.

"Just for now, accept it, Varian," Kymora whispered.

Her words were like a release and permission all rolled into one. He exhaled a shuddering breath, and in between one heartbeat and the next, peacefulness filled him. Where she touched him, it bled into him through the pores of his skin. The deeper he breathed, the faster it rushed through his veins. He almost groaned with the sensation.

"This is temporary, Kymora." He exhaled a shuddering breath. "It'll disappear once I step outside your door. . . ."

"Then I hope you'll find me or send me a message, and I'll come to you. It's what friends do. They're there when you need them, Varian."

"But you have your Temple duties. . . ."

A smile curved her lips as her fingers eased the frown on his brow. "Let's live in this moment, and worry about everything else later."

She made it too easy to comply. That he sat naked on a cold tile floor while the most influential spiritual leader in all human territory knelt at his feet didn't seem to matter. It would later, but for now Varian wanted to ignore the future and enjoy the present.

He reached to cup her cheek, chest aching at the tear tracks marking it, and smoothed his thumb over them. No one, except perhaps for Hesia, had ever cried over him before.

"You care too much," he stated, grimacing at the hoarseness of his voice.

"I've been accused of that many times. It's just who I am, Varian." Kymora smiled and placed her hand over his.

A simple gesture but one that tugged something loose inside him. She stroked his knuckles, caressing each one with her fingers as if she were memorizing every crease and indent. While her touch wasn't sexual in nature, there was a sensual element to her actions. One his nerves were beginning to fire and come alive with. A look at her face assured him she wasn't doing it deliberately.

He wished she would.

He liked her hands on him. He'd never thought any woman would make him feel the way she did. It was contentment, satisfaction, hunger, desire, and lust all tangled together. His appetite for them all was a growing addiction.

He wanted more.

Varian twisted his hand under hers, gripped her wrist, and drew it to his mouth. He placed a kiss on the underside of her arm, where the skin was soft and warm. A faint flush stained Kymora's cheeks, and her scent deepened into a rich floral sweetness. The serene expression on her face changed to raw anticipation.

"I like you touching me, Varian." Her scent confirmed her statement, yet she made no move toward him like he thought she might.

Was she waiting for confirmation of the direction he wanted to go with her? Where did he want to take this moment?

Images and sensations crowded his head, vivid and explicit. Some he'd already experienced with her, others he didn't even know if they were possible. Fast and hot, arousal raced through him, a powerful jolt that hardened him in a matter of seconds. He swallowed a groan.

Varian released it as he reached for her, unable to resist. He buried his hands in her hair, tilting her head up so he could place his mouth on hers and taste. Her lips opened and her sweetness exploded on his tongue.

*Merciful Mother*, she was nectar and honey, spice and heat.

The contact between them could have been minutes or just seconds. He didn't know or care. Not when her tongue twined with his, tasting, taking, teasing him to the point of breathlessness. She made a soft sound, like a sigh, and the firestorm of need seething inside him erupted.

He wrapped his arms around her, and without losing contact with her mouth, pulled her over him so that she straddled his hips. He groaned as her weight settled on top of him. There was no way she could miss what he wanted, not with his erection caught between them.

Sliding his hands from her waist to her behind, he spread his fingers and cupped the taut curves of her rear, savoring the smooth heat of them through the folds of her robe. He gripped her hard so that he could feel the heat of her through her dress, then worked her in a slow, hot gliding motion against him.

Kymora cried out, breaking their kiss, and a small tremor traveled the length of her body. Varian sucked in a shocked breath, as unprepared as her for the delicious heat that seared him. He could smell her desire, a concentrated, heavy scent he tasted in their next kiss.

When she started tugging at the folds of her robe, he stilled. "What are you doing?"

She issued a breathless chuckle. "I thought that would be obvious." Her hands shook as she plucked at the tie. "I want to feel you skin to skin."

It dawned on him then that they were still on the floor of her bathing room. He grimaced. Cold tiles were no place for her or what they were doing. "Put your arms around my neck."

Once upright, he bent to grasp the hem of her robe and pulled it over her head and let it drop to join his clothes on the floor. The pleasure of just looking at her held him spellbound for several long seconds.

She stood before him, her skin flushed with a rosy hue, her long hair settling around her shoulders in a dark wavy curtain. Her breathing was as erratic as his and drew his attention to her breasts. It took every ounce of control not to reach out and cup them, to feel their weight, to stroke the dark-pointed tips of her nipples.

He wanted to savor the pleasure he'd brought her. The swollen wetness of her lips, the hard thumping of her heart, the fragrant heat glistening in the curls that covered her sex.

Sinking back onto one knee, he pressed a kiss to the curved flare of one hip. "*Mother of Light*, you're so beautiful."

As he closed his teeth over her flesh in a gentle bite, her fingers threaded through his hair and dug into his scalp. He banded his arms around her hips and back and scooped her up against him.

Kymora gave a startled cry as he lifted her from the ground and headed out of the bathing room. Her hands gripped his shoulders and squeezed. "Where are we going?"

Besides the door he'd entered through to come into her apartment, there were three others, all closed. "Where's your bedroom?"

"Second on the right." She buried her head into the crook of his neck, her breath hot against his skin. As he started in that direction, her lips pressed against his throat.

The sensation made him growl and she laughed softly in his ear. By the time he'd entered her room and kicked the door closed with his heel, she'd sampled both sides of his neck and left a stinging bite of her own just above the hollow of his throat.

Varian dropped her onto her bed, grinning at the small scream she issued as he let her go. She landed with a bounce, then huffed as she levered herself up on her elbows.

"You did that on purpose!" she accused him.

He placed a knee on the end of her bed and a hand on the soft blanket near her ankle. With a gentle nudge he parted her legs.

"Why would I"—he began, and starting at her feet, kissed and licked and sucked and bit his way up her calves and thighs—"want to bruise this body?" Past her hips. Her stomach. "I can think . . ." Her breasts. Her throat. ". . . of so many other"—her soft moan thrilled him—"more desirable ways"—she was squirming beneath him as he reached her lips—"to mark you."

Her scent was so rich and thick it made his mouth water. Their uneven breaths mingled, and from the corner of his eye, her hands fisted the blanket into wrinkled wads. He was surprised the heat pouring off both of them didn't set the fabric alight.

"I can sense how much you like teasing me." A sensual smile curved Kymora's lips. She slid one leg up the side of his, then locked it around his hips. In a single motion, she flipped him onto his back so their positions were reversed, the action so smooth it reminded him she trained daily in combat. "You can't feel how much I like it, but I can show you."

She angled her hips so the heat of her core pressed against the base of his erection, an intimate meeting of flesh. A slow drag of her hips along his length startled a groan out of him. Her wet heat coated him.

*Lady's Breath!*

With a hiss, he arched upward. "Kymora . . ."

Her kiss cut him off. She nibbled at his lips, tongue sneaking out to taste them, the depths of his mouth. She was fire and sweetness and desire. And focused totally on him, on driving him to the edge with everything she did.

Her teeth closed on the soft lobe of his ear, an erotic nip that twisted the temperature inside him so high he felt like he'd been thrust into a potter's furnace. A growl erupted from his chest; his hands clamped on her shoulders. He gazed up at her, then froze, stiffening with shock.

Kymora's skin and everything around her had turned a light shade of crimson.

# Chapter 33

VARIAN'S fingers dug into Kymora's upper arms, and beneath her he stilled. A hoarse cry exploded from his lips even as she sensed the powerful surge in energy coming from deep within him.

"Kymora, get off me!" His voice had dropped, deepened into the familiar gravelly growl associated with battle rush.

Her breath caught as strands of sensations whipped at her mind, a maelstrom of rage, desire, loneliness, hunger, sorrow, and agony, all shadowed by a cloud of desperation and need.

"No, wait, Varian." She gripped her legs against his flanks to stop him throwing her off. "Let me feel this. Don't move."

"I don't want to hurt you!" Varian's panic slammed into her.

She clasped his head between her hands. "Focus on my voice." His hands clamped around her wrists. His breath heaved in and out of his lungs. "I can sense your other half. It wants something."

"It's angry." His voice came through gritted teeth.

"Yes, I know." Her heart thundered in her chest, but she kept her voice calm. "Kiss me." His head shook from side to side. "Trust me. Do it. Now!"

Their lips locked, the kiss lacked the heat of their previous ones, but it served the purpose she intended. She felt pressure against her aura. Pushing, straining.

"It's reaching . . . for this," she whispered against his mouth. "Our pleasure. Our joy. Can you feel it?"

Her heart constricted as she understood the why of what was going on. The *Lady* had designed all *Na'Chi* to have both human and *Na'Reish* traits, but *She'd* never intended them to live one without the other. Circumstances and thoughtless behavior had created the problem Varian, and the other scouts, now faced.

He'd rejected part of himself for so long, only drawing on it when he needed it to protect or ensure the survival of his people, and now all the emotions associated with those actions were mostly negative.

A child raised on harsh discipline would crave the gentler emotions, but having never experienced them, it made sense he would feel threatened when confronted by them. Controlling and twisting that particular situation to something more familiar, yet ultimately harmful, was logical. For him.

It explained the anger and more destructive feelings Varian's other half showed in times of high emotion, but it also accounted for the desperate need buried deep beneath them.

Feed it and the balance would be restored.

Kymora laughed softly. It made sense. She lifted up on her knees and reached down to clasp Varian's erection. His grip on her wrist tightened.

"Trust me, Varian. Focus on what I'm doing and what you're feeling as we make love."

Fear stained his aura; she could sense it swirling around the edges of the maelstrom inside him. She waited, not willing to push him into this. *Lady* help her, she was asking a lot, but what waited on the other side of the storm was something she hoped would be worth the risk.

Varian's hold gradually slackened. "Just go . . . slow."

"I will." Her stomach fluttered with nerves as she took a deep breath. "Remember, focus on us and only us."

As she brought the head of his erection to the heat between her legs, she slid him against her, gently at first, then when his hips started thrusting upward, with more friction. Her mouth dried at the hard, steely heat of him gliding against her. She was wet, covering him and her fingers with her cream.

"All right?" she asked, the pleasure shortening her breath.

"There's fire in your touch, Kymora." Varian's hands dropped to her hips, then skated over the curve of her rear to grip the flesh behind her thighs. "It brands me."

His words scorched her. She swallowed hard, her whole body heating, tightening, needing something more. While she knew what that more was, actually knowing and doing were two separate things.

Biting her lip, she settled herself against him and lowered herself down. Her mouth parted on a gasp at the blunt feel of him stretching her, the sensation unfamiliar. With every slow push, her body wept to accommodate him. There was heat and pleasure from working him a little deeper every time.

Against her mind, she felt Varian's aura pulsing, twisting, one moment giving off a thousand sparks, the next sucking inward like a vortex. A struggle between desire and the need to cause pain.

Varian fought to keep his gaze on Kymora. Every gentle movement of her hips, the incredible heat of being taken by her, the way her thighs trembled as they spread over his hips, tested his resolve to keep his eyes open.

Concentrating on their combined pleasure was one of the toughest battles he'd ever encountered. Her every movement threatened to shatter his control, yet to lose it would mean endangering her.

Through gritted teeth, he growled, "This burns all the way to my soul." The words helped ground him. He stretched a hand up to cup her arm and steady her. A fine sheen of sweat dampened her skin. "I didn't think it would be this good."

Kymora smiled and her fingers dug into his forearm. "Good? *Mother*, this is more than I think I can handle. . . ." Her husky voice trailed off on a laugh that hitched and altered into a moan.

On the next rise, she hesitated a moment, then dropped down on him fast. She cried out, a sharp painful sound. Something inside her gave as the friction whipped like lightning along his shaft and straight up his spine. His head jerked back and the crimson world around him flared.

Vision swimming, lungs working like a pair of bellows, Varian forced himself to focus once more on Kymora. She remained seated on him, unmoving, her brow creased in a frown, a slight grimace on her face. His heart thudded hard as he realized the significance of her last action.

"Breathe, Kymora." His gruff reminder drew a shaky smile from her. She was tight around him, furnace hot. "I need to touch you."

She gave a jerky nod. With one hand, he parted her wet folds and stroked her with his thumb. She shuddered and her inner muscles clamped tight around him. Her hips rolled toward him.

"More, please," she gasped.

Watching her shiver and respond to what he was doing continued to help him focus. Slowly she started moving again, rocking against him, falling and rising. Her soft cries grew louder.

Varian tried to let her set the rhythm, but the heat of her consumed him. He couldn't help thrusting up to meet her every other stroke. He lost himself in the incredible sensation of her muscles gripping and releasing him. The sounds, the scents, the burning tension tightening between them centered him. Then there was nothing except pure pleasure rushing through him. At the edge of his hearing, Kymora cried out, her body convulsed against his, and she peaked with him.

Their mutual pleasure took him hard, surging over him like a wave of fire. One after another. Each stronger than the last, then finally ebbing.

When he regained some sense of his surroundings, he discovered a warm, limp weight draped across his body. Kymora. His lips curved. The heavy spiciness of their scents mingled, a satisfying accompaniment to the satiated exhaustion afflicting his limbs.

Varian blinked, breath catching. "I see color. . . ."

And he did. The inky blackness of Kymora's hair, the rich deep blue of the blanket, the stark whiteness of the walls. His throat tightened.

Kymora's hand pressed against his damp chest. "And what do you feel inside?"

Focusing inward, he was startled to discover there was no surging darkness, no tearing fury or anger threatening to consume him, no hollow emptiness waiting within. Just a salve of contentment spread over his soul.

How had she known what to do? The gift she'd given him was overwhelming.

"Breathe, Varian." There was a smile in her voice.

With a shaking hand, he cupped the back of her head, unable to find the words to speak.

"There's no need, Varian," she whispered. "Not when I can feel your heart."

# Chapter 34

"YOU'RE thinking too hard." Kymora paused in brushing Varian's hair.

Kneeling behind him on the bed gave her a height advantage. A quick pull to free her dress from under her knees, and she looped her arms around his shoulders to hug him. His shirt still carried a light herbal wash odor, but beneath it was Varian's unique fragrance. A clean, outdoor, woodsy scent.

"You're not having second thoughts about this dinner are you?"

His large, warm hand closed over both of hers. "I won't say I'm comfortable with the idea, but I said I'd go." He took a deep breath. "I need to see Lisella." Kymora nuzzled his cheek as pain slashed through his aura. "And I should also talk to the other scouts."

Kymora's heart squeezed tight. There was an edge of vulnerability in his tone, but in typical Varian style, he was preparing to take action to protect those he loved. She truly loved his strength and determination.

"Since Arek discovered the secret of our shared history with the

*Na'Reish* in Zataan's journal, Kalan's had our historians searching the archives for more information about the times before the first war." She returned to brushing his hair. "He wants to know more about what life was like when we all lived together. Human and *Na'Reish* and *Na'Chi*. That information might also explain more about you and the other *Na'Chi*."

"Don't you think that past Councilors who kept the secret from everyone would have made sure nothing remained?"

"I'm sure they destroyed a lot of documents and journals, but obviously some were overlooked. Perhaps more will be uncovered in time." Placing the brush aside, she smoothed her fingers over his temple braids, unable to resist also tracing his *Na'Chi* markings before tucking the strands behind his ears. "I love touching your hair. It's so soft." She rest her hands on his shoulders. "Actually, I love touching you anywhere. You're a feast for my fingers."

Varian's snort drew a grin from her. The bed creaked as he shifted next to her. He caught one of her hands in his.

"And you bring me peace like I've never felt before." Spoken low, the words were rough and thick. Her breath caught as his lips kissed the pads of her fingers. Soft and warm. There was a lightness to his aura that reflected his statement. "You have such faith and strength. It humbles me, priestess."

"And here I was thinking the same thing about you, *Na'Chi*." Her own voice wasn't too steady.

His kiss held heat and hunger, but it wasn't hard or aggressive, just a tender melding of lips. One that made her wish they didn't have to attend the dinner she and Lisella had planned.

As they finished getting ready, Kymora reflected on the past few hours. So much had happened. They both needed time to sort through everything. And more than anything, she needed to explore what loving Varian meant to her.

*Merciful Mother*, the gift the *Lady* had given her was one she'd long dreamed of but never expected to happen. Not since taking on the calling as *Temple Elect*. For most it meant a lifetime of serving *Her*. It was a future she'd never considered changing until now, and it left her feeling more vulnerable than she'd ever been before, yet an incredible joy tempered it.

The uncertainty of giving up her vocation still weighed heavily on her mind. After nearly twenty years, the last eight as *Temple Elect*, she'd never imagined a life outside *Her* order. Routines, structure, discipline, timetables, all of these things gave her independence. She'd be giving up the familiar. And that was what probably frightened her the most. But did it mean she'd become too reliant on them? Too set in her ways? That in itself was a form of dependency.

No closer to making a decision about her life, Kymora accompanied Varian to the *Na'Chi* apartments to join the others for dinner. A handful of orphans from the city and those the *Na'Chi* had agreed to shelter were among those she and Lisella had invited.

Kymora spent time before dinner talking to the children and other adults while Varian spoke to Lisella and the scouts. Even half a room away, she could sense his apprehension, but as the minutes passed, it eased to a much healthier level.

"Of all the people here, I never thought to see my sister so somber. If you're not careful, the light will change and that expression will freeze on your face."

The childhood superstition drew the corners of her mouth upward. "Only you believed in that tale as child, brother mine," she replied.

A soft puff of air rushed across her face, carrying with it a light masculine odor with a hint of *Vaa'jahn*. Kalan's warm body brushed against her side as he joined her on the bench running the length of the wall. He pressed a cool mug into her hand.

"*Cheva*-juice," he told her, then, keeping his voice low, "Jole told me what happened. How is Varian?"

"Better." Kymora sighed. "There are a few things I need to tell you, Kalan."

As concisely as possible, she filled him in on what she and Lisella had discovered. The exact details of how she'd helped Varian she kept to herself though.

"So, integrating the *Na'Chi* is now paramount," he mused, then, "I presume Varian's informing his scouts of just what you've revealed to me?"

"Yes. He knows they can't afford to ignore this problem."

Her brother grunted. "Varian's a strong leader. Resourceful and flexible when he needs to be." His tone lightened and a finger teased the skin low on the side of her neck. "So, is this bite mark a part of the solution and not the result of a battle rush attack?"

Her blood heated and rushed to her cheeks. "What are you talking about?" Her hand collided with his as she tried to feel it.

"There's a mark there, Kym. I swear." His low chuckle was accompanied by a hug. "I'm just glad I don't have to call on Varian to account for it."

Kymora aimed a swift elbow into his ribs. A soft "Oof" was accompanied by more chuckling.

"Don't you dare say anything to him," she hissed, succumbing to a reluctant smile.

"I wouldn't dream of interfering, unlike someone I know who decided to give her two chits' worth of advice when Annika and I were—"

"Kalan, I love him." Her brother fell silent, his aura rippling with surprise. "So, there's no need for you to dispense any advice."

He pressed a gentle kiss to her temple. "And what about Varian?"

"I don't know," she admitted. "I doubt with everything that's happened he's even considered what our relationship means to him."

Kalan's hair brushed her cheek as he nodded. "*Lady* willing, you'll both find a way to deal with this." His comment jerked her upright in her seat. "Kymora? What's wrong?"

"It was only the start of my Fourth Journey," she murmured. Excitement fluttered in her stomach. "Oh, *Mother of Light*, I've been so blind!" She sipped her drink, needing it for a suddenly dry throat. "Kalan, do you remember my first account of the *Lady's* instructions to us all concerning the *Na'Chi*?"

"*She* warned us that there would be opposition, but *She* welcomed them as *Her* children."

"Yes, but *She* also said, '*My children must survive.*'" She shook her head. "I assumed she meant just the *Na'Chi*. What if I've interpreted that wrong? Now that we know the *Na'Reish* once lived peacefully with us, and that our three races share common blood, what if she was referring to all of us?"

"How does this affect your Fourth Journey?"

"*She* foretold it'd begin with the arrival of the *Na'Chi*, and it did."

"You made the decision to live with them in their village."

"Yes. I thought my Journey would end once we came back here." She wet her lips. "It doesn't." A shiver worked its way up her back. "I sought the *Lady's* guidance after Councilor Elamm's little perform- ance. *She* said something to me I didn't want to hear. *Her* words were, 'You serve me whether you wear the Temple Elect robes or not.'"

Kymora gripped her brother's hand, unsurprised to find her own shaking.

"I can't help the *Na'Chi* nor serve our people if there's conflict over my spending time with them. I can't serve *Her* faithfully if I ignore *Her* mandate about them." She sucked in an unsteady breath. "I *can* give up the position of *Temple Elect* and fulfill both."

Kalan's aura flared with shock. "You'd resign?"

"Now isn't the time for more instability, I know, but you know me, *Chosen*."

Given the gravity of the situation, it seemed a little surreal to hear the sounds of children laughing, the clatter of crockery, and chairs scraping on the floor, all so familiar and reassuring in the silence that followed her announcement.

Kalan's thumb smoothed over the knuckles of her hand. "I do know you, *Temple Elect*." Hoarse and a little deeper than normal, his voice still remained strong. "To give up your calling for the unknown and follow *Her* will take great faith. You're one of the strongest people I know."

"*She* brought the *Na'Chi* to us. They're meant to be with us. We need each other to survive. My future lies with them, not the Temple. Not any longer." Kymora turned her face into his shoulder. "It scares me not knowing what lies ahead."

His hand tightened around hers. "You can deal with fear, Kym; you've done it so many times already in your life. Just as long as you're happy with this decision."

"Anxious is a better word, but there's now a sense of rightness to it that I haven't felt until tonight."

"When will you announce this?"

"Not until I've spoken to Varian about it."

The evening progressed and Kymora pushed her decision to the back of her mind to enjoy the company of good friends. During dinner when Varian took her hand and laced his fingers among hers and rested them on his lap, her heart soared. His positive action just reinforced the decision she'd made. While no one commented, she sensed some surprise but mostly good will.

As conversation and the children's energy ran down, many began to call it a night.

"I'd better gather the children and take them back to the orphanage," Lisella stated. A chorus of protests came from those still awake.

Seated beside her at the table, Varian spoke up. "I'll help you."

"No need, it's only a short walk."

Kymora listened to the tired chatter of a dozen children as they all headed down the corridor with Lisella.

Varian leaned in to her shoulder. "Do I need to accompany you back to your room?"

An innocent enough question, but what she sensed from his aura was anything but. Kymora ducked her head as heat flushed her cheeks. After a few farewells, she allowed him to help her from her chair and waited until they'd reached the archway to the corridor before replying.

"I think I'd rather accompany you to yours. It's closer."

His harsh indrawn breath and the way his arm tensed beneath her hand made her smile, particularly when he said nothing but guided her right instead of left, and along the corridor leading to his room.

# Chapter 35

"VARIAN!" A muffled voice and a loud knocking woke Varian.

He propped himself up on one elbow on the bed. Darkness still filled the room, and a quick glance toward the window showed no light coming through the crack in the shutters.

The warm body curled up beside him underneath the blanket stirred. Kymora. The light scent of spiced honey mixed with the heavier scent of musk lingering in the air. A stimulating combination that reignited all of his senses, the most vivid being the memory of making love to her as soon as they'd reached his room after the dinner.

He leaned down to kiss her. She mumbled incoherently.

"Someone's knocking on my door," he murmured, just as more rapping on wood echoed through his apartment.

"Again?" Her disgruntled tone brought a smile to his lips "Maybe we should have gone to my room."

Perhaps they should have. The cooler air prickled his skin as he pulled on his breeches. Zaune stood in the doorway of his apartment, half dressed like himself. The young scout's head snapped up. The flecks in his eyes were black and his scent bore the sharp, caustic odor of fury. Varian frowned.

"You need to get to the hospice." The low growl in Zaune's voice sent ice crawling across the back of his scalp. "Lisella's been attacked."

He sucked in a jagged breath. "I'll get Kymora."

Kalan and Candra were waiting in the hospice vestibule. The human leader's tight, grim expression and Candra's drawn features escalated his fear.

"Where is she?" His pulse tripped in his veins.

Kymora's hand tightened on his arm in quiet support.

"Inside with Annika." Candra's scent was masked by the heavy odor of *Vaa'jahn*. She caught his arm as he headed for the curtained doorway. "Varian, there's no easy way to tell you this. Lisella was raped and beaten on her way back from the orphanage."

Beside him, Kymora gasped; her fingers dug into his arm. A shudder ripped through him. The air in the room suddenly seemed to disappear, and his thoughts narrowed down to the woman lying in a hospice bed beyond the curtain.

Her face appeared in his mind, her slender features softened by dark wavy hair, with the gentle smile he'd seen only hours ago. The woman he'd spent a lifetime with, sharing a thousand conversations, listening to her temper a hundred arguments and sooth as many hurt feelings. The gentlest soul among the *Na'Chi*.

The light of his people.

Sister of his heart.

*"I'd better gather the children and take them back to the orphanage."* Lisella's voice and the chorus of protests from the children she cared for echoed in his head.

*"I'll help you."*

*"No need, it's only a short walk."*

He flinched at the memory of the relief he'd felt when she'd declined his offer. Relief because he'd been more concerned with making love with Kymora than helping someone he'd sworn to protect.

Nausea rolled heavily in his gut. She'd suffered because of his complacency. Anger fireballed into fury. He sought the darkness within.

It stirred.

"Varian!" Kymora's voice came from a great distance. The darkness howled and writhed against her soft tether. Every instinct screamed for him to find whoever had hurt Lisella and tear them apart. "Varian, we need you."

He blinked, the motion a deliberate one, a slow movement of lid meeting lid. He lifted his head, and Kymora's anxious face snapped into focus. Her hands pressed against his chest. Her lips parted on a gasp, as if she were sensing something, then her arms wrapped around his waist tight.

"Oh, thank the *Mother of Light*."

He glanced down at the hands gripping his arms, one on either side. Candra and Kalan.

"Breathe deep, warrior," the elderly healer advised. "Lisella needs you, not your anger."

"Who was it?" His gravel-throated question made all three humans wince.

"Lisella shared some details before Candra gave her an herbal sedative." White lines of tension etched Kalan's eyes. "They identified themselves as rebels. City folk, not Light Blades."

"How many?"

"Five."

Crimson tinged the edges of everything in the vestibule. Varian curled his fingers into fists. He *wanted* their blood on his hands. Kymora stroked his chest, her hands gentle. Her action centered him. He sucked in a deep breath, every muscle shaking.

"We'll start searching for them tonight," Kalan promised, his jaw flexing. "The gates to the city have already been closed. There hasn't been enough time since the attack for them to flee." The grip on his arm tightened. "I was on my way out to wake the barracks to get the search underway, but I wanted to wait until you arrived."

Varian swallowed hard. "Take Zaune with you; he's one of our best trackers." The warrior gave a brusque nod. "Tell him . . ." And here he had to pause as the demand for retribution clawed at his innards like a predator savaging its prey. His gaze locked with the human's, steady and fierce. "Tell Zaune I want the rebels brought back alive."

Surprise swirled in the depths of the warrior's gaze. "I was expecting you'd demand blood-justice."

"I'd be delighted to see them all dead, *Chosen*," he growled. "But that decision will be Lisella's." He waited for Kalan to nod in agreement before turning his gaze on Candra. He tried to soften his tone. "Can I see her?"

The woman nodded. "For a short time." Her gaze turned apologetic. "I'm sorry, Kymora, but he has to go in alone."

"I'll wait for you here." She released him after a final hug.

Half a dozen oil lanterns dimly lit the main hospice hall. A handful of patients slept in the beds closest to the vestibule. Candra led him to the curtained-off area where Kalan had spent a week healing. Cast on the fabric, a distorted shadow of a woman leaned over a bed, then seated herself.

"Annika's healed most of Lisella's injuries, but she'll be groggy from the broth I gave her to help her rest," the woman murmured. She squeezed his hand tight. "Remember, she needs your empathy, not your anger."

As he pushed through into the curtained area, Annika rose from her seat next to Lisella's bed. On the way out, she touched his arm in mute support. He took her place.

His breath shuddered into his lungs. Raw bruises mottled one side of Lisella's face and neck, and newly healed cuts formed a latticework of red marks on her lips, her brow, and her jaw. She'd have fought, and fought hard, but even her *Na'Chi* strength hadn't helped against so many attackers.

His heart clenched tight, knowing exactly what sort of blows would have caused the sort of damage he was seeing and wished he didn't. He was grateful the blanket hid the rest of her body. The urge to howl and scream and tear something apart quaked inside him, his control blade thin.

*Mother of Light*, why hadn't he accompanied her to the orphanage?

"I know that look. . . ." Soft, slurred words snapped his gaze to Lisella's face.

Dazed violet eyes were half open, the pupils dilated. Her arm came out from beneath the blanket. His gut churned. *Dear Mother!* Finger marks ringed the flesh on her upper arm and wrist. Black bruises covered her knuckles. Gently, he grasped the hand she held out to him.

"You can't have anticipated this, Varian." Her fingers trembled. "They did it to stop the alliance. . . . Don't let them. . . ."

"Shh, just rest, Lisella." She flinched at his low, ragged tone. He ground his teeth together and sucked in a deep, calming breath. "We're hunting them. The Light Blades. Zaune."

"Promise me"—tears welled in her eyes—"you won't give up. . . ."

"I won't. We'll find them. I swear it."

"No . . ." The flecks in her eyes flashed green. "Promise me . . . you won't let Hesia's dream die. . . ."

Fury raged through his veins.

*Hesia's dream.*

How could she want him to pursue something that had brought them only pain and suffering? The dream had turned into nightmare after nightmare.

"I promised to protect you, little sister. . . ." Broken words, just like the vow he'd made.

"You have." Lisella's throat bobbed. "Don't give up. Have faith in *Her* journey for us. . . ."

The *Lady*. His lip curled. "*Her* path for us has brought us nothing but sorrow and death!"

"Then have faith in Kymora and those who are our friends."

"Faith is for fools!" He regretted his angry reply, and his heart twisted in his chest as it proved too much for Lisella.

Her chin trembled, and while she tried to remain composed, a sob wrenched from the depths of her soul. Then another, and another. Each was a sharp blade thrust into his chest.

His throat closed over as he forced his next words out. "I'm sorry, Lisella."

The helplessness of watching her cry ate away at him, but he swallowed his tears. She needed his strength, not a sign of weakness.

Her sobs quieted to soft, uneven hiccups as whatever medication Candra had given her took effect. When her eyes finally closed and her hand relaxed in his, Varian dropped his head, unable to keep up the facade of strength.

*Blessed Mother*, what a horrific mess.

Perhaps Rystin had been right, maybe they shouldn't have left *Na'Reish* territory. The others were going to be looking to him for answers. For guidance. For vengeance. For assurance.

His thoughts twisted and darted around in his mind, chasing one another around and around. Frenzied, tangled. Just below the chaos lurked guilt, but he pushed it away. If he started that path, he'd spiral into the darkness and never resurface. Varian took in a slow breath, trying to calm the ache in his heart and soul.

He laid Lisella's hand down on the bed. How could he fix this?

He was tempted to seek guidance from Kymora. Some of his tension faded with the thought of her. But his resolve hardened. She was too involved already. Too at risk.

"I'll find a way, sister," he murmured, and smoothed a fingertip over Lisella's bruised cheek. He watched her sleep a moment longer, then rose. "I swear it."

On silent feet he left, his strides picking up pace as fast as his resolve hardened. He bared his teeth in a savage grin.

It was time to go hunting.

# Chapter 36

KYMORA jerked upright, woken from her doze by the hard thud of footsteps and muted voices. She recognized many of the scouts' voices. The myriad emotions shimmering amidst their auras made it hard to decipher who was in the group.

Throwing off the blanket covering her, she scrambled to her feet and groaned as her body protested. Sleeping in an upright chair did nothing for the muscles. She reached for her staff. Someone pressed it into her hands.

"They're back, *Temple Elect*," Tovie said, his young voice barely a whisper. "They don't look happy."

"Is Varian with them?" She smoothed a hand over the boy's head.

"He went past here a moment ago. I think he went straight to his room."

She smiled her thanks and headed out of the common room, nodding as some of the scouts addressed her with somber greetings. How long had it been since the search began? If Tovie was awake, then it was at least breakfast time. Inhaling, she detected the faint odor of cooked mash, the popular milk-boiled grain of choice for the *Na'Chi* children, wafting along the corridor from the direction of the communal kitchen.

When Kymora reached Varian's apartment, the door was wide open. She hesitated, her fingers playing with the beveled edge. Away from the crowd, Varian's aura seethed and throbbed, the heat in it scorching the edges of her mind.

"Varian?" she called. A chair scraped to her right. Something metal clattered onto the wooden table. "What's happened?"

"Kalan's called a break to the search." His tone was just short of scathing. She pulled in a slow, silent breath, knowing he was angrier over the situation than disrespectful of her brother. "He sent us back here to eat."

"I'll get you some breakfast."

"I'm not hungry."

Her temper sparked at his bluntness. "You sound like a five-year-old harpy." She stepped in and pushed shut the door until the latch clicked. "A simple 'no, thank you, Kymora,' would have sufficed."

Silence met her scolding, then Varian issued a drawn-out sigh. "My apologies, Kymora." Weariness etched every word. "We spent five hours tracking the blood-scent only to have it disappear near Waterside Dock."

"Blood-scent?" Kymora reached the table and found him in the end chair. She pulled up the one next to him.

"Lisella injured at least one of her attackers. The blood splatters were few, but the scent was strong." Varian's braids made a soft, hollow clinking sound, like he'd run a hand through them. "Kalan is now sending messengers all over the city warning that anyone who's found sheltering the rebels will face imprisonment. We'll continue the search in another hour."

"Did you see people gathered outside the hospice on your way in?" she asked. *Lady* knew some good news might lift his spirits. He grunted. "They're all visitors for Lisella. Candra won't let them see her yet, not until she's ready, but they've all left messages and well-wishes for her."

"*All* of those people are there to see her?" He sounded shocked.

Kymora smiled. "She's made a lot of friends out in the city. Guilders, traders, refugees, workers at the orphanage, Councilors' families. They're outraged by what's happened to her. Many of them want to help in the search."

He grunted again. "The more who search, the better our chances of finding those who attacked her."

Her fingers grazed his arm. Muscles tensed at her touch. "Go bathe for a little while, relax. . . ." Here she wrinkled her nose at the fishy odor emanating from his clothes. "Soak away the remnants of the Dock and I'll bring you some tea."

"There's no need, Kymora." Varian's chair scraped, strident and loud, as he rose from the table. His aura held less heat, but there was a strange hardness to it now. "I'll just catch a half-hour nap."

"I'll join you."

His boot scuffed on the floor. "Why?"

Kymora frowned at the wary tone. What was going on? Sure, she could understand his anger and frustration. The assault on Lisella had everyone on edge, but Varian seemed . . . distant ever since they'd left the hospice.

"No particular reason . . . I just thought you'd appreciate the company." She offered him a half smile. "It's what you do for someone you care about. . . ." She gathered her courage. "For someone you love."

She fiddled with a fold of her dress, waiting for him to answer, hoping he would. Telling him she loved him could've been timed better, but the hardness in him worried her. It had a barrierlike feeling. Sensing his emotions was more difficult, like finding them through fog. She needed to reach him again. But the silence drew out well beyond what was comfortable.

*"It's what you do . . . for someone you love."*

An ice-cold shudder tore down Varian's back and he took a hasty step backward. Two days ago he'd have cherished those words, begged Kymora to repeat them, allowed them to sink into his soul and warm him as he would by putting his hands close to a fire. And then he'd have made love to her so slowly, giving pleasure, sharing it, showing her just how much she meant to him.

"You can't love me." His reply was flat, hard.

Kymora flinched as if he'd struck her. She rose from the table, her face losing color. "I love you, Varian." Her chin lifted in familiar defiance. "You can tell me not to all you want, but you can't stop me."

*Lady's Breath*, he couldn't deal with this right now. He'd never wanted anything more than to be loved by a woman like her, yet circumstances made it impossible. What they'd already shared were moments stolen in time. Precious moments, but that's all he could ever allow them to be.

When the *Na'Chi* had fled *Na'Reish* territory, Hesia, the mother of his heart, had stayed behind so she wouldn't slow them down.

At the village in the mountains, Geanna and Eyan, two young lives—gone—taken well before their time.

Rystin, his brother-in-arms, in the leadership challenge—dead by his hand.

During battle, Arek, a man he respected and admired, sacrificed himself to save friends.

And now, Lisella, who gave so much of herself to others, suffered, her life torn apart by violence and hatred.

Varian shook his head and took another step away from Kymora. The price of loving someone was too high. Life had hammered home that message, and as usual, he'd been slow to learn the lesson, but at least he'd woken up to the fact before something had happened to her.

"You can be the strongest leader there is and make the best decisions you possibly can, others may look to you for guidance, but there's no guarantee things will work out right, Varian." Her compassionate expression hit him low in the gut. "Lisella isn't going to blame you for what happened. Do you honestly think she would?"

Her quiet question ripped away the hard veneer he'd tried to maintain in the hours since leaving the hospice. Beneath it, the tiny embers of anger he'd kept tempered burst into wild flames that seared and tormented every nerve in his body.

"I made a promise to protect her!" Low and rough, his voice was almost a snarl. "If I couldn't do that for her, what chance do I have of protecting you?"

Kymora blinked back tears at the raw agony in his voice, the harsh rasp of his breathing. Briefly his pain broke out from behind whatever barrier he'd erected around his aura.

"Did I ever once ask you to protect me?" she asked, quietly.

"You don't have to!" His boot steps thudded hard on the floor, as if he paced, needing to vent through movement. "There was no need to. I always protect those I . . ."

His words cut off on a harsh breath. Kymora held hers, wishing he'd continue. Would he finish his statement? She bit her lip, swallowing her disappointment, which grew the longer the silence between them lasted.

"Varian, don't we deserve a chance?"

"*Temple Elect*, there's no point. There never was."

She sucked in a hard breath. The cold bitterness in his tone was like a spike to her heart, sharp and piercing, tearing at her, shredding the memories of them loving each another as if they'd meant nothing to him.

*Merciful Mother*, surely he didn't really feel that way?

"Don't you dare belittle what we have." Anger made her voice hoarse. "What we have is good. I'm happier than I've ever been when I'm with you. Why can't you believe in us like I do?"

"There's no future for us. Can't you see that, Kymora?" Varian's voice shook, as torn as hers had been a few moments ago. "You've dedicated your life to serving the *Lady*. You belong to *Her*. I won't let you choose between *Her* and me."

Another excuse. Telling him she would no longer be the *Temple Elect* seemed futile now. He'd see it as an attempt to change his mind.

"I've never wanted a man more in my life than you. Never. You know I love you. *Lady* willing, I want to share everything with you. The blessed times, the heartbreaks, the trials that will test us. Everything, Varian." Kymora shook her head, the movement jerky. "You don't get to end what we have because you think you know what's best for us, and don't you dare thrust the *Temple Elect* role in my face. That doesn't even factor into this!" She dragged in a shuddering breath, a heartbeat away from tears. "Refusing to take a risk to save yourself from getting hurt is the easy option. The Varian I love isn't a coward."

His aura flared red hot, but she ignored the sizzle and heat. Every hair on her arms tingled with energy. She used it to push past the hurt.

"If you don't want me . . . If you don't love me"—here her voice trembled—"then you're going to have to say it, Varian. That's the only way I'll accept your reasons."

Again she waited for his response. Any response. None came. Nothing leaked from his aura. He'd shut down. She gripped her staff so hard her fingers went numb.

Kymora turned away from him, her hand reaching blindly for the table. There was no point arguing any further. The door to his bedroom creaked open as she reached for her amulet and jerked it, breaking the leather thong. Carefully, finger by finger, her pulse pounding heavy and hard, she laid the disc on the smooth surface of the table, her fingers tracing the etched sun one last time.

"When you decide what my love is worth to you, let me know."

She couldn't manage more than a whisper but knew Varian's *Na'Chi* hearing would pick up her voice.

Then she left.

Out in the corridor, Kymora focused on the solid wooden warmth of her staff and the soft scrape of it on the stone floor. Fear clutched at her shoulders like a sky-scavenger, casting its beady eye on her battered heart, on the hope she left behind with her amulet. On the future she felt crumbling down around her with every step she took away from the man who had become her life.

She'd done all she could to convince Varian he meant the world to her. The journey was now his to walk. The decision to join her or leave her to go on alone was his.

Kymora shivered and pushed the thought to the back of her mind. Outside the *Na'Chi* apartments, her two Light Blade guards were waiting for her.

"Where to, *Temple Elect*?" Ehrinne inquired.

The question gave her pause. She needed some time to meditate, to restore her calm, but returning to the Temple wasn't an option. Once there she be swamped with duties she hadn't the patience for at the moment. The prayer room would be full of those completing morning petitions. The gardens were just as popular, a good place for quiet thought, and her apartment held too many memories.

"Let's walk, just around the compound," she replied. "I need some fresh air."

The pathway they took curved behind the Temple and away from the apartments. While the morning was warming, the shadows thrown by the buildings cooled the air. She breathed deeply, keeping her pace steady, letting the tap of her staff on the gravel walkway settle into a soothing rhythm.

Lost in meditation, Kymora wasn't sure when she realized the crunching sound of their footsteps had tripled in volume. Ten separate auras, all focused and intent, brushed against her mind. She half turned to ask who had joined them when Ehrinne shouted out.

"*Temple Elect!* To your left and behind!"

Kymora spun, her staff already swinging when somebody tackled her from the side and took her to the ground. The impact stunned her. She lost her staff. It clattered away across the stones. The clash of weapons and cries filled the air.

Hands shoved her onto her stomach and wrenched her arms behind her back. The odor of sour sweat washed over her. She bucked but whoever pinned her to the ground weighed twice as much. Coarse rope wrapped around her arms, then the rest of her body.

"Gag her! Hurry!" A second pair of hands grabbed her hair. Her head was pulled back. A length of material was forced between her lips and wound around her head. All sound deadened as whatever was being used covered her ears.

*Lady's Breath, no!*

She screamed, the hoarse tone smothered by the thickness of material in her mouth. The body astride hers shifted. Something heavy covered her head, smelling dust dry and grainy, the texture thick and rough. A miller's bag? It was jerked down over her shoulders.

Her world shrank fast to the pounding of her heart and her rapid breaths sucking in through her nose. Hands lifted her. She grunted as something dug into her midriff. A shoulder? Then jolting, lasting minutes or seconds. She had no way of measuring, not with panic eating away at her sense of time. Where was she being taken?

Tears burned in her eyes. Kymora tried to force them back. If she cried, her nose would block. She'd be unable to breathe. She'd suffocate. She tried to slow her breathing.

One thought filled her head.

*Survive.*

# Chapter 37

VARIAN pulled on a fresh shirt as he crossed the floor in the main room. Tucking it in, he reached for his weapons belt sitting on the middle of the table, and then frowned. A golden sun disc with a broken thong rested next to it. It was Kymora's *Temple Elect* amulet.

*"I've never wanted a man more in my life than you."* Such passion and torment wrapped into her voice. Her every word had pierced his soul, hacked and slashed at it until nothing remained but tatters.

*"When you decide what my love is worth to you, let me know."*

He winced at the memory of her standing with her back to him, hunched over, as if warding off a blow. Her pain had left him feeling lower than the dirt under his boots. He'd wanted to close the distance between them, pull her into his arms, and beg her to forgive him.

But he'd done the right thing by letting her go. It was the only way he knew to keep her safe. His hand shook as he picked up the amulet and fingered the design. Why had she left it behind?

A knock sounded on his apartment door. His fingers curled around the amulet.

"Enter!" he called, more than willing to be distracted from his thoughts.

The door swung opened.

"Varian." The hoarse strain in the deep voice snapped his head up to look at his guest. Kalan stood there, his forest green gaze, so like Kymora's, turbulent and dark. Tight lines of tension grooved the lines on his tanned face. He clutched a rolled parchment in his fist. "I need your help."

The sour stench of fear assailed his nostrils. He'd never seen the human leader so anxious, not even when he'd been wounded and facing death. Uneasiness crawled across the back of his neck. What had him so afraid?

"What's wrong?" Varian motioned the human to take a seat and took the one opposite. "Is it the search?"

The older man shook his head and scraped a hand through his dark hair. It looked like he'd done that several times already.

"That no longer has priority." Varian stiffened and took a breath. Kalan held up a hand, stalling him and placed the piece of parchment on the table. "This is a letter from the rebels demanding the release of Davyn." His voice lowered. "It was found pinned with a Light Blade dagger on the ground next to Kymora's two slain bodyguards."

Shock ricocheted through Varian, searing every cell and nerve in his body. The beast inside him roared. His vision darkened, and half a heartbeat later it lightened, only this time with crimson overtones.

Kalan's hand gripped his forearm. "Don't lose it, *Na'Chi*. I need you." His fingers dug into his muscle. "Kymora needs you."

Varian locked gazes with his. "Kymora?"

"The rebels want to exchange her for Davyn."

"They have her?" The thought of her in their hands . . . He shied away from the dark images hovering at the back of his mind. He didn't dare let them surface. A shudder tore through him. "Where?"

"I don't know. That's why I've come to you. I need your skills in tracking and you know her scent better than anyone." The warrior's gaze never flickered, but the knowledge of his and Kymora's relationship was there. "We need to find her fast. They've given us until midday to free Davyn and open the city gates."

The threat to Kymora piggybacked on his words.

A shiver grated along Varian's spine. "That's only a few hours from now."

His gaze dropped to the amulet in his fist as emotions and memories poured through him, the most recent ones of their argument. They hurt. They ached and burned so fiercely he wasn't sure he could bear it. The metal edge bit into the skin of his palm.

"Who else knows about the letter?" Gravel grated in his voice.

"Just the Temple acolytes who found the bodies, the watch on duty in the compound who was alerted by them, me, and you. I haven't announced this to the Council yet. I can't." Kalan's lips pressed into a hard, thin line. "It would mean civil war."

Varian let out a ragged breath and glanced down at the disc in his fingers.

Kalan's indrawn breath was harsh. "That's Kymora's amulet."

"She left it here this morning." He could feel the warrior's stare. "We . . . argued." The admission twisted his gut.

"About what?"

Varian averted his gaze. "Us. The future. She told me she loved me." A derogatory sound welled deep in his throat as a cold empty void yawned inside him. "And I shut her down. Told her there was no us. No future."

"Why?"

"Everyone I've ever loved has been hurt." It hurt to breathe. "I didn't want the same happening to her. I thought by doing what I did, it would keep her safe." The coldness inside him grew. "I failed."

He stared at the swirling grain pattern on the top of the table, waiting for Kalan's anger, expecting retribution for his failure, prepared to accept it.

"No." The grip on his arm firmed. "You made a mistake. That's human." Varian looked up. A wry smile curved Kalan's lips, but then his expression grew serious. "Do you love Kymora?"

He frowned. Opened his mouth. The words stuck in his throat. He forced them out. "More than my own life, *Chosen*."

And that was the *Lady*-sworn truth. Declaring his love for Kymora left him feeling exposed, like a *lira* out on the plains, but there was no denying the rush of peace he felt after saying it. It was like she held him in her arms. He could almost feel the palm of her hand pressed against the center of his chest.

"Did she tell you why she left the amulet?"

Varian shook his head. "I found it a moment before you walked in."

"The tie is broken." Kalan ran a finger along the frayed ends of the thong. "Anyone who wishes to end their service with the *Lady*— Light Blade or Servant—has only to break the chain of their amulet. It doesn't mean they've put aside their faith, just whatever position they hold."

Varian's jaw loosened, his lips parted in shock. "Kymora's resigned as *Temple Elect*?"

"She told me yesterday. She asked me to say nothing until she'd spoken to you."

"Why would she break her service? The Temple is her life!"

"Kymora follows the *Lady's* will." A gentle smile curved the warrior's mouth. "She walks the path of her Fourth Journey. Her path is now with you. With the *Na'Chi*."

Kymora had chosen him over her role as *Temple Elect*? Why hadn't she said something to him this morning? But he knew why, and wished he could relive that time over again.

"*Blessed Mother*, I've done this all so wrong," he groaned.

"Then let's go make it right, my friend." Kalan squeezed his forearm. "Gather your scouts and let's begin the hunt."

Varian nodded, and as he rose, he tied the broken amulet around his neck. For safekeeping and to feel Kymora close to his heart. He was going to need her strength, because he couldn't find her alone. He was going to need the senses and skills of his darker half. As much as that scared him, he was going to have to gamble everything—his life, his heart, his soul—to succeed.

And Kymora's love and a future with her were worth that risk.

KYMORA counted, for time didn't exist. Whoever had kidnapped her was gone. Wherever they'd taken her, they'd abandoned her there. Whatever she lay in left her no room to move in any direction. She'd tried. Escape wasn't possible. The rope, the canvas, whatever she was locked in, it kept her immobile.

*Helpless.*

No movement.

No sound.

No auras.

Almost no sensation.

Someone had made a hole in whatever covered her head, near her nose, big enough to let blessed, fresh air in, but that was it.

All that remained in her world was nothingness. And terror, with its chilly fingers wrapped around her throat.

What had happened to Ehrinne and Nendal? Had the warriors survived? Her kidnappers had to be rebels, but what did they want? Had anyone noticed she was missing yet?

Her heart raced.

What if they never found her?

Mother of Light, *please hear my plea and deliver me from fear and despair.*

Her simple prayer became a mantra. She fought to stave off the panic that threatened to shut her in ice. Succumbing would leave her trapped in her mind.

Or she would give in to her tears. She couldn't cry.

Madness or death.

Kymora shuddered. She'd come so close to both during the fever-induced darkness brought on by Claret-rash.

She'd survived that.

She would endure this.

Mother of Light, *please hear my plea and deliver me from fear and despair.*

# Chapter 38

"THE blood-scent ends here, Varian." Zaune crouched at the cross section of two streets, one hand framing a ruby-colored stain on the cobblestoned roadway. He tilted his head into the slight breeze, nostrils flaring, then shook his head. "All I can smell is human waste and rotten garbage."

Varian wrinkled his nose, agreeing with the young scout. The stench was almost overpowering; he could taste the foulness of it at the back of his throat. The renegade Light Blade they were tracking bled arterial blood, the scent of it fresh and strong. He was surprised the warrior had made it this far.

Perhaps death had already claimed the warrior, and his companions had taken him with them to keep his identity a secret. Dark satisfaction coursed through his veins. One less rebel would suit him just fine.

"Where do these roads lead, *Chosen*?" he asked.

Kalan peered down each, his brows dipping into a frown. "The one headed west goes back to Bartertown. That one with the burnt-out dwellings curves southeast but ends up taking you to the Guild storage factories. Ahead leads straight to Waterside Dock."

Varian exchanged a look with Zaune. They'd lost the trail of Lisella's attackers near Waterside Dock. The similarity of circumstances couldn't be just coincidence, could it? Pivoting, his gaze strafed the ramshackle buildings.

Most were poorly constructed and only a handful were taller than a single story. Very few were made entirely of the same material, and all of them were joined together so that they formed one long row of connected houses.

They were like the homes constructed by the human slaves within the *Na'Reish* fortress. Some had small overhanging roofs. The odd bench or chair congregated like bleaters beneath them. All empty of people but that didn't mean they weren't at home. Faces peaked out dirty windows, but no one came out onto the street to greet them.

Kalan drew level with him. "Coppertown has the largest population of all the sectors in Sacred Lake." He pointed with his chin to a tunnel-like corridor twisting its way into darkness beneath a section of dilapidated two-story buildings. "With so many alleyways and snickleways, this place is like a digger-warren. Easy to get lost in, and even easier to hide within."

Movement caught the corner of Varian's gaze. A young boy with a shock of blond hair, a few years older than Tovie, sidled around the edge of the darkened snickleway. His pale eyes surveyed them all with a wariness well beyond his years. He scrubbed a dirty foot against the damaged wall, then leaned against it, his posture deceptively lazy.

"Would those living here aid Light Blades?" Zaune inquired, tone low. "They weren't particularly helpful this morning during the search."

"If you paid them enough, they'd do almost anything," Kalan replied, dryly. "Unfortunately, those who live here are either the very poor, the destitute, or are lawbreakers and the chit holds sway over their conscience, not empathy." He grimaced. "But when you're hungry, you'll do anything to survive, even if it means sacrificing your morals."

His softly spoken statement rang true with all of them. Clouds chose that moment to cross the path of the sun. The resulting dimness and cooler conditions sent a shiver skipping down Varian's spine. It could take them days to search every inch of this place. Kymora didn't have that sort of time.

"What now?" Jinnae asked, her thin face drawn tight.

"Kalan." Varian nodded to the man's left, toward the boy observing them.

The Light Blade swiveled but made no move to go toward the boy. "Seen anything interesting around here this morning?" he asked.

The corners of the boy's mouth twitched. "Lotsa interestin' things. Me mam chasin' me brother with his britches . . . took her half the mornin' to catch 'im." He shrugged a thin shoulder and came to the edge of the porch. "He don't like wearin' 'em."

His scent carried to Varian on the breeze. Beneath the unwashed odor of dirt and sweat, he detected the sharp scent of interest.

Kalan's eyes crinkled. "How old is your brother?"

"Three."

"My mother had the same problem with me." He took a step forward. "What's your name?"

The boy straightened. "Ryn."

"I've two chits you can earn, Ryn."

"What for?"

"Have you seen any Light Blades anywhere near here this morning? Anyone with a woman who was blind?"

"Light Blades. Nah. Didn't see none. No blind woman, either." The youngster's mouth pulled to one side. "Saw almost a dozen people, fancy dressed like you though."

Kalan flipped him one chit. "Where?"

Ryn caught it, then pointed down the road headed to the docks. "The alley by the portico." Two more chits tumbled through the air. His face lit up in surprise as he caught them.

Kalan gave a nod. "Let's go."

"Hey!" Ryn took a step off the porch. "That group I seen? One of 'em was carrying a bag over 'is shoulder. It were the size of a woman. . . ."

Barely three people wide, the alley's cobblestones were coated with all sorts of filth that squished underfoot. A gutter ran along one side and putrid slimy water gurgled into a busted drain farther along. Varian took the lead, trying to filter through the countless odors assaulting his nostrils. Some of them were stale and weeks old. As they passed a shadowed doorway, a dank draft wafted out.

"Varian!" Zaune's hiss came at the same time he scented fresh blood. He backtracked to the door. The younger scout's gaze glowed crimson. "The renegade was carried in here."

A quick scan of the building showed the doorway to be the only entrance. He pressed his ear up against it. Very faint scuffling sounds came from within. Humans or rodents?

"Taybor, Jinnae, you stay with the *Chosen*. Do not leave his side," he ordered, voice low. He glanced to Kalan. "There will be no guarantees. If they threaten you or one of us, we'll take them out."

The warrior's emerald gaze gleamed in the ambient light. "Do what you have to."

Varian closed his eyes and drew in a deep breath, then turned his thoughts inward, toward the darkness in his soul. The beast was there, lurking, the anger and fury contained but seething, waiting for the chance to rise, rend, and take revenge.

He released the leash. It surged; violent emotions crashed through him, racked his body, all reacting to the knowledge that Kymora's life was in danger. A scream of rage echoed in his mind. With every rapid beat of his heart, adrenaline pumped through his body, his skin began to heat, his senses intensified.

The faintest, familiar fragrance of honeyed spice lingered in the air. Every hair on his neck rose.

"She's here." Gravelly and rough, his voice still quavered with excitement.

Varian opened his eyes; this time he welcomed the crimson- and red-edged hues in the objects around him. A single thought, the image of Kymora as he'd last seen her, filled his mind. Within half a heartbeat, the chaos inside him changed; the energy morphed from a need for vengeance to the desire to protect what was his. For the first time, he and his darker half were in agreement.

Zaune's hand grasped his shoulder. His mouth curled into a grim smile. "Let's hunt."

# Chapter 39

THE barest flutter of sensation, a vibration, brushed against Kymora's mind. She cried out, quivering as she held her breath, praying the sensation hadn't been a figment of her imagination, but as her pulse settled into a steady rhythm again, tears prickled behind her eyes.

She was going mad. Shewasgoingmad. *Shewasgoingmad.* . . .

She sucked in air through her nose. Rapid, short, sharp breaths. *Slow down.* Breathe in, hold, breathe out. Her inhalations lengthened, became more deliberate. Cool air filled her lungs.

Control each breath. Control your thoughts. Control your body.

Exhaustion hovered at the edge of her mind, but to give in and sleep carried the risk of missing someone nearby.

Kymora focused again and continued whispering one of her favorite scriptures against the gag in her mouth. "We all look to you, *Mother of Wisdom and Mercy, You* are the provider of all things good, *You* give us Light and deliver us from Darkness, *You* are our Strength—"

A spike of terror stabbed at her mind. She froze. There was no way that had been her imagination. It had depth and intensity. She counted her breaths, waiting. Who was out there? How close were they?

Another harsh gouge punctured her shield. More bombarded her, deluging her Gift like a glass of water drunk too fast. She flinched but soaked in the fierce sensations, glorying in the agonizing touch of reality after enduring its absence. The ensemble of impressions lacked harmony. She couldn't sort through them to figure who might be out there.

She didn't care. She screamed, hoping whoever it was could hear her. And she kept screaming, determined to last as long as the sensations kept coming, too frightened to stop and return to the darkness in her mind.

THE building proved to be one where several houses joined together in a bizarre melding of workmanship. The first three rooms were each a house with a door cut into its back wall. That door led to another house.

Pausing by the fourth one, Varian tested the air for Kymora's scent. It was getting stronger and it mingled with other odors. Cooking food, people, blood. The murmur of voices also came from the other side of the thick wooden door.

With a throat-shredding roar, he shouldered his way through it. One swift glance showed him nearly a dozen men and women scattered around the room, some seated in front of a small fireplace, others at a table pushed into a corner, some lying on pallets on the floor.

The closest humans to the door clambered to their feet, reaching for their weapons. Shouts, the scraping of metal from leather sheaths, and *Na'Chi* war cries filled the air. Behind him the other scouts launched into the fray.

The darkness inside him exulted in the heat and rush of the fierce fighting. His first opponent, he knocked out cold with one powerful back sweep of his fist. The second he hauled from her feet and sent her crashing against the wall. When she hit the floor, she never moved. The next warrior came at him with a dagger drawn.

A silent snarl shaped the man's mouth, his broad face flushed with hatred. Varian blocked his first thrust and caught the other arm in a forearm clinch. He twisted. The man howled. Bone snapped. The renegade dropped to his knees. Varian locked both hands around his other arm and twisted again. Bone cracked. He shoved the man away from him, sent him sprawling onto his back.

Honey and spice, thick and rich, coated his senses. He could taste it on his tongue as he sucked it into his lungs. Left, right. Stronger to the right. Beyond the chaos of bodies locked in combat, there stood another door. Frustration clawed his gut. The place was worse than a digger-burrow.

Avoiding the struggling combatants left on their feet, he strode for the doorway. It gave under his shove. Thick with shadows, the room reeked of blood and death. A dark figure lay in one corner. Heart pumping, Varian rushed to it, but as he rolled it toward him, he knew it wasn't Kymora.

Kalan appeared in the doorway, flanked by Taybor and Jinnae. "Is it . . . ?"

"No," he grated out. "His scent belongs to the Light Blade we've been tracking. He's dead." Unsurprising. Satisfying. He shot a savage grin toward the human leader. "One less rebel to worry about, *Chosen*."

"Then where is she?" Tension threaded every word.

Zaune shoved his way into the room, blood streaming down his face from a split across his brow. "Six dead, four down. All rebels accounted for," he panted. "Yari's injured but all right. Everyone else is fine. Surprise certainly helped us."

Varian nodded, swiveling on his knee in the dust as he scanned the floor. "What's that?" A small square section of floorboards lay at a right angle to the rest. He unsheathed his dagger and pried at the niche. The wood creaked but lifted to reveal a hole. Cool air brushed against his hands. Someone passed him a lantern from the other room.

Kalan joined him, kneeling on the other side of the hole. "Looks like a catacomb." He grunted. "They're used to bury the dead. See the holes in the walls?"

Varian handed Kalan the lantern. "Kymora's scent is strongest here."

He dropped into the catacomb. His boots hit the hard-packed floor with a sharp thud. A millennia of dust puffed out from underneath them. The place smelled of the dead, dry and musty. Despite the dimness of light, he counted just over a dozen holes in the walls. Wrapped bodies filled eight of them.

Inhaling again, he traced Kymora's scent to the only shroud-covered body on the bottom row. There was no odor of death.

His gut clenched. *Blessed Mother*, had they buried her alive? The cold logic of the rebel who'd planned this ripped through him. Had their plan succeeded, they'd have freed Davyn. If it'd failed, Kymora might never have been found. A growl rumbled in his chest.

He reached into the hole. Hooking his fingers into the canvas, he pulled. A muffled scream stopped his heart.

"Kymora!" He gritted his teeth, and with one final yank, she was free of the grave.

He tore open the head covering. Her dust-coated face appeared. Her emerald eyes were wide open, terror haunting their depths. He placed trembling fingers to her cheek. Her body convulsed, then arched. Tears welled in her eyes. He pried the rags from her mouth, then tore them from her head.

Gagged, bound, and shrouded.

The horror of what she must have endured ripped into him. Just how close he'd come to losing her sank in. He wanted to yell and howl, but the terror shaking her body kept his fury contained.

"You're safe, Kymora," he whispered, and peeled more of the shroud away from her head, freeing it so she could feel the air on her hot cheeks.

Her lips were stretched wide in a silent scream, her voice so hoarse he could barely hear her. He stroked her sweat-soaked hair back off her face.

"You're safe." He threw back his head. "Zaune get down here. I need your help."

In minutes she was free. Her legs wouldn't hold her, so he gathered her against him, supporting all of her weight as he cradled her against his chest.

His heart ached as she ran her hands over him, tears pouring down her cheeks. Her fingers shook so badly he had to help her place them on the side of his face. Her touch never felt so good.

"Varian!" The whisper of sound came from a tortured throat. "Thank the *Lady* . . ."

"Shh, don't speak." He smoothed a finger over her lips. "I'm here. Kalan's here. You're safe." He pressed a kiss to her temple. "I love you. Let's get you home."

# Chapter 40

"YOU said you loved me, *Na'Chi*."

The soft, lilting voice came from behind Varian and alerted him to another visitor on the wall walkway running behind the Light Blade compound. Not that he hadn't heard the gentle *tap-tap-tap* of her staff as she made her way up the flight of stairs or caught her honey and spices scent on the late afternoon breeze.

The glacial lake made a stunning backdrop to the activities going on along the shoreline, but he turned away from it and took in another of nature's beautiful creations as she made her way toward him.

"I did." The gut-freezing vulnerability was easing the more he admitted to loving Kymora. To himself. To her and to those dearest to them. Denying or hiding his love for her was no longer an option, not after coming so close to losing her. Nothing could be worse than that.

After getting her out of the catacomb and to the hospice, he'd spent a long night sitting vigil over her as she recovered from her ordeal. Not even Candra's halfhearted threat of infecting him with pox could move him from her side. He'd wanted to be there when she woke from a nightmare, to comfort her, to wipe the tears from her face and then hold her and whisper how much he loved her until she fell asleep again. Every time she needed him.

The blessed times. The heartbreaks. The trials.

From now on, he wanted to share everything with her.

With unerring accuracy Kymora walked straight up to him and slid her arms around his waist to squeeze him tight. He shut his eyes and counted, a grin pulling at his lips.

"Well?" she asked. "Will you tell me again?"

The wind chose then to eddy around them. The gust caught the long strands of Kymora's hair and whipped them around her face. He caught them and curled them around his fist until his hand cupped the back of her head.

Varian placed his forehead against hers. He inhaled her scent and let it wrap around his heart, more than willing to be tied to her in such a unique way. Even his other half craved that connection now. Melding would take time but it was working. Kymora had helped him see that his other half wasn't something to be feared.

"I love you, Kymora Tayn," he murmured. She'd taught him that it was all right to care and that to let someone into your heart was one of life's most precious gifts. "Your love is worth every year of my life. They're yours if you want them."

He heard her breath hitch, then her hand slid to the center of his chest, her fingers spreading flat to claim him. "Yes, I'll take them, Varian, every single one of them and consider myself blessed."

"I'm the one blessed, Kymora." He took a moment to appreciate the feel of her against him, to savor the peace her love had brought him.

Shouts and giggles carried on the breeze. Kymora shifted in his arms and turned toward the lake.

"I can hear Kalan's voice." Her smile stretched wide; her eyes sparkled. "What's going on down there?"

"Rissa conned Kalan and half the adults into a game of flutter-tag," he explained, tone dry. "Even Councilor Elamm's joined in."

Her delighted laughter made him grin. "See?" She prodded his chest. "The *Lady* does perform miracles. There's hope for you yet."

He grunted. "*Her* paths to achieving *Her* goals are . . . complex." He took a cleansing breath. "I never would have expected such an outpouring of support from so many different people as I've seen in the last few days. For the *Na'Chi*, or us, or Kalan and Annika."

"The alliance is working, Varian." Her arms tightened around him. "There's still more to achieve, but now, with so many walking the journey with us, it'll be easier."

As much as Lisella's ordeal and Kymora's kidnapping still pained him, the incidents had thrown the rebel movement into disfavor with many humans. Kalan still had a job winnowing out Davyn's supporters, but they were no longer such a threat with their own people turning against them.

Progress of a sort, and it gave him hope.

Kymora's fingertips found the amulet that used to be hers around his neck. "So, *Na'Chi* Light Blade, what's it like being in the service of the *Lady*?"

"It might take some getting used to," he admitted, his laugh rusty sounding.

The *Chosen* and Sartor, the *Lady's* newly approved *Temple Elect*, had inducted all the *Na'Chi* scouts in a ceremony just that morning on the training grounds.

"We'll work on your faith. Who knows, that might be your Fourth Journey," she teased.

Varian thought back to the day when Hesia told him it was time to seek sanctuary with the humans. He'd left *Na'Reish* territory with a heavy heart, anxious about the future ahead, uncertain that an alliance could work.

He looked out over the wall at the people gathered below, *Na'Chi* and human, then glanced over his shoulder at the sprawling city behind them. Much had changed since that day. The timeline of events, and the faces of friends lost flickered through his mind.

The price of freedom and sanctuary.

"It's come at a cost," he murmured.

Kymora tilted her head toward him, puzzled amusement creasing her brow. "What has?"

"The *Na'Chi's* new home." He cradled her face. "But it was worth it because I found you."

She gifted him with her smile, and the warmth of it outstripped the sun. Varian placed his mouth over hers and kissed her with all of his heart, mind, and soul, both halves, dark and light.

He'd found a new home, at last.

And love . . . Her name was Kymora.